Alan Blackwood ... emigrated to the US with ... was 12. He graduated in Applied Psychology from Florida State University and has worked for several major companies on Florida's Space Coast, specializing in the psychology of flight and guidance systems. He now lives and work in Los Angeles, where he is a consultant for an interactive computer company. *Kingdom of the Blind* is his first novel.

KINGDOM
OF THE BLIND

Alan Blackwood

CORGI BOOKS

KINGDOM OF THE BLIND
A CORGI BOOK : 0 552 14645 5

First publication in Great Britain

PRINTING HISTORY
Corgi edition published 1998

Set in 11/12pt Plantin by
Phoenix Typesetting, Ilkley, West Yorkshire.

Corgi Books are published by Transworld Publishers Ltd,
61–63 Uxbridge Road, London W5 5SA,
in Australia by Transworld Publishers (Australia) Pty Ltd,
15–25 Helles Avenue, Moorebank, NSW 2170
and in New Zealand by Transworld Publishers (NZ) Ltd,
3 William Pickering Drive, Albany, Auckland.

.Reproduced, printed and bound in Great Britain by
Cox & Wyman Ltd, Reading, Berks.

For the three ladies whose inspiration and enthusiasm made this book come to life: my wife Susan Blackwood; my agent Wiescka Masterton; and my editor Averil Ashfield. And of course a very special thank you for Michael Halperin.

Rancho Santa Fe, Southern California, September 24 1942

Somebody stumbled against the dressing-table stool. Instantly, Dr Gathering switched on the bedside light and sat up in bed, groping on the nightstand for his glasses. Next to him, his red-haired wife Gina blinked open her eyes and said, 'Lionel . . . what is it?'

Three men in black balaclavas and black coveralls were standing at the end of the bed, like figures in a shadow-theater, pointing guns at them.

'Who the jumped-up Jesus are you?' Dr Gathering demanded. 'Get the hell out of my house!'

One of the men walked quickly around the bed and pointed his automatic at Dr Gathering's head. 'We have no time to waste, Dr Gathering. Please to dress.'

'What's going on?' Dr Gathering retorted. 'You can't just come in here and—'

'Dr Gathering. We have very little time. Please to dress.'

Dr Gathering peered at him shortsightedly. 'Are you *Japanese*?' he asked, incredulously.

The man gripped the neck of his balaclava and pulled it off, revealing a surprisingly sensitive-looking young face with a triangular scar. 'Major Genji Nishino, Imperial Marines. Please to dress now, Doctor, or I will kill your wife. No wait.'

Mrs Gathering clutched at the sleeve of her husband's blue-and-white pajamas and said, 'No! Don't, Lionel, you mustn't!' But Dr Gathering pried her hand away and eased himself out of bed, without once taking his eyes off Major Nishino. 'Please to dress. Quick as possible. Please to dress very warm.'

'It's 75 degrees, for Christ's sake.'

'Not on ocean.'

'What the hell are you doing?' Dr Gathering shouted at him. 'Are you *kidnapping* me?'

Major Nishino checked his chronograph. 'Please to be quick, Dr Gathering. *Isoide*! In thirty second I have to shoot.'

'Lionel—' Mrs Gathering began, but Major Nishino straightened his arm until the muzzle of his Taisho automatic was less than an inch from her forehead.

'Twenty second, Dr Gathering.'

Dr Gathering didn't hesitate. He opened the doors of his closet and took out a heavy green sweater and a pair of thick corduroy pants. He tugged them on over his pajamas, and buttoned up his fly.

'Two pairs sock,' said Major Nishino.

Dr Gathering sat on the end of the bed and

8

pulled on two pairs of long walking socks.

'Now sneaker. No shoe.'

In less than a minute, Dr Gathering was dressed. Major Nishino said to one of his men, 'Take him to the car. I won't be long. Tell Lieutenant Miwa to be ready to leave.'

The commando took hold of Dr Gathering's arm and pushed him toward the bedroom door.

'If you so much as *touch* her!' Dr Gathering shouted at Major Nishino.

'Quick, go!' Major Nishino ordered, and Dr Gathering was hustled from the room.

Mrs Gathering sat up in bed with the blanket tucked under her chin, staring up at Major Nishino with tear-filled eyes.

'What are you going to do to him?' she asked. Her face was white, sprinkled with cinnamon freckles. 'You're not going to kill him, are you?'

'You don't worry. I have order from high command to keep him safe.'

'But where are you taking him? You can't just *take* people, not like that!'

'Necessity of war, madam. Like this.'

With that, Major Nishino shot her through the head. She was flung back against the pillow like a Raggedy Ann doll, and blood sprayed up the wall. It made extraordinary characters, like the writing on a Japanese scroll. An epitaph, in the language of her killer.

Outside, Lieutenant Miwa and the rest of his commandos were waiting in the Nash with the engine running. Major Nishino climbed in, and they slithered away from the side of the road in a shower of dust and pebbles. In the back seat, Dr Gathering had already been handcuffed and gagged. Major Nishino turned around to him and said, 'Your wife is wise, Doctor. She has agreed not to call the police, or the military. Because of this I was able to spare her.'

Dr Gathering's eyes bulged and he made muffled grunting noises underneath his gag, but that was all he could do. Major Nishino turned back, and didn't bother with his captive after that. This was a war, and Dr Gathering was a prisoner of war, and Mrs Gathering had been one of its casualties.

They swerved their way through the eucalyptus trees and the lemon groves. The moon was so bright that they hardly needed headlights. At last they crested the hill that overlooked Solana Beach, and saw the ocean glittering in the near distance like hammered glass.

At 00:42:23 the conning-tower of submarine *I–17* broke the surface of the Pacific Ocean at latitude 117° 26' W and 33° 1' N, about a mile off Solana Beach, and their small rubber boat was already waiting for it, tilting and bobbing on the waves.

Commander Tagami appeared, his cap still turned peak-backward from using the periscope. 'Please hurry, Major,' he said. But then he saluted. 'You have done us a great honor here tonight. This will not be forgotten.'

Major Nishino helped Dr Gathering onto the knotted-rope ladder. Dr Gathering tried to turn his head around to take one last look at the California coastline.

'Don't look back, Doctor,' said Major Nishino. 'From now on, you will be living a very different life.'

1

When a true genius appears in this world, you may know him by this sign, that the dunces are all in confederacy against him – Jonathan Swift

St Cloud, Florida, July 23 1998

Hurricane Hubert was only two hours away now, although the National Hurricane Center computer was still uncertain how hard it was going to hit the suburbs east of Orlando. The evening sky was filled with dirty, scurrying clouds, and sheets of newspaper were tumbling through the parking lot and clinging to the fences. The lid suddenly lifted off a trashcan and rolled noisily across the street. The pressure was dropping like a stone: and everywhere windows were rattling and doors were juddering as if they were all in a panic to get away.

Guido came into the starkly lit kitchen, took off his tight black coat, and said, 'Come on, you guys, *pronto*! We have to close up!'

Micky was still struggling with the cheese dishes. Guido stalked up to him and watched him with a hugely exaggerated expression of patience. 'Mother of God,' he said, at last. 'They didn't build Rome in a day. Maybe they didn't build it in a week. But they built it quicker than you wash up dishes!'

'Hey come on, this is mozzarella, all caked on,' Micky protested.

'I *ha*-know what it is,' Guido told him, standing so close beside him that Micky could smell the steady invisible streams of garlic puffing out of his nostrils. 'But you don't have to know what it is. All that you have to do is clean it off, and we have to close up. This is your *ha*-job.'

'Yes, sir, Guido, sir,' said Micky. He didn't even attempt to argue. Guido may have behaved like a highly stressed band-leader, with his shiny black hair and his clipped mustache. But it was his restaurant and he was paying the wages, there was nothing that you could do. Except, of course, give him the single finger as he walked out of the room.

'You know what your trouble is, *ha*-Micky,' said Guido, without moving any further away. 'You don't have the right brain to wash dishes. You keep thinking how many more you got to do. You shouldn't think how many more: concentrate on what you got in the water.'

Micky stacked another plate onto the drainer. 'The agency didn't mention anything about Zen,' he said.

'What you say, Zen?'

'Look, if I'm kind of slow, I'm sorry; but it's only my second week and I don't have the karmic attitude you obviously need to clean caked-on mozzarella. Not yet, but – you know, give me time.'

Guido stuck his stiffened finger under Micky's

nose. 'You know what your trouble is? You think you're some kind of *ha*-genius?'

'Hey, look,' said Micky. 'I think I've cracked it. If I gently tap this cheese dish while holding it under a continuous stream of lukewarm water, all the cheese slides off without scrubbing. Magic.'

He lifted the dish out of the sink and held it up, sparkling and clean. Guido looked at him as if he had just interfered with his sister. He turned without a word and went across to the other side of the kitchen, where he screamed at Rashid for putting the cherries into the icebox next to the swordfish steaks.

'You never hear of mingling?' he demanded.

'Someplace in China, isn't it?' Micky put in.

Although Micky found washing dishes totally nauseating – all that pale spaghetti floating in the water like sea-snakes – and although Guido was such a pain in the rear end, this job was just what he needed. It was steady; it didn't pay too badly; and most of all it didn't require concentration. He could think about other things while he was swabbing off bolognese sauce – think about songs and lyrics and whatever other creative flotsam drifted into his mind. On the day shift, too, he could look out of the kitchen window and watch all the rollerblading girls glide by, and some of them were Bettys. Apart from that, there was always plenty of food left over at the end of the night, pasta and *sfincuini* and, if Guido wasn't watching, a tuna steak or a pork cutlet, or even a steak. Tonight, for instance, Micky had carefully wrapped up a

14

large portion of cannelloni in aluminum foil.

Better than the food, though, was the fact that Guido's was only a nine-minute drive away from the house which Micky was renting on Canoe Creek Road. He could roll out of bed at 11 a.m. and have his hands in hot water by twenty minutes after.

His father (his plain-speaking, serious-faced father) had badly wanted Micky to join him in the family shoe-repair business, Life & Sole, in Poindiana; but Micky had played in his father's store ever since he could crawl and he had an over-whelming aversion to the smell of leather and human feet. Besides, he didn't think he *looked* like a shoe repairer. He had inherited his father's darkness, and his height, but he looked mostly like his mother, with a thin, almost haunted face with very sharp cheekbones, a long straight nose, and eyes the color of sky, when you see it reflected in rainwater.

He was into his black period at the moment, and so he was hardly ever seen in anything but black T-shirts, black jeans, and black cowboy boots. He could have been a very minor saint, painted by El Greco.

He sang as he finished off the last of the dishes. '*I thought I saw you . . . beside my bed . . . you climbed in next to me . . . but I was dead.*' He had always wanted to be a rock star. He could imagine melodies in his head and he could think of what he wanted to say, but so far he had never been able to play those imagined melodies on his guitar, or write down what he really wanted to say in words. All the same, he kept on practising, and he and his friend

15

Mingus had at least half a band going. They talked for hours about what they were going to do when they were rich and famous. Micky was going to buy a Dodge Viper and Mingus was going to buy a Ferrari, and they were going to race each other along Daytona Beach.

Micky would buy his girlfriend Roxanne a diamond as big as a Cheerio, so that she could wave it under the noses of all of her friends.

He emptied the sink, hung up his apron, took his cannelloni and walked through the double swing doors into the restaurant. The main dining-room was paneled in varnished wood, with a photographic mural of Lake Como at one end, and plastic ivy leaves hanging from a trellis on the ceiling. Heng, the Chinese busboy, was putting up all the chairs on the tables. Mario the chef was shrugging on his coat and arguing with Guido about tomorrow's dish of the day. Mario was huge, with a heavy black mustache and thick black curly hair like a rug. He was Guido's brother-in-law and they always argued.

Guido believed that the customer was always right, even if the customer wanted tomato ketchup on his *torta di carciofi*. Mario thought that the customer was little more than a cockroach who shouldn't be allowed to crawl all over his sacred preparations. How could you give *luganega* sausages and boletus mushrooms to people who could actually stomach airline food, and McDonalds, and that rubbery Peking Duck they served at Panda Express?

★   ★   ★

16

Out front, Guido's shield-shaped sign clattered in the rising wind. The pressure kept on dropping and dropping, and Micky began to feel as if all the air in the restaurant were being dragged outside, and swept along with the papers and the Dr Pepper cans and the whipped-up whirls of dust.

They heard a loud bang and a squealing of tires. Three blocks to the west, the gold fiberglass dragon that advertized the Szechuan Palace had taken an abrupt nosedive into the street, causing a minor collision and flattening its face.

'One hundred years' bad luck,' remarked Heng, with considerable relish. He used to work at the Szechuan Palace.

Up above them there was a tearing noise, followed by a violent flapping. The shingles were flying from the roof. Guido said, 'Come on now, people; it's time to put up the shutters.'

On the boardwalks outside, five of them wrestled to close the storm-shutters and fasten them tight. Micky found Guido's tabby cat hiding under a heap of empty vegetable crates. She scratched his hands, but he brought her inside, mewing and shivering. 'Stupid cat,' said Guido. 'You want a one-way flight to Cocoa Beach?' But he gave Micky an appreciative nod, and said, 'Take a bottle of Frascati with you . . . it'll go good with all that cannelloni you've stolen.'

Micky smiled back at him as if somebody had pinned the corners of his mouth with hair-grips.

Guido locked and bolted the doors behind him, and Micky hurried out into the night, his wine and his cannelloni swinging in a plastic Publix bag. The

17

National Hurricane Center had forecast that Hubert's full force would swing well to the south of Kissimmee, and Vine Street was still busy with traffic, but all the same Micky wanted to get back home and shut himself in before the big blow really got up to strength.

He climbed into his battered red Camaro with the one blue door, and pulled out onto the street with a loud blare from his punctured muffler. He switched on the radio and turned up the volume to Almost Deaf, and slapped his hands on the steering-wheel in time to Sugar's 'Hoover Dam', occasionally joining in the words in a high, strangled whine.

It took only a few minutes to drive as far as St Cloud, passing under the concrete arches of Florida's Turnpike. The wind buffeted the car and whistled through the gap in the ill-fitting side window. Micky was about to turn right down Canoe Creek Road when he remembered that he'd run out of coffee, and he wasn't sure that he had any fresh bread, either. He turned into the brightly lit parking lot outside Winn-Dixie, switched off his radio and climbed out of the car.

Dog food, too, dammit, he'd forgotten dog food. His Labrador Orbison would be waiting for him with his eyes all expectant and his tongue hanging out like a wet dishrag.

He had almost reached the entrance to the store when he heard somebody shouting: hoarse, and high-pitched. He stopped and turned around, and saw three men scuffling together, next to a black Lincoln with its engine running and its doors wide open, and its headlights on, high beam. Micky thought: ferr-get it, man, somebody else's problem, and went into the store. But as he did so he heard more shouting, and one of the men suddenly broke free from the other two, and started hobble-running toward the store, waving both his arms.

Now that the man was closer, Micky could see that he was quite elderly, early seventies probably, with spectacles and white, close-cropped hair. The other two were much younger. They caught up with him and knocked him to the ground. Then they took an arm each and started to drag him back toward the Lincoln, his knees buckled, his shoes scraping on the asphalt.

Micky hesitated. He wasn't physically strong and he wasn't particularly brave, but it upset him to see an old man like that being pushed around. He went back out into the wind and called out, '*Hey*! Hey, you! What the hell do you think you're doing?'

The men didn't even turn around, so Micky called out again. 'Hey, you guys! What's going on?'

They continued to ignore him, so he started jogging toward them. They had already reached the Lincoln and they were trying to force the old man into the back seat. He was clinging onto the door and shouting, 'Get off me, goddammit! Get off me! Leave me alone!'

Micky came up to the car and gave one of the men a sharp shove on the shoulder. 'Hey, what's going on here?'

The man turned around. He was wearing a smart yellow Italian sport coat, but he had a chest like an oil drum and no neck at all. His eyes gleamed like the heads of freshly hammered nails. 'Butt out,' he recommended.

'I just want to know what's going on. It seems to me like this gentleman here isn't too keen on taking a ride.'

The wind sent a stray hubcap rolling across the parking lot, and the Lincoln bucked on its suspension. The old man said, 'Please, help me! Please! You have to! These men are—'

The second man pried his fingers off the car door, gave him another push, and slammed the door shut. He was tall and gingery-haired, with a pale bony head like a horse's skull. 'He's a loony, okay?' he told Micky. 'Touched, if you know what I mean. We're taking him back to the funny farm. Thanks for your interest.'

The old man was beating with his fists against the window. Micky looked from one of the men to the other, and didn't know what to do. Either one of them could have done him a severe injury without pausing for breath. Together, they could kill him. 'I still think maybe we could call a cop,' he suggested.

'Believe me, not necessary,' said Oil-drum, climbing heavily into the front passenger-seat.

Horse's-head gave Micky a grin full of malice and Scrabble-tile teeth, and walked around the front of the Lincoln to the driver's door.

'Hey, wait up,' said Micky. 'This old guy is really distressed.'

'Of course he is. He doesn't like to be caught. The doctors will give him a sedative, okay? Now thank you very much and goodnight.'

20

Micky took a step back. He really wasn't sure about this. But as the Lincoln backed out of its parking-bay, the old man managed to open his window two or three inches and shout out, 'For God's sake, help me! They're going to kill me!'

Oil-drum twisted around in his seat and smacked him across the head, knocking his glasses off; and that was all the incentive that Micky needed. No genuine psychiatric nurse would beat up on a patient like that. And no genuine psychiatric nurse would swerve his car around and head for the exit with his tires howling. Micky ran for the Camaro, threw himself into the driver's seat, started up the engine, and came skidding out of his parking bay in a tight screeching semicircle.

The Lincoln bounced out onto the main road, and took a sharp right amid a cacophony of car horns. Then it immediately cut left across the intersection with Canoe Creek Road, barely catching the traffic signals. Micky went after it, blaring his horn and flashing his headlights. He was met by a barrage of cars and pick-ups coming the other way, and blaring their horns at him in return; but he managed to maneuver his way around them, left and then right, and then left again, before kicking down the Camaro's gas pedal and speeding after the Lincoln with an earsplitting crackle from his badly tuned 5.7-liter engine.

Up ahead, the Lincoln had been delayed for a moment at Neptune Road, but now Micky could see it pulling out from the line of traffic and over-taking three and four cars at a time. Some of them protested by blowing their horns, and then protested even more loudly when Micky overtook them, too. The next five miles of Canoe Creek Road were almost totally straight, but they were narrow and badly lit, and now the sky was covered in inky, tumbling clouds, and a furious crosswind was blowing. Palm fronds flew through the air and lashed against Micky's windshield. Surrealistically, a flimsy wooden chicken-coop with a white rooster in it came tumbling across the road, and Micky had to swerve to avoid crushing it.

The Lincoln was traveling at well over 60 m.p.h., but Micky was gaining on it. He didn't really know why he was chasing it, or what he was going to do if he caught it. But he was so keyed up that he couldn't have stopped now, even if somebody had given him a very good reason. He pressed his foot even harder on the gas pedal, and the Camaro rewarded him with an extra surge of rough, un-diluted power.

They passed the entrance to Lakeside Acres, the last suburban enclave between here and Kenansville, and the sign for Lakeside Acres went past in a flash. From here, the road grew even narrower and even more rural, and the Lincoln began to spew out clouds of dust, which the wind lifted into a high, swirling banner. The blacktop was pitted and uneven, and Micky's car bounced and banged on its worn-out shocks.

In less than two miles, Micky was so close to the Lincoln that he could see the old man sitting in the back seat. He flashed his headlights and leaned on his horn, but the Lincoln slewed from one side of the road to the other so that he couldn't overtake.

He tried edging nearer, until their bumpers were almost touching, but the Lincoln managed to accelerate out of his reach. His engine was hammering and he knew that he was blowing out smoke, and he had to admit that he was never going to catch this turkey, not in an out-and-out race.

It was then that he saw two tiny red lights, way up ahead in the darkness. Another car, maybe? But they were coming up so fast that they couldn't be a car. Gradually, he saw what the Lincoln's driver must be seeing too. A tractor, with a trailer, stacked up high with bales of hay. It couldn't have been traveling at more than 5 or 6 m.p.h., and it was swaying drunkenly in the wind, with fragments of dried grass flying from it. The Lincoln braked, with a red flare of lights, and that was all Micky needed to push his Camaro forward and nudge its back bumper.

There was a Wagnerian chorus of tires as the Lincoln swerved from one side of the road to the other. The driver regained control, but Micky was close enough now to hit him again, much harder this time. There was a deep, satisfying crunch of metal and plastic and broken glass, and one of the Lincoln's lights went out. Micky kept the Camaro's nose rammed up against the Lincoln's back bumper, and the Lincoln began to wander wildly onto the wrong side of the road.

The tractor was now less than a hundred feet away. The Lincoln's driver desperately tried to avoid it, but it was being blown so hard by the wind that it was halfway across the road. Micky saw a collision coming up and hit his brakes. The Camaro slid sideways and then spun on its axis, so that Micky saw the night going around like a carousel. He came to an abrupt stop and banged his forehead on the steering-wheel. As he did so, he saw the hay-trailer tip up on its side, right across the road, and the Lincoln drive straight into it, with a spectacular explosion of hay.

Bruised, shaking, Micky climbed out of the car. The wind was shrieking now, a weird high-pitched wail that sounded like a pack of hounds straining against their choke-chains. He struggled across the road, his collar flapping up and repeatedly slapping his face. The Lincoln was half buried in hay, its lights still blazing but its engine dead. A bony young man in denim dungarees and a red Ford cap was stepping his way through the wreckage.

'It weren't my fault,' he appealed. 'The wind just catched my trailer and there wasn't nothing I could do.'

Micky didn't say anything but wrenched open the Lincoln's back door. The old man was sitting with his head in his hands, and there was blood dripping steadily from his nose. Next to him, Oil-drum was slumped awkwardly against the door, his face squashed against the window. His cheeks were ashy gray but Micky could hear him breathing, a horrible harsh little *heee . . . heee . . . heee*. In the driver's seat, Horse's-head sat slumped forward into his deflated airbag, and even if he wasn't dead he was certainly unconscious.

'You saw what happened,' the young man insisted. 'There just weren't no warning at all.'

Micky said, 'Call an ambulance, why don't you?'

More cars were beginning to reach the scene of the wreck, and the road was lit up with headlights. 'Somebody must have a car phone.'

He reached inside the Lincoln and tried to feel the old man's pulse, but he wasn't exactly sure where he should put his finger. The old man lifted his blood-smeared face and frowned at him. 'Are you a doctor?' he asked, thickly.

'Well, no sir. I was the one who tried to stop these men from taking you away.'

The old man looked around the interior of the car. 'We've crashed,' he concluded. He touched his nose with his fingertips. 'Christ, that hurts. I hope it's not broken.'

'There's an ambulance on its way, don't worry about it.'

The old man retrieved his glasses from the floor. They had been badly twisted but he managed to fit them back on again. 'Can't *you* take me to the hospital?'

'Well, I don't know. Supposing you've been whiplashed, something like that? Or you've got some kind of internal injury. I could kill you, if I moved you.'

'For Christ's sake, I have a nosebleed, that's all. Now why don't you drive me to the nearest hospital and let the paramedics deal with these two jokers.'

'But, listen, I really don't think—'

The old man heaved himself out and faced Micky unsteadily, holding onto the roof of the car for support. 'I'm just asking you to get me out of here,' he breathed. 'You wanted to save me, so *save* me.'

25

Micky glanced around. People were starting to climb out of their cars and walk toward them to see what was going on. The bony young man in the denims caught their sleeves and pointed out the wreckage to each of them in turn. 'See that? The wind catched it, and over it went.' He was holding onto his cap to stop it from blowing away.

Micky helped the old man across the road and into the passenger seat of his Camaro. 'Come on,' the old man urged, 'let's go before the law get here.'

'You got some kind of problem with the law?' Micky asked him, dubiously.

'Not really, no. I just don't want . . . complications, that's all.'

Micky thought for a moment, then shrugged, and closed the passenger door. If the old man didn't want complications, who was he to argue? And he might as well finish what he'd started. He dropped behind the wheel, started the Camaro's engine, and gunned it hard.

'Your timing-chain needs adjustment,' the old man told him, matter-of-factly.

Micky flashed him a quick, curious look, and then reversed the Camaro across the road so that he could turn around and head back toward St Cloud. 'You some kind of auto-mechanic?' he asked, as they gathered speed.

The old man was dabbing his nose with his bloodstained handkerchief. 'Unh-unh. I'm what you might call a jack-of-all-trades. Little bit of this, little bit of that. You know what I mean.' He had a curiously flat, formal way of talking. Micky glanced at him from time to time as he drove and he was impressed by his slimness, and his wiriness. He had the look of a retired doctor or a defrocked priest. His short-cropped hair was stone white, and his neck was withered. Micky would have guessed that he couldn't be younger than 75. Yet he looked alert and fit, and he had the inner tension of a much younger man. He had a lean, oval face, large distinctive nose, and very dark eyes. He was wearing a slate-gray coat, a loose charcoal-gray shirt and black pants, all of which looked expensive. He had something else expensive, too: a gold Rolex Oyster wristwatch worn slightly too loose.

'I want you to know that I very much appreciate what you've done,' he told Micky. 'You took a risk and you didn't have to.'

'It was nothing. I think I even enjoyed it.'

'I never thought they'd ever find me, to tell the truth.'

Micky waited for him to explain further, but he didn't. As they approached the lights of St Cloud, he said, 'How's your nose? You want to go to the hospital?'

'I'll live. It's stopped bleeding now.'

'You want me to drop you someplace? Is your car back in the parking lot?'

'Yes, but – let's make a little reconnaissance first, if you don't mind.'

Micky drove up to the main road and stopped at the traffic signals. The old man peered cautiously across the road toward the Winn-Dixie parking lot.

'Well?' asked Micky, trying to be patient.

'Yes – I can see my car. But there's another car

not far away and it looks as if two men are sitting in it.'

'Another two? What the hell did you do?'

The old man disregarded that question. Instead he said, 'Would you mind driving me home? I'm pretty sure they haven't found out where I live, otherwise they would have gone for me there.'

'What about your car?'

'Forget it, I can't use it again, now they know that it's mine.'

'Forget it? Just forget it? Which one is it?'

'The blue Mercedes, see it?'

Micky followed the direction in which he was pointing and made out a Mercedes SL600 roadster in gleaming metallic blue.

'Just *forget* it?' he said. 'That must have cost you fifty or sixty grand.'

'One hundred and twelve thousand nine hundred sixty, and thirty-eight cents.'

Micky looked at him. 'I'm impressed. This baby cost me $480 cash.'

The old man smiled. 'Well, that shows how stupid I am, doesn't it? Instead of my Mercedes, I could have had 235 of these, and $160.38 change.'

The lights changed to green, and a pick-up truck behind them started hooting, and Micky had to say, 'Which way? Which way?'

'Left. You know the way to Winter Park?'

'Sure. Not that I go there too often.'

'Summerland Avenue. I'll direct you.'

They drove back along Vine Street, under the concrete columns of Florida's Turnpike, and passed Guido's restaurant, which was all closed and shuttered now, like most of the restaurants along the strip. The golden dragon had been retrieved from the road and was being ceremoniously carried into Szechuan Palace by six windblown waiters. There were far fewer cars on the road. The wind had risen noticeably since Micky had left work. Dust and debris were blowing across the sidewalks like dark, twisting snakes. A large piece of tarpaper roof came flying through the air like Batman and cartwheeled across the highway in front of them.

'Wild night,' said the old man. 'By the way, my name's Lügner . . . Dr John Lügner.'

'Micky Frasier . . . pleased to make your acquaintance. You a doctor of anything special, or a doctor doctor?'

'As I told you, I'm a jack-of-all-trades. A doctor of this and a doctor of that.'

'I keep getting this rash on my arm, see?'

Dr Lügner peered at it. 'Nummular eczema. What do you do for a living?'

'Wash dishes. Well, just for now. I'm a musician really.'

'Try wearing rubber gloves when you wash; and don't have the water too hot. If it persists, use a detergent substitute with benzalkonium chloride.'

'Right,' said Micky, lifting his arm and looking at his rash as if it had already healed. 'Thanks for the tip.'

They drove into Winter Park and Dr Lügner said, 'Don't forget the speed limit. It's 25; and it's strictly enforced. Even when there's a hurricane blowing.'

'Got you,' said Micky. He dropped his speed and they burbled along Park Avenue, empty and immaculate. On either side stood solid, handsome, turn-of-the-century business buildings, and restrained modern stores. There was scarcely any trash tumbling across the road here because there was scarcely any trash to tumble. This was one of Florida's wealthiest and most traditional communities, where the City Commissioners did everything they could to prevent growth and development. Beyond Park Avenue sprawled a haven of hugely expensive lakefront houses and tree-canopied streets, where the residents could safely walk at night – although tonight the trees were wildly thrashing like tribal dancers, and the residents had obviously decided to shutter themselves up.

Dr Lügner directed Micky to Summerland Avenue, which was lined on both sides by enormous estates, most of them hidden behind trees and bushes. 'Make a left here,' he said; and Micky found himself driving between lofty wrought-iron gates, and up a long, red-asphalt driveway. His headlights illuminated beautifully trimmed privet hedges and a massive magnolia, which was shedding its white, waxy petals in the wind, and strewing them all over the lawns.

He drew up in front of a large turn-of-the-century house of pale honey-colored brick, with a pillared portico and impressive double oak doors. The windows had all been shuttered, but the house still looked handsome and inviting. Micky thought of his shabby two-bedroom place out on Canoe

Creek Road and wondered how anybody could say that the Lord thy God is a just God.

'How about a drink?' Dr Lügner suggested.

'No, thanks, I have to get back. My dog hates any kind of storm. I don't want him panicking and tearing the place apart.'

'Come on, one drink. It's the least I can offer you.'

Micky reluctantly climbed out of the Camaro and followed Dr Lügner up the front steps. 'Some place,' he remarked, as Dr Lügner went to a stainless-steel alarm panel and punched out a series of four numbers, saying them out loud as he did so. After a few moments the double doors swung open. 'Oh . . . don't try memorizing the numbers,' Dr Lügner told him. 'The sequence changes every time the door opens.'

Micky said, 'I couldn't remember them anyway. Hey, I can't even remember my own telephone number most of the time. Good thing I never need to call myself up. Hna!' then wished he hadn't snorted at his own joke.

They stepped into a high-ceilinged hallway, decorated in buttery yellows, with gilded mirrors and a polished marble floor. As they walked across it, one of the side doors opened and a delicate young woman in a scarlet sari appeared. She could have been Thai, or Indonesian. She was dark-skinned, and very graceful, with long black hair pinned up in a ponytail; and she brought with her a strong fragrance of patchouli. She greeted Dr Lügner with a wide smile. 'I was worried about you, Doctor,' she said. 'What happened to your nose?'

'I'm fine, Suna. Just a bump. Here – I want you to meet a new friend of mine, Micky Frasier.'

Suna bowed her head and said, 'I am honored to meet you, sir.'

'Well, the honor's all mine,' said Micky, embarrassed by her formality. 'Really nice place you have here. Comfortable, you know. Smart. Pricey, I'll bet.'

'Yes,' smiled Dr Lügner, 'pricey.' He laid a hand on Micky's shoulder and led him through to a formal sitting-room. The walls were painted pale turquoise and the floor was highly polished oak. There were French windows all along the left side of the room, and by the end window stood a grand piano, in a natural oak veneer to match the floor. There were huge varnished paintings all around, including a vivid scene of New York on a snowy winter's night, with bustled women and derby-hatted men, and horsedrawn carriages.

'Have a seat,' said Dr Lügner. 'What would you like to drink? I have some pretty good bourbon. I had the Jack Daniel distillery prepare it to my own specification.'

'You're kidding me.'

'Absolutely not. They wanted to market it, too, but there was too much legal wrangling over percentages.'

Micky sat down on a long gilded sofa upholstered in gold and silver brocade. He had never been in a house so opulent before, and he didn't know whether he felt excited or anxious, or a little of both.

'You been here long?' he wanted to know.

'Too long,' said Dr Lügner, handing him a heavy square crystal glass filled with a generous measure of bourbon. 'Sometimes it feels more like a penitentiary than a home.'

'You don't get out much, then?'

'I travel as often as I can. I was in Vienna last month for the conference on cancer research, and I'm hoping I can get to Malta in October. But every time I show my face I'm taking a risk. You saw what happened tonight.'

Micky put his nose into his bourbon glass and inhaled deeply. He had never smelled bourbon like it before. It was aromatic, strong, with a smooth smoky finish. He sipped it, and shook his head in appreciation as it slowly burned down his throat. 'This is something. You really invented this?'

'I didn't invent it. I blended it. I *composed* it. I worked out which flavors were the most appealing, and in what comparative strengths, and the rest was easy.'

Micky sipped some more. 'All I can say is . . . eat your heart out, Old No.7.'

'*I'm* pleased with it,' said Dr Lügner, not trying very hard to be modest. He sat on a single armchair facing Micky and crossed his legs. 'I *could* market it, I suppose. But then why should I? What do I need with a whiskey distillery?'

'Oh, well, sure,' Micky agreed. 'Just more worry, I guess.' He couldn't work out this Dr Lügner at all. He was obviously rich; he seemed to know everything about more or less everything; and yet he was cautious about traveling and he was obviously frightened that tonight's kidnap attempt was going to be repeated. A sudden gust of wind blew deep and hollow down the chimney, and the shutters rattled.

'You're a musician, then?' Dr Lügner asked him. 'What do you like to play? Chopin? Rachmaninov?'

Micky gave him a shrug. 'Not exactly. I mean, don't get me wrong. I like some of the classics. That one with the cannons, you know. But I'm more of a Sugar man myself. You heard of Sugar?'

'Sugar? Yes, I like Sugar.' Dr Lügner walked around to the piano, put down his glass of bourbon, and opened the lid. He tinkled a little while, and Micky thought he was going to play something classical, like *Eine kleine Nachtmusik*. But without warning he launched into a hammering version of 'Slick', playing it note-perfect all the way through, and even singing the words. He finished it up with a grand symphonic flourish, running his fingers all the way across the keyboard and playing a last thunderous chord that was still sounding when he stood up.

'Sugar?' he asked Micky, with a smile, even though his spectacles were twisted and the bridge of his nose was swollen up like a boxer's.

Micky couldn't help laughing in amazement. 'That was incredible. You don't want to jam with my band, do you?'

Dr Lügner shook his head. 'I don't think so. I have more challenging things to do than play cover versions of Sugar songs.'

'Is there *anything* you're no damned good at?'

'Well, now you come to mention it, I'm hopeless at volleyball. No interest in the outcome. And I'm not particularly good with women, either. I guess it's a question of conflicting interests. I want to talk about quantum physics; but they'd rather spend the evening criticizing their best friend's new dress.'

'You're not married?'

'I was . . . a long time ago. But I guess once was enough.'

'What about those guys who tried to kidnap you? Who are they?'

'I suppose they'll get me in the end. They're closer now than they've ever been before.'

'But who the hell *are* they?'

'I'm sorry, Micky, I can't tell you that. It wouldn't be fair.'

'Listen, I saved you, didn't I?' said Micky. 'It would be kind of interesting to know what from.'

Dr Lügner sat down on the sofa next to him. 'They're a paradox. I don't know why they're so persistent. *I* know what they want, but I don't think *they* do.'

'If they don't know what they want, how do they know that they want it?'

'I think they want *me* to answer that.'

Dr Lügner took a large swallow of bourbon and then stood up again. 'Let me show you the library,' he said. 'Do you like books, or are you just a music man?'

Micky brought his drink and followed him out of the sitting-room, across a corridor, and into a book-lined room that was only a little smaller than Micky's entire house. There were shelves of books all the way up to the ceiling, thousands of them, and a sliding library ladder so that they could be reached. In the center of the room stood a large antique partner's desk, with a green leather top, and an IBM personal computer. Next to the computer was a neat stack of paper with the title *Nicotine Mimicry of Acetylcholine*.

'You writing this?' said Micky, and when Dr Lügner nodded, he said, 'Incredible. I couldn't even pronounce that, let alone write a book about it.'

Also on the desk was a small bronze statuette of a 1920s fan dancer, a Cartier clock, and a silver-framed photograph of a woman standing in a garden.

'My late wife,' said Dr Lügner.

Micky looked up, surprised. The woman in the picture couldn't have been older than 27 or 28.

'I'm sorry. She was a good-looking lady, wasn't she?'

'Yes, she was. I still miss her. I never even had the opportunity to say goodbye.'

Micky walked slowly around the library while Dr Lügner sat on the edge of the desk and watched him. Micky had the feeling that Dr Lügner wasn't sure if he had done the right thing, letting him into his home. But he also had the feeling that Dr Lügner was extremely lonely, and that it was rare for him to have found anybody who was prepared to help him, and talk to him like a human being, too. With all of his piano-playing and book-writing abilities, his friends probably treated him more like a party trick, rather than a man. That's if he had any friends.

At the far end of the library there was a tall glass-fronted case of books all identically bound in green leather with gold-blocked titles. 'Hey . . . there's a book on sea-fishing here,' said Micky. 'Do you like to fish?'

'Well, I'm a little too old for it now. But I used to.'

'My friend Mingus and me went fishing for blackfin tuna last year, off Key West. That was the coolest. All we caught was two stupid mackerel and a barracuda . . . well, half a barracuda. The other barracuda kept jumping up and biting chunks out of it while it was hanging on the line.'

'Don't worry about it, barracuda taste disgusting, and they can give you a very nasty disease called ciguatera. You should try shark. I worked on some very interesting ways of catching shark. I compounded a chemical gel that dissolved in the water and affected their thinking processes. It made them hyper-aggressive to the point where they attacked the bait without any of their usual caution. It had some similarities to Prozac. And I'll tell you something really interesting about sharks—'

Dr Lügner talked about sharks and shark-fishing for nearly a quarter of an hour. He had caught mako, blue pointer, tiger and hammerhead sharks, all of them man-eaters. Then he digressed into a revolutionary new resin that he had invented for making fiberglass fishing poles that were virtually unbreakable. Micky nodded and listened, and listened and nodded, and soon began to understand why women might find him boring. Not only did he *know* everything: he seemed to have *done*

37

everything, too, and ten times better than anybody else. Women might find him boring: men would find him unbearable.

Micky's eyes wandered back to the bookcase. There were no other books about sea-fishing, although there was *The Geography of Salmon Breeding*. Other titles ranged from *Mozart and Spatial Reasoning Skills* to *Napoleonic Battle Strategy*; from *Advanced Orthodonty* to *Gastronomic Cookery*.

'Pretty serious collection,' Micky admitted. 'Makes me wish I had more time to read.'

'Do you want to borrow something? You're quite welcome.'

'Well, no, I don't think so. Somebody lent me *The Shining* two years ago, and I'm still on page two. If I borrowed any of these books, you'd be dead by the time you got them back.'

The wind shook the shutters and somewhere outside there was a sharp clattering sound, as if a garden chair had blown over.

'Listen,' said Micky. 'Thanks for the drink and the guided tour and everything, but I think I'd better be getting back. My dog and all.'

'There's just one thing—' said Dr Lügner, as if he had suddenly made up his mind about something. 'If they do manage to find me . . . there's something I want you to do for me.'

'Be glad to.'

'They've come this close, so there's quite a high probability that they'll be able to track me down. If they do, I'll arrange for you to receive a package, special delivery. A Sugar cassette, how about that?'

'I don't get it,' Micky frowned, and he didn't.

38

'All you have to do is play it,' said Dr Lügner. 'Play it, and listen to the words.'

'And then what?'

'Then you can make your own decision. You won't be under any kind of obligation.'

Micky said, cautiously, 'Whatever it is you're asking me to do, remember that you hardly know me.'

Dr Lügner gave him the faintest of smiles. 'I know a lot more about you than you think. There are very few people who have the spontaneity to act the way that you did today. I wish there were more people like you.'

'So do I, but my girlfriend won't come off the pill. *Hna*!'

'Well, very well,' said Dr Lügner, tolerantly. 'But will you do that for me?'

Micky looked around the library. Whatever Dr Lügner was into, he was cultured, he was wealthy, and he was polite. What was more, he was going to send him a Sugar tape. Pretty hard to say no.

So he said, 'Okay. Sure. If that's what you want.'

'Just remember that I trust you,' said Dr Lügner, taking hold of his arm in a gesture that was oddly fatherly. 'Those men would probably pay you a great deal of money for that cassette. But if you keep it to yourself, it'll bring you much more than money. It'll bring you things you never even dreamed of; and that's a promise.'

'Still – let's hope they don't find you,' said Micky, trying to sound optimistic.

Dr Lügner guided him to the front doors. 'They nearly caught me today. I don't want to sound melodramatic, but believe me – if it hadn't been for you, I would probably be lying in a swamp some-place, keeping the gators company.'

'And you still won't tell me who they are?'

'I promise you: it's better that you never know.'

'So how do you think they found you?'

'The car, probably. It was leased under another name, but they must have realized that other name was me. I'm not usually so careless.'

'And you can't call the police?'

'Are you kidding me? I might just as well stick a gun in my mouth and have done with it.'

'Aren't you *scared*?'

'Sometimes. Sometimes I feel like God has forgotten about me. Sometimes I feel like I've lost my faith. But I still pray sometimes, as a very last resort. I still pray for peace of mind. "The Lord is my Shepherd, I shall not want."'

Suna the maid came out of the kitchen and bowed her goodbyes. Micky wondered if Dr Lügner were sleeping with her. She was so sweet and pretty that he wouldn't have blamed him.

'I owe you, Micky,' said Dr Lügner. 'But – please – don't talk to anybody about what happened tonight, and don't ever mention that I brought you back here.'

'Don't worry,' said Micky. He turned up the collar of his coat and stepped out into the hurri-cane, so that he had to shout. 'I won't tell a soul!'

As he climbed into his car he gave them a final wave, and then drove off, shaking his head. He reckoned they were just about the strangest couple he had met in his entire life.

2

What is your aim in philosophy? To show the fly the way out of the fly-bottle – Ludwig Wittgenstein, *Philosophische Untersuchungen*

By the time he reached Canoe Creek Road, the wind had risen so much that he had difficulty steering. It had started to rain, and his windshield wipers couldn't keep up. He parked well away from the utility pole that stood outside his house, in case it was blown down during the night. Then he hurried to his front porch, holding a copy of *Guitar Player Magazine* over his head. As soon as he put his key in the lock, he heard Orbison barking furiously and hurling himself at the door.

He let himself in and stood panting and dripping in the tiny hallway, with Orbison jumping up and circling all around him. 'Okay, boy. Settle down, will you? I've had enough rough stuff for one night.'

He took off his coat and hung it on the peg next to the mirror with the curly wrought-iron frame. Behind him, looking over his shoulder, he could see a framed picture of Alfred E. Neuman, the gap-toothed boy from the cover of *Mad* magazine. His girlfriend Roxanne knew a former *Mad* artist, and had given it to him for his last birthday.

He went into the living-room and to his surprise Roxanne was there, sitting on the red-upholstered couch, drinking Dr Pepper and watching *Beavis & Butthead*. She turned around and said, in that little Pan-pipe voice of hers, 'Hi, Micky! You took your time! I've been waiting for you for *hours*!'

'I didn't even know you were coming around,' said Micky, leaning over and kissing her on the top of the head, while Orbison tail-lashed him around the calves.

'I didn't know, either. But they let us off work early; and in any case Mom's staying with Aunt Mercy for the next two days. They need to catch up on some serious family gossip.'

Micky had met Roxanne seven months ago, at a Christmas party in Orlando, mostly for Sea World employees. Roxanne had just quit Sea World because they never gave her a chance at training the killer whales, and she was sick of her hands smelling of fish. Now she worked for Sav-Mart while she trained by mail order to be a reflexologist: she had answered an advertisement in *Woman's Own* that had promised her $30,000+ per year and 'the dignity of self-employment'.

She was just 22, with an over-abundance of long cornstalk-colored hair that she had to keep sweeping out of her face. She was pretty in a slightly elf-like way, with eyes the color of wintergreen Life Savers, and a mouth that was always right on the verge of a sulky pout. She was slim and petite, only 5 feet 4 inches, but she was very full-breasted, and

42

Micky was always telling her that she ought to write off to *Playboy*.

What he loved about her most of all, however, was her dazzling honesty. She had only the haziest knowledge of politics and geography and world issues. She thought that deforestation meant shaving your armpits. But she had views of her own. She adored animals and didn't believe in eating meat. And she always meant exactly what she said and she always, *always* told the truth.

'You eaten yet?' Micky asked her.

'Alfalfa sandwich, cheese Ritz and a Snickers bar.'

'Hey – all three food groups in one meal: that sounds healthy. I brought back some cannelloni but it's beef. How about an omelet? Tomatoes and cheese? With just-a da eentiest sprinkling of cilantro?'

'Okay . . . that sounds cool.'

Orbison started jumping up again and whining. 'Oh, shit,' said Micky. 'I forgot to buy anything for Orbison. That was the whole reason I was held up.'

The small house rumbled ominously as the wind caught it, and palm fronds slapped against the roof. Micky called it a 'house' but it was only a prefabricated plywood building with a flat tarpaper roof. He had a living-room, a kitchen, two cramped bedrooms, and a bathroom with a shower. The bathroom was so small that he had to climb over the toilet to get into the shower.

The kitchen wasn't much more spacious. If there was anybody in the kitchen when Micky wanted to open the icebox door, they all had to shuffle out of it. He looked in the freezer compartment and was relieved to find a pack of eight economy burgers. 'It's okay, boy. Look, *haute cuisine!*'

He switched on the grill, broke eggs into a Pyrex bowl, and sliced up tomatoes. As he worked, he glanced out of the kitchen door and saw his second-hand Fender Stratocaster propped against his one and only armchair. He thought of Dr Lügner sitting at his piano playing 'Slick' as if he had composed it himself: driving and assured, his foot tapping, his eyes closed. What kind of man could understand quantum physics and write books about chemicals that Micky had never even heard of, and at the same time play rock music like a professional? Roxanne came into the kitchen, sat on the single vinyl-topped stool, and started nibbling at shreds of grated cheese and slices of tomato. 'They said on TV that the hurricane looks like it's dying out.'

'Just as well. This place is going to do a *Wizard of Oz* with us, else.'

'Hey, baby, where did you get this bruise?' said Roxanne, lifting his hair and touching his forehead with her fingers. 'How did you do that?'

'It's nothing. I had a little jolt in the car, that's all. Hit my head on the steering-wheel.'

'What, you had an *accident*? You should put butter on that. That's what my granma always did.'

'Listen, it's nothing, really, and I don't want butter on it. What do you think I am? Some kind of human bagel?'

'Okay, okay, suit yourself.'

Micky poured the eggs into the pan, and stirred

44

them around. 'I met this guy tonight,' he said. 'This really strange guy.'

'Oh, yeah? *How* strange?'

'*Very* strange. But friendly. Like, he was incredibly talented and brilliant. But he was a great guy, too.'

'Well, they say that opposites attract.'

'Oh, come on, Roxanne. I'm being serious.' As he tilted the skillet, he told her all about Dr Lügner and Dr Lügner's incredible house; and how Dr Lügner had given him a whiskey that he'd blended himself, and then played the piano for him.

Roxanne stared at him. 'Are you making this up?'

'It's true. I swear it.'

'Oh come on, you're making it up. And if you don't watch out, those eggs are going to turn into like shoe leather.'

'I swear on my mother's life that it's true,' Micky told her, scattering tomatoes and cheese and cilantro into his omelet. 'I couldn't believe it myself. The guy had a brain like a goddamned encyclopedia; and he could do like *anything*. I mean, he'd even invented some kind of new fishing pole that you couldn't break.'

'A *fishing* pole?' said Roxanne, wrinkling her nose in disbelief.

'I promised I wouldn't tell anybody but, Jesus, I had to tell *somebody* otherwise I would have thought I was losing my marbles. Look – it's ready. Hand me those plates, would you?'

He folded up the omelet and slid it out of the skillet. Roxanne said, 'How about a beer to go with it? I brought some over.'

45

She perched on her stool forking up omelet while Micky finished grilling the economy burgers. He dropped them straight into Orbison's bowl, and Orbison had to lunge at them and juggle them with his paws because they were so hot. 'You're so cruel to that dog.'

'He's stupid, that's why. If he wasn't stupid, he would have learned how to eat with a knife and fork.'

'The only reason that Orbison doesn't eat with a knife and fork is because he doesn't have any hands. And I bet he's got a higher IQ than you.'

'Oh, yeah? Come on, Orbison, what's 378 times 506?'

'That's not fair. You don't know what it is yourself.'

'Of course I don't know. But Orbison doesn't even *know* he doesn't know.'

'I still think you're cruel to him.'

They finished their omelets and left the plates in the sink. Then they took the rest of the sixpack into the sitting-room and sprawled on the couch together, legs loosely intertwined. Orbison's economy burgers had now cooled down sufficiently for him to be able to gulp them down the way he usually did – like a jackal that hasn't eaten in a week. The wind had subsided, and was now doing nothing more than sucking sulkily around the window frames, but the wind had been followed by a steady torrent of tropical rain, and every corner of the ceiling was dripping steadily, onto the coffee table, into the plant-pots, and wrinkling up Micky's *Guitar Player* magazines.

Even the René Magritte poster on the wall started to buckle.

Micky used the remote control to silence David Letterman. 'This old guy I met today . . . I couldn't help thinking he was such an outsider, you know? He must have been a multimillionaire. He had everything you could think of. But it was like he didn't belong to the rest of the world. You know, like the kid at school who's brainier than everybody else and nobody ever talks to him.'

'Are you going to see him again?'

'I don't know. The whole thing kind of confused me.'

Roxanne kissed him, and rubbed noses with him, Inuit-style, and grinned. 'I always said you were easily confused.'

'So how was your day?' Micky asked her. 'How's that lovely supervisor of yours?'

'Godzilla? Just the same. Breathing fire and stomping on everything that comes her way.'

'Don't worry . . . so soon as you get your reflexology business up and running, you'll be able to tell her where to get off.'

Roxanne snuggled up close to him and started to play with the cowboy buckle on his belt. 'Then you and Mingus are going to be famous, right? And rich. And then we can tell *everybody* where to get off.'

Micky thought of writing a song about a man who knew everything but lived in a house on his own because nobody wanted to know *him*. '*I met a man* . . .' he began singing. '*A man who had the world in his head . . . he lived alone . . . with no young girl to lie in his bed . . .*'

Roxanne pushed her hair aside and looked up at him. 'He upset you, didn't he? This Loognah guy?'

'I don't know. Like I said, he confused me. I always thought I was bright, but today I met somebody who was so bright he was off the map. I'd give my right arm to play the piano like that – well, no I wouldn't, because then I wouldn't be able to play the piano like that. But all those other things he could do. But he was so damned lonely. Leastways, he seemed like he was. So what's the point of being brilliant if you're so damned lonely?'

Roxanne nuzzled his neck and kissed him. 'You're brilliant; but you're not lonely.'

'No,' said Micky, and kissed her back. 'No I'm not brilliant; and no I'm not lonely.'

They were woken up by somebody beating at the door. Not just beating it, *kicking* it, too. Micky sat up in bed, blinking. It was still raining heavily, and the rainwater that ran down the window threw corrugated shadows on the wall.

'What's that?' asked Roxanne.

'Somebody knocking, for Christ's sake. What time is it?'

She turned over and picked up the white plastic clock beside the bed. 'Twenty after three! Who the hell knocks on your door at twenty after three?'

Micky rolled out of bed and groped around on the floor to find his jeans. The beating went on, loud and unrelenting, punctuated by occasional kicks. There was a bellpush by the front door, but whoever was knocking had either failed to see it or didn't want to use it. Micky hopped and stumbled into his jeans, shouting, 'All right, for Christ's sake! I can hear you!'

Roxanne switched on the bedside lamp. Her hair was heaped up like a corn-rick, and her eyes were completely unfocused. She wore contact lenses and she had left them in the bathroom. 'Micky, be careful! It could be anybody!'

'They've got the wrong house, that's all.' He negotiated his way around the couch until he reached the hallway. The beating went on, louder and louder. Micky switched on the light and he could see that the door was visibly shuddering.

'Hey come on, man, I heard you already! That's my door!'

He opened the latch, keeping the door on the security chain. As he did so, however, somebody gave it a devastating kick, and the chain burst its screws. The door was thrown open, racketing back against the wall, and two men strode with great ferocity into the house. One immediately went to the bedroom while the other slammed the front door shut so that Micky couldn't run away. Not that he would have done, with Roxanne to protect.

'Leave her alone!' he shouted, dodging back toward the bedroom. 'You even breathe on her, man, and I'll fucking kill you, I promise!'

'Hey,' said the man by the front door. 'Why don't you fucking take a chill?'

'Well, what the hell do you want?' Micky shouted at him. 'Do you know what time this is?'

Roxanne screamed, 'Get off me!' and Micky charged back to the bedroom, knocking his shoulder a bruising blow against the doorframe.

Roxanne was sitting up in bed in her pink Minnie Mouse T-shirt. The second man was sitting on the bed next to her, with his left arm draped almost casually around her shoulders, but his right hand firmly gripping her wrist. Her eyes were wide with fright.

'Don't you hurt her,' Micky warned him. 'Don't you dare hurt her.'

The other man came into the bedroom, thoughtfully popping his knuckles. He was short and stocky, but he was smart, in a 1960s *Man from U.N.C.L.E.* style, with a shiny blue mohair suit and a button-down collar and a tinily knotted necktie. His face was bland and round and featureless, more like a bowl of dough than a face. He could have been a life-size Cabbage Patch doll.

The man on the bed looked as if he were Cuban. He was very gaunt, and he wore a sharp black deconstructed suit but the same kind of tinily knotted tie. His black gelled hair was combed back directly from his forehead, and he had an obsessively trimmed mustache. Micky noticed that he was wearing very expensive green crocodile-skin shoes.

'What is this?' asked Micky, after a long moment of silence. 'A robbery? What?'

'Oh, no – no robbery,' said the Cabbage Patch man. His accent was Bostonian or thereabouts, languid, archly voweled, and surprisingly cultured. 'We're not here for profit' – pronounced *praw-fit* – 'Well, not directly, anyhow. All we want to do is to ask you some questions.'

'What questions? Questions about what?'

'You were involved in a little fracas today, yes?'

'I don't know what you mean.'

The man came up and stood very close to him. His nose only came up to the level of Micky's chin, but his physical presence was tremendous, like a steam boiler about to burst. His featureless face made him even more alarming. 'You instigated an accident, yes? just down the road here. I got witnesses. Not only that, the front of your automobile is looking pretty sorry for itself.'

'That was done weeks ago. A crate of oranges fell off the back of a pick-up.'

'Oh, come on, now. You were seen. The farmboy saw you. Six other people saw you.'

'So – even if I was there, what does it have to do with you?'

'I'll tell you what it has to do with us, smart boy. Two friends of ours were in the other vehicle, and one of them broke both his ankles. Apart from that, there was somebody else in the vehicle, too, and that somebody else was seen to be driven away from the scene of the accident in a red Camaro with one blue door.'

'Are you police?' asked Micky. 'If you're police, let's take a look at your shields.'

'Police? Do we look like police? We're just interested parties. And what we're interested in is where you took that somebody else after the accident. Whatever he looks like, whatever he told you, he's a dangerous felon and we have to find him.'

'Your friend said he was a mental patient.'

'That's right. He's a dangerously felonious mental patient.'

But Micky shook his head. 'Unh-unh. I'm sorry, I can't tell you where I took him. I gave him my word.'

'Oh, did you? Well, I give you my word that if you don't tell me where you took him, your life is going to be something less than idyllic from here on in.'

'What the hell are you talking about? This is nothing to do with me! Your friends were beating up on this guy, that's all. What was I supposed to do, look the other way?'

'It would have been healthier for you if you had.'

'Well, I can't help you. I'm sorry.'

Without any hesitation at all, the Cabbage Patch man slapped Micky twice across the face, so hard that he staggered back against the nightstand, spilling Roxanne's glass of water and knocking the alarm clock onto the floor.

Roxanne shouted, 'Stop it! You bastard! Stop it!' and tried to wrestle herself free, but the Cuban hooked his left arm around her neck and pulled her back. The Cabbage Patch man gripped the front of Micky's T-shirt and dragged him to his feet. Micky's ears were singing and he felt as if his lips had swollen to three times their normal size. His mouth was filled with the pewter taste of blood.

'Now you listen very carefully,' said the Cabbage Patch man. He was so close that Micky could smell the dry grassy aroma of his aftershave. 'This may be none of your business, but if you want it to stay that way, you'd better tell me where you took that old buzzard.'

He nodded to the Cuban over Micky's shoulder, and then he turned Micky around. The Cuban had taken out a long double-edged knife and was holding the blade up close to Roxanne's right eye. Micky attempted to wrench himself away, but the Cabbage Patch man twisted his T-shirt into a knot and held him tight. 'I want a little co-operation. That's not much to ask, is it? Otherwise, I'm going to ask my friend to start his long-delayed career as an amateur opthalmic surgeon.'

'Okay, okay!' Micky told him. 'I took him to the airport. He said he was catching a flight to New York.'

'Sorry, stupid answer,' said the Cabbage Patch man. 'Orlando was closed at five o'clock yesterday because of the hurricane, and they haven't re-opened it yet.'

The Cuban held the knife closer to Roxanne's eye and started twisting the blade in the air, grinning widely. Roxanne squeezed her eyes tight shut and clenched her teeth.

'Don't think he wouldn't do it, smart boy,' said the Cabbage Patch man. 'I've seen him do worse than that. I've seen him cut a man's hamstrings, and slit a woman's nostrils, all the way up. She didn't look like a supermodel after that, believe me.'

Micky wiped blood from his mouth. He didn't have any option. After all, what did Dr Lügner mean to him? For all he knew, he *might* be a dangerous lunatic.

'Summerland Avenue, Winter Park,' he said. 'I don't know the name of the house, but it was a couple of houses east of 1300. Big, with pillars, and those curly metal gates.'

'You'd better be telling me the truth,' said the Cabbage Patch man.

'It's the truth, for Christ's sake. That's where he lives. His name's Dr Lügner, right?'

'Dr Lügner? Is that what he told you? *Lügner?*'

'Sure. What's wrong?'

The Cabbage Patch man laughed and slapped Micky hard on the back. 'Come on,' he said to the Cuban. 'Let's leave these good people in peace.'

'What's so damn funny?' Micky wanted to know, as the Cuban sheathed his knife and got up off the bed.

'You, that's what's funny,' smiled the Cabbage Patch man. 'But at least I know you're telling me the truth. You wouldn't have had the nerve to say that his name was Dr Lügner, otherwise. Lügner is German for liar.'

Micky sullenly stood aside while the two men went to the door. On the stoop, the Cabbage Patch man turned around and said, with emphatic jabs of his finger, 'We were never here, you never saw us, and you never went to Winter Park in your life. If I ever hear that you've mentioned this little visit to anybody, *ever*, then you can rest assured that we're going to come back, and then it's going to be white-stick time for both of you.'

They went out into the night and Micky slammed the door. For a long time he stood with his back pressed against it, taking deep steadying breaths. Roxanne stood in the middle of the sitting-room staring at him, ashy-faced.

'Oh, Jesus,' said Micky. 'Oh Jesus, Jesus, Jesus!'

He took Roxanne into his arms and held her as tight as he could. She was shivering all over, and she was so shocked that she couldn't even cry.

'Oh, Jesus,' he kept on repeating. He couldn't think of anything else to say. Then suddenly he let go of Roxanne, went to the back door, unlocked it, and stormed out into the yard. It was still raining, although not as torrentially as it had been before, and the sky was beginning to clear.

Micky went up to Orbison's kennel and banged the roof with his fist. Orbison scrabbled onto his feet and wuffled in surprise.

'You stupid son-of-a-bitch!' Micky raged at him. 'You stupid, lazy, good-for-nothing waste of space! You're supposed to be a guard dog! You're supposed to guard, you asshole! You're not supposed to lie there like a goddamned log while people break into the house and almost cut our goddamned eyes out!'

Orbison retreated into the darkness at the back of his kennel, whining. Micky gave the kennel a kick with his bare foot and almost dislocated his toe. He hopped back to the house, still cursing, pushed past Roxanne and went into the bedroom. He took his wallet and his car keys off the top of the night stand and crammed them into his pocket. Then he dragged on a maroon Dolphins sweatshirt and went searching under the bed for his trainers.

'Micky, what are you doing? You're not going out!'

'I let the guy down, didn't I? He made me promise not to tell anybody where he was, and I did. I'm just going to try to warn him.'

'Are you *nuts*? What do you think they're going to do to us if they find out?'

'They won't find out. I'll just try to get to his house before they do. If they're already there, I'll forget it.'

Roxanne held him tight. 'Micky, don't. You'll never manage to get there first.'

'Listen, the way I can drive—'

'Exactly. That's why I don't want you to go. It's wet, it's dark. If those two guys don't kill you, you'll probably end up killing yourself.'

Micky ran his hand through his tousled hair, and sighed. 'You're right, of course. I just feel so bad about it.'

'You didn't have a choice, did you?'

'No, I guess not. Story of my life.'

Roxanne went through to the kitchen and came back with two large tumblers of Jim Beam. 'Here,' she said. 'I think we need this. I think Orbison could probably do with one, too.'

They sat together on the bed and swallowed whiskey. Roxanne started to cough.

'You look like a goddamned ghost,' said Micky.

'Oh, yes. And what about you, Casper?'

'I just wonder why those guys want to find Dr Lügner so bad. I mean, *he* wouldn't tell me. Said it was safer if I didn't know.'

'Don't get involved, Micky. Whatever it is, it's really dangerous.'

Micky looked around the bedroom, with its lilac-painted walls and its cheap fluffy rug and its faded framed photographs of me and the guys at Busch

Gardens and me and the guys on Daytona Beach. He thought of the shiny hardwood floors in Dr Lügner's house, the mirrors and the gilded furniture, and the piano that was almost big enough to live in.

What had Dr Lügner said to him? '*It'll bring you more than money. It'll bring you things you never even dreamed of, and that's a promise.*'

They finished their whiskey in silence. Then Roxanne went back to bed. Micky jammed a chair under the front door-handle: the frame was too badly splintered to screw the security chain back into place. Then he went out into the yard and apologized to Orbison.

The next morning was hot and humid, and the air around St Cloud was golden with traffic pollution. Micky and Roxanne left the house just after eight. The roads were strewn with broken branches and debris, and there was a Mississippi delta in miniature right across Neptune Road, where the rain had washed the topsoil out of the adjoining fields.

Micky gave Roxanne a kiss and dropped her outside Sav-Mart.

'What time do you finish tonight? Maybe we could go for Chinese.'

'I don't know. I'll call you. Sandy wants me to fix her hair.'

He watched her walk into the store and wave to one of her friends. He loved the way she wiggled when she walked. Then he sat still and thoughtful for a moment, wondering whether he was about to do the right thing. He didn't want to put Roxanne at risk. He didn't want to put *himself* at risk. But he had to know what had happened to Dr Lügner, even if his name did mean liar. You couldn't just betray a man's trust and then forget all about him, for ever.

He drove across the highway to the Winn-Dixie shopping center on the other side. As he circled around the parking lot, he saw orange lights flashing, and a small crowd standing around. A pick-up truck was winching up the rusty-colored burned-out hulk of a pale blue Mercedes SL600. Now Micky knew that he had to go to Winter Park.

Traffic was slow because of the clear-up after yesterday's hurricane, and it took him almost forty-five minutes to get there. He cautiously turned into Summerland Avenue, turning his radio down. He burbled along at walking speed, the same as all the other law-abiding citizens of Winter Park, although he was ready to take off at any moment if he saw any sign of the Cabbage Patch man and the Cuban. The air was beginning to clear now, and the sun sparkled through the tall trees that surrounded the Summerland Avenue estates.

He reached Dr Lügner's house and slowly cruised past it. The driveway was empty and there was no sign of life. He stopped, backed up, and then drove in between the wrought-iron gates. His heart was beating like a washing machine full of galoshes.

He climbed the front steps and pressed the door-bell. He could hear it chiming inside the house, but there was no reply. He went to the large living-room windows and peered inside, but all the ground-floor windows were protected by white-painted wrought-iron grilles, and it was difficult to see anything through the nets except the reflection of the sun on the polished floor, and the silhouette of one of the sofas. He was about to go around the back of the house when he heard the sound of a car drawing up in the road outside. Oh, Christ, if this was the Cabbage Patch man!

He was already hurrying back to his Camaro when two men in light gray uniforms appeared. They wore peaked caps and their belts were hung about with flashlights and nightsticks and hand-cuffs and guns. They jingled officiously as they walked. One of them was young and black and the other was middle-aged and white, with spectacles. Private security guards, goddamnit.

'He'p you with something, mister? This is private property.'

'Yes, I know that. I was looking for Dr Lügner.'

'Dr who?'

'Lügner. I was here yesterday, paying him a visit. There was something I forgot to ask him.'

'No Dr Lügner here, my man,' said the black security guard. 'This here's the Snow property.'

Micky frowned. 'You sure about that? He told me his name was Dr Lügner. But that does mean liar, in German. Lügner, you know – liar.'

The white security guard stared at Micky with a face that looked as if it had been carved out of a curbstone. 'We're going to have to ask you for some ID, my friend. Is that your vehicle parked there?'

'That's right. Listen, if this is a mistake, it's a genuine mistake. I gave the guy a ride home

59

yesterday evening and he invited me in. If he gave me the wrong name – well, that's not my fault, is it? Maybe he was just playing games.'

'Games?' said the black security guard, as if he had never heard the word in his life before.

'Let's see that ID,' the white security guard insisted.

'In the car,' Micky told him. He began to walk carefully back toward the Camaro, keeping his hands in plain sight. Both security guards had unpopped the strap on their holsters, and the last thing he wanted to do was give them an excuse to shoot at him. He reached over the sun-vizor and came back with his driver's license and his pink slip.

He was just about to hand them over when the front doors of the house unexpectedly opened. They all turned around, and to Micky's horror, the Cabbage Patch man appeared, in his shirtsleeves but still wearing his tinily knotted necktie. He stood on the steps and stared at all three of them as if he were waiting for an explanation.

'Pardon me, sir,' said the white security guard, walking across to the porch with his big rump protruding. 'We found this character standing outside here in a suspicious kind of way that could have been interp'eted as loitering. Do you happen to be familiar with him, sir?'

The Cabbage Patch man gave the bleakest of smiles. 'I wouldn't say I was familiar with him, officer, but I do know who he is.'

'And how about him being here on this property, sir?'

'No problem at all.'

'Well, sir, that's all settled then. Just doing our job, sir. Sure you can understand that.'

The Cabbage Patch man didn't answer, but came down the steps and approached Micky along the driveway until he was standing less than two feet away. He looked Micky directly in the eyes but *his* piggy little eyes were unreadable.

'It seems as if the good doctor anticipated our coming,' he said, clearly, but not loudly enough for the security guards to be able to hear him. 'You wouldn't have called to warn him, by any chance?'

'How could I? I didn't know his number. Christ, I only met him that once.'

'Do you know something?' said the Cabbage Patch man. 'I believe you. But let me tell you this: if you ever hear from him again, and I find out that you've heard from him again and you haven't told me, then it's *King Lear* for you, smart boy.'

'*King Lear?*' asked Micky, baffled.

'Shakespeare. They put out some guy's eyes.'

At that moment, a gray panel van came to a halt outside the house. The Cabbage Patch man put his hand on Micky's shoulder and said, 'Time for you to leave. Just remember what I said. Listen – here's a card with my telephone number on it. You ever see or hear from your Dr Lügner again, you give me a call pronto.'

Micky thought: *in your dreams, pudding-face*, but he kept his mouth shut. He climbed into his car and started the engine. The Cabbage Patch man leaned against the roof and said, 'Sorry about the fat lip . . . but, you know, let's face it, you *were* pissing me off, weren't you?'

Micky slammed the Camaro into reverse and backed away with a high squeal of tires, so that Cabbage Patch almost overbalanced. He swung round into the road, and drove noisily back toward the center of Winter Park. He felt angry, frightened, but strangely excited, too, as if he had accidentally stepped into a completely different universe in which anything was possible. He felt almost as if he were on TV.

He reached his first red traffic signal, and stopped. His mouth was dry and he would have done anything for a cold Dr Pepper. He drummed his fingers on the steering-wheel and glanced into his rearview mirror from time to time to make sure that he wasn't being followed. Across the street, with all the patience of daily routine, a man in a gray suit approached a small camera store, took out his keys and unlocked the door.

The signals turned to green, but Micky stayed where he was.

The man had unlocked the door.

And it occurred to Micky for the first time: how had Cabbage Patch managed to get into the house? Dr Lügner had a special constantly changing code to open the door, and all the windows were barred.

There was no other traffic around. He U-turned in the middle of the intersection, and drove back toward the Lügner house. On his way, he passed the two security guards in their Chevrolet Caprice, and they didn't even give him a second glance. But as he passed the Lügner residence, or the Snow residence, or whatever it really was, he saw that the gray panel van was now parked right outside the porch, and that its rear doors were open.

He parked a hundred feet further up the road, and then he climbed out of the car and walked back toward the wrought-iron gates. Keeping himself pressed close against the hedges, he was just in time to see four men in gray coveralls come out of the front door carrying a gurney, with a gray zippered-up bag lolling on top of it. They lifted it into the back of the van and slammed the doors. Jesus. A body bag. Micky had never seen one in real life, but he recognized it from *Homicide: Life on the Streets*.

He ran back to his car, slid into the driving seat and drove off, breathless. He could guess now what Cabbage Patch had done. Rung the door chimes, and kicked his way in as soon as the door was opened, and killed whoever had tried to stop him. If Dr Lügner had escaped, it was probably Suna, his maid. That poor little Asiatic girl with the pony-tail. Jesus.

He drove to work through a nightmare of stop-start traffic, and arrived fifteen minutes late. He parked, and pushed his way through the squeaking swing doors into the restaurant. As he came in, Marcella was sweeping the floor and Guido was arguing with Mario about the dish of the day, *salsicce con le cipolle*, sausages smothered in onions.

'It's peasant food.'

'So? That should suit you down to the ground.'

'If you want to cook sausage, what about *salsicce col vino rosso e i funghi secchi*?'

'We don't have any *funghi secchi*.'

Guido snatched Micky's sleeve without even breaking rhythm. 'Where you been, hah?' Then, to

63

Mario, 'You should have thought of *funghi secchi* last time you went to the market.'

'Sorry, Guido,' said Micky. 'The traffic was a bastard.'

'You look sick. Why do you look so sick? Hurry up, there's baking trays to clean up.'

Mario threw his arm up in annoyance. 'I didn't want no *funghi secchi*! Today I cook *salsicce con le cipolle*, and tomorrow I cook *pollo in fricassea all marchigiana*!'

Heng said, 'Holy shit. This place is worse than one of those operas.'

But Micky didn't say a word. He went through to the kitchen and found his apron and his yellow latex gloves, and then he stood in front of the stainless sink swallowing and swallowing like a man who is trying desperately hard not to regurgitate his breakfast.

3

America is not so much a nightmare as a non-dream – William Burroughs

It was a classic sting. John and Neville were sitting in Room 239 at the Howard Johnson's at Mill Valley, just north of San Francisco, when there was a discreet knock. John nodded to Neville, who levered himself out of his armchair and went across to the door.

'Who is it?' he asked, turning back toward John and giving him a wink.

'The Merchant of Venice,' came the reply. John liked that password. It had a nice ironic taste to it; a nice classical smack of betrayal and greed and ultimate justice.

Neville slid back the security chain and opened the door. Immediately, in stepped a balding middle-aged man in a beige Sta-prest suit and a wide brown necktie, carrying a large sport bag. He was sweating, even though the hotel was fiercely air-conditioned. He hefted the sport bag onto the bed and took off his glasses so that he could wipe them with the end of his necktie.

'Well, Myron, it looks like you came up with the goodies,' said Neville. Neville was black and always immaculately dressed in a blazer and sharply creased pants.

'Believe me, it wasn't easy,' Myron complained. 'Security stopped me at the gate and I thought they were going to search me. It turned out one of my tires was running flat.'

'No profit without a little risk,' said Neville. 'Do you want to open her up, so that we can take a look?'

'I thought maybe the money first.'

'Oh come on, Myron. This isn't crack we're dealing with here. Either you got the goodies or you don't.'

'All right, then,' said Myron. He tugged open the zipper and turned the sport bag upside-down, and shook it. Two dozen plain white cardboard boxes were scattered across the bedspread.

'There you are,' he said. 'The whole range, two boxes of each.'

John stood up and came across to the bed. He picked up one of the boxes and examined it closely, turning it this way and that. Then he opened it up, tore open the inner wrapper, and sniffed it. 'Smells good,' he agreed. Myron watched him tensely as he wet his finger and dipped it inside. He examined the brownish powder that came out, and then licked it. 'Tastes good, too.'

'You can check them all if you like,' said Myron. 'I promise they're all 100 percent. And as soon as I get proofs of the labels from the printers, you can have those, too.'

John checked the typewritten label on the side of the box. Old Mother Brown's Pecan and Toffee Cake Mix, with Pecan Crackle Frosting. He picked up one or two more boxes. Old Mother Brown's Strawberry and Walnut Cake Mix, with Strawberry Snow Frosting. Old Mother Brown's Chocolate Fudge Crunch Cake Mix, with Double Chocolate Frosting.

'Old Mother Brown's sure been busy,' said John. 'Surprised she gets a moment's rest.' He reached down beside the bed and produced a briefcase, which he laid on the bed next to the cake-mix boxes and snapped open. Inside were sixteen bundles of brand-new $100s and $50s. They were so new that they smelled, and Myron visibly salivated. 'There you go, $175,000 in low-denomination bills, as requested. Do you want to count them?'

Myron picked up one bundle and flicked his thumb down the side of it. 'I don't think that'll be necessary, thanks. I can trust you, can't I?'

John and Neville said nothing as Myron closed the briefcase and picked it up. They almost had enough. John laid his hand on Myron's shoulder and escorted him toward the door. 'I'll bet this is the first time you ever got 175 big ones for a few cartons of cake mix,' he smiled.

'Money for old rope, isn't it?' laughed Myron. 'Well, money for Old Mother Brown.'

He started to open the door but John slammed it shut again with the flat of his hand.

'Hey, what's going on?' Myron protested, lifting up the briefcase and clutching it close to his chest. 'We had a deal here, plain and simple. You got the

67

cake mixes, I got the money. Now let me out of here.'

John slowly shook his head. 'Sorry, Myron. No can do. The deal wasn't quite as plain and simple as you thought it was going to be.' He laid his hand on top of Myron's bald patch, and twisted his head around so that he was looking toward the dressing table. On top of the dressing table was a leather toiletries bag – or what appeared to be a leather toiletries bag. Neville pointed to the front of it, and now Myron could clearly see that a circular hole had been cut into the end of it. 'See that, Myron? That's called a hidden camera. Everything you said and did in this room has been faithfully recorded on videotape; and later this afternoon I'm going to take that videotape and show it to your esteemed president Mr Peppard Falmer.'

'You bastard,' said Myron. His face was totally drained of blood. 'You four-flushing bastard.'

'Sorry, Myron, you walked right into it. Any professional would have noticed the toilet bag. Like, we're not staying here, are we? What would we need with a toilet bag?'

Myron hesitated for a moment. Then he suddenly swung sideways and made a desperate grab for the toilet bag. But John blocked him and pushed him away. '*You bastard!*' Myron screamed at him. '*This is my whole life! You bastard!*'

He tried to swing a second time but John dodged aside and twisted the briefcase out of his grasp. 'Give me that!' Myron demanded, his voice rising from a scream to a shriek. But John slung it casually across the room to Neville; and then he punched Myron directly in the nose.

Myron staggered back and sat on the bed, his hands cupped over his face. 'You're a sad case, Myron,' said John, and laid his hand on his shoulder. 'I'm sorry I had to hit you.'

He would have expected Myron to give in at this point, and burst into tears, and go through all the miserable litany of debt and repossession and delinquent children and a wife whose thighs couldn't be opened with a crowbar. But after a few congested sniffles, Myron abruptly sprang up and started hitting John with arms that flailed like a windmill.

'You tricked me! You fucking tricked me you bastard! I was going to go to Hawaii you bastard and you tricked me!'

John punched him again, and then again, and Myron was catapulted back onto the bed. The boxes of cake mix burst, and various-colored powders showered all over the bedspread, pink and brown and bright yellow. Myron tried to lift himself up, but John was angry now, and he climbed onto the bed and punched him again and again, until the air was filled with cake mix, and the whole room smelled of strawberry and chocolate and lemon meringue.

Neville came over and caught John's wrist. 'Hey. Enough already. Look at him.'

John climbed off the bed, panting. Myron was lying spreadeagled amongst the broken boxes, his face pierrot-white, his brown suit dusted with cocoa powder. His nose was bleeding and his left eye was closed up like an overripe apricot.

John rubbed his knuckles, and then he dusted down his coat.

'You shouldn't have done that,' said Neville. 'The guy's lost everything anyhow.'

'Tell that to Old Mother Brown,' John replied.

He came up the white-painted steps of his second-story apartment to find a very tall, dark-haired woman waiting for him on the deck. She was sitting back in his white-painted sunlounger, smoking a cigarette and tapping the ashes into his geranium pots. Her appearance was exceptional. She had strong bone structure, distinctive cheekbones, and eyes that were hooded and almost completely colorless. Her hair was cut in a severely angled bob. She wore a linen suit with a mandarin jacket and loose, flowing pants.

She didn't get up, not even when John took out his keys and unlocked his door. All she did was lift her hand to shade her eyes against the late-after-noon sun. 'Looking for me?' he asked her.

'That's right, Mr Huntley. You don't keep very predictable hours, do you?'

'I don't have a very predictable job.'

He opened the door and went into the kitchen. The marmalade-colored sunlight shone on the copper pans that hung from the ceiling, and turned the skeins of onions into ripe oranges. He laid his briefcase on the pine-topped table, along with a shopping sack containing veal chops, bunches of fresh thyme, and a bottle of red wine. His tortoise-shell cat Molière came strolling in to see him, stretching himself and scratching his claws on the raffia matting that covered the floor.

The tall woman stood in the open doorway, still

smoking. Behind her was the hazy outline of down-town San Francisco, looking like one of those distant, ephemeral cities that are seen in the clouds.

'You want to come in?' John asked her. 'How about a cup of coffee, or a beer?'

'I'm fine, thanks,' she said. She stalked across the kitchen with all the giraffe-like grace of a super-model, drew out a chair, and sat down very close to him, entwining her legs and leaning on one elbow. She wore a very strong perfume, Giorgio or Poison. 'I suppose I'd better introduce myself. I'm Sara Lake. I'm vice-president in charge of personnel for Broussard Guidance Systems, in Cocoa Beach, Florida.'

John went to the icebox, stored his veal chops, and took out a cold can of Pabst Blue Label. He popped the top and took a deep swallow. 'That's better. One of those days.' Then, 'Tell me, what does Broussard Guidance Systems in Cocoa Beach, Florida, want with me?'

'You were highly recommended, Mr Huntley. *Very* highly recommended.'

'Well, thanks for the compliment. But I don't work freelance any longer, I couldn't make enough to feed Molière here. If you want to hire me, you'll have to contact my office. Here – Western Eye Industrial Investigations, Sansome Street. We're running a special this month. Two betrayals inves-tigated for the price of one.'

'I won't be contacting your office, Mr Huntley. This is purely a personal request.'

John smiled and shook his head. 'Sorry . . . like I said, I don't do those any more.'

71

'Maybe you'll change your mind when you hear just how much Mr Broussard can offer.'

'Wait a minute . . . before we go any further, and you tempt me with untold millions, would this personal request involve my actually *going* to Cocoa Beach?'

'It would obviously mean a trip to Florida, yes.'

'In that case, don't say any more. I decline, but thank you for thinking of me.'

'Mr Huntley, we're talking $250,000.'

John nodded, tightly. 'Yes. I knew it would be something like that. That's why I said no first.'

'It's not just the money, Mr Huntley. It's a fascinating case.'

'So what's happening? Some treacherous egghead is selling off all your R and D so that he can take his secretary off on a luxury cruise? Some unauthorized underling is playing guidance systems with Mr Broussard's wife?'

'I think it's more interesting than that,' said Sara Lake, looking up at him with those pale, negative eyes. 'You must have heard of Broussard . . . we took over Hoshi International last August, one of the biggest single takeovers of a Japanese corporation by a US multinational in the past ten years.'

'For sure. There was a long article about it in *Fortune*. Or was it *Reader's Digest*?'

'Both. We paid over $878.9 million for Hoshi. And the reason we paid so much is because they had developed a missile guidance system that was totally unlike anything we had ever seen before.'

'Damn clever, these Japs,' said John, dragging out a chair and sitting down.

'You don't know the half of it. I guess you've heard of Tercom, the system they use to guide Tomahawk cruise missiles? This system makes Tercom look positively Stone Age. It's called MiGR8 – pronounced "migrate" – because it actually uses the same processes that birds use whenever they fly south.'

'I'm impressed, I think. But what's your problem?'

'You won't believe this. After our people had spent four and a half months familiarizing them-selves with Hoshi's research, they came right up against a brick wall. MiGR8 had been demon-strated to them several times in Hoshi's simulator before the sale went through, and it worked like a dream. All the computer models were 100 percent functional. But when our people came to fitting the MiGR8 unit into a real missile, it simply didn't work. It was programmed, it was active, but it wasn't passing any guidance information to the missile's flight control computers.'

'So what did your people do?'

'They went storming right back to the Hoshi people, of course. At first there was all kinds of talk that Hoshi had pulled off an incredibly inventive scam to sell off an ailing business for nine times what it was worth. But after a whole lot of shouting and arguing and lawyers' letters it turned out that nobody at Hoshi had ever completely understood how MiGR8 worked.'

'*They* didn't know how it worked? They devel-oped it, didn't they?'

Sara Lake shook her head. 'It turned out that

MiGR8 had been devised by an outside scientific theorist who had hardly ever visited the Hoshi facility in person, and who had disappeared not long after the takeover went through, leaving no forwarding address. Mr Broussard practically went into meltdown. It was like buying Microsoft and finding that Bill Gates had quit.'

'That *is* interesting. That's pretty funny, too. Do you have a name for this missing theorist?'

'You're going to laugh when you hear this, although Mr Broussard didn't. He called himself Dr Bakayaro. We couldn't understand why the Japanese kept tittering behind their hands every time we asked where he was. In the end, we found out that Bakayaro is Japanese for damned fool.'

'I see,' said John, swallowing beer. 'Not such a damned fool, though, if he could devise a guidance system like that. And not such a damned fool if he could vanish without anybody being able to find him. Mind you, *I* could find him, if that's what you want.'

'Oh, we *did* find him, as a matter of fact. At least we're pretty sure we did. We've had seven of our security people looking for him for nearly a year now. They connected him with a scientific paper that was published in *Navigational Systems Review* in May. It was published under the name of Professor William Cicero, University of North Florida at Jacksonville. Needless to say, there's no such professor. But the paper discussed the possibility of using bird genetics in navigational and guidance systems; and some of the ideas were so close to MiGR8 that they couldn't have been a coincidence.

'Then about a month later, a routine computer check discovered that a certain Mr William Cicero had leased a Mercedes roadster from Daytona Beach Mercedes. Two of our investigators saw the car in St Cloud, which is just east of Orlando. They tried to pick him up, but some local hero got the wrong idea and intervened, and Cicero got away. We found his house, but he was long gone by then.'

'Again without leaving a forwarding address, I imagine?' said John. Outside, the sun was going down, and the bay had turned to dazzling gold, so bright that he could scarcely look at it.

'You're interested?' asked Sara Lake, uncrossing and recrossing her legs. The soft zizz of expensive pantyhose. She had a strongly erotic presence, as if she were talking about technology but thinking about sex.

John said, 'Of course I'm interested. It's a very interesting story. Why does a man who can invent a revolutionary guidance system choose to run away and hide? Why does he take to using all these stupid aliases? Why does he submit papers to scientific journals when he must *know* that your people are keeping a weather eye out? What else do they put into frankfurters apart from ground-up chickens' feet?'

Sara Lake took a pack of More out of her purse and tucked one between her lips. 'You'll take it, then?' she asked, her cigarette waggling as she spoke.

'Unh-hunh. Not for me, thanks. I'm totally snowed under. I've just wrapped up a major bust for Old Mother Brown's authentic American cake recipes. But somebody's been stealing the secret recipes for Chef Vincenzo's canned soups, and I'm hot on the trail.'

'You're kidding me.'

'I'm serious. We're talking about a multimillion-dollar espionage racket here. Chef Vincenzo's Lobster Bisque is the best there is, and if anybody was to find out that they use freeze-crystallized lobster shell to give it that extra-lobstery taste . . . well, it could mean financial disaster.'

'They really do that?'

John nodded. 'It saves on real lobster meat. It means they can use more "other fish" and still taste better than their competitors.'

'And after everything you've done in your life, you find that kind of work sufficiently rewarding?'

John didn't answer. Instead, he said, 'You're sure you don't want a beer? How about a glass of wine? We could take it out on the deck.'

'All right, then,' said Sara Lake.

He opened a bottle of Verdicchio which had been lying on the bottom shelf of the icebox since the last time Maggie had been able to come around. It was superstitious to save it: he could always buy another bottle, if she managed to stay the night again. He opened it with the elk-horn corkscrew that he had been given by Elk Insurance Corporation in Toronto, and stepped out onto the deck with two mismatched wineglasses jingling.

They sat back on their sunloungers for a while,

saying nothing. This was the time of day that John enjoyed the most – with the sun going off on its stately journey across the Pacific, and the hills of San Francisco still whispering and roaring with the noise of homegoing traffic. Across the bay, seagulls wheeled and screamed like unhappy wives. John had lived here for most of his 36 years and he still loved it. He had so many friends and acquaintances and they had saved his life more than once. If ever he was feeling off-balance there were a dozen bars or restaurants where he could find somebody to talk to; from the Mark Hopkins hotel to the kitchen at Salvatore's.

He was stocky, although he moved very lightly on his feet. His short blond hair was beginning to turn ashen at the edges. He had a squarish, Scandinavian-looking face, with blue eyes that sometimes looked colder than he wanted them to. He had a battered appearance, for his age, and there was a sharp hook-shaped scar on his left cheekbone, so that he was often thought to be ten years older than he really was.

He still dressed like a freelance, in washed-out jeans and a white Oxford shirt, but these days he carried a khaki Armani coat slung over his shoulder, and a paisley necktie, too, in case of an urgent need to look respectable. Western Eye Industrial Investigators had some important clients, including City Hall and several major banks, such as Pacific Rim Credit and Wells Fargo. You couldn't go to meet any of them looking like Jack Kerouac.

Sara Lake said, 'This could really enhance your

career, you know, if you find this guy.'

'I don't know. I don't think I *want* to find this guy. He sounds like he's better left alone.'

'You're not thinking straight, Mr Huntley. We're talking about national interests. Broussard has been contracted to supply the guidance systems for a whole new generation of selective-attack missiles, based on their MiGR8 prospectus, and right now they simply can't deliver. That means that our country's defense capability is going to be severely compromised for ten to fifteen years to come. We may never catch up.'

'I'm sorry, Ms Lake, I'd like to do the right thing, but – you know, Chef Vincenzo needs me more.'

Sara Lake blew out smoke, and it whirled into the early-evening wind. 'They told me that was what you would probably say.'

'Who told you?'

'All the people I met who ever knew you.'

'What people?' he asked, defensively.

'Oh . . . you know. People who liked you a lot and people who spat when they heard your name.'

'My ex-wife, I suppose.'

'Well, she is a little bitter about you, yes. But understandably.'

John let out a short, wry snort. *Understandably*! That was the understatement of the century. Almost exactly fifteen years to the day, he had been right at the very top of his profession. Cool, efficient, smart, and beginning to grow reasonably wealthy. He had invested in all of the latest electronic equipment: bug detectors, ultraviolet scanners, video cameras. He had three assistants and two Caprice station wagons with his name emblazoned on the side. Huntley Security had been the first choice of any large corporation which suspected espionage or vandalism or any kind of petty corruption.

His wife Lorna had complained about the long hours he had worked; especially the all-night stake-outs. Their son Jamie was only four, and apart from the fact that John was hardly ever at home to play with him, Lorna very rarely had time to herself. So one night John agreed to stay home and baby-sit while Lorna went to see six or seven of her college friends in Sausalito.

And that was the night that John received an anonymous tip-off that two men would be trying to break into Kreussman Electronics with the intention of stealing more than $3.5 million worth of computer software. In a hurry, he hadn't been able to find a substitute babysitter, so he had wrapped Jamie up in a blanket and taken him along, too.

The story was tragically simple. As John had arrived at the Kreussman works, he had surprised the thieves outside the building, trying to neutralize the alarm system. One of them had fired a single shot at him, which had missed. It had passed straight through the rear offside door of John's Caprice and hit Jamie in the head.

Jamie hadn't been killed, although there were many times when John wished that he had. He was in a clinic in Santa Cruz now, unable to walk, unable to talk – unable to do anything except lie on his side and stare at the wall. The doctors kept assuring John and Lorna that there was brain activity, but what kind of activity? Did he have dreams, this inert, dark-haired young man, with his limbs like a fallen goat? And if he ever did, what did he dream of? His life that might have been, but never would?

After that night at Kreussman, John's marriage had collapsed, his business had fallen through, and he had taken to spending weeks in seclusion in a cottage in Mendocino, up the coast. During one of those sojourns, in the middle of the night, he thought that he saw Jamie dancing and laughing on the seashore, and ever since then he had believed that disabled people had ghosts, who carried on the happy, active lives of which their owners had been deprived. That was one of the reasons why people thought that John was a little crazy.

'Understandably, your ex-wife also told us about Mrs Scarbeary,' said Sara Lake.

John gave her a long, old-fashioned look. 'That doesn't surprise me. Whatever she said, I deny. Mrs Scarbeary is my employer's wife and all I feel for her is friendship and respect.'

'Of course. That isn't the card I came here to play. How about I offer you some more money – say, 300,000, plus all expenses?'

'Ms Lake, I really don't want to go to Florida. And I really don't want to get involved with people who use blackmail as a method of persuasion. Now, how about finishing that wine and let's say *hasta la vista*.'

'You found Dieter Waxman. Nobody else could, not even the FBI.'

'That was in 1986. Besides, Dieter Waxman was

a criminal. He stole computer data and that's just like stealing somebody's purse. It doesn't seem to me like this guy you're looking for has committed any crime, unless it's a felony to annoy your precious Mr Broussard.'

'Mr Huntley, get this straight. We have to find him and we think you're the only person who can do it. Other people want him, apart from us, and some of those people want him dead.'

'So what's this now? An appeal to my fundamental humanity? First it's bribery, then it's blackmail, then it's praise. Now you're trying to make me feel guilty. It won't work, Ms Lake. I don't want to leave San Francisco and I don't want to go looking for this genius of yours.'

'All right,' said Sarah Lake. She tipped the dregs of her Verdicchio into one of the geranium pots. 'If you can't be persuaded, that's it.'

She stood up and held out her hand. John noticed that she had phenomenally long fingers, and lacquered red fingernails to match. 'If you change your mind . . .' she told him, looking at him intently with those colorless eyes, and she tucked a visiting card into the pocket of his shirt.

He watched her negotiate the steps in her stiletto heels, and teeter off to her car. A rental Mercedes sports coupé, expensive. When she had driven down to the bottom of the street, and turned off left, he went back inside and poured himself another glass of wine. He walked through to the sitting-room and sat down on the green-and-white couch. On the main wall hung a huge reproduction of a

Tom Wesselmann painting. *Great American Nude No. 98.* There was no nude in it, only a woman's overpainted mouth, a smoldering cigarette, and an orange. Lorna had hated it. Maggie hated it. But it reminded John of being 24 years old, and that was sufficient justification for keeping it there.

He called Maggie. It was a long time before she answered, and when she did, she sounded very guarded. 'Can you talk?' he asked her.

'A little. My sister's here.'

John told her about Sara Lake's offer to go to Cocoa Beach.

Maggie said, 'Cocoa Beach? That's Florida, isn't it? You're not going?'

'Of course I'm not going.'

'Danny's up to his ears. I don't know how he'd cope if you went away.'

'Hey, I wouldn't dream of it. Besides, I'd miss you too much.'

'I can maybe come round later tonight. Say about eleven.'

'What's Danny doing tonight?'

'He's running through six years of accounts at Killian Industries. It's going to take him hours.'

'Oh, yes. The phantom payroll. Could you believe that one, when you heard it? One hundred seventy imaginary people with imaginary social security numbers and imaginary jobs. Real salaries, though. Amazing.'

Maggie said, 'I'll see you later.' Then, very softly, 'I love you, John.'

'Ditto,' he told her, and hung up.

* * *

While he waited for her, he logged onto his computer to see what he could find out about Hoshi International and MiGR8. Hoshi had been founded in 1968, making cheap transistor radios from a small factory in Hiroshima. In 1974, however, it had suddenly switched to navigational systems, from inertial guidance to phased-array radar. It had won seven contracts from American companies to supply components and auxiliary equipment.

In October 1995 it had announced the successful development of MiGR8, which was going to turn the whole of the guidance industry into turmoil. MiGR8 was based on the genetic codes of migratory birds, combined with a highly sophisticated interpretation of the Earth's magnetic field, and an artificial pecten: a frond-like projection from the retina of a bird's eye which acts as a sextant. What was more, MiGR8 would be capable of making tactical choices of its own – altering its own course according to the weather or enemy anti-missile activity, and even making last-minute decisions about the feasibility of hitting its assigned target.

Not only that, MiGR8 would possess 'a strike accuracy second to none'. There was a speculative story in *Scientific American* that a MiGR8-guided missile could be targeted to a single window in a multi-story block in the center of a heavily built-up city.

In short, MiGR8-guided missiles were at least twenty-five years ahead of the most advanced known weapons-delivery system. Or they might have been, if Professor Damned Fool had been around to show his people how to connect them up. That's if they *could* be connected up. It was beginning to look more and more as if Broussard had paid $878 million for a piece of equipment which – as it stood – was totally worthless. 'It is becoming increasingly apparent that Broussard Guidance have bought the warp drive for the *USS Enterprise* without having Scottie to get it working,' *Omni* magazine had remarked.

The more John read about Professor Damned Fool, the more intrigued he became. According to company records, he had joined Hoshi's Seattle plant in September of 1973 as 'guidance advisor', on a declared salary of $27,350 a year. His real name was given as Stratford Hering, an honours graduate from the Massachusetts Institute of Technology; but when John searched MIT's rolls for the past thirty years, the only Hering he could find was Janice Hering, who had dropped out of computer studies in 1982. Even the professor's real name wasn't real.

John leaned back in his chair. He was intrigued, but he wasn't intrigued enough to fly to Florida. He had done too much of this kind of work. In spite of his success in finding Dieter Waxman, and quite a few others, he knew only too well that if somebody didn't want to be found, then 99 percent of the time they *wouldn't* be found. It had taken eleven months to locate Waxman; and it would probably take years to locate a wily old man who had the intellect to fly missiles as if they were homing pigeons. In fact they would probably never find him at all.

He was settled now; and he didn't want to lose Maggie, for all that she was another man's wife. Quite apart from that, there was Jamie to visit, two or three times a week.

He was still working on the computer when there was a sharp rap on the kitchen window. It was Maggie. He opened up the door for her, and invited her in. The first thing she did was to sniff sharply, and declare, 'I smell perfume. Poison, if I'm not mistaken.'

'Well done, Holmes. That was her. The woman who came to see me from Broussard International.'

'That's your excuse. It smells like you've had forty whores in here.'

John laughed, and took her in his arms, and kissed her. Maggie Scarbeary was the woman he should have married instead of Lorna, and the fact that she was married to Danny Scarbeary, his employer and one of his oldest friends, didn't make his life very much easier to bear. She was small and blonde and drop-dead pretty, even though she was three years older than he was. She was very slim. She had the smallest breasts of any woman he had ever known, little fairy tits he called them. But she was passionate and funny and very, very smart. She actually understood *A Brief History of Time*, or most of it.

They had kept their affair an hermetically sealed secret for nearly four years now. They both loved Danny and even though they knew how hypocritical they were, they didn't want to hurt him. Lorna had found out about them only by accident, when Jamie had suffered a serious fit and she had rushed around to John's apartment in the middle of the night. She had never told Danny. She had kept that possibility hanging over them; but John had volunteered to pay her more alimony, and that seemed to have kept her settled.

John poured Maggie a glass of wine. 'I couldn't tell you everything over the phone. This Sara Lake woman knows about you and me. Yes – she did her homework before she came to call, and she talked to the lovely Lorna.'

'So she knows. What's she going to do about it?'

'It's hard to say. She said it was a card that she didn't want to play; but if she didn't want to play it, why mention it at all?'

'She really wants you that bad, huh?'

'It seems like it. She's willing to pay me 300,000 plus expenses, just to locate this one guy.'

'But you don't want to do it?'

'I don't know. Christ, I could use the money. But this doesn't feel right. If what this Lake woman told me was true, this guy's a genius, practically. He's turned the whole radar industry right on its head. He could be a billionaire, if he co-operated with Broussard Guidance. But he's chosen to vanish – to go into hiding. Now, why?'

'He's eccentric?'

'Yes, well, maybe he is. But this Lake woman told me that there were other people after him, too – people who might want to kill him. I didn't know whether to believe that or not.'

'I thought you *knew* if somebody was telling you the truth, just by looking into their eyes.'

'Not with this lady. You look in her eyes and

all you can see is yourself, staring back.'

Maggie took hold of his hand. 'You're not smitten, I hope?'

John leaned over and kissed her. 'All that I'm worried about is that she'll go tell Danny what she knows, just to get me back to Florida with her.'

Maggie reached up and touched his face. 'Why don't you go? It can't be for long.'

'I hate Florida. It's nothing but red-raw tourists and golfers and withered old women. Not only that, I don't like the feel of this Broussard business. I don't know . . . there's something skewed about it.'

He paused, and took two or three very deep breaths. Then he said, in an unexpectedly constricted voice, 'Besides, you know how fragile Jamie is. If anything happened and I wasn't there – well, if I'm going to lose him, I want to be there, holding him. I don't want to be three thousand miles away, climbing into somebody's second-story window in Cocoa Beach.'

Maggie stood up and came around the table and put her arms around him. 'He'll survive, John. God will take care of him.'

'Sometimes I wish that God would just take him. The worst of it is, I don't want him to die. But I can't bear to see him lying there, knowing what I wanted him to be, and what I did to him, because of my own damn selfishness.'

Maggie kissed his face all over. 'Don't give up, John. Please.'

He wiped his eyes with the heel of his hand. 'Well, you can't, can you? Life goes on.'

*   *   *

She stayed that night until two o'clock in the morning. There was a waxing moon, and it filled his bedroom with silver. She lay naked on the bed as slim and as small as a dancer, and when he made love to her he felt that he might crush her; so after a while he rolled over onto his back, and let her move up and down on top of him, her neck arched back, her hair shining, her eyes filled with tears.

Danny took him around the corner to the Coffee Shop. The morning was busy and sparkling bright. They ordered cappuccinos and blueberry muffins and sat in the back where the *Chronicle* reporters congregated, along with the whiskered gentlemanly customers who read newspapers on sticks, and the pale sulky boys in Versace jeans and no socks.

Danny Scarbeary was ex-everything manly that you could think of. Ex-college football star; ex-Marine; ex-police; ex-physical training instructor. He was short and muscular with a handsome head that was a little too large for his body, like an actor. He was good at industrial counter-espionage because he was logical, and immensely self-disciplined, and he knew the market value of everything, from the most advanced computer software to the exact formula for Beech Nut strained carrots. Once you understood the value of certain commodities, you knew who would be looking for what, and you could stop them before they stole it.

One of Western Eye's most successful coups had been to catch three cereal-company employees trying to sell the technique for sticking colored sugar crystals onto stars of wheat. The process had been worth more than $55 million.

Danny dipped his spoon into his cappuccino. 'How long you been working with me now?' he asked.

'Six years,' John told him, cautiously.

'Enjoyed it?'

'What?'

'Enjoyed it? Have you enjoyed it?'

'You know I've enjoyed it. I love it.'

'So . . . when you look back on it, you won't have any regrets?'

John didn't reply. He could sense what was coming – he could sense it in the pit of his stomach. That goddamned Sara Lake woman, she'd talked to Danny already. She hadn't even given him the chance to say yes or no.

Danny ate the chocolate flakes from the top of his coffee. The sun was shining through his ears and John suddenly thought how babyish he looked, a very old, dejected baby.

'Listen,' he said, 'I'm not a stupid man. I've known about you and Maggie right from the very beginning. It's my job, knowing things like that. If I can find out that the president of Sunset Hotels is having an affair with his sister-in-law in Santa Barbara; and that the editor-in-chief of *San Francisco Woman* is carrying on with the publisher's chauffeur; how can it possibly have escaped me that my loyal deputy is screwing my own wife? I mean, how? Answer me!'

John was silent for a very long time. Then he

tossed aside his spoon, and said, 'Shit, Danny. I'm sorry.'

'You're not sorry! You've been at it for over four years. If you were sorry, you would've stopped doing it. But you went on, and on, and you loved every minute of it, and so did she. And before you say it first, I know you love me, too, the both of you, and that's why you tried to keep it a secret, and that's why Maggie never left me, and you never tried to take her away.'

John had never felt so crappy in his whole life. All he could do was stare into his cappuccino, and say nothing.

Danny said, 'I was angry at first, but I learned to live with it. And do you know why? Because I didn't want to lose either of you. I love you both, the same way you love me; and so long as it was a secret, and nobody else knew, I thought, well – at least my pain isn't public. I can tolerate being a cuckold if they don't put a billboard up in Union Square. But then yesterday evening some woman came along and told me all about it. Some total stranger knew that Maggie and you were regularly getting it on; and I didn't know which was the worse humiliation – to say that I didn't know, or to say that I did.'

Danny looked away, and there were tears in his eyes. 'She said she had a job for you in Florida. I recommend that you take it. There isn't any job for you here.'

John nodded. He was close to tears himself. 'I'm sorry it had to finish up this way,' he said.

Danny cleared his throat, and shrugged. 'Things like this, they always have to finish up this way.'

John stood up, and laid his hand on Danny's shoulder. Danny shrugged him off. 'I'll say goodbye, then,' he said, and walked out of the Coffee Shop leaving his cappuccino undrunk and his muffins untouched, the way people do in movies.

When he reached home, there was a message waiting for him from Sara Lake.

'Mr Huntley? How are you? Meet me at SFX at eight. American Airlines desk. You don't have to pack very much. Shirt, pants, swimming shorts. Look forward to seeing you. Bye.'

He looked around him. He guessed there were times when we all have to admit that we've been outmaneuvered. He could have told Sara Lake to forget it, but he needed the money. All he had to do now was find somebody to take care of Molière.

4

You're not thinking. You're just being logical –
Niels Bohr

It was raining torrentially when they arrived at
Cocoa Beach. The roads were flooded and they had
to creep through the traffic with their windshield
wipers frantically flapping from side to side.

'Welcome to the Sunshine State,' said the black
driver, with a cackle. John didn't need jokes. He
was feeling edgy enough already. Their flight had
been delayed for two and a half hours, and he
hadn't been able to sleep at all. Apart from that, his
steak had been tough. And the movie had been
some sentimental garbage about a man who had
fallen in love with a married woman, and he
had actually found that tears were sliding down his
cheeks; and to his embarrassment Sara had seen
them, too.

The silver stretch Lincoln wallowed its way into
the parking lot outside Broussard Guidance
Systems, a glassy box-like building on A1A, just
south of Cape Canaveral. Red fluorescent lettering
on the side of the building said GUIDING AMERICA

INTO SPACE. Most of Broussard's profits came from selling maritime navigation systems to South Korea and Eastern Europe, but Sara laconically remarked that GUIDING POLAND'S SHIPS STRAIGHT wouldn't have quite the same heroic ring.

'I don't know why I'm doing this,' said John, as the automatic glass doors opened and they walked into the chilly air-conditioned lobby, with its polished marble floors and its potted palms. 'As if you haven't screwed up my life enough already.'

'You're doing it because you're a professional and a patriot,' said Sara. Her heels rapped on the floor like castanets. 'And, come on, don't tell me you're not just a little bit turned on? Missing scientists are a whole lot sexier than cake mixes.'

'Mrs Scarbeary was a whole lot sexier than either, thank you.'

Sara gave his hand a quick, unexpected squeeze. 'Don't be bitter. You couldn't have gone on like that for the rest of your life, now could you?'

They went to the security desk and John was issued with a visitor tag. 'I'll introduce you to Mr Broussard, and then Michael will drive you to your hotel. Before we go any further, we have to get you a Grade 5 government security clearance. Oh, don't worry – *we* know you're clean, we checked you out. But the Pentagon is *very* twitchy when it comes to state-of-the-art defense systems.'

Sara led the way to the elevator bank. The left-hand elevator was marked GB Only. Sara swiped her security card down the slot by the door, and the elevator opened. As they rose to the seventh story,

John could see countless reflections of Sara and himself in the burnished bronze mirrors that surrounded them on every side.

'I'm still wondering what a girl like you is doing in a deadly dull business like guidance systems.'

She gave him the strangest little smile – a smile that unaccountably made the small hairs rise up on the back of his neck. 'It's the power, John. That's what it is. It's the only thing that really makes me come alive. High technology may seem deadly dull to you, but there's more power in it than politics, there's more money in it than oil, and there's more sex in it than rock music.'

'Seems like I chose the wrong profession.'

'Well, you think of this man you're looking for,' said Sara. 'Think of the brain he must have, to conceive something like MiGR8. Think of the influence he's going to have on people's lives. Think of the money he could make.' She licked her lips so that they glistened. 'Why do you think that women adore Stephen Hawking?'

'Stephen Hawking isn't in hiding. Our man is.'

The elevator came to a smooth stop and the doors slid back. 'Oh, you'll find him,' said Sara. 'I just know you will.'

Gene Broussard's office occupied more than half of the seventh story. It had ceiling-to-floor windows that overlooked A1A – and beyond, to the Atlantic. It was thickly carpeted in periwinkle blue, and furnished in a style which could only be described as Florida Opulent, with gigantic sofas and armchairs with chrome arms and white leather seats. On one side of the office was a circular glass conference table that could have doubled as a skating rink. On the interior walls were hung three extensive modern abstracts. John didn't have to look at the signatures to know that he was looking at work by Jasper Johns, Allan D'Arcangelo, and Franz Kline, several million dollars' worth in all.

He went to the window and looked out. The rain was beginning to clear and the clouds were tumbling away. Off to the north he could see a grayish-yellow gleam of sunshine over the Banana River, where the Kennedy Space Center was located. The ocean was still charcoal-gray, but he could see surfers crossing the street with their boards under their arms, so the forecast was probably hopeful.

He was still looking when Gene Broussard came into the office. For some reason, John had been expecting somebody very tall; but Gene Broussard wasn't more than 5 feet 8 inches. He walked directly up to John and grasped his hand with one of those bone-crushing grips that John always hated. You don't have to maim me to prove you're sincere.

'John . . . so pleased you could make it. How was your flight?'

'We went up. We came down.'

Gene said, 'Sit, why don't you. How about something to drink? I have some wonderful bourbon creole coffee. Just the thing for jetlag.'

He picked up a phone beside the sofa and said, 'Velma? How about some coffee in here? And some of those pecan cookies I like.' Then he sat back, crossed his legs, and stared at John with twinkling eyes and a friendly but completely fixed smile that made John feel like saying '*What?*'

Gene Broussard was sallow-skinned, as if he had failed to keep up a suntan. His head was almost a perfect sphere, with thinning, brushed-back hair and flattened-back ears. His curved eyebrows gave him an expression of permanent amusement, like a French comedian. He wore a white shirt with a white vest and a white double-breasted coat, tightly buttoned up.

His only obvious flamboyance was a cerise silk necktie, but John wouldn't have been surprised if he were wearing cerise silk undershorts, too.

After almost a minute's staring, he said, 'I want to apologize for the way we recruited you, John. It was unfair, and unethical, and I can't promise that we'll ever be able to make it up to you.'

John said, 'It's done now.' But he was already beginning to believe that maybe Sara was right. He and Maggie couldn't have gone on like that for the rest of their lives, betraying Danny and yet never really fulfilling their own love for each other. Perhaps that was why he hadn't found it as difficult to accept Sara's offer as he'd expected. He had at last been forced to make a decision; and although he was deeply upset, he was also unexpectedly relieved. His only regret was leaving Jamie so far away.

Gene Broussard said, 'I guess Sara's given you the general picture as far as Hoshi International is concerned. You wouldn't believe that anybody could be so stupid, would you – spending $878 million on something that you can't get to work?

But there's nobody to blame. The theory was so complex that it took our technicians months to understand it, and with Hughes making a rival bid, we didn't have months to spare.

'The system itself is amazing – totally amazing. Theoretically – and under the right circumstances – you'll be able to program a missile to go find somebody. Just *one* person,' he said, lifting his index finger. 'Can you imagine what we could have done with a missile like that in Iraq? Saddam Hussein hears a noise outside, opens the door, and *foof*! the missile hits him right between the eyes.' He gave a high, hissing laugh, and repeatedly tapped his index finger against his forehead. 'Right between the eyes, John! Right between the eyes!'

A busty, redheaded girl in a very tight crimson dress came in with a silver tray of coffee and several plates of pecan and cherry cookies. 'You see this young lady?' said Gene Broussard, with proprietorial pleasure. 'She used to strip at the Golden Feather Club. But one day I got talking to her, and I found out that she was very, very bright. In fact she has an IQ of 135. I offered her a job as my personal assistant and here she is today, running my schedule like the genius she is.'

'Still making the coffee, I see,' John remarked.

'Who are you, Gloria Steinem?' Gene Broussard lashed back. 'There's nothing demeaning about making coffee! When Velma's busy, *I* make the coffee. I get a thrill out of allowing people to realize their full potential, John. I like to take ordinary people off of the streets and show them how *extra*-ordinary they really are. But you have to be *rounded*,

97

do you know what I mean? Just because you're Archimedes, that doesn't mean you're excused from cleaning off the ring round the tub.'

'Gene came from a very poor background,' Sara put in, by way of explanation.

'Well, you don't want the whole story about that,' said Gene. 'But suffice it to say that I'm never too proud to undertake a menial task for the good of the whole community and I don't expect those around me to be too proud, either.'

'Gene's a Baptist,' Sara added, as if that settled everything.

Gene poured the coffee himself. It smelled rich and strong. 'You haven't been granted your security clearance yet, but we're working on that as fast as we can. What I can say to you, though, is that we've had six men looking for this William Cicero and they've come within a whisker of catching him. We've located his house, so you can take a look at that. But we can't afford to be too leisurely, John. Time's running out on us and that's why we've asked you to join the team.'

'What's the hurry?' asked John. 'I thought it took years to develop a guided missile.'

'For sure. Usually it does. But now that the Russians have de-targeted all of their ICBMs, defense spending is being cut back to the bone. MiGR8 is nearly three times more expensive than conventional systems, and unless we can show within the next eight weeks that we can get it up and running, and that it genuinely works, the Department of Defense is liable to pull the plug on us. We'll still be able to develop MiGR8 for commercial airlines and maritime navigation, but it's the defense contracts that are going to make us the big bucks.'

'Is there a missile ready to fit MiGR8 into?'

Gene didn't stop smiling. 'Right now, that's classified information, so far as you're concerned.'

'I'll assume, then, that you do.'

'Don't assume anything. Just find this guy, okay, and bring him back alive. You can have whatever facilities you need. Sara's allocated you an office downstairs with a PC and a separate fax line. There's a car waiting for you in the basement. I've arranged for you to have a working lunch with two of our people at 12.30 p.m. this afternoon. They'll be able to give you a progress report, and get you up to speed.'

John put down his coffee cup. 'I have just one question.'

Gene spread his hands, inviting John to tell him what it was.

'Supposing I find your William Cicero and he refuses to work for you?'

'I think you can leave that to us.'

'What makes you so sure that you can persuade him?'

Gene turned to Sara and smiled, and then turned back again. 'We persuaded *you*, didn't we?'

The morning had turned hot and sunny as John drove out of the basement of Broussard Guidance Systems in the white Eldorado that Sara had provided for him. He switched on the radio and listened to the local news for a while; then he turned it over to a country station and listened to 'Achy, Breaky Heart'. Tell me about it, he thought.

He drove down as far as Melbourne Beach, where Sara had booked him a suite at the Breakers Hotel. It was a grandiose 1950s building painted violent pink. The inside was as tasteless as the outside, with potted yuccas and waterfalls and pink-painted basketwork lounge chairs. An unsmiling black bellhop carried John's bag up to the sixth floor.

'You in the auto racing business?' he asked.

'No. Why?'

'It's a hobby of mine to guess people's perfessions.' He paused for a moment, and then he said, 'You wouldn't be a priest by any chance?'

'No, I'm not. How come you think I'm either?'

'Because you look like a man who likes to take a risk; while at the same time you look like you got your spiritual side, too.'

He showed John to his suite. It was enormous, with a pink shagpile carpet and an emperor-size bed with a ruffled pink satin throw over it. The bathroom was tiled in pink and white and echoed like a concert hall. There were so many mirrors in it that when John stepped in to have a look, it appeared as if five other people came in with him.

With a flourish, the bellhop drew back the net curtains to reveal a view of the beach, and the foaming breakers of the dark blue Atlantic. 'Private stretch of beach, Breakers guests only,' he said. 'Trouble is, most Breakers guests are verging on the senior side. Walk a quarter-mile south to the pier if you really want to meet some babes.'

John gave him $10. After all, Broussard Guidance Systems was picking up the tab. 'How do you know I'm not gay?' he asked.

The bellhop still didn't smile. 'I can tell that, too; a mile away.' He went to the door, opened it, and then turned around. 'You ain't a mortician, are you? I can sure feel the sense of death.'

He unpacked the few utilitarian clothes that he had bought – chino slacks, button-down shirts, sneakers. Then the six of him had a shower. He stood staring at himselves in the mirrors and tried to understand who he was and what he was doing here. His life had never changed so abruptly before. It was like walking through a door in a funhouse, and unexpectedly finding yourself back out on the street.

He called Maggie, but it was still early morning in San Francisco and Danny answered, so he hung up.

He climbed into bed and slept for exactly two hours. He had developed a facility for doing that on all-night stakeouts. He could sleep for five minutes or round the clock, to order. At twelve he woke up, dressed, and went out onto his balcony. The sea breeze was warm and salty, and the seagulls were suspended in it with their wings outstretched, not moving.

He went back inside and tried Maggie again. This time she answered at once.

'Maggie? It's me.'

'John? Where *are* you?'

'Florida, a little place called Melbourne Beach. I

wanted to call you before I left but I didn't have time.'

'So you took up that woman's offer?'

'I was tempted to tell her to stick it where you don't need Ray-Bans, but what was the use? I'd rather be deeply resentful than deeply broke.'

'John – I'm going to miss you so much.'

'Me too you. How's Danny?'

'Not as happy as you'd think. In fact he's pretty miserable. I think he's going to miss you as much as me.'

'Come on, Maggie. It had to happen one day.'

'I know,' she said. She was swallowing back the tears. 'I just didn't want the day to come so soon.'

They talked for a while, then he told her he loved her and hung up. He thought of what O. Henry had said: 'Life is made up of sobs, sniffles, and smiles, with sniffles predominating.' He took his beige linen coat out of the illuminated walk-in closet, and went out to meet Gene's 'people' for lunch.

They had chosen the Blue Pelican, a family restaurant only two minutes' drive up the strip. He parked beside the sign, a huge fiberglass pelican winking one eye. Inside, the restaurant was gloomy and the air conditioning was set to Nome, Alaska. He asked for 'Broussard' and a blonde waitress in a short blue-checkered dress guided him through an archipelago of empty tables to the far corner of the room.

Gene's 'people' were there already, leaning conspiratorially over the table and talking to each other. When John arrived they didn't get up, and they didn't make any attempt to shake his hand, either. John sat down between them and the waitress asked him if he wanted a cocktail.

He glanced at what the 'people' were drinking. It could have been vodka-tonic or it could have been 7-Up. He risked it and asked for a Bloody Mary, heavy on the Worcester sauce.

'I won't pretend that we like this situation, Mr Huntley,' said one of the men. Of course John didn't know it, but it was Micky's Cabbage Patch man, in a tight buttoned-up suit of steely gray viscose and a tight white shirt with a gold pin through the collar. 'We're *that* close to finding William Cicero already; but having a newcomer on the team isn't going to make matters any easier.'

John was surprised how cultured his voice was, compared with the way he dressed. Perhaps he had been living in Florida too long.

'Well,' said John, 'the decision wasn't mine. I would rather have stayed in San Francisco, chasing recipe robbers. But since I'm here, maybe we can just agree that you don't like the situation and neither do I, and do the best we can to get along. After all, the sooner we find this guy, the sooner we can all collect our money and go home.'

'We're on Mr Broussard's *permanent* security staff,' said Cabbage Patch, with undisguised contempt.

'Oh well. Every life has its lumps in it.'

Cabbage Patch explained how they tracked William Cicero down through the Mercedes-Benz database; and then discovered an account in the name of William B. Cicero at the First Florida Bank next to the Winn-Dixie shopping precinct in St Cloud. 'We waited for him outside the bank for six and a half weeks, and then two days ago – *pozah*! – he showed.'

'Good work,' said John. 'You said you'd located his house.' His Bloody Mary had arrived, and he sucked up a chilly, generous mouthful through his straw. It was so spicy that he had to cough.

'That's right. But while his maid or whatever was opening the front door, he was running out of the back.'

John took out his ballpen and made a note on a napkin. 'I'll want to talk to this maid or whatever.'

'That could be difficult. She barely managed to get the door open. She died about two minutes later.'

'No sign of what did it, neither,' said the second of Gene's people, the Cuban. He was wearing a purple designer coat with ledge-like shoulder-pads, white linen pants and white kid loafers with no socks. He looked like a merengue dancer on his day off.

'No bruises? No contusions? No smell of poison? Nothing round the neck?'

The Cuban shook his head.

'Where is she now?' John asked him.

'Her body?'

'Of course her body.'

'We took her to a private mortician. The last thing we wanted was the cops involved.'

'Was there anything in the house that gave you any indication of where Cicero might be?'

Cabbage Patch shook his head. 'We found

stuff from all over – Europe, Africa, Japan.
Letters, too, from people all over the world. At
first we thought he was just a postcard collector,
because they were all addressed to different people.
Then we realized that all of those people must
have been him. That guy has more names than the
goddamned telephone directory.'

'Did he have a computer?'

'Oh, sure. But he crashed everything before we
got there. Everything. He must have been prepared
for it. All you get is this cryptic message saying –
here it is, I wrote it down: "*A equals x plus y plus z*."'

'Hmm,' said John. 'I think I'd better start with
the house. Do you have a key?'

'The doors are protected by some kind of coded
combination lock. We couldn't crack them so we
blew the lock off the rear door and replaced it with
our own lock. Here.' He fished a keyring out of his
pocket, and worked one of the keys off it. 'Don't
lose it. That's a top-rate security lock, they won't
cut you any copies.'

The waitress came over to take their orders. John
asked for *fajitas*, while Cabbage Patch ordered a
patty melt and the Cuban went for green peppers
stuffed with goat's cheese on a bed of greens.

Cabbage Patch said, 'It's incredible the way this
guy has managed to stay undetected for so long.
He's been writing books and scientific papers on
every damned topic you can think of, and having
them published, too. He has this huge house . . . I
don't yet know how long he's been living there, but
you'd think that *somebody* would know something
about him.'

105

'How about his neighbors?'

'Summerland Avenue isn't exactly the kind of place where people talk to each other over their backyard fence. The house on the west side belongs to some guy who made a fortune out of plastic containers; and the house on the east side belongs to a wealthy old widow who talks like Mr Magoo and makes about as much sense.'

'Have you talked to the City Commissioner's office?'

'We've talked to everybody – from the City Commissioner herself, right down to the letter carrier's dog. A few people knew William Cicero socially, but he kept his life very compartmentalized.'

'Is it possible he's left the country?'

'With this character, anything's possible.'

The waitress came back with their food. As she was giving Cabbage Patch his patty melt, however, she accidentally knocked John's drink with her elbow. It fell over and tipped vodka and tomato juice onto his knee.

'Oh, I'm so sorry!' she flustered, trying to wipe it with a paper napkin. 'I just hope that isn't going to stain!'

'It's okay,' John told her. 'I'll just go to the men's room and rinse it with a little cold water.'

He made his way between the tables to the front of the restaurant. In the restroom he dabbed his pants with a damp towel, and then gave his hair a quick comb-through. As he came out again, he saw two men walking across the restaurant, both dressed in medium-gray suits. They approached

106

Cabbage Patch and the Cuban and started talking to them as if they knew them.

For some reason, John found himself holding back. He stayed in the reception area, watching the men through a screen of trailing plants, next to a softly bubbling tank of tropical fish. There was something about the way in which the men were dressed; something about the gliding, measured way in which they had walked across the restaurant. Who wore a gray office suit on a late summer day in Florida, and kept it buttoned up?

John could see that Cabbage Patch was shrugging. The Cuban tried to stand up but one of the men placed a hand on his shoulder and forced him to sit down again. The other man kept turning toward the reception area as if he were expecting John to return at any moment.

The waitress came past the screen where John was standing and said, 'Oh, good . . . you managed to clean it off. I'll bring you a fresh drink, shall I? On the house, of course. And you'd better get back to that *fajitas* . . . you're supposed to eat it while it's sizzling hot.'

John gave her a quick smile, and nodded. He was probably being paranoid. But he was about to step out from behind the screen when he saw one of the men reach down toward his coat button *with his right hand*. John had frequently carried concealed weapons but he had never worn a shoulder holster because all men open their coat buttons with their left hand and there is no other interpretation of the *right* hand diving toward the coat button than going for a gun. Instantly, he stepped back again, almost colliding with the waitress, who was bringing him a fresh Bloody Mary.

'Hey!' she laughed. 'You're determined to get yourself splashed in this stuff, aren't you?' It was then that both men drew long-barreled revolvers out of their coats. Cabbage Patch leaned back in his chair and flung up one arm to protect himself, but there was a sharp, nasal whistle and a neat circular hole was punched into his forehead. His chair tilted and he fell heavily to the floor. The Cuban turned his head away, as if he didn't want to watch his own execution. There was a second whistle and part of his brain was flung against the restaurant window.

Without hurrying, the two men holstered their guns, buttoned up their coats, and walked back out. They passed within two feet of the place where John was standing, but they looked neither right nor left. They were of almost identical height, 5 feet 10 inches or thereabouts, with short hair and the kind of bland, corporate faces that would be instantly lost in a crowd.

For a moment, the restaurant was shocked into silence, except for a gluey orchestral version of 'Moon River.' Cabbage Patch was lying on his back in a widening lake of very dark blood. The Cuban's face was resting in his plate, and he was staring at his greens in astonishment.

A woman screamed. A man shouted, 'Oh my God!' Then the whole restaurant was in chaos, with families tipping back their chairs, gathering their children and their belongings, and jostling each other for the exit. John stayed where he was, behind the screen, thinking how illogical people are when they panic. Cabbage Patch and the Cuban were in no position to do them any harm: they were dead, and it was highly unlikely that their killers were going to come back. Yet everybody was scrambling out of the restaurant in the same direction that the killers had gone.

He waited until the restaurant was almost empty. The manager was phoning the police; the waitress was sitting on a chair, shivering and white. Outside, people were milling about like bees around a smoked-out hive. Eventually, very quietly, causing no disturbance whatsoever, he walked out of the Blue Pelican into the parking lot.

The midday sun hit him like a halogen lamp.

Over the years, he had learned how to make himself inconspicuous. It was a skill just as refined as karate or kung fu. He walked through the crowds of panicking onlookers with no more substance than a ghost. Police cars were arriving already, their sirens whooping and droning, their tires shrieking, and a hot wind was ruffling across the parking lot like a freshly opened furnace.

He reached his Eldorado and was taking out his keys when he felt a sharp prickle of alarm and knew that he had made a mistake. The gray-suited men in the restaurant had continually glanced toward the door. They must have known that Cabbage Patch and the Cuban were expecting somebody to join them; but they couldn't have known what he looked like, or else they wouldn't have walked right past him in the reception area. So why had they come into the restaurant *then*? Why had they thought he was there?

109

Either they had been tipped off that he was expected; or else they knew what car he was driving, and had seen it parked outside.

He pocketed his keys and veered away from the Eldorado as if he had never seen it before. He stepped over the low blue-painted cinderblock wall that surrounded the parking lot and started walking nonchalantly toward the strip, stopping at the pedestrian crossing with his hands in his pockets like a man with all the time in the world. The traffic stopped, and he started to cross. Behind him, the parking lot was crowded with police cars, and now a television van and an ambulance were drawing up outside. These days, you get media attention faster than medical attention, he thought, wryly. He crossed the street and started to walk southward, back to his hotel.

He hadn't walked more than three blocks before he became conscious that he was being followed. Just as he had learned to become inconspicuous, he had learned what makes other people stand out. In this case, it was the regular rhythm of their feet on the sidewalk – a drumming rhythm of people coming in pursuit, unlike the amble-shuffle-hesitate of most of the tourists and surfers and amiable geriatrics who crowded the strip at this time of day.

He started to walk faster. He knew that amounted to an out-and-out admission that he was the man they were after, but he had seen the way they dealt with Cabbage Patch and the Cuban, and if they were prepared to shoot two men dead in a busy restaurant, they certainly wouldn't hesitate to drop him in the street. He reached a side turning that led toward the beach and broke into a jog, his footsteps echoing against the painted stucco buildings. A small white dog yapped at him until its owner dragged it away. He ran through a private parking lot, over a grassy bank, and onto the beach.

The afternoon was hot but the wind was still strong and the Atlantic breakers were royal blue and thunderous. John glanced behind him and saw that the two men in gray suits were just vaulting over the parking-lot pole. There was no pretense any more. These guys plainly meant business. They were walking toward him with the smooth unhurried gait of men who know what they want to do and aren't afraid to do it.

He kicked off his right loafer, then his left, and paused for a moment to pull off his socks. Then he started running.

He wasn't as fit as he used to be, when he played football. But he still kept himself in trim by jogging most mornings, and he and Danny had regularly competed at raquetball. The sand was deep and soft and very hot, but he sprinted the first quarter-mile before settling down to a long, easy lope. He had almost reached the pier before he allowed himself the luxury of looking back.

What he saw made him immediately anxious. Only one of them was coming after him. That meant that the other one must have gone back to their automobile, with the intention of heading him off. There were plenty of cut-throughs to the beach from the main highway, and if one of them got in front of him he wouldn't stand a chance. His

111

pursuer hadn't tried to catch up with him. He was keeping a respectable distance between them, which made John all the more sure that his partner was on his way by car.

This part of the beach was crowded with swimmers and surfers. Their shouts and laughter competed with the cries of the gulls. But it was obvious that the two men didn't care about minor details like witnesses, and the risk of hitting innocent bystanders. They would shoot him down wherever he was.

John started to run faster. He had to leap over a girl sunbathing on a towel, and she shouted out, 'Watch where you're going, you bozo!' when he sprayed her with sand. He looked back again and his pursuer was running faster, too, although he still kept his shoes on and his coat buttoned up.

John reached the pier and elbowed his way through a crowd of chattering South American nuns, whose habits were noisily flapping in the wind. He ran up the ramp and around the souvenir shops, and headed for the White Gull Restaurant at the very end of the pier. As he did so, he heard a long howling of tires, and he turned around to see a gray Buick slide to a halt by the asphalt ramp that led down to the beach. The second man climbed out, slammed the door, and came hurrying toward the pier, aggressively peeling off his sunglasses as he did so.

John ran the rest of the way along the pier, blurting out 'pardon me, pardon me,' as he dodged past strolling couples and babies in buggies and old people in sunhats. At last he reached the entrance to the restaurant, and pushed his way through the heavy glass swing doors into the reception area. A waitress came forward with a wide well-capped smile and a menu. 'On your own, sir?'

'That's right. Table for one, please.'

She looked down at his bare sandy feet. 'The manager does normally ask for footwear, sir.'

'Oh, yes, hey . . . I lost my shoes in the sea, I left them on the beach and they were washed away. I'll tell you what I'll do . . . I'll keep my feet hidden under the tablecloth.' Although he was hyper-tense – although he expected the two gray-suited men to come bursting into the restaurant at any second – he managed to give her his most winning, provocative grin.

'Well, okay, then,' she said, and led him to a corner table overlooking the ocean. 'The special today is red snapper. If you don't want fish I can recommend the chicken potpie.'

John glanced quickly toward the doors. He couldn't yet see any sign of his two pursuers, but it looked as if there was some unusual jostling activity among the sightseers along the pier. A little girl lost a large red balloon and it went dipping and swooping into the wind, staying quite close to the railings, but tantalizingly out of reach.

'You want a cocktail?' asked the waitress.

'What?' said John, distracted. 'Oh – just a beer, please.'

'Coors, Bud, or Heineken?'

It was then that he saw the first of the men struggling his way past a young man in a wheelchair. He was delayed by a moment's argument with the

113

young man's friend, but then he came jogging directly toward the White Gull.

'Erm, Bud,' said John. Then, 'Men's room?'

'On your left, past the ship's wheel. But remember –' she said, with a conspiratorial wink ' – discreet with the feet.'

John left his table and crossed the restaurant to the men's restroom. The door was emblazoned with a picture of a bearded merman. He went inside and locked himself in one of the two stalls.

The window was made of adjustable slats of frosted glass, in an aluminium frame. John balanced on the toilet seat, opened his penknife, and took out the six cross-headed screws that held the window in place. They came out easily, because the window was comparatively new. He lifted it down and rested it against the wall. Then he quickly stripped off his shirt, unbuckled his belt and dropped his pants. He tucked the key that Cabbage Patch had given him into his billfold, along with his car keys. Wearing nothing but his white undershorts, gripping his billfold between his teeth, he climbed back up onto the toilet, and maneuvered himself out of the window.

There was nothing outside the window but a narrow sill with flaking white paint on it, and then a sheer 30-foot drop to the ocean below. The surf was crowded with swimmers, but it was so white and foamy that it was impossible to tell if the water was deep enough to dive into. He decided to climb down until he was hanging by his hands from the sill, and then drop. He might break an ankle, but that was better than diving in headfirst and breaking his neck.

He heard the men's room door open, and the door of the first stall being flung back. Then a furious pounding on the second stall.

He hung on until he saw a huge breaker surging in toward the shore, and then he dropped.

There was a moment of breezy falling. Then he crashed into white, boiling surf. His feet hit the bottom, and he went down onto his knees, but the force of the breaker was more than enough to cushion his fall, and to sweep him inshore with no more injury than bruises and a noseful of stinging seawater. He took his billfold out from between his teeth and he had almost bitten through it.

His first instinct was to wade back onto the beach, but he stayed in the surf, surrounded by scores of other swimmers, and began to wade underneath the pier so that they wouldn't be able to see him. Most of the other swimmers had seen him drop from the toilet window; they gave him an odd stare and kept their distance, but that didn't matter as long as the gray-suited men couldn't pick him out from the crowd. *Be invisible. Give nobody any reason to look at you.*

He swam and waded southward. They wouldn't expect him to go this way, because it was over 18 miles to the next causeway back across the Indian River to the mainland. But first of all he wanted some clothes, and to get in touch with Sara Lake.

He waded almost a mile. Then he stopped for a while, waist deep, shading his eyes with his hand,

and looked back toward the pier. As far as he could make out, the gray Buick had gone, and nobody appeared to be following him. He licked his lips and they tasted of salt.

Slowly, he made his way to the beach. He was only halfway out of the surf, however, before two young girls shrieked at him, and called out, 'Mister – hey, mister! Your shorts are falling down!'

Florida has everything, he thought grimly, as he trudged through the baking sand. The sun and the moon, both.

5

A man of action forced into a state of thought is unhappy until he can get out of it – John Galsworthy

Next morning, Micky came out of the front door to find that the flag on his mailbox was down. He very rarely received letters because he never wrote them, and he stood staring at the mailbox for a long time before he opened it. Orbison looked up at him with his head tilted to one side, and made a little whining noise.

Inside the box was a subscription copy of *Guns & Ammo* which the previous tenant had failed to cancel, and a small padded envelope.

With Orbison trotting close behind him, Micky went back into the house and tore the envelope open. There was no letter inside, only a compliments slip from Lance, Peutus & Evangeline, P.A., Corporate Law Consultancy. And a cassette of *Copper Blue*, by Sugar. He called Lance, Peutus & Evangeline; and was eventually put through to Mr Lance. 'You've sent me a Sugar cassette.'

'That's absolutely right,' said Mr Lance, in a

dismissive, single-nostrilled voice. 'We did it on instructions from one of our clients. He said that you'd be aware what to do with it.'

'Listen, I'm worried about this. I don't even know the guy's real name. And every time I try to help him, I seem to end up in trouble.'

'He *is* elusive, I'll grant you. But maybe you should listen to the tape and make up your own mind what you want to do next.'

'I'm late for work. My boss is going to kill me.'

'In that case, problem solved,' said Mr Lance, snidely, and hung up.

Micky hung up, too. He stood in the sitting-room and said, 'Shit.'

He spent a long time tapping the unwrapped cassette against his thumbnail. He knew that as soon as he played it, he would be involved; he would be compromised; and Roxanne would be, too. But it wasn't too often that something like this came along, not in his life, not in anybody's life. A chance to do something different. A chance to do something exciting, and a little dangerous. In truth, he was quite proud of the bruise that the Cabbage Patch man had inflicted on his left cheekbone. It showed that there was more to his life than washing baked-on mozzarella and trying to write songs which never came to anything.

The phone rang. It was Guido. 'What's the matter with you – you still asleep? We got baking tins to clean!'

'I'm coming. I'm sorry. Give me ten minutes, okay?'

'This is the last time, Micky. Next time you fire.'

'Listen, I'll stay late, I promise. I'll lick the kitchen floor.'

He hung up. He hesitated for one moment more, and then he broke the shrink-wrap that covered the cassette, opened up the box, and took out the tape. It looked perfectly normal. He held it up against the light, but there was no sign that anybody had tampered with it. He opened up his cassette player and dropped it in.

The first two tracks were just like the original album – 'The Act We Act' and 'A Good Idea'. Micky knew them so well that he fast-forwarded them.

It was only when the tape ran into the third track that anything happened. Right in the middle of 'Changes', the music and the singing slowly faded away. There was silence for a while, and then Micky recognized Dr Lügner's voice. Orbison cocked up his ears and started to whine.

'*Hallo again, Micky,*' said Dr Lügner. His voice sounded so clear and close that Micky felt a prickling sensation up the back of his neck. '*I'm sorry that you've gotten yourself mixed up in all of this. I know that you were simply trying to do a good deed, and save an old man from some obvious thugs, and that you may not wish to take your involvement any further. But one good deed deserves another, as they say, and I think that you deserve the gift that I am going to give you.*

'*I might escape; I might not. But whatever happens, my lifetime's work can continue, within you. To put it simply, I devised a drug that enhances the action potentials within the human brain. Within a very short space of time, anybody who injects this drug will become*

119

intellectually brilliant – a genius, almost – with all of the advantages that go with being mentally superior – quickness, brightness, creativity, and boundless self-confidence.

'This drug has the potential to change the intellect of the entire nation . . . if not the world. Ignorance and stupidity will one day be eradicated in the same way that cholera and smallpox were eradicated.

'I don't need to go into technical details right now – although you'll be interested to know that the scientific community has potentially had the capability to produce this drug since 1944 – if only they had been bright enough to think of it. If you choose to carry on my work, you'll be able to grasp the principles with no trouble at all.

'What I'm offering you, Micky, is a series of doses of my drug, so that your intellect will equal mine. It's a secret that I've kept to myself for longer than I care to think. If they catch me and kill me, it'll be lost for ever. The circumstances under which I developed it could never be repeated.'

There was a pause, and then Dr Lügner said, '*Go to the Kindred Animal Health Laboratories on Fowler Avenue in Tampa. Talk to Dr Richard Keene. He'll be expecting you. Tell him what fish you caught when you went deep-sea angling off Key West . . . that's just for security's sake. I've worked with him for two or three years; but, remember, he thinks my name is Smollett . . . and he also thinks that you've been assisting me with my experiments in animal psychosis. You don't have to get yourself involved in any discussions on the subject. But Keene will give you a set of ampoules from his refrigerator.*

'You take the drug by injection . . . 15 millilitres once a day for seven days, strictly in numbered sequence. Dr Keene will give you ten doses altogether, but I'll explain about the extra ampoules later, after you've decided to take it. It may bring you out in a slight rash, but that's the only side-effect that I've ever come across. If you believe in yourself, Micky . . . if you believe that we can all be much greater than we are . . . that every man and woman on this planet has an astonishing intellectual birthright, including you . . . then you'll take it, you'll try it, and you'll never, ever look back. When you're ready for everything that I can give you, your own mind will open up the door.'

The music faded back in again, and that was all. Micky switched off the cassette and sat down on the sofa and stared at it. *Quickness, brightness, creativity and boundless self-confidence?* He wasn't at all sure that he wanted all that, even if it were possible. His life wasn't particularly rich or special at the moment, but it had its certainties, and it had its hopes, and apart from that he didn't particularly approve of drugs, except for a late-night joint or two when they came back from dancing at the Cracker House, or met their friends for a party.

He didn't see anything in a complicated way, although he was quite aware that there *were* complicated ways of looking at things. He believed in God, and straightforward songs that came from the heart, and V8 engines, and loving your girlfriend the way she loved you. He wasn't at all sure that he wanted his life to be any different.

To Micky, what Dr Lügner was offering him sounded scary rather than stimulating – especially when he thought of the Cabbage Patch man and the Cuban, and the gray body bag slackly wobbling from side to side on the gurney.

He took the cassette out of the player, tucked it into his shirt pocket, and went to work, leaving Orbison tied up in his kennel with a bowl of water and a squeaky vinyl bone.

Guido shouted at him because he was so late. The pizza trays and the lasagne dishes were already stacked up on either side of the sink. A special company birthday party had been booked in for lunchtime, which meant thirty extra covers and all the washing that went with it. Rashid was in a bad mood because his girlfriend had left him for a tall blond ex-Marine who worked in a T-shirt printing shop. Heng had a headache; and Mario, the chef, had cooked dozens of *spiedini all' uccelleto*, veal and sausage brochettes, flavored with sage, and nobody had ordered any.

By 1.30, the skies had dramatically clouded over. The air conditioner in the kitchen was making loud clattering noises and the heat was so oppressive that Micky was dropping beads of sweat into the washing water. Lightning flickered to the northwest, over Disney World. The disturbed summer weather that had brought them Hurricane Hubert still hadn't settled.

'Why you take so long?' Guido demanded, coming up to the sink.

'Usual problem, Mr Guido, sir. The old baked-on mozzarella.'

'You can't find no fresh excuse?'

'You can't find no fresh mozzarella?'

'Everything here is fresh!'

'Oh, sure, except the atmosphere. Do you know how hot it is in here? Even my sweat is sweating.'

There was a hairy crackle of lightning right across the street, and a deafening explosion of thunder. Rain started to speckle the sidewalks and patter against the windows. The lightning flashed again; and in that flash, Micky saw the kitchen lit up as if it had been photographed, every single sordid detail. The greasy pans stacked up, the ladles hanging from the range, the cream-painted walls streaked with condensation. He saw Guido with his dyed hair and the bags under his eyes. Mario with his black woolly arms and his heavy cook's belly.

And he thought of Dr Lügner's house; Lügner the liar; with its cool polished floors and its elegant rococo tables; and its piano big enough to live in.

He finished his shift. The skies cleared just as he stacked away the last dish. The kitchen was filled with sunshine. Guido came in and apologized for the air conditioner, and thanked everybody for what they had done. Mario ate two portions of unwanted *spiedini all' uccelletto*, right off the skewer, and even Heng was laughing.

All the same, though, Micky had journeyed to Damascus during that lunchtime; and he knew for certain where he was going that afternoon.

He missed his friend Mingus by only two or three minutes. Mingus had gone out to meet his public, and to pose for photographs. Micky walked up Main Street looking for him, weaving his way between strolling adults and clusters of excited children. The afternoon was hot now, after the rain, and the air was filled with that damp, sweaty smell of drying vegetation.

He found Chip 'n' Dale by the entrance to Tomorrowland. He waded knee-deep through the crowd of bemused toddlers and said, 'Hi, Vance, Hi, Terry. Seen Mingus anyplace?'

Chip shook his head but Dale pointed toward Frontierland.

'Thanks,' said Micky. 'Bet you guys could use a cold beer.'

'Fucking tell me about it.'

He found Mingus by the popcorn stand overlooking the 'Mississippi River'. As Pluto, he was easier to approach than some of the other characters, but all the same the lower part of his costume was thickly studded with popcorn where dozens of small sticky children had been patting him.

'Hi, Mingus, how's it going?'

'Ennui unlimited, man. What do you think?'

'Are you going to have some time off in a minute? I have to talk to you.'

'I'll tell you something, if that kid pats me in the crotch one more time—'

'It's important,' said Micky. 'Something's happened and I want you to come to Tampa with me.'

Mingus said, 'No way. My shift doesn't finish till five.'

'Can't you call in sick? Tell them you're going down with distemper.'

A small boy in a pink stripy T-shirt said,

'Mommy, how come that man is talking to Pluto and Pluto never said anything to me?'

'Come on, man,' said Mingus. 'You're going to get me the sack.'

'Yeah, how about it?' said a huge red-grilled man with his baseball cap on backward. 'My kid here said hi and you never even said a word.'

'Pluto's a dog,' Micky explained. 'Dogs don't generally speak.'

'He's speaking to *you*,' the man retorted, aggressively.

'That's different. I'm his vet.'

He met Mingus fifteen minutes later outside the staff quarters. A popcorn-encrusted Pluto had turned into a lean young black man with close-shaved hair and two gold earrings. He had a broad, well-made face, and a kind of amused, defensive sparkle in his eye that always reminded Micky of Sidney Poitier when he was trying to act persuasive. Mingus' real name was Dexter Wells, but his father had been such a modern jazz fanatic that he had always called him after his favorite musician. Ironically, Mingus hated jazz, especially Mingus, and much preferred soul and blues.

'I was nearly fired on the spot there, man. You know we're not allowed to talk. It makes us seem like we're not real.'

'A six-foot yellow dog walking around on its hind legs, that's real?'

'It's a real job that pays real money.'

Micky said, 'Listen, you know I called you yesterday and told you all about that Dr Lügner guy? Well, he sent me the tape. He says he's invented some kind of drug that can make anybody into a genius.'

'So, what about it?'

'He wants me to take it, so that I can carry on his life's work.'

'How can you ever do anything like that, man? That's advanced science. The only thing you didn't flunk at school was registration.'

But Micky shook his head impatiently. 'Don't you get it? If I take the drug, then I'm going to be brainier, right, and when I'm brainier, I'll understand how to carry on making the drug for myself, and developing it, or whatever.'

'You're crazy, do you know that? What if it has some kind of terrible side-effect, like makes you a fruit-loop for the rest of your life, not that anybody would notice the difference. I mean, it could kill you, man, and then where would you be?'

'I still want to try it,' said Micky. 'I saw my life today, Mingus. I looked into that sinkful of greasy water – you know, like Bambi when he looks into the pool in the forest and he sees he's grown these antlers and stuff. I saw what I *could* be, like Dr Lügner, playing music, writing articles about things that nobody knows what the fuck I'm talking about.'

'Nobody knows what the fuck you're talking about anyway. Well I sure don't.'

'Listen . . . I have to go to Tampa to get this stuff. Will you come with me?'

Mingus blew out his cheeks in exasperation. 'If I lose this job, man . . .'

'You won't, I promise. I'll call up personnel myself and say that I'm your father, and you've gone down with heatstroke.'

Mingus pursed his lips. He didn't look very happy about it, but he nodded. Micky said, 'Great! Get your stuff and meet me outside the front gate. We'll make the call from there.'

As he turned away, Mingus caught his arm. 'I hope you know what you're doing, man. I'm serious.'

'Me too,' said Micky, and walked back toward the main entrance. As he went out through the turnstiles, the Disney railroad blew its whistle, and a brass band started to play. The *whooommpp-whhooompp-whooompp* of its bass drum echoed across the acres of glittering cars.

It took them just over an hour and a half to reach the outskirts of Tampa. The animal health laboratory was a low, flat building with reflecting glass windows, set well back from the main road and surrounded by trees.

As Micky drove his burbling Camaro into the front entrance, he was stopped by a security guard in a pale blue uniform and detergent-white gloves.

'Name's Frasier. Come to visit Dr Keene,' said Micky.

'Oh, yes. You're expected.' He looked down at his clipboard. 'I'm supposed to ask you what fish you caught.'

'A king mackerel and half of a barracuda.'

'That's right. Who the hell thinks of these things?

127

Park outside the main entrance, then go inside for your visitor's tag.'

Inside the Kindred building it was chilly and bright. It might have been an animal health laboratory but Micky couldn't see any sign of any animals, apart from a steel logo on the wall depicting a man's hand resting caringly on a spaniel's head. A highly groomed receptionist with scarlet fingernails and huge yellow-tinted glasses gave them an identity tag each, and then directed them to the third floor. The only sound they could hear as they walked along the cold, polished corridors was the squelching of their own sneakers.

They reached a door marked RICHARD M. KEENE, DEPARTMENT OF VETERINARY TOXICOLOGY. Micky peered through the small wired-glass window and saw a young, bald, bespectacled man sitting at a desktop computer. He knocked, and in they went.

Dr Keene raised his hand for a moment, to indicate that he was busy. Then he rattled away at the keyboard with two fingers. Eventually he said, 'Hum . . . not *at all* what I expected,' and turned around to greet them.

'You must be Dr Smollett's protégé,' he smiled.

'That's right. Micky Frasier, and this is my assistant Mingus.'

'Pleased to know you,' said Dr Keene, dismounting from his lab stool. 'Quite a character, Dr Smollett. Fish, for a security check! Was that really all you caught? A king mackerel and half a barracuda?'

'Well,' said Micky, embarrassed, 'that was two or

three years ago. We weren't really taking it very serious.'

Dr Keene looked Micky up and down and blinked, as if he wasn't at all sure about his black T-shirt and his black jeans and his pointed black cowboy boots with the curled-up toes. Not the kind of research psychologist that *he* was used to. All the same, he said, 'Dr Smollett was very complimentary about your work on canine paranoia.'

'He was?' said Micky. 'Oh, sure . . . yes, he was.'

'He promised to show me the work you did on dogs with feline persecution mania.'

'Oh . . . right. Well, why don't I send you a copy?'

Dr Keene winked and clicked his tongue and said, 'I'd *like* that! I've been studying cat behaviour for almost six years now. I'd like to see it from the other side of the fence, if you know what I mean. The *canine* point of view.'

Micky looked around the laboratory. It was over 80 feet long, with a single bench in the middle, crowded with chemical glassware, as well as tripods and test-tubes and flickering burners. But there was much more sophisticated equipment along the wall: spectrographs and critical-path analyzers and toxic intensity scanners.

'We're state-of-the-art here at Kindred,' Dr Keene enthused, as he led them along the length of the laboratory. 'We're primary consultants to 39 percent of the US petfood industry; as well as world leaders in veterinary pharmaceuticals. Hydra was invented here – right here in this laboratory.'

'What's Hydra, when it's at home?' Mingus asked him.

'It's a worm tablet for dogs,' said Micky, the voice of experience.

'Best and most effective on the market,' added Dr Keene. 'Flushes out *nematoda* before they can blink. I mean, not that they *can* blink.'

He went to the door at the far end of the laboratory and beckoned them to follow him. They found themselves in a storeroom that was lined on one side with shelves – each shelf stacked with folders and books and computer disks. On the other side stood a large glass-fronted laboratory refrigerator, crammed with jars and bottles and phials of different-colored liquids, as well as three cans of Diet Coke and half a Swiss cheese sandwich. Dr Keene reached to the back of the middle shelf and took out ten small glass ampoules, embedded in a Styrofoam tray. Each contained a small quantity of colorless liquid, and each had a number written beside it in felt-tip pen.

'You're very, *very* lucky to be working with Dr Smollett,' said Dr Keene. 'I never knew anybody who could solve a toxicological problem so quick. Or *any* problem, for that matter. He helped us develop a treatment for bovine spongiform encephalopathy that was *light-years* ahead of anything that anybody else was doing. He could understand how the nemavirus was *thinking*, you know, and just what it was going to do to protect itself.'

Micky took the ampoules and tried to give Dr Keene a serious, understanding nod. Dr Keene made him sign a docket, then shook him briskly by the hand. 'You won't forget to send me that paper?'

'Oh, sure, no problem.'

'Tell me one thing, though. Do you think that breeding kennels leave a permanent imprint on a dog's psychology? I mean, in their later relationships with their owners, is there always some degree of anxiety and mistrust, because they're subconsciously suspicious that their owners may not be their natural parents?'

There was a long silence. Then Mingus nudged Micky's arm and said, 'Go on. Answer the man.'

Micky lifted up the tray of ampoules. 'Erm, well, that's what we're hoping to find out. That's what *these* little babies are for.'

They shook hands again, and then they left as quickly as they could, their shoes squelching even more loudly along the corridor.

'What was all that about?' asked Mingus, as they climbed back into Micky's Camaro and drove away.

'I guess he wanted to know if Orbison gets upset because I'm not his real dad.'

'And does he?'

'I don't know. He hasn't said anything about it so far.'

They drove back to Canoe Creek Road, stopping off at the pharmacy to buy a pack of disposable hypodermic syringes, and then at Winn-Dixie to pick up a sixpack of cold beer and two giant-sized pepperoni pizzas. Roxanne had gone to her mother's for the evening, so they could sprawl around and drink beer and play their guitars without annoying her.

Micky put down the ampoules in the kitchen, next to the pizzas. Mingus said, 'I still think you're nuts to try that stuff. It could be anything.'

'He said it would change my life.'

'Well it certainly would if it killed you.'

They went into the living-room, popped open two cans of beer, and picked up their guitars. They strummed for a while, and then Micky tried to get into the new song that they had been working on, 'The Devil You Don't'. He had an exact idea of what the opening chords should sound like, but he simply couldn't get them right. He wanted a *gerr-annggg*! sound, a G with an F on top of it, but wanting it was a whole lot different from playing it.

Mingus joined in with the basic riff, and played it in a choppy, bluesy way that was much better than Micky's playing, but still not right. In the end they went back to their own version of ZZ Top's 'Gimme All Your Lovin' which was about the only song they could play note-perfect. They turned up the amps until they screamed with feedback, and they played so loud that the window frames rattled and their beer cans started to edge across the table. They were really getting into it when there was a ring at the doorbell, followed by a furious knocking.

They stopped playing immediately. Mingus looked at Micky in alarm. 'Who's that? You're not expecting anybody, are you?'

'The stuff,' Micky whispered. 'Hide the stuff, for Christ's sake.'

'Where?'

'Second kitchen drawer. In back of the cutlery tray.'

132

Mingus hurried to the kitchen while Micky went to the front door. He opened it up, and his next-door neighbor was standing on the stoop, a hugely obese man with greased hair, orange Bermudas and a purple undervest.

'Hi Rhett,' Micky greeted him. 'How's things with you?'

Rhett shifted his chewing gum, and then he said, 'I'm only going to tell you this the one time, Micky. My kid's going to be a doctor some day. He has two hours of homework to finish. So you and your friend shut the fuck up.'

'Sure Rhett. Sorry Rhett. Guess we just got carried away.'

'You don't shut up, you *will* be carried away. On a fucking stretcher.'

Micky gave him a little finger-wave and then closed the door. Mingus came in and said, 'What?'

'We were disturbing his kid's homework, that's all.'

'So what? This is a free country. Do you think James Brown worried about disturbing some kid's homework?'

But Micky swigged some more beer, and then he said, 'He wants to be a doctor. He's this little fat kid that all the other kids bully. His father drives a dumpster and his mother works in the laundromat, and he wants to be a *doctor*.'

'So?'

'So he wants to improve himself. He wants to be something better than his old man.'

'So?'

'So I want to improve myself too. You should

133

have seen Dr Lügner's place, Mingus. Beautiful furniture, books, paintings. A grand piano. How many years do you think I'm going to have to wash dishes at Guido's to get a place like that?'

'Don't worry about it. You're going to be a rock star, man.'

'Oh, sure. Me and ten million other no-hopers. You've heard me, Mingus. It's all in my head but I can't get it out through my fingers.'

Mingus gave him a long, bruised look. Obviously, he couldn't think what to say. But they both knew that they had no chance of turning professional, not ever. Mingus & Frasier had been nothing but a sustained fantasy, a way of avoiding the mundane, unpalatable truth: that Mingus would be shuffling around in his Pluto costume until the Magic Kingdom decided he was too long in the tooth; and that Micky would be washing dishes until the flesh fell off his fingers.

They had talked for months of demo tapes and agents. They had tried to imagine what it would be like to appear on TV. They had even designed their own logo, M&F entwined, and drawn the sleeve for their début album. But suddenly it had all gone flat. The fat kid next door wanted to be a doctor, and he had shown them up for what they really were.

Micky went into the kitchen and retrieved the ampoules from the cutlery drawer.

Mingus followed him. 'I warn you, man, if anything goes wrong here, I'm not taking the rap. If you drop dead on me, or go out of your head, that's nothing to do with me.'

'You want a written indemnity?'

Micky unwrapped a hypodermic syringe. He snapped the neck from one of the ampoules, inserted the needle, and drew up the plunger until the ampoule was empty.

'Don't get no air in that, man,' Mingus cautioned him. 'Spray some out; that's right; and tap it.'

Micky took a deep breath, and said, 'Right. This is it.' He pointed the hypodermic toward his left arm; but then he paused.

'What's wrong?' Mingus asked him. 'You change your mind, or what?'

'I never did this before. I don't know how.'

Mingus let out a long sigh. 'I don't believe this is happening, man. But you're right about one thing. If anybody needs to be brainier, it's you.'

'Just help me, will you?'

Mingus pulled the belt out of his jeans, lashed it around Micky's upper arm, and tightened it. 'Make a fist . . . let's see those veins bulging. There you are. Now slide the needle into the vein . . . that's right. Draw it out a little so that you can see that blood flow. Then push the plunger.'

It hurt, but it was surprisingly easy. When he had done it, Micky looked at Mingus and smiled in triumph.

'Well,' said Mingus. 'Are you brainier yet?'

'I don't feel anything.'

'No rush? No buzz?'

'Nothing.'

Micky gave him his belt and they went back into the sitting-room. 'You sure you're okay?' said Mingus. 'You're looking kind of wishy-washy, if you ask me.'

'I'm fine. Let's have some more beer. How about trying 'The Devil You Don't' one more time, with the amps turned down?'

'I don't know, man. Maybe we should call it a night.'

'I'm *fine*, okay? Maybe I'm just hungry. I haven't eaten anything since breakfast.'

'In that case, o forty-million candlewatt brain, why don't you put in the pizzas?'

Micky returned to the kitchen to switch on the oven. He took out a baking-tray, and picked up one of the boxes of pizza to open it. He was surprised how glaring the picture on the box appeared to be: yellow cheese and green capsicum and red slices of pepperoni. The colors were so strong that he could hardly bear to look at them. The cheese was like a mustard field on a hot summer's day. The capsicum was as green as an overwatered golf course. The pepperoni was bright as bull's blood, in a Tijuana arena, at noon.

The light in the kitchen seemed to be brighter, too; and growing brighter all the time. Micky looked up at the fluorescent strip and he was dazzled.

He was about to say 'Mingus—' but then, without warning, his eyesight folded inward like a black umbrella, and he was blind.

He dropped the pizza. He stumbled sideways trying to catch it but he had lost all sense of balance. He tried to shout out but he couldn't make his vocal cords work. *I'm blind*, he thought. *That fucking drug's made me go blind*. He swung his arms around, trying to find the kitchen counter, trying to find the walls. He touched something smooth and cold, which felt like the icebox. But then it collapsed in his hands like soft chilly toffee, sliding away; and the floor slid away, too.

He thought he managed to scream '*Mingus!*' just once; but then he pitched forward and he didn't even put out his hands to save himself. He felt as if he were pitching from the top of a shot tower, in total darkness, with no idea of how far he was going to fall.

He had a dream in which it was raining. He was sitting at a long table eating pieces of white fish with chopsticks. A man was sitting opposite him with his head in his hands. The rain made a sprinkling noise against the window. Outside, the landscape was glowing yellowy-green as if it were radioactive.

The dream seemed to go on and on. The rain sprinkling. The tap of the chopsticks. The low, swelling throb of the radioactive landscape. There was a terrible feeling of boredom and death.

Without warning, his mind surged with fountains of dazzling white light, one after the other, higher and higher. He lifted his hands to cover his eyes but the light was inside his head and it was his brain that was being blinded. He screamed again because he didn't know where he was or what was happening to him, and he was sure that he was going to die.

The fountains sprayed higher still, until they seemed to be reaching up to infinity. Then they collapsed, and Micky was plunged back into darkness again. He tried to turn around, tried to balance himself, but he didn't seem to have a body any more.

What's happening to me? Oh God, don't let me die . . .

He began to feel a thick buzzing sensation in the back of his brain, as if it were host to a giant beehive. Then something flew past his line of sight – a spark, a cinder, a blazing bee. The next thing he knew, his whole consciousness was swarming with a million million fiery particles, flying in every conceivable direction.

The swarm grew thicker and thicker. He felt as if he were going mad. He tried to let out another scream but he didn't know where his voice was.

Gradually, however, the sparks began to clog and cluster together and form distinctive glittering shapes – spirals and cones and stars. And it was then that something extraordinary began to happen. Micky suddenly felt an *idea* gliding toward him, a geometrical concept. He knew it was a geometrical concept although he didn't know *how* he knew. But instead of being a jumble of figures, it had a visible *shape*, like a globe, glowing and sparkling as it came nearer and nearer. He felt that he could almost reach out and touch it. And more than that, he could *understand* it.

Space consists of the surface of a sphere.

Yes, he thought.

The only lines are great circles of the sphere and all great circles intersect.

Exactly.

Therefore there are no parallel lines anywhere in the universe.

The globe seemed to pass right through him and into his memory. The sensation was cold and shrinking and prickly – like the feeling you get when you're very, very frightened.

Before he knew it, another idea was approaching him, a shining construction like the complicated branches of a tree. Then another, like a nautilus shell. And another, like a box within a box. Within less than a minute he was overwhelmed by a slow-moving torrent of glittering understanding.

He heard crashing, discordant music. He heard voices like a thousand people singing in the dark. He heard mutterings and whispers. He heard recitations, proclamations, dissertations, discussions. He saw extraordinary colors and indescribable shapes.

It was more than his brain could take. He tried to shut out the deluge of noise and color and music, but he had no eyelids to close and no ears to cover.

Help me! he shouted. *Help me!*

But the ideas kept on pouring into him. They poured into him for day after day, and all he could do was drown in them. At last, however, the ideas died away, and the darkness came swelling back, and this time he knew for sure that he was dead.

He opened his eyes and Roxanne was leaning over him. Her head was covered in a red bandanna, and she was wearing large dangly earrings that caught the light.

He looked around and realized that he was lying on top of his bed. It was still dark outside, but he had no idea how long he had been lying here. He

139

felt exhausted, as if he run all the way to Guido's and back, and his head throbbed.

'How long have I been here?' he said. His mouth was so parched that he could barely speak.

'A couple of hours, that's all.'

'A couple of hours? I thought it was days. Is Mingus still here?'

'No, he had to split. But he told me what you did.'

'Oh. And now you're mad at me.'

Roxanne took hold of his hands. 'Micky . . . I'm not mad at you. I love you, that's all. I don't want you to kill yourself or get sick, just because of this wacky doctor you met. Don't you think he's given you enough trouble already?'

Micky closed his eyes for a long moment and then opened them again. 'I saw . . . all kinds of things. Really weird things. It was like being in space. Shit. It was *frightening*, you know?'

'Come on, honey, you're okay now. Do you want something to drink?'

'Anything. There's a big bottle of Gatorade in the icebox.'

Roxanne brought the whole bottle and Micky gulped down almost a third of it straight from the neck. Afterward, he sat on the side of the bed, his eyes watering, repeatedly burping.

'Promise me one thing,' said Roxanne. 'You won't inject yourself with any more of that stuff.'

'I don't know,' he told her. 'I don't know how I feel about it yet.'

'It hasn't made you any smarter, has it?'

He shook his head. 'I feel like somebody hit me with a hammer, that's all.'

'Well, just have a rest. Do you want me to make you a sandwich or something?'

'No – no thanks. I'm all stuffed up with elliptic geometry.'

'Mingus didn't tell me you'd eaten already.'

'No, no. Elliptic geometry is numbers. Mathematics. It's one way of disproving Euclid's fifth axiom. Well, *postulate*, more than axiom, if you're going to be picky about it. The thing is—'

He suddenly stopped talking and stared at Roxanne like a man who's blurted out the fact that he's having an affair.

'How did I know that?' he asked her.

'I don't know. I don't even know what it *means*.'

He stood up, panicky, and stalked from one side of the bedroom to the other, and back again. 'I don't know anything like that. How could I know anything like that? But I do. I do know it.'

'Maybe it's just, like, *shock*, you know? I mean people say some pretty crazy things when they're in shock.'

'But that's the whole point. It's not crazy. It makes sense. I don't only *know* it. I *understand* it.'

He cupped his hands over his mouth and inhaled two or three times. Roxanne put her arms around him and held him close. 'It'll fade, honey. I'm sure it will. I can remember stuff sometimes – you know, like my shopping list – and then I forget it completely.'

'This is scary,' said Micky. 'This is really, really scary.'

'Honey, you took some kind of drug you shouldn't of took, that's all. It was just a bad trip.'

'Oh, sure, it was a trip all right. Like I hallucinated and everything. But what kind of trip makes you understand everything so easy? What kind of a trip – ' he searched for the words to describe the sudden clarity in his mind – 'What kind of trip makes you understand what sunlight does when it shines through your window? Or why things fall downwards, instead of up? Or how to work out the size of a circle in your head?'

Roxanne slowly took her arm away from him.

'Hey . . .' he said, drawing her back again. 'I'm really going to need your help here, sweetheart.'

'Maybe you should see the doctor,' she suggested. 'You don't know what that stuff's done to your head.'

'I'm beginning to. I'm beginning to. Ask me a question.'

'What kind of a question?'

'You know – like a math problem. The hardest one you can think of.'

'I don't know any math.'

'Just make it up. Any old big number divided by any old other big number.'

'I don't know. What's 3,078 divided by 2,552?'

Without any hesitation at all, Micky said, 'To the nearest four decimal places, 1.2061.'

'Do you think that's *right*?' asked Roxanne.

'I *know* it's right. It came into my head, that's all. It was like *whrrrp!* and there was the answer.'

'All right. What's 9,442,187 divided by 671?'

'Fourteen thousand seventy-one point eight one three.'

'What's 13,895,602 divided by 77?'

'One hundred eighty thousand four hundred sixty-two point three six.'

Roxanne shook her head in amazement. 'I can't believe you can *do* that. You're not just making the answers up, are you?'

'Go get my calculator; we can check.'

Roxanne went to the kitchen drawer where they kept all those vital objects that don't fit into any particular category, such as out-of-date Chef Boy-ar-dee coupons and lengths of string and plastic stoppers for half-empty wine bottles. She came back with Micky's calculator and sat down beside him.

'Okay, let's try some more.'

'No, let's check the other ones first.'

'I can't remember them. Don't tell me that *you* can.'

'For sure. Easy. The first one was 3,078 divided by 2,552; the second was 9,442,187 divided by 671; and the third was 13,895,602 divided by 77.'

They sat and talked until it grew dark, and Orbison came scratching at the back door. Roxanne gave Micky question after question: division, multiplication, square roots, cube roots, percentages, everything that she could remember from school. He answered every single one of them instantly, and every answer was correct. Then he memorized a column of text out of his guitar magazine, simply by reading it through once. Then a whole column of the telephone directory.

He felt as if his brain were lit up like a fairground, with all of the rides working. He felt both excited and afraid – the same way that he used to feel when he approached fairgrounds when he was a small boy. The sparkling lights, the roaring of the generators, the screaming of the girls on the roller-coaster.

He had no idea what his new brightness was going to bring him. But he already felt a hunger for more. He felt that he could have sat down right here and now and read dozens and dozens of books, on any subject whatsoever.

Orbison, however, was scuffling around his ankles and Orbison didn't want books, but dog food. Micky opened a can, went out into the yard, and spooned it into Orbison's dish. He held the empty can in his hand, scanned it for a split second, then dropped it into the trash. He came back into the kitchen and said, without any hesitation, 'Meat and animal derivatives, cereals, ash, bakery products, protein 6.5 percent,' and then all the details of the dog food manufacturer, right down to its zip code.

Roxanne tried to smile.

'Goddamnit, he was right,' said Micky, hugging her. 'Dr Lügner was right. He said it was worth more than money. It *is*. It's fantastic. I can remember everything. I can remember what you were wearing when I took you out with Fran and Phil – you remember that? We went to Capriccio on International Drive, and you wore this red kind of ruffled top and this short black skirt and a red ribbon in your hair. Jesus – I can even remember what I *ate*, and that was three years ago! I can even remember what *you* ate; and Fran; and Phil.

You had the angel-hair pasta with tiger shrimp and Phil had the mesquite pizza.'

'Micky, slow down!' said Roxanne. 'You sound like you're going to explode!'

'No way! I haven't even started yet!'

She kissed him. 'Hey, memory-man,' she said, trying to soothe him. 'How about some coffee? I could do you some waffles if you're hungry.'

'Sure, sure. That would be good. I can't believe this! I'm like some kind of genius!'

He phoned Mingus to tell him that he was okay; and that Dr Lügner's drug appeared to have worked. 'It's totally radical! I'm so damned smart I don't even feel like *me* any more!'

'That's great, man. Just don't get *too* smart for the rest of us.'

Micky agreed to meet Mingus later, and then he hung up. His urge to read was almost uncontrollable. But what did he have to read, except *Guns & Ammo* and a stack of old *Guitar Player* magazines? It was more frustrating than the day he had passed his driving test, and hadn't owned a car. What he needed was reading material, and lots of it. Encyclopedias, history books, science manuals, atlases.

Then he remembered something that Dr Lügner had said on his tape. '*When you're ready for everything that I can give you, your own mind will open up the door.*'

He had assumed that 'the door' was a metaphor for the way to the future. But maybe Dr Lügner had meant a real door – the door to his house, where all

145

his books were kept. Maybe he had given him an invitation to go to his library and fill his mind with all of the knowledge that was stored there.

Your own mind will open up the door. Dr Lügner had opened it with a series of numbers, and Micky suddenly found that he could remember what those numbers were. He picked up a ballpen and wrote them in the margin of *Guns & Ammo*: 89 – 144 – 233 – 377. The trouble was, Dr Lügner had said that there was no point in memorizing them, because they changed every time. But they appeared to be a sequence; and if he could work out what the sequence was, maybe he could discover a continuation of the same sequence which would open the lock.

'Waffles up!' called Roxanne, from the kitchen. 'Do you want syrup on yours?'

But Micky didn't answer. He had worked out the sequence almost immediately. Each number was the sum of the two numbers preceding it, and he could work it out backward all the way to 1: 1 – 1 – 2 – 3 – 5 – 8 – 13 – 21 – 34 and so on. He also saw that the ratio between 144 and 233 was 1.618 and that the ratio between 233 and 377 was 1.618, too. His mind teemed with figures and calculations – so many figures that he was literally breathless. He had just realized that 1.618 was the only number in the universe which could be squared by adding 1 to it when Roxanne came in.

'Are you feeling all right?' she asked him.

He nodded. 'I feel scared. But good. In fact, I don't think I ever felt better.'

He followed Roxanne into the kitchen. He

146

picked up a waffle in one hand and the phone in the other.

'You're dripping syrup!' Roxanne told him, tearing off a piece of kitchen tissue.

Micky pushed more waffle into his mouth and sucked his fingers. His mouth was still full when Guido answered.

'Guido's, how can I help you?'

'Guido, this is Micky. Look, something's happened, man.'

'What's the matter? You're sick?'

'No, no. Nothing like that. It's just that I can't wash dishes for you any more.'

'You quit? How can you quit? I'm busy to the top of my head.'

'Sorry, Guido. I just can't do it any more.'

'Oh, well,' said Guido, philosophically. 'What you going to do now?'

'I don't know, man. I really don't. But it won't involve baked-on mozzarella, I can promise you that.'

6

Eppur si muove [It moves for all that] – Galileo
Galilei

From the cramped phone booth in back of the
Laughing Lobster Restaurant on New Haven
Avenue in West Melbourne, John put in a call to
Sara Lake. He had been trying to contact her since
yesterday afternoon, but every time her secretary
had said that she was 'away from her desk'.
John had given it up, and gone to book himself a
room in a small privately owned hotel on Minton
Road, under his regular alias of Thomas H. Benton.
He had chosen the name because of its anonymity
and its faint familiarity. Only art enthusiasts would
recognize the name of one of America's greatest
painters; and John was rarely pursued by anybody
who knew anything about modern baroque.

He had rented a car, too: not from an auto-rental
company, but a used-car dealership on Kissimmee
Highway. A five-year-old Honda, metallic brown,
with Florida plates. The dealer had let him have it
for $25 a day. 'But if it breaks down, tough shit.'

He waited impatiently while the switchboard

148

tried to put him through, listening to Vivaldi's *Four Seasons* and drumming his fingers on the sticky cedar-effect Formica paneling. Somebody had scrawled on the paneling in black felt-tip: *Damn the consequences*. He wondered what the hell it meant: it gave him a feeling of mild paranoia, as if it had been written specially for him to see.

At last, Sara said, 'John? Is that you? Where are you? Are you all right?'

'I'm still living and breathing if that's what you mean.'

'John – I'm so sorry I wasn't here yesterday. The police kept me tied up till seven or eight in the evening. Trudy told me you called. I tried to get back to you at the Breakers but they said that you weren't in your room.'

'You really expected me to be sitting in my room, after that? Those goons wanted to waste me, Sara, the same way they wasted your friends. It was sheer luck that I went to the men's room when it happened.'

'Where are you now?' Sara asked him. 'Do you want me to come pick you up?'

'Right now I'm someplace anonymous, and I intend to stay that way for a while. But I think you owe me an explanation, don't you? I'm supposed to be looking for some missing egghead, that's all. I didn't count on being chased by two gun-toting homicidal maniacs.'

'John, believe me, I don't know why this happened. I can only think that Kevin and Jesus had made some bad enemies before we employed them.'

'Kevin and Jesus? That was their names? They were fish in a bucket, Sara: they didn't stand a chance. But why did they come after me?'

'You were a witness,' Sara suggested.

'The whole restaurant was crowded with witnesses: why didn't they shoot everybody in sight? And another thing: they knew that I was there, but they didn't know what I looked like. They didn't start chasing me till I went toward my car.'

'I don't know what you're trying to say.'

'I'm trying to say that they didn't know me by sight but they knew which vehicle was mine. How? That car was rented through Broussard Guidance systems, wasn't it?'

'Well, yes, but—'

'But nothing. For Christ's sake, Sara, those two guys were shot right in front of me, and I almost got killed myself. I don't want any part of this job. You've screwed up my personal life and lost me my job. If you think I'm going to lay down my life for Mr Gene Broussard and his dud missile, you'd better think again.'

'John . . . we need to talk. We can't do this on the phone.'

'I don't want to talk. I'm not interested any more. I'd rather go back to $250 a week and a poky room on Polk.'

'John, let's just *talk*. Those men – they must have made a mistake.'

'Listen, Sara, it's just as fatal when you're killed by mistake as it is when you're killed on purpose.'

'You're not suggesting that anybody at

150

Broussard Guidance Systems had anything to do with this? That's *absurd*. Kevin and Jesus were two of our best investigators. Our own people. Kevin got us closer to William Cicero than anybody ever did before.'

'I'm not suggesting anything. I'm just withdrawing my services, and thanks for the one-day vacation. See Florida and die.'

'John – please let me meet you. You can't just quit.'

'I quit. Period.'

'Won't you even think about it?'

'What's to think about? A bullet through the head is a bullet through the head.'

'John, please. This has implications way beyond a simple missing-persons case. This could affect the whole of national security.'

'What about *my* security?'

'You won't ever be secure until we find out who killed Kevin and Jesus, and tried to kill you. If they want you now, they could come after you at any time, couldn't they? I mean, go back to San Francisco if you want to, and a poky room on Polk, but who's to say they won't track you down, even when you're there?'

'I quit. K - W - I - T, quit.'

'Think about it, please. Get back to me.'

She wasn't just asking him, she was pleading. John hesitated for a moment, and then he said, 'Who thought of hiring me? It wasn't you, was it?'

'Well, of course not. It was Gene. I didn't even know who you were. Gene plays golf with Bob Prizer . . . the president of Prizer Pharmaceuticals.'

151

'I get it. That was why I was so highly recommended.'

'You did find Dieter Waxman, when nobody else could.'

'I can find anybody, if I want to. But I don't want to find William Cicero.'

Sara was silent. In fact she was silent for so long that John thought that she had hung up. But eventually she said, 'If I lose you, John . . . I could lose my job. This is my whole career we're talking about here. If we can't get MiGR8 to function, we're set to lose millions and millions of dollars, and you don't think that *Gene*'s going to take the blame, do you?'

A gray-haired woman with hugely magnifying spectacles and a turquoise jogging-suit peered into the telephone booth. 'What are you doing in there? Dictating your memoirs?'

He gave her a wave to indicate that he was nearly through. Then he said to Sara, 'I'll call you later. This is something I have to think about.'

'That's all I ask.'

He hung up. He stood there for a while, his hand thoughtfully covering his mouth. There was something badly wrong here; and it wasn't just the killing of Kevin and Jesus. He had the feeling that his own involvement in Broussard Guidance Systems was nothing more than the tip of the tip of the iceberg: and that there were cold and massive depths to this case that he could only guess at. Still, it happened before. Dieter Waxman had discovered that Prizer Pharmaceuticals were involved in manufacturing a nerve-paralysis drug, and he had tried to sell it to the Iraqis in the interests of 'the balance of world power'. But who was guilty? Where did the moral responsibility really lie? The Department of Defense had denied all knowledge of Prizer's experiments, but who had financed them, and why would a private pharmaceutical corporation invest years of research in a totally unauthorized project?

He had never found out; and in just the same way, he would probably never find out why the Cabbage Patch man and the Cuban had been killed, Kevin and Jesus. He didn't really *want* to find out.

The gray-haired woman irritably tapped a dime on the glass door of the phone booth. John slid back the door and stepped out.

'I'm sorry,' he said. 'My grandmother just died.'

'Took her sweet time,' the woman complained, and slammed the door behind her.

John crossed the street and went back toward the Palm Hotel. It was a small, square 1960s block of dark-brown brick with a single dusty palm on the sidewalk outside. The morning was blazingly hot, and his shirt was already clinging to his back. After he had waded out of the sea yesterday, he had stopped at Buster's Vacationwear at Melbourne Shores and bought himself a new pair of jeans and two short-sleeved shirts, but he would have to buy some more clothes later. He wasn't going to risk returning to the Breakers. He thanked God that he had managed to hold onto his wallet, otherwise he would have been walking around in a pair of sandy undershorts.

He had planned to drive to Miami and take a late flight back to San Francisco. If the people who were looking for him were any good, they would be keeping an eye on Orlando International. They might even be watching SFX, too, but that was a risk he was prepared to take. It depended on who they were, and who was paying them, and what they wanted. So far he didn't have the slightest idea, except that they seemed determined to put a stop to Broussard's search for William Cicero.

He was nearing the hotel when he noticed an automobile parked on the opposite side of the street, a gray Buick, just like the car that had chased him onto the beach. The engine was running to keep the air conditioning going, and a man was sitting alone in the passenger seat.

Of course there were thousands of gray Buicks; and it wasn't particularly unusual to see a man sitting alone in a car. But it wasn't all that *usual*, either. It was kids and elderly relatives who sat alone in cars. This man must have been waiting for the driver, and yet there were no offices along this block, no dry-cleaners or convenience stores or print shops. Nowhere that you would stop off quickly to buy cigarettes or pick up cleaning or photocopy a letter, while your friend waited in the car. Only restaurants and hotels; and why would you quickly stop off at an hotel? To check if they had any vacancies, maybe; or to collect or deliver a package; to ask directions; or to find out if the desk clerk had seen a certain person that you were trying to locate.

Maybe he was being over-cautious, but John

walked straight past the Palm, glancing into the lobby as he did so. It was hard to see inside, because the street was reflected so brightly in the glass, but he was sure that he could see a man in a gray suit standing by the reception desk, talking to Mr Hunsacker, the hotel's white-haired proprietor. He kept on walking until he had nearly reached the end of the block. Then he stepped into the doorway of Carden Arts, which was shaded by a semicircular awning. If he stood in shadow, he would be very much harder for them to see.

He waited with the stony patience which had taken him fifteen years of detective work to acquire. He didn't move at all: not even to change the weight on his feet or look at his watch. A woman appeared on the other side of the art store window, a pale woman, watching him between the paintings and the pottery. He didn't return her stare. He didn't even blink.

After a while she came outside and stood next to him. She was very thin, with lots of silver bangles and a blue muslin dress. Her eyes had been painted as black as a panda's.

'You're welcome to browse,' she told him.

He didn't answer, but kept his eye fixed on the Buick.

'We have some wonderful new seascapes by Felicity Frewen. They could cost you $3,000 each if you bought them at auction.'

'No thanks. I'm just keeping out of the sun.'

She frowned. 'No, you're not. You're watching something. What are you watching?'

She stepped out onto the sidewalk and peered

along the street. 'I can't see anything,' she said. At that moment, the gray-suited man came out of the Palm Hotel and crossed over the street. John was sure that he recognized him as one of the men who had shot the Cabbage Patch man and the Cuban. He had a hunched, determined way of walking, with his legs criss-crossing like scissorblades; and a big boiled-looking face. He climbed into the Buick and slammed the door but he didn't drive away.

That was a bad sign. If they weren't going to drive away, that could very well mean that they knew he was staying there, and that they were prepared to wait for him.

'What's the matter?' asked the panda-eyed woman. 'You look so *worried*, for goodness' sake.'

John kept his eyes on the Buick. 'Do you think you could do me a very great favor?' he asked her.

Her eyelashes flapped, and she pressed one hand against her chest. 'Well, I don't know. It depends what it is.'

'Do you happen to know Mr Hunsacker, who runs the Palm?'

'Of course. We're old friends. The last time he remodeled, he bought twelve Daphne Screeds for his bedrooms. Originals, too. Not prints.'

'Do you think you could go along to the Palm and ask Mr Hunsacker who that man was, and what he wanted?'

She stared at him. 'You're not a fugitive, are you?'

'Private investigator.'

'This isn't a divorce case, is it? I can't help you if

it's anything to do with divorce. I've always believed in the absolute freedom of physical expression, whether it's in wedlock or not.'

'Please . . . this isn't anything to do with divorce.'

'Well . . . I don't know why, but I will. You'll have to watch the store for me. It's too complicated to lock up.'

'I'll watch it, I promise.'

'But don't try to sell anything.'

'I promise.'

She was away for only two or three minutes. 'Come inside,' she said, 'it's cooler.'

John followed her into the store. There were paintings and prints hung on all sides, and several more displayed on easels. Most were of the School of Mawkish Sentimentality – animals and sunsets and white stallions leaping through the surf – but there were one or two well-drawn nudes, and some strong bronze figures of dancers.

'Mr Hunsacker said the man came from some government security agency. He showed him ID and everything, and asked him to call a special number if he wanted confirmation. He said he was looking for a man called John Something. Hunter, I think it was. But he went by another name, too, like Benton.'

Shit, thought John. *They've discovered my credit-card accounts.* He had four 'Thomas H. Benton' cards – American Express, Mastercharge, Visa and Exxon. Apart from that he had $1,650 in the Wells Fargo Bank.

'It's not *you* they're looking for, is it?' asked

the panda-eyed woman. 'You're not armed and extremely dangerous, are you?'

'I wish. Did the man say *why* he was looking for this John?'

'He's just *wanted*, that's all. Something to do with national security.'

John went over to the window and looked out. The Buick was still there. 'It *is* you, isn't it?' the woman asked him.

'Yes, it is. But it's nothing to do with national security. Those guys are killers, that's all. They're out to whack me and I don't even know why.'

The woman came and stood very close to him. She must have been beautiful once, but now her skin had the texture of withered leaves. 'They want to *whack* you?' she said, almost whispering.

'They want to rub me out. Eliminate me. Sanctioning, they call it in the security services.'

'What are you going to do?'

'I'm going to get out of here as quick as I can, that's what I'm going to do. But I'm going to need your help. My car is parked in back of the Palm, and if you could possibly go get it for me, and bring it here . . .'

The panda-eyed woman looked uncertain. 'I'm not so sure that I should. After all, if those are government agents, who knows what you've done? If I were to help you, couldn't they arrest me, too?'

John took hold of both of her hands. 'What's your name?' he asked her.

She hesitated, and then she said, 'Constance. Constance Carden. Why do you want to know?'

'Because, Constance, I wouldn't ask for your

help without knowing your name and I wouldn't ask for your help unless I was innocent of any crime and I really needed it. You're too fine a woman for me to take advantage. Look at this business of yours. Look at you.'

'You're flattering me,' she told him. But the way she coyly lowered her head to one side showed that she liked it.

He took the car keys out of his pocket. 'It's a bronze Honda . . . it's right at the very back of the parking lot, next to the fence. All you have to do is drive it around to the door, and you won't ever have to see me again.'

She raised her head and looked him squarely in the eye. 'All right,' she said. 'I don't really know why. Maybe I need the excitement.'

He bent forward and kissed her on the forehead. 'When I meet people like you, I know that life is worth living.'

She took his car keys, but before she left the gallery, she went to the counter and came back with a circular enameled pendant on a chain. It was cobalt blue, with a silver footprint embossed on it. 'Here, have this,' she said. 'It'll help to protect you.'

'I can't, really. Not without paying for it.'

'No, take it. Nothing much ever happens to me. I get up, I open the gallery, I sell a few paintings. Twice a week I go to exercise class but every other night I go home alone and I sleep alone. You see the footprint on this pendant? That's very significant. The foot supports a man upright; and it's supposed to be symbolic of the human soul. The Danes always made their treaties by sprinkling each

other's footprints with their own blood; and
Pythagoras forbade damaging a man's footprints,
because if a man's soul lies in his feet, then
tampering with his footprints can do him great
harm. This is *your* footprint, to keep you safe.'

'Okay, then,' John smiled, and bent his head
forward so that she could hang it around his neck.

'Good luck,' she said, in the quietest of voices,
and left the shop.

John went to the door and watched her walking
back to the Palm Hotel. It was almost noon now,
and the heat was wavering off the concrete pave-
ment so that it appeared to be flooded with bright
silver puddles. Constance walked through them
without getting her feet wet. She reached the hotel,
and turned down the ramp to the parking lot.

Several minutes went by. How long did it take to
find his car and start it up? He kept glancing
anxiously at the men in the gray Buick, for any sign
that they had noticed her. He felt more isolated and
more vulnerable than he had ever felt before, even
in those days after Lorna had left him and his business had collapsed. In those days he had at least
been in charge of his own life, miserable and frac-
tured as it was. But now he felt as if he were a white
rat in a laboratory maze, hurrying desperately
toward a future that had already been contrived for
him.

Suddenly, the Honda appeared at the top of the
ramp, paused for a moment, and turned toward
him. The men in the gray Buick didn't seem to pay
it any attention, which could mean that they
didn't know that the car was his. He prayed – for

160

Constance's safety, and his own – that they hadn't traced his rental transaction.

Constance drove sedately down the street and stopped outside the shop. John hesitated, and then he stepped out of the shadow of the doorway, into the brilliant sunshine. As he did so, the Buick's engine bellowed into life, and it swerved out from the curb. John wrenched open the Honda's passenger door and shouted, '*Go!*' right into Constance's face.

Constance had been unbuckling her seatbelt, and at first she couldn't understand what he meant.

'*They've seen us!*' John told her. '*Just hit the gas and let's go!*'

'Oh, my God,' said Constance. 'I'm not that much of a driver.'

All the same, as the Buick wildly U-turned in the middle of the street behind them, she put down her foot and the Honda lurched forward like a mule.

'Come on, hit it!' John urged her.

'Which way shall I go? Which way shall I go?'

'Doesn't matter – right here, that's it.'

They screeched around the corner and almost knocked down an old man in a Panama hat who was trying to cross the street. 'You hoodlums!' he called after them.

'Up here,' John told Constance. 'Then hang another right.' He brought down his sun vizor so that he had a rear view in his vanity mirror. They had almost reached the next intersection when the Buick appeared, sliding round the corner with its suspension bucking up and down. Constance

161

turned right, and headed up toward the Kissimmee Highway.

'You're slowing down – don't slow down.'

'But it's only 25 along here.'

'Believe me, if these guys catch up with us, a speeding ticket will be the least of your worries.'

'Whatever you say,' said Constance, and pressed her foot down again. 'I think I'm beginning to enjoy this.'

They sped across the following intersection at over 60 m.p.h. and a large old Lincoln had to slew around in a howling circle to avoid hitting them.

'Red light!' said Constance, anxiously, squinting up ahead.

John twisted around in his seat and saw that the Buick was still following them. 'Run it!' he told her.

'What?' she said, staring at him in horror. 'Suppose there's somebody coming the other way?'

'Run it! We don't have any choice!'

They reached the red traffic signal just as two motorcycles came speeding across the intersection from their right and a pick-up truck came jouncing across it from their left. John didn't even have time to think *shit*. Constance hit the brakes and the Honda went into a dry sideways slide, its tires screeching and flibbering on the concrete.

John snatched at the wheel in a last-ditch effort to steer them out of their skid, but one of the motorcycles hit them in the trunk with a deafening bang. The rider flew over their heads, all arms and legs, and landed in the back of the pick-up truck. The other motorcyclist wavered wildly off course and rode straight into the open door of a travel agency.

The pick-up collided with their Honda head-on, ramming it up the curb and onto the sidewalk. They demolished a mailbox and two newspaper stands before they were forced into the huge plate-glass window of the Sun State supermarket. John didn't see his whole life flashing in front of his eyes. All he saw was a red-and-yellow banner announcing SPECIAL ON PRIME RIB. Then the supermarket window exploded like a bomb, showering glass everywhere, and the Honda was pushed sideways through the stacked-up sacks of barbecue charcoal and dog food, ending up against the photo booth and the last checkout counter.

There was a moment of total silence. Then a piece of aluminum window frame dropped onto the hood of their car with a sharp clang, and John said, 'Constance? Constance? Are you okay?'

Constance stared at him with her eyes wide. 'Oh my goodness,' she said.

'Listen, Constance, you're not hurt or anything?'

She patted herself all over. 'No . . . I don't seem to be.'

'Come on, we have to get out of here. Those goons are right behind us.'

A young crewcut store assistant opened up John's door. 'Are you hurt, sir? Do you need an ambulance?'

John unlatched his seatbelt and climbed out. He had bruised both knees, but apart from that he was unhurt. A checkout girl was helping Constance. Shoppers were crunching bemused through the shattered glass.

'I'm fine,' said John. 'I'm absolutely fine.'

163

Just outside the window he could see the pick-up driver still sitting in his cab with blood on his forehead. His injury didn't look any worse than concussion, but it would keep him out of their way. The motorcyclist was being carefully lifted out of the back by four utility workers and laid on the sidewalk.

'Don't take off his helmet,' John heard one of them saying. 'His head might come off with it.'

The Sun State store manager came from his office at the back – a small gingery man with a bristly mustache and a white short-sleeved shirt. He stared at the damage and kept on shaking his head.

'I've heard of drive-in shopping,' he kept repeating. Then he turned to John and said, 'I'm going to have to take your name and particulars, sir. And you, madam, since you were the driver.'

But at the moment they heard a scream of tires outside and it wasn't the police or the paramedics. It was the gray Buick. It slewed to a halt on the opposite side of the street and the two men in gray suits snatched open their doors and came running across to the supermarket.

John took hold of Constance's hand and pulled her through the nearest checkout and into the aisles. Together they hurried down the whole length of the store until they reached the deli counter. They hid behind a large display for Doritos while the deli assistant stared at them balefully through heavy-rimmed glasses. John turned to her and pressed his finger to his lips. The assistant gave him a ghastly smile and edged away as quickly as she could.

The two men in gray suits quickly approached the broken window and stepped in over the glass.

'Hey there – excuse me – we're closed for business!' said the manager, trying to head them off.

'That's all right, asshole,' said the taller of the two men. 'We're not planning on buying anything.'

'I'm sorry, you have to leave the store. We have a wrecked vehicle here. There could be a fire.'

The men ignored him and hurried through the checkouts. When they reached the aisles they hesitated for a moment and then they split up – one of them making for the chill cabinets on the left-hand side of the store and the other weaving his way through the fruit and vegetables.

'Give the cops another call!' the manager called out. 'And the fire department! I don't know what the heck's going on here but I don't like it one little bit!'

John led Constance across the store, ducking low, dodging from aisle to aisle. He could hear a chorus of sirens not far away, so he knew that the men in the gray suits didn't have very long to find them. But he could hear their rubber-soled shoes squeaking quickly and softly on the supermarket floor and he didn't count on the cops getting here before one or other of them had a clear shot.

They had almost reached the fruit counters when one of the men suddenly appeared around the corner gondola.

'*They're here!*' the man shouted, and whistled. John pulled Constance into the petfood aisle, and they hurried to the other end. The manager saw them as they turned the corner by the checkouts and called out, 'Hey! Hey, you! Come over here!' But John didn't take any notice of him. The second gray-suited man had just appeared three aisles in front of them, and he had to tug Constance past the shelves of cereals and sodas.

They were only halfway down the aisle when the man fired a deafening shot. Beside them, a box of Cheerios burst open. The man fired again, and there was a soft explosion of Cream of Wheat. The third time, the bullet sang so close to John's left ear that he felt its draft.

He had only seconds to think. He collapsed onto the floor, twitched, and then lay still. Constance, distraught, knelt down next to him.

'John! John!' Her voice was like the shrilling of a snared bird. 'They haven't killed you, John! Don't say they've killed you!'

Without opening his eyes, John hissed, 'I'm okay. They missed me. But make out I'm dead. And – quick – this is what you have to do.'

The police and fire sirens were howling all around the building in a hallelujah chorus. Constance stood up, and stepped away from John's body, her hands clutched together in apparent anguish. The man in the gray suit came hurrying up, thrusting his automatic back into its shoulder-holster.

'You've killed him,' said Constance. 'You terrible men. You've killed him.'

'Shut up Grandma or you'll get the same.'

The second man appeared and said, 'Let's get out of here. There's a door out back.' He turned and made his way toward the deli counter.

At that moment, however, Constance took two large bottles of Perrier water off the shelves next to her, whirled them in each hand like Indian clubs, and struck the first man two hard knocks on the back of the neck, one after the other, so fast that he had dropped to his knees before the second man even started to turn around.

When he did, he found John standing right in front of him. He didn't even have time to register surprise or resignation before John punched him between the eyes, and he fell backward onto the supermarket floor and hit his head with a sickening crack.

He tried to sit up, but then he fell back again and hit his head a second time.

'Police!' called an echoing voice. 'Whoever you are, drop your weapons and come on out!'

'Time to leave,' said John, squeezing Constance's hand.

They negotiated the deli counter and found their way into the storeroom. They walked past the refrigerators, and out through the back door into the dusty, sunbaked parking lot. A stray dog barked at them but Constance shooed it away. They walked out onto the street as casually as they could, until at last they had turned the corner.

John said, 'Where the hell did you learn to handle soda bottles like that?'

'Seniors fitness class. I told you I go twice a week. You should see me with a medicine ball.'

John said, 'You're a star, believe me. But I shouldn't have gotten you into this. I'm sorry. Let me take you back to the gallery. You can forget it ever happened.'

'I don't want to forget it ever happened.'

John didn't know what to say. The two men would have been picked up by the police, no doubt about it. But unless there was any way in which they could be materially connected to the killing of Kevin and Jesus, he doubted if they could be held for anything much more than blowing some holes in a few boxes of cereal. The way they acted, he guessed that they had friends in high places – and, if they did, they would probably be coming after him again.

'I'll have to rent another car,' he said. 'Do you have a credit card?'

For almost twenty minutes, John and Constance drove westward in silence. The warm wind buffeted into the car. Constance glanced at John from time to time, and he glanced at her.

'What are you thinking about?' John asked her at last.

She smiled. 'I was thinking – my God, if only my grandchildren could see me now.'

They reached William Cicero's house at Winter Park a little after three in the afternoon, and parked a short distance away beneath the shade of a large lignum vitae. John had seen the signs warning of security patrols, and he took a long look around before he beckoned Constance to follow him to the back of the house. The gardens were warm and fragrant, filled with azaleas and camellias and

Oriental magnolias. The lawns were beginning to look straggly, and some of the vines needed cutting back, but there was still a deep air of wealth and peace.

John took out the key that Kevin had given him and went up the three brick steps to the back door. The replacement lock was stiff, but he managed to turn it, and step inside.

'No alarm?' asked Constance, as she cautiously followed him.

'Kevin and Jesus deactivated it.'

They walked across a large breakfast-room, with white-painted basketwork chairs, and desiccated palms. 'It's a beautiful place,' said Constance, admiring a large oil painting of a woman in blue.

'I know. You wouldn't think that the guy who lived here invented a guided missile that could target individual people, would you?'

'I could have used one of those when I divorced my first husband.'

They entered the library. John slowly shook his head in disbelief, and walked all the way around the shelves, running his fingertips against the backs of the leatherbound books. Then he went over to the glass bookcase where all the green-bound books were kept. 'Look at this . . . *Mozart and Spatial Reasoning . . . Fermat's Last Theorem . . . Nyungar Tradition in Western Australia* . . . pretty eclectic kind of collection.'

They went through to the living-room, with its grand piano and its huge oil paintings. It was there that they found a young man asleep on one of the yellow silk-upholstered sofas, with an open book spread across his chest. He was dressed in black jeans and a black shirt. He was thin and pale-faced and he was whistling slightly in one nostril. 'Who do you think he is?' Constance whispered. John circled the sofa, and then looked at the book. '*Fibonacci Numbers and the Golden Ratio*,' he said. 'Pretty heavy reading for a guy who looks like he just got off a Harley.'

He walked over to the window and looked out through the net curtains. As he did so, the young man stirred, and dropped his book on the floor. Then suddenly he sat up, and looked around, and said, 'Jesus – who are you?'

'I think we could ask you the same question,' said John. 'Or how about I call for security?'

'Hey . . . I only came here to read,' the young man told him. 'I was invited by Dr Lügner. Well, kind of invited.'

'Dr Lügner?'

'It's not his real name. I don't know what his real name is. The security people said that he was called Snow, but – you know – who knows?'

'If we're talking about the same person, we call him William Cicero,' said John. 'You don't happen to have the remotest idea where he is, do you?'

The young man looked at him narrowly. 'You're not anything to do with that Cuban guy, are you, and the other guy with those tiny little knots in his necktie?'

Kevin and Jesus thought John. But the suspicious way in which the young man had asked him was a caution for him to shake his head. 'Doesn't mean anything to me. Why?'

170

'They've been trying to track Dr Lügner down, that's why.'

'Ah . . . I think I've heard about you,' said John. 'You're the local hero who saved William Cicero from being kidnapped.'

'How do you know that? Who are you?'

'I know it because I've been looking for William Cicero too. And it seems like I'm not the only one.' He held out his hand. 'John Huntley, I'm a private investigator. Licensed, look. Here's my ID. This is Ms Constance Carden. She's an art dealer and the worst getaway driver in Central Florida.'

Micky shook his hand, still looking suspicious. 'Don't ask me where Dr Lügner's at, because I genuinely don't know.'

'So what are you doing here?' John asked him.

'I don't know . . .' Micky demurred. 'I'm not sure how much I ought to tell you. I don't even know if Dr Lügner is dead or alive.'

'But you're here, reading a book on advanced math.'

'Sure: it's all about Fibonacci numbers. That's a sequence of numbers where every number is the sum of the previous two numbers. I was reading about it because the code to the front door lock is a sequence of Fibonacci numbers.'

'Oh, really?' said John, looking around the room.

'Sure . . . and it says here that if you count the clockwise spirals on the head of a sunflower, and then count the anticlockwise spirals on the same flower, the figures won't just be Fibonacci numbers, they'll be consecutive Fibonacci numbers.

It's the same with plants, the way their leaves grow.'

'Well, good; that's real handy to know. But I still don't really understand what you're doing here.'

'Just like you said, I'm reading a book on advanced math. After that I'm going to read a book on music. Then I'm going to read a book on physics. I'm going to keep on reading until I know everything.'

'Until you know *everything*?' John repeated.

'Until I know everything that I can find out here. Then, well, who knows. There are plenty more books out there.'

John said, 'There must be 10,000 books here. How long do you think it's going to take you to read them all?'

'I'm a real fast reader. Getting faster all the time. I've got a good memory, too. Do you know what it says at the top of page 113?'

He handed the book over. John hesitated, and then opened it up.

Micky said, 'Got it?' and then began to quote. '"Successive ratios in the Fibonacci series converge on the number 1.618033989, which is the Golden Ratio known to mathematicians since at least 300 BC. When a Golden Ratio rectangle is divided into a square and a rectangle, it repeats the same proportion; and if the smaller rectangle is divided again, the same proportion is repeated in the even smaller rectangle. If the points where the squares and rectangles meet are joined by semicircles, they will form a logarithmic spiral which exactly matches the spiral on every snail shell on the planet."'

John gave the book back. 'Pretty good.'

'Pretty good? You know that's a whole lot more than "pretty good".'

'All right, it's amazing. How did you do it?'

Micky hesitated. 'I don't think I ought to say any more until I know, like, *why* you're looking for Dr Lügner. After all, I didn't save his life from one bunch of thugs just to help another bunch to track him down. You know – not being offensive or anything.'

John said, 'Listen, we can choose to be paranoid or we can choose to trust each other. Either way, it doesn't make much difference to me.' He explained what Gene Broussard had hired him to do; and all about the MiGR8-guided missile that couldn't fly.

'Well, that's why *you're* looking for him. Why are all these other guys looking for him, too?'

'I don't know. Maybe he's invented something *else* that won't start until he's there to push the button.'

'Well, that sure sounds possible,' said Micky. 'He's a total genius. But I mean he's not just your average genius like Albert Einstein or Thomas Edison or Max Planck. He's a genius at *everything*. He's your, like, Renaissance genius.'

John looked at Constance and raised an eyebrow. Here was a skinny young man in cowboy boots tossing off the names of three of history's greatest minds as if he had known them. 'Here, let me show you,' said Micky, and led the way back to the library. John and Constance cautiously followed him.

'I found out that all of these green-bound books

he wrote himself, under different names. I found a catalog, but you can work out that it was him, because every name is an anagram of a Florida city. Look – *Deep Sea Fishing* by O. Roland – that's Orlando. And, here, *Infrared Photography* by Ben Rigs – that's Sebring. Here's my favorite so far, though – *Marine Sponges* by Walter Cera – that's Clearwater.'

John picked up one of the books and flicked through the pages. It was obvious from the dense type and the copious footnotes that this wasn't the work of a gifted amateur or a weekend hobbyist. This was factual, fully annotated argument by somebody who had researched his subject exhaustively.

'One man can write all these books and still find time to invent the most advanced missile guidance system in the world?' John asked, rhetorically. Then, '*How*?'

Micky shook his head. 'Don't ask me. I only saved his life.'

'He found the time to write all of these books and now you're finding the time to read them? I mean, what's going on here? I don't like to be rude, but you don't look like your average polymath.'

'I have a good memory, that's all. What's a polymath?'

John gave him a narrow look, but Micky changed the subject by saying, 'Take a look at these paintings on the wall. Dr Lügner did all of these. They're fantastic, aren't they?'

On one of the library walls hung three Florida landscapes, in a rich, highly finished style reminiscent of Maxfield Parrish. Constance nodded. 'I've been admiring those. To tell you the truth, I think I've even sold one or two paintings by the same artist. Charles Babson, isn't it? His work commands *very* high prices.'

'He's signed some of them Charles Babson,' said Micky. 'But these two are signed by Arthur Friend . . . and *this* one's signed by Davis Watkins. They're all his, though. He has them listed. And that isn't all. He's written music, and poetry. He's made sculptures. He's done just about every creative thing you could think of. I've only been here – what – three and a half hours, and some of the stuff that I've seen already . . .'

'It makes you wonder why he's not famous, doesn't it?' said Constance.

Micky shrugged. 'I guess he's not famous because he never wanted to be famous. And I guess those guys who were trying to find him were something to do with it. The way he talked, it sounded like he'd been running and hiding all his life.'

John went over to Dr Lügner's computer and switched it on.

'You won't find anything in there,' said Micky. 'He erased everything before he disappeared. All you get is that.'

On the screen, in red letters, was the message '*A equals x plus y plus z.*'

'Do you know what that means?' asked John.

'It's a quote from Albert Einstein. He said, "If *A* is success in life, then *A* equals *x* plus *y* plus *z*. Work is *x*; *y* is play; and *z* is keeping your mouth shut."'

John grunted in amusement and switched the computer off. 'Seems like you're taking his advice. At least as far as your Dr Lügner is concerned.'

'I can't tell you where he is because I don't *know* where he is. I can't even *guess* where he is. I've looked through some of his papers and some of his notes, but he hasn't left any kind of clues. Well, none that *I* could see.'

John stood still for a moment, thinking. Then he said, 'We're going to have to find him, you know, and we're going to have to find him first. I told you a lie, Micky. I *do* know those guys you were talking about, the Cuban and the guy with the tiny knots in his necktie. Their names were Kevin and Jesus and they worked for Broussard, same as me, except they were part of Broussard's permanent security staff.'

Micky turned to him, furious. 'Shit, man! That Cuban threatened to cut my girlfriend's eyes out! And the other guy hit me, right in the face! Then they came around here and somebody got taken out in a body bag. Dr Lügner's maid, I think. I mean, did these Broussard people tell you that? Shit. I can't talk to you any more.'

'Micky, for Christ's sake. I didn't know anything about any of that, I swear it. It all happened before they asked me to join them. Well – before they put me into a position where I *had* to join them, more or less. Kevin and Jesus – they didn't really hurt you, did they? I guess they thought they were tough guys.'

'So what are *you* going to do? Hit me with a cushion?'

'Look, Micky . . . both Kevin and Jesus were shot dead yesterday. Two men came up in a restaurant and blew them away, right in front of sixty witnesses. It was only by chance they didn't whack me, too.'

Micky said, 'Whoah,' in alarm. 'That's heavy. But what? You want me to be sympathetic? They were, like, animals.'

'They probably were. But they're dead now, so that's pretty much beside the point. The point is that Broussard Guidance Systems are obviously not the only people who are looking for Dr Lügner or William Cicero or whatever he's calling himself now. We don't just have hunters hunting the hunted here. We have hunters hunting the hunters.'

'Maybe we do. But you're still working for the same people who kidnapped Dr Lügner, and threatened Roxanne and me. Come on, man – how do you expect me to trust you?'

'It's up to you,' John told him. 'I came clean, didn't I, and told you that I knew Kevin and Jesus. As for working for Broussard, like I told you, they made me an offer which wasn't easy for me to refuse. But somewhere along the line, somebody set up Kevin and Jesus, and me, too; and I'm not going back to Broussard until I find out who that was. I think that you and I could do each other a favor. I think that we could help each other to locate our William Cicero, and then see who's been trying to find him, and why.'

'I don't know,' said Micky, reluctantly. But John came up and stood over him. 'You listen to me, friend. If we don't find this William Cicero before

177

everybody else, we won't have anything to bargain with. You know in the movies, when they say that somebody has to be rubbed out because they know too much. Well, you and me, I think we know too much. We may not know what it is that we actually know, but the trouble is we know it. And I don't think we're ever going to be safe, *ever*, unless we locate this genius friend of yours, if he's still alive, and locate him first.'

Micky said, 'I don't know, man.' He still felt suspicious. He couldn't decide whether he liked John or not. He was middle-aged, and square, and a bit too authoritarian for Micky's liking. He probably listened to REM, too. But he was the kind of guy who had the corners knocked off him and he seemed to be sincere. Constance seemed to trust him, too; and Constance was giving Micky a motherly, encouraging smile. He looked around the library and he realized that here was a gift that couldn't be wasted. All these years, Dr Lügner had tried to keep himself hidden. But when you can write – when you can paint – when you can work out complex elliptic theorems – you can't keep your work to yourself. Otherwise it means nothing. It would be like Mark Twain writing *Huckleberry Finn* and throwing the pages into the Mississippi before anybody else had the chance to read it. It would be like Monet taking a match to his paintings or Caruso singing in the shower and no place else.

Dr Lügner hadn't been able to resist publishing all of his works and selling most of his paintings. He hadn't been able to resist travel, and conferences, where he could eavesdrop on his colleagues' conversations and hear how brilliant he was. Micky was beginning to feel the same way. In a few hours he had already developed an extraordinary memory, and he could work out astronomical sets of figures in his head. A whole garden of new abilities was blossoming inside his brain like a speeded-up movie of flowers opening out. This morning he had found that his handwriting had improved beyond recognition and that he could accurately sketch. Yesterday he had only been able to draw pin-men. Today he had drawn Roxanne's face on a notepad in Dr Lügner's library, purely from memory, and it had been such an exact likeness that he had sat smiling at it for almost ten minutes, unable to believe what he had done.

Out of respect, out of caution, he had tried not to rummage too comprehensively through Dr Lügner's house, but there was so much here. So much art, so many musical scores, so many books, so many scientific instruments. At the rear of the house, he had discovered a large airy conservatory fitted out as a physics laboratory. He hadn't understood any of the experiments that were set up, but there was something that looked like a cross between a transparent car battery and a human brain. Even if he didn't understand it now, he knew that he *could* – and that, eventually, he would.

It was more than he could keep to himself. In spite of his fast-breeding intellect, or maybe because of it, he had to share the experience that had changed his life. What did it really matter? Dr Lügner was either dead, or disappeared; and the secret that he had bequeathed to Micky was too enormous for Micky to keep to himself.

'What is it?' asked Constance, as if she could tell how troubled he was.

Micky said, 'I might be betraying a trust here. I don't know. But Dr Lügner never made any stipulations. He never said don't tell nobody.'

'So what was it that he never said you shouldn't tell?' John demanded.

'He discovered something – or invented it, I'm not sure which. It was a kind of a drug which could make your mind work better.'

'So what are you saying to me? That all of these paintings, and all of these books, and all of his scientific developments . . . he was able to do them because of some drug?'

Micky said, 'It works, believe me.'

'How do you know?'

'At school. I didn't even get past the fourth grade. Now I can work out *pi* in my head. How many decimal places do you want?'

'*You* took it?' asked Constance.

'You're putting us on,' said John, circling around him, looking at his eyes, his ears, the back of his straggly, unconditioned hair.

'It *works*,' said Micky. 'Listen to me! I've been having thoughts in my head that I never considered possible. I've been solving problems that I didn't even know existed. You want to give me a Rubik's Cube? I'll finish it in five seconds flat. You want to give me a sheet of white paper? In ten seconds flat, you'll have yourself an origami horse with a rider in the saddle.

'It's like – it's like an explosion in your head,

man. It's as scary as all hell. But it's like you've been asleep all your life and you've suddenly woken up. You can't *help* but tell people all about it.'

'Your Dr Lügner didn't tell anybody about it, though, did he? He kept it to himself.'

'Well, I don't know why. Maybe he had a good reason. But the things he's done . . . he's touched on everybody's life. He invented food coloring that doesn't upset hyperactive children. He invented some kind of gas for putting out fires on oil rigs. He's written *symphonies*, for Christ's sake.'

'Isn't it *interesting*, though?' said Constance. 'If he *had* put his drug on the market, so that *everybody* could have had some . . . well, *everybody* could have been a genius.'

'If you ask me, that's just what he didn't want,' said John. He took a stick of eucalyptus gum out of his shirt pocket and folded it into his mouth. 'You know what they say. "In the kingdom of the blind, the one-eyed man is king." Supposing you had *two* eyes, in the kingdom of the blind. You'd be really something, wouldn't you? You'd have a power like nobody else.'

'But that's my point,' Constance put in. 'He *does* have the power, but he never really used it. He didn't make any attempt to market this genius drug, did he? Why did he paint his paintings under false names? Why did he write books under silly anagrams, and use false names for all of his scientific papers?'

'Well, who knows? Maybe he had some kind of persecution complex. Maybe he got his rocks off being brainier than everybody else.'

'I don't think so,' said Constance. 'I think he was frightened. Pure and simple.'

'Frightened?' John wanted to know. 'Frightened of what?'

'Come on, man!' Micky protested. 'Of course he was frightened. He was kidnapped. He said those guys were going to shoot him in the head and throw him in the swamp.'

'But if he hadn't been so secretive – if he'd have come out years ago and said that he'd invented this genius drug, then he would have been a household name, wouldn't he? The Martha Graham of the intellect. He wouldn't have had anything to be frightened about. Nobody could have touched him.'

'But he didn't,' said Micky.

John came over and nodded. 'That's right, Micky. He *didn't*. And I think that the reason he didn't is the answer to this whole damned puzzle. Why did he leave Hoshi International so suddenly after it was taken over by Broussard Guidance Systems? Why are all these guys in suits looking for him? Why are all these guys in suits looking for me? Who *are* these guys in suits? Somebody must be paying them. Guys in suits don't go around whacking people for nothing.'

'Well, like you say, if Dr Lügner is still alive, we have to find him. We have to work out some kind of a plan. You're a private detective. What do *you* think we ought to do?'

'You mean you're willing to trust me?' John demanded.

There was a very long silence. Then Micky said,

'I don't have anybody else to trust, do I?'

'Supposing I don't trust *you*?'

Micky stared at him. 'What do you mean? Of course you can trust me.' He clapped his hands against his Grateful Dead T-shirt. 'I'm *me*.'

John turned to Constance and there were three different expressions on his face. Disbelief, relief, and a deeply suppressed need to laugh. 'All right,' he said. 'We'll formulate a plan. But I think our most urgent priority is self-protection. Whoever's looking for William Cicero or Dr Lügner or whatever his name is, they're more than ready to blow us away. Don't think law and order; don't think conscience. These guys will drop you as soon as look at you. I only saw killers like that once before, and they were just released from San Quentin. You can't win against somebody who literally doesn't care whether they live or whether they die.

'Over the next few days, we have to search this house from attic to basement. We need just one clue to what might have happened to William Cicero. Just one. A diary note. A letter. A jotting on the end of the blotter.'

He said to Micky, 'This could take a couple of days. You don't know anyplace where I could stay, do you? The more anonymous, the better.'

'What about me?' Constance demanded.

'What about you? I thought you were going back to Melbourne to sell some more art. Those guys won't connect you with me.'

Constance stiffened. 'I risked my life for you, John. I wanted an adventure; and I'm determined to have one.'

183

'Constance, we had a few exciting moments back there in Melbourne. But from here on in, I promise you, this is all going to get very procedural and very boring. We have to search through William Cicero's papers. We have to look at all of his notes, all of his receipts, all of his credit-card records. How do you think I found Dieter Waxman? Patience, endless patience. The next few days, really, they'll send you to sleep.'

'I'd rather sleep with you than on my own,' Constance protested. Then she flushed, and said, 'You know what I mean. I feel I've invested something into this case. I want to stay and see it through. All I need to do is call my sister and ask her to take care of the gallery.'

Micky said, 'There's this Italian restaurant where I work, Guido's. He has a couple of rooms in back . . . they use them when their relations visit from Italy. You could stay there, I guess. And eat there, too, you wouldn't have to take the risk of going out too much. The linguini's great.' He paused, and then he said, 'My girlfriend works at Sav-Mart . . . if you need a couple of changes of clothes, you know, and some toiletries . . .'

'It would really be safer if Constance went back home,' John insisted. But at that moment, Constance drew back the net curtain and said, 'There's a car out there.'

John went to the window, too. Half hidden by the trees that lined the driveway, he could see the rear end of a black-sapphire Chevrolet Caprice. It paused for a few moments, its six rear lamps flaring red through the bushes, then it disappeared.

'I think it might be advisable if we got out of here,' said John, quietly.

'My car's parked around the side of the house,' Micky told him. 'How about yours?'

'It might be better if we left ours right where it is.'

'Okay, then . . . let's go out the back way. We can lock up, too.'

But they were only halfway across the living-room when they heard the sound of pattering feet. John glanced back, and saw three men in black suits running toward the house. It was difficult to see them very clearly through the net curtains, but they had their arms raised in that distinctive triangulated way that told him they were carrying guns.

'*Down!*' he barked.

Constance said, 'What?'

'*Down on the floor, for Christ's sake!*' he shouted at her, and pushed her over. She fell against a side table, toppling a large Sèvres vase and smashing it into thousands of pieces, just as the first volley of gunfire shattered the windows and sent the net curtains flying wildly up and down like the wings of panicky geese.

7

It is not everyone who changes shape, possesses magic boots, exhibits suprahuman strength or meets prodigious tests – Theodor H. Gaster

For over a minute, the living-room was swept by a blizzard of bullets. They tore into the pale yellow watered silk that covered the walls; they blasted bits off the plaster acanthus. The gilded antique furniture exploded into matchwood and kapok stuffing, and the grand piano thundered out a deep discord. Paintings dropped from the walls; vases exploded; books were blown into moth-eaten shreds.

John lay flat on his face against the polished parquet, with one arm extended to keep Constance pressed to the floor. Micky lay a few feet away, flattened against the skirting board. Two dozen bullets hammered against the wall only inches above his head. Then mirror-glass cascaded all over him, and he was showered with splinters of gilded abura.

Suddenly, the pattern of bullets ran right up the wall, and into the ceiling. With a catastrophic crash, the huge crystal chandelier came down, and exploded on the floor. Slivers of glass glittered in all directions, and they covered their faces with their hands.

Almost immediately, the shooting stopped. Micky didn't try to get up, but he twisted his head around so that he could see John and Constance. 'You guys okay?'

'We think so. How about you?'

'Fine, so far. What the hell have they got there?'

'Ingram Mach 10s, by the sound of it.'

'What are they?' asked Constance, in a chalky-white voice.

'Submachine guns,' John told her. 'They can fire a whole magazine of thirty bullets before you've had time to blink. One thousand, one hundred rounds per minute. You could cut an elephant in half.'

'They're serious, then?' said Micky. He was frightened, but he felt strangely elated, too.

'I should say so.'

'And they don't work for the same people as you? These Broussard Guidance people?'

'Micky, I told you. I don't know who's hunting who. I just want to find this William Cicero and keep my ass in one piece.'

'Most people's asses are in two pieces.'

'For Christ's sake, Micky, stop being so academic. We just need to get out of here.'

'I know, I know. I'm thinking, that's all. Did you lock the door behind you when you came in?'

'Unh-hunh.'

'Can you go do it now? We need to delay them. But get back here as quickly as you can.'

John started to climb to his feet, but Constance said, 'I'll do it.'

'You can't. It's too dangerous.'

'John – that's the whole reason I'm here.' And with that, she hurried out of the living-room in a crouching run.

'That's some old lady you've got yourself there,' said Micky, shaking his head in admiration. 'Now, I'll tell you what we're going to do. Those guys are not going to come in by the front door, are they? It's solid oak; and it's got that Fibonacci combination lock. So they'll probably come in by the back.'

'So what can we do to stop them?'

Micky pointed to the ceiling. 'You see that chandelier hook? How much do you think that could take?'

'I don't know. Eight, nine hundred pounds. It's a main structural beam, isn't it?'

'That's what I thought. So come on, quick.'

Micky climbed to his feet and went over to the window. He dragged down the thick, braided curtain cords, yards and yards of them. With his feet crunching in inches of shattered glass, he criss-crossed them under the grand piano. Then he climbed on top of the piano lid and said to John, 'Hand me that chair.'

'What the hell are you *doing*?' John hissed at him. 'We have to get out of here.'

Micky tapped his forehead. 'We will, man. But this whole situation is scissors-cut-paper-wraps-rock. These guys have machine-guns. What do we have?'

John hefted up a heavy colonial armchair, which Micky placed on top of the piano. 'Now pass me the ends of those cords.'

It took less than a minute for Micky to climb up onto the chair and tie a complicated arrangement of curtain cords to the hook which had held the chandelier. While he was engrossed in knots and loops, Constance came back. 'They're definitely out there,' she said. 'I saw one of them crossing the lawns. It looks like they're making up their minds what to do next.'

She watched Micky jump down from the piano and drag eight of the curtain cords over to the window. He threw them one by one over the curtain rail, and then divided them into two bunches of four.

'Braided silk,' said Micky. 'It's as strong as a ship's hawser, this stuff. Here – ' and he handed four of the cords to John – 'This is where we're going to need some brute strength. But not as much as you'd think.'

John and Micky each wrapped their cords around their wrists, and then together they began to walk backward across the living-room floor. The cords tightened around the grand piano, and then it began to creak.

'We can't *lift* it,' said John incredulously. 'It must weigh over a third of a ton. You need cranes to lift these things.'

'Can't you see?' Micky grinned at him. 'That's exactly what we've got.'

They stepped back, inch by inch, and at last the piano's legs teetered and rose off the floor. It swung slightly as they raised it higher and higher. When it was head-height, Micky said, 'Stop . . . okay, that's enough. Just hold it there for a moment.'

'Hold it? On my own?'

'You won't drop it, I promise. I was reading all about this, this afternoon.'

'Reading about what, for Christ's sake?'

'How they built the Pyramids. They used ropes to make pulley arrangements, the same as these. You can lift tons if you get it right.'

There were ominous crackings and creakings from the ceiling, but Micky ignored them. If the ceiling was going to come down, the ceiling was going to come down, and there was nothing he could do about it.

He tied another curtain cord to one of the legs of the grand piano, and looped that over the curtain rail, too.

'Okay,' he told John. 'All we have to do now is swing the piano up to the ceiling.'

John wouldn't have believed it if he hadn't seen it with his own eyes. But between them, using a cat's cradle of cords, they lifted the grand piano right up through 90 degrees until its keyboard touched the ceiling, and it hung there, right above their heads, like something out of a surrealistic painting. The ceiling groaned, and the plasterwork was starred with cracks, but Micky clapped John on the shoulder and said, 'So long as it stays up for two more minutes.'

'I don't know how the hell we did that. It didn't seem to weigh anything.'

'They worked it all out in Ancient Egypt, when they were building the Pyramid of Cheops. They needed to lift all these granite blocks right up to the top. That was 2560 BC. Can you imagine that?

They didn't have hydraulic cranes so they worked out ways of using pulleys and ropes.'

Constance shook her head. 'What on earth do you think you can do with a grand piano?' she wanted to know.

'Didn't you ever see *Home Alone?*' said Micky. 'This is the same principle, different method. Now, let's get ourselves out of sight. Behind this couch should do it.'

They crouched behind the gilded sofa like children playing hide-and-go-seek, and waited. Inside, the house was silent, but then they heard somebody trying the front door. They thought they could make out voices, too, but it was impossible to understand what they were saying. Up above them, the ceiling made a deep complaining sound, and the piano lurched a little, and swayed. 'Steinways would have a heart attack if they could see what you've done,' said Constance.

Suddenly, there were two brief blurts of automatic weapon fire – one at the front of the house and one at the back. Then a longer and much more concentrated burst from the back, and the sound of kicking. Glass shattered, timbers were split. They heard the back door kicked from its hinges, to slam flat-bang onto the floor. Somebody shouted, 'Vince – check that side room! Cal, you come with me!'

Now they could hear their attackers walking cautiously through the library. 'Nobody here, Moody. They must be in the living-room.'

'*Yes,*' whispered Micky, under his breath. But the ceiling was making even more ominous splitting

191

noises, and a heavy lump of plaster dropped to the floor.

'What was that?' said one of the voices. 'Did you hear that?'

'Quiet . . . there's somebody in there. I can feel it.'

Very softly, the men came padding across the corridor. They stepped into the living-room – three tall, dark-haired men wearing conventional gray business suits and conventional white shirts – each of them carrying a small, black, boxlike machine-gun, with a silencer attached. They had pasty, plain faces which reminded Micky of the downtrodden 1960s 'organization men' who used to be satirized in old copies of *Mad* magazine. They looked around at the shattered glass and the ripped-up upholstery. They kicked aside the torn-apart cushions and the smashed antique figurines.

Then they stopped, and stared.

'What the fuck's that doing up there?' said one of them, lowering his gun. 'They've hung a piano from the ceiling, for Christ's sake. What the fuck did they do that for?'

He took one more step forward and then he found out. Micky released the cords, and the piano swung down in a 15-foot arc, all 335 kilograms of it, and hit him directly in the chest. One of the men tried to duck aside, but a piano leg caught him between the shoulder-blades and sent him sprawling. The third man simply stood transfixed as the piano hurtled toward him and smashed him against the wall. With a thunderous chord that sounded like the finale of the loudest symphony ever written, his skull cracked and his blood was sprayed in crochets and semiquavers all over the yellow silk wall-hangings.

'Oh my God,' said Constance. But John took hold of her hand and said, 'Let's get the hell out of here, pronto.'

The piano was still rumbling to itself as they hurried across the living-room and out into the corridor. 'What about their guns?' asked Micky. 'Shouldn't we take them with us?'

'What are you going to do with an Ingram?' John retorted.

'I don't know. Protect myself from people with other Ingrams.'

'Bull. You don't need a machine-gun, do you, so long as you've got a grand piano handy.'

Until they had reached Micky's Camaro and were driving away from Winter Park, John didn't realize that – for the first time in a very, very long time – he had paid somebody else a compliment.

Micky drove John and Constance to Guido's. Guido was in a foul mood because a party of twelve had canceled at a half-hour's notice, and one of his waiters had called in sick. Apart from that, Mario wanted to cook *calamari ripieni con funghi secchi*, squid stuffed with wild mushrooms, which was Guido's idea of the *secondi* from hell.

'These are two friends of mine,' said Micky. 'I wonder could they stay here for a while?'

'I cook what I like!' Mario shouted, through the kitchen hatch.

'You cook what my customers like! You cook

193

what I like! My customers don't like rubber socks filled up with toadstools, and neither do I!' He turned to Micky, and said, 'You should come back to work here. I thought *you* were slow with the pots, but this new kid . . . he should win the Slow Olympics.'

'What do you say, Guido? It's only for two or three nights.'

Guido looked at John and Constance with the suspicious, slitted look that he usually reserved for judging the freshness of calves' liver. They were both hot and bedraggled, and they were quite an odd couple – a battered-looking man in jeans and a nervous lady twenty years his senior. It was even odder that they should both be friends of a frustrated young rock 'n' roller like Micky. But he found their very oddness reassuring. They didn't look as if they would steal the cutlery or hold all-night parties.

'Okay then,' he agreed. 'Thirty-five dollars the night. Italian breakfast.'

'What's an Italian breakfast?'

'Last night's spaghetti, what do you think?'

'I cook what I like!' Mario repeated.

Guido showed them through to their rooms. They were plain, but very clean, with pine furniture, checkered bedspreads and Italian travel posters pinned to the walls. 'You see there?' said Guido. 'Terracina. That's where my father was born. Beautiful. Heaven on earth.'

After he had left, John sat on the bed and said, 'We're going to have to think what we're going to do next. I mean, it's obvious that somebody is deadly serious about preventing us from locating William Cicero . . . and they're not going to let us go with just a warning.'

'Maybe it's the Russians, or the Chinese, or the Iraqis,' Micky suggested. 'Somebody who doesn't want this new missile to work. Or somebody who wants to pick Dr Lügner's brains, and doesn't want *us* getting to him first.'

'There's only one person who can tell us for certain,' said John.

'Well, yes, for sure. But how do we go about finding him?'

'It won't be easy – especially now that we can't search through his house any longer. First of all I have to track down some people who might have known him.'

'I know his lawyers, if that's any help.'

'Are you kidding me? You know his lawyers?'

'For sure. Lance, Peutus & Evangeline, in Orlando. After Dr Lügner disappeared, they sent me a tape telling me where I could find the genius drug, and how to take it.'

'Did you ask them how you could get in touch with him?'

Micky shook his head. 'They were pretty abrupt. I could call them again, if you like.'

John said, 'Never mind about that. Can you get me access to a PC?'

'Sure . . . my friend Mingus had one for his birthday. He never uses it much. Well, he plays a lot of *Seventh Guest*, but that's just about it.'

'As quick as you can, then. The sooner we find out who's been after us, and why, the sooner we can find out how to protect ourselves.'

Mingus lived just off Emmett, in the quieter back streets of Kissimmee, where his family shared a small red-and-yellow house with his mother's cousin and *her* family. There were always children playing in the yard and running up and down stairs. There was always something boiling or baking and the sound of music. Outside, three vehicles were parked: a Firebird, an old but shiny LTD, and Mingus' bright yellow pick-up with its chromed exhausts.

Mingus' mother was in the kitchen, making a chicken potpie. She was a big, pretty woman with the sweetest singing voice. Mingus' sister Dauphine was sitting crosslegged on a stool, watching *Sesame Street*.

'You looking for Mr Noise?' asked Mingus' mother. 'He's in his room, giving me the earache.'

Micky listened, and heard the sudden *chong-kerchong-kerchong* of Mingus' guitar. He went through to Mingus' bedroom and knocked loose-wristed on the door. The bedroom was small, but it was Mingus' own, and it had a door that led right out onto a brown brick loggia, where there were earthenware pots filled with flowers. On the walls were oil paintings of James Brown and Bo Diddley and John Lee Hooker: amateur, but strong.

Mingus was sitting on the bed, playing his guitar with the amplifier turned right down.

'Hi, Mingus. How's it going?'

Mingus laid down his guitar in exasperation and smoothed both his hands back over his head. 'I don't know, man. No place, fast. I've been trying to work out this bridge and it's just all over the place.'

'Play it for me.'

Mingus picked up his guitar again and started strumming their new song 'Rats Run Free'. The bridge started off vivid and clear, but then it just fell apart. Mingus stopped playing and threw his guitar onto the bed. 'It's crap, man. It's total *crap*. *I'm* crap. I can see my future clear as day: sweeping the sidewalks outside of McDonald's, or sitting in a ticket booth at Gatorland.'

'What the hell's wrong with you?' Micky asked him. 'You nearly got it. Listen.'

He took the guitar, played two or three chords and retuned the G and the F. Then he started playing, and Mingus sat back and stared at him in amazement. From the moment he started, his playing was inspired. There was a deep, bluesy power to it: an oily, dirty, earth-and-locomotive sound that pushed it relentlessly forward. But as he continued to play, the upper registers began to grow huge wings, and rise from the earth, and soar. Eyes closed, head tilted back, he came out with one breathtaking phrase after another, lifting the song higher and higher, until Mingus had to stand up, with both his fists clenched in excitement, and say, 'Yes, man! That's it, man! That's wicked!'

Mingus' mother opened the bedroom door and stood there with her arms folded. 'Excuse *me*,' she said, 'but your sister can't hear a word that Ernie and Bert are saying to each other, and they're her favorites.'

Micky stopped playing and handed the guitar back. 'I'm sorry, Mrs Wells. Got carried away.'

'Hmph,' she said with a smile. 'You may deafen a person, but you're good. About time you learned to play that good, Mingus.'

When she had gone, Mingus said, 'I never heard you play anything like that before. It's that brain drug, isn't it?'

Micky lifted both of his hands and turned them this way and that as if he couldn't believe that they were actually his. 'It just seems like everything's so *easy*. Everything's so *understandable*. And what really gets to me is that everything always *was* easy, if only my brain had been working properly. Like, if Albert Einstein could understand the general theory of relativity, then why the hell shouldn't I?'

'General theory of relativity, hunh? That's what? Like, all your aunts and uncles and stuff?'

'$E = mc^2$, dummy.'

'Dummy yourself, that was supposed to be a joke. Listen, I have to go to work in five minutes. Why don't I come around to your place later and we'll play some more?'

'I don't know . . . I kind of got involved in something today.' Haltingly, he told Mingus what had happened at Dr Lügner's house.

'You're kidding me,' said Mingus, as he wrestled his way into a clean T-shirt. 'Come on, man. Machine-guns? You're putting me on.'

'I wish I was.'

'Come on, you're kidding me, right?'

'I'm serious, Mingus. I mean it. That's why it's real important that we find Dr Lügner as soon as we can. Do you think that this guy could borrow your computer?'

Mingus said, 'My computer? I don't know. That cost my folks a fortune.'

'He'll take good care of it, I promise.'

'Well . . . okay. But if he breaks it, you've got to buy me a new one.'

'If he breaks it, I'll buy you two new ones.'

'And you have to teach me how to play the guitar the way you just did.'

'If I can, man, I will.'

'Go on, then, play that "Rats Run Free" again. Play it real loud. Mom won't mind. Well, she won't mind much.'

Micky picked up the guitar again, and turned up the amplifiers so that they hummed with feedback. Then he launched himself into the opening chords, and the song jumped into life – a song of protest and discontent – a fierce declaration of youthful disaffection. He started to sing, too, and the words came out as if they had been written already.

'Lovers are trapped in their love lives
In glances and gestures and smiles
Birds are all caught in their cages
Although in their minds they fly miles
But the dark and the bad and the beautiful
They seem so alluring to me
Rats are the bearers of death and destruction
But rats run free'

Micky played until the glass in the windows vibrated; and all Mingus could do was to sit back on the bed watching him and shaking his head. When he came to the final chord, Mingus said, 'Shit, man. I never heard anything like that before. You're going to make it so big.'

'*We're* going to make it so big. Frasier & Wells, okay?'

'Oh, yes, and what's everybody going to say? What's a genius musician like you doing with a frankfurter-fingered backing guitarist who can't even play "House of the Rising Sun" without making eighty-five mistakes?'

Micky said, 'Mingus, we're friends.'

'We *were* friends, when we were both equally stupid.'

'We're still friends, for Christ's sake.'

Mingus stood up, and took back his guitar. 'Sure,' he said, although he didn't sound convinced. 'I'll help you carry the computer out to the car.'

Micky picked up Roxanne from Sav-Mart at a quarter after six. The evening was warm and clear, but there were distant indigestive rumblings of thunder. Roxanne was wearing tight white pedal-pushers and a shiny pink short-sleeved top, with lipstick to match.

'Hi-i-i!' she greeted him, catching hold of his arm and giving him a kiss. 'How's my egghead this evening?'

'Okay, I guess. I've had one of those days you'd rather forget. And I wish you wouldn't call me egghead.'

'So what went wrong? Did you go to Dr What's-his-name's house? You were so keen to read all of his books.'

'Well, I looked around some; and I read maybe two or three books.'

'In *one day* you read two or three books?'

'Sure, yes. But they weren't too highbrow or anything.' Only *Taniyama-Shimura and Modular Function* had given him any serious trouble. But that was right at the leading edge of abstract math, and many of its conclusions were still beyond proof, even to the world's most advanced mathematicians.

'What do you want to do this evening?' asked Roxanne. 'I could cook you a corned-beef hash. You know, with all the crispy bits. Maybe we could rent out *Babe* again.'

Micky found himself looking at her with an unexpected sense of detachment. She was just as pretty as yesterday. She smelled just as exciting. Her blonde hair shone in the early-evening sunshine. Her breasts bounced under her satin top. But corned-beef hash? And *Babe*? And another evening sprawled in front of the television with a bottle of cheap domestic wine?

'What's wrong?' she smiled, but her eyes weren't smiling.

'I don't know. Nothing.'

'You're not having any side-effects?'

'No,' he said. 'I guess it's just me.' He was tempted to tell her what had happened at Dr Lügner's house but he decided against it. She had been frightened enough by the Cabbage Patch man and the Cuban. He opened the car door for her, with its distinctive groaning hinges, and drove down Canoe Creek Road.

'Do you ever think about getting married?' she asked.

He glanced at her sideways. The sun was right behind her, giving her a radiant reddish-gold corona. 'I'd like to marry someday, for sure. And have kids. I don't want the Frasier name to die out for ever. Why do you ask?'

She smiled at him coyly. 'I was just wondering what qualities you'd be looking for in a wife.'

'What's this? Fishing for compliments?'

'Just interested, that's all.'

'Well . . .' he said, 'she'd have to be blonde, and blue-eyed, and extra-specially pretty, and have a figure like a centerfold. She'd have to cook good, and like rock music. She'd have to have a mind of her own. No yes-woman for me. And she'd have to be a trainee reflexologist.'

'Okay, then,' she said, snuggling up close to him. 'Why don't you propose?'

'You want me to propose? You're serious?'

'You're not upset, are you?'

'Why should I be upset? I'm flattered. It's just a surprise, is all.'

'We've been living together since the dawn of time, almost.'

'Sure, but marriage. You know, Mr and Mrs Frasier.'

He pulled down his sun vizor and studied himself in the vanity mirror. 'I'm not sure that I look like a husband.'

'I think you'd make a gorgeous husband. No two ways about it.'

Back home, Orbison was waiting for them with his tail madly flapping. Roxanne went into the kitchen to put away her shopping and to bring them some beers, while Micky stood in the middle of the living-room for a moment, feeling strangely alienated, as if he didn't really live here. He looked at the painting of Alfred E. Neuman on the wall, *What, Me Worry?* and he found that he was irritated by its brazen stupidity. It was like an advertisement for being dumb; and who the hell wanted to be dumb?

Roxanne came out of the kitchen with their beers. 'You haven't switched on the TV.'

'No, well. I guess I haven't.'

'But *Home Improvement*'s on! You love *Home Improvement*!'

'Sure. Yes. Let's watch *Home Improvement*.'

She kissed him, but then she frowned. 'Are you *sure* you're not feeling any after-effects? Maybe you should go see your doctor.'

'Hey, I'm fine,' he told her. 'I really feel good. You know *good*. Full of energy. Raring to go.'

'You want to go? We only just got back.'

'I mean metaphorically raring to go.'

She kept on staring at him and it was then he realized that she didn't know what 'metaphorically' meant. But then neither had he, until he had taken Dr Lügner's drug.

'Let's watch *Home Improvement*,' he suggested.

They sat on the couch and watched television for a while. Roxanne loved *Home Improvement* and couldn't stop laughing. Micky sat with his arm around her, trying to smile. Outside, the sun went down, and the sky was the color of dark blue glass. Less than 24 hours ago, he would have been laughing, too. But he couldn't help worrying about Fermat's Last Theorem. It had been mentioned only in passing in one of Dr Lügner's books, but it had snagged his imagination like a fishing-fly caught on a rough tweed coat.

$x^n + Y^n$ *never equals* Z^n *if n is a whole number greater than 2.* In other words, two squared numbers can sometimes add up to another squared number, but two cubed numbers can never add up to another cubed number; and two numbers to the fourth power can never add up to another number to the fourth power. And so on, for ever, no matter whether you multiplied the two numbers to the fifth power, or the sixth power, or the seventy-zillion-and-first-power.

Pierre de Fermat was a seventeenth-century French mathematician who had devised this tantalizing theorem, and then written, 'I have discovered a truly remarkable proof. However, this margin is too small to contain it.' And for three hundred years he had left his fellow mathematicians desperately trying to work out what the proof could possibly be. This afternoon, Micky had turned back to Fermat's Last Theorem again and again. For Christ's sake, any two numbers could be multiplied by an infinite number of numbers. How could you actually *prove* that none of them would ever add up to another number that was multiplied to the same power? I mean, *ever.*

A British mathematician had proved it, but only by using modern, state-of-the-art math. How had Fermat worked it out?

Roxanne said, 'Suzie's put on weight. She eats so many potato chips.'

'She should try those new weight-watchers' chips. They fry them in this artificial fat that slides right through your gut without you digesting it.'

Roxanne punched him. 'You're so disgusting!'

'That's not disgusting, that's science.'

Roxanne was silent for a moment, watching him. Then she said. 'You're not going to get all brainy on me, are you? You're not going to start making me feel that I'm stupid or something, just because you took that shot?'

He squeezed her bare foot. 'Of course not. So I can do sums in my head. So my memory's gotten better. That doesn't make me a different person, does it?'

'And what you said about marrying me?'

'Just take a master's degree in applied math and I'll marry you tomorrow.'

'You bastard!' she laughed, and punched him again.

'Hey, you're going to get your diploma in reflexology,' he told her. 'That'll do just as good.'

He kissed her. She was very pretty, in the dancing light from the television. 'You'll help me, won't you, start up my reflexology business?' she asked him.

'Come on, you know I'll help you, whatever you want to do.'

She kissed him again, and started to unbutton his

shirt. 'You're the bestest guy I ever met. Just think, I could have been throwing fish to killer whales, instead of doing this.'

He kissed her in return. Her mouth tasted sweet, as it always did. His tongue ran around her smooth white teeth, and then they had the briefest flicker of tongue-fights. He kissed her more deeply, and held her tight. She was so soft-skinned and fragrant and feminine that he sometimes felt that she couldn't be real: she should have been running across the screen in *Baywatch*, a flickering fantasy rather than the girl who fried him corned-beef hash and popped his beer cans for him.

He reached down and grasped her tight shiny top.

'Oh, my,' she breathed, in a pretense little-girly voice. '*You're* a little forward tonight.'

'Better than being a little backward.'

She lifted her arms and he tugged the clinging pink satin over her head. Underneath – although she was so big-breasted – she was wearing only the skimpiest of plain white nylon bras, through which her nipples showed as a wide pink flush. He kissed her again, and then kissed her cleavage. He almost swallowed the little silver crucifix which she always wore around her neck, and went '*pttff*!' and laughed.

'You're not going to rape me, are you?' she said. Her eyes were very bright.

He slid apart the hooks and eyes which held her bra, and took it off. Her breasts swung free with a heavy, complicated sway. He held them in his hands, feeling their warmth, feeling their weight, and circling his thumbs around her nipples until he could feel them crinkle and rise.

'Rape you? What makes you think that? I'm a genius. Geniuses never rape people.'

'Well, in that case . . .' she said, and lay back on the couch. Micky grasped the elastic waistband of her pedal-pushers and started to tug them over her hips. He rolled them down her suntanned legs until she was naked. She never wore any panties. She had read somewhere that the world's most famous women in history had never worn underwear – Catherine the Great, Marilyn Monroe – and in any case she thought that a visible pantie line was almost a mortal sin. 'No P, no VPL.'

Micky reached up and squeezed her breasts, so that her nipples bulged between his fingers. Then he ran his hands down over her golden stomach, with its tiny golden hairs. He trailed his fingertips around her thighs, then drew them lightly between her legs. She had waxed off all of her pubic hair except for one blonde, bravura plume, and her vaginal lips were smooth and bare and gleaming with moisture. Her body was full of youth, and health and eagerness; and the look in her eyes told the same story.

Micky smoothed his hands back down her legs, past her knees, right down to her ankles. He lifted up her feet, and tickled the soles. She whooped and kicked, but he held her feet fast. 'Hey, hey . . . I read something about reflexology today.'

'What are you doing, making love to me, or tickling my feet? You know I hate you tickling my feet.'

'I'm not tickling your feet. I'm just interested in reflexology.'

'You *massage* your feet in reflexology, stupid. You don't tickle them.'

'Massage? Like this?'

'That's better – no, no, no, stop, you're still tickling! You have 72,000 nerve endings in your feet right? and they're all connected to different parts of your body, okay? Your heart, your liver, your eyes, your ears. Like your big toes are connected to your head; and your second toe is connected to your sinuses. You can massage your second toes and you can unblock your nose just like that.'

'I read that there was one place that you could massage, and it would give you an orgasm?'

'I don't know. There's nothing about it in *my* course.'

Micky slowly massaged the balls of her feet with his thumbs. 'Oh, for sure. It said that it works for both sexes. A man can massage a woman's feet until she has an orgasm, and a woman can do the same for a man. Without even *touching* anyplace else.'

'Well, I don't know about that,' said Roxanne. 'I think I prefer to have my orgasms the normal way.'

But all the same, she snuggled herself down onto the couch with a sensual wriggling of her hips, and when Micky continued to massage her insteps and then worked around to her toes, she gave him a deep, warm smile and she didn't ask him to stop. Even though he had glanced at it for less than thirty seconds, he could remember with complete clarity the chart that he had seen when he looked up reflexology in Dr Lügner's house. He massaged Roxanne's pinkies, to ease any stress in her shoulders, and she said, 'Mmmmm . . .' and closed her eyes. Then he moved slowly across her upper soles, gradually increasing her heart rate and stimulating her chest and lungs. Almost immediately, he could see the skin across her chest begin to flush. Her nipples knurled, and she began to breathe more quickly. Her response had an effect on him, too. He found that he was breathing harder, and his penis was rising inside his shorts. He was tempted to forget about her feet and make love to her immediately, urgently, then and there – but he was equally excited by the sense of discovery, the sense of control, the idea that he could give her so much stimulation just by massaging her feet.

He took hold of the third toe of each foot and began rhythmically to work his thumb around and around, while his middle finger stroked the shaft of the toe itself. Roxanne was breathing in light, quick gasps now, and tightly clutching the cushions on the couch. Her eyes were tight shut, her head was arched back, and she was gritting her teeth with pleasure. At first she opened her thighs wide apart, and Micky could see the glistening of her response. But then she brought them back together again, and began to squeeze them tight.

'Oh, Micky,' she panted. 'Oh, Micky, what are you doing to me?'

He kept on massaging, even as her orgasm came nearer and she curled and stiffened her feet. Her bare body was shining with perspiration, and her nipples had risen so much that they cast little dancing shadows in the flickering light from the TV screen.

There was a moment when Micky felt that he and Roxanne were almost wired together – as if her nerves ran all the way down her body and into her feet and into his fingers. It was an even closer connection than anything he had ever felt with her before – even closer than intercourse – because they were not only physically connected and emotionally connected, but *electrically* connected, too, nerve impulses flowing from one to the other in a shared stream of sheer delight.

Roxanne was usually noisy when she climaxed; but not tonight. She gave a quiver that went fathoms deep, and began to quake, and quake, as if she would never be able to stop. It was almost ten seconds before she relaxed, and then she let out a long, long sigh.

'Oh, Micky . . .'

He eased himself up and lay next to her, and kissed her. She kissed him back, and stared up into his eyes. 'I think you're the one who deserves a diploma in reflexology . . . that was amazing.'

'Why don't we try it the usual way, just to make sure?'

They made love slowly, in languid silence; because in their way, they were both already in a state of peace. Afterward they lay on the couch holding each other.

'What are you thinking about?' Roxanne asked, after a while.

'Nothing much.' (Fermat's Last Theorem, again.)

'How about some ice-cream?'

'Sure. There's some Cherry Garcia in back of the freezer.'

'Micky?'

'What is it?'

'You love me, don't you?'

He kissed her. 'Of course I love you. Especially your feet.'

'I feel like there's a part of you that isn't here.'

He took hold of her hand, and squeezed it. 'I'm all here, sweetheart. It's just that I've discovered something inside of myself that I didn't know I ever had. Like being poor all your life and finding a million dollars under your bed.'

'But if you found a million dollars under your bed, you could share it. This is all inside your head, and you can't.'

Roxanne went into the kitchen. Micky sat back and opened another beer. Orbison sat in the corner and watched him with his head cocked on one side. Today, Micky had read about James Clerk Maxwell, a brilliant nineteenth-century Scottish physicist who described electromagnetic waves two decades before anybody was able to prove that they existed. Maxwell used to work out his theories by holding imaginary conversations with his dog Tobi, even in the middle of noisy parties.

'You want to discuss some calculus?' he asked Orbison.

Orbison whined and retreated behind the chair.

'Jesus,' Micky complained. 'I even have a dumb *animal*.'

★   ★   ★

That night, when Roxanne was asleep and Orbison was back in his kennel, Micky went to the icebox and took out the ampoules of Dr Lügner's formula. He took out his hypodermic syringe, too, and fitted a clean needle.

He had started out on a huge adventure and it frightened him. But what frightened him even more was the thought of losing all of this mental ability; of going back to what he was before. It gave you so much *power*, to have your head full of knowledge and information and theory and facts. Forget the rock stars and the heavyweight boxers and the Hollywood actors. What did they know? *They* didn't know that there are so many molecules in the Earth's atmosphere that, every time you take a breath, you take in some of the same molecules you breathed the day you were born, and some of the same molecules that Julius Caesar breathed, and Abraham Lincoln breathed, and every other person in history.

They didn't know about pulsars and quarks; or how to make a bomb out of a kitchen apron; or how to win millions of dollars by probability theory; or how to live to be 120. They didn't see their potential. They couldn't see themselves for what they were. They were born; they grew up; they lived their lives and then they died; and they never once realized that inside their heads they were carrying around the greatest single glittering treasure in the whole goddamned known universe: the human brain.

He bound his upper arm with a Space Coast tea-towel until the veins stood out; and then he carefully prodded the needle into his skin. It hurt, but it wasn't that difficult. He hesitated for a second, and then injected himself with the contents of the second ampoule.

Afterward, he stood in the kitchen staring at his reflection in the window. It looked as if his own ghost were standing in the yard, watching him. His ghost appeared thoughtful; his ghost never smiled.

That night he dreamed that he was in a foreign country, with jagged black mountains in the distance. The sky was the color of pewter; and it was raining. He was sitting on a veranda, over-looking a muddy path filled with pewter puddles. A young girl in a straw hat was walking barefoot along the path, driving a noisy collection of ten or eleven ducks.

He could smell smoke on the wind; not the kind of smoke he was used to. It was fragrant and sharp, like bamboo burning.

Another man came out onto the veranda and stood behind him. He didn't have to turn around because he already knew who it was.

The man said, 'Doesn't it ever stop raining?'

'The ducks like it,' Micky remarked. He took out a cigarette, untipped, filled with very loose tobacco. He lit it, and then picked off a shred that had stuck to his tongue.

'I feel as if I've been here all my life,' the man remarked.

Micky leaned back in his creaking wickerwork chair. 'One day, you and me, we'll look back on this, and we won't even be able to believe that it ever happened.'

The rain continued to make circles in the puddles. The girl with the ducks disappeared along the lane. As she did so, Micky was suddenly conscious of the number *731*. He didn't see it. He didn't hear anybody saying it. But he thought 731 – 731 – 731 – and he was flooded with a cold and inexplicable feeling of deadness and regret.

He woke up and lay quite still for almost five minutes, almost convinced that he had really been there, on the veranda, with the jagged mountains in the distance. But where? And what was '731', and why had it made him feel so bad?

It was six o'clock, and the sun was shining through the blinds. He climbed out of bed and went to the icebox. He took out a bottle of Dr Pepper and drank it straight from the neck. It was flat and it tasted disgusting but at least it was cold and wet. He rummaged around for something to eat but he didn't feel like solidified cannelloni. In the end he found a box of Golden Grahams and leaned against the counter eating them by the handful.

The phone rang. He tucked it under his chin and said, 'Yo.'

'Micky? This is John Huntley. Listen – how soon can you get round here? I could use some help.'

'Give me fifteen minutes, tops. Did you locate you-know-who?'

'What? I can't hear you. There's some kind of crackling on the line.'

'Sorry, that's just me eating cereal. I wanted to know if you'd found our friend.'

'Oh, right. I've narrowed it down. But we're still left with a whole lot of questions.'

'I'll get around to you as soon as I can.'

'Okay . . . but make sure that you're not being followed. And watch out for cops, too. There was a TV report this morning about our little private war at Winter Park. They've traced my rental car back to me, and they're also looking for a blue sports car with a mismatched door.'

'That's all I need.'

He kissed Roxanne, who flapped at him with one drowsy arm. Then he hopped into his jeans, dragged on a T-shirt, and left. Not without writing a note, however, that said *Please feed Orbison for me and don't under any circumstances open the door for anybody*.

Underneath, he added, '*You may be a vegetarian, but don't forget the little piggies who had roast beef!*'

215

8

*I believe that a large portion of the mythological
conception of the world which reaches far into the
most modern religions is nothing but psychology
projected to the outer world* – Sigmund Freud

John had been up since five. He was unshaven and
the table which he had borrowed from Guido
was cluttered with half-empty coffee cups. He was
sitting in front of Mingus' computer, his eyes red-
rimmed and unblinking, as if he had been
lobotomized.

'Where's Constance?' asked Micky, as he
squeezed in between the end of the bed and the
back of John's chair.

'Still asleep, as far as I know.'

'You're not going to let her stay with you, are
you?'

'Hmh? Of course not. So soon as she's had her
breakfast, I'm sending her right back to the safe and
genteel world of art.'

'She's something, though, isn't she? I mean she's
got plenty of go for an old rock hen like that.'

He didn't realize that the door was still half-open, and that Constance was just outside. She pushed her way in and said, 'Old rock hen? Thanks very much.'

Micky jumped up and blushed. 'Hey, listen, Constance, I'm sorry. Listen, I'm *really* sorry. Rock hens, they don't ever get too old, do they? So, like an *old* rock hen would still be a pretty young rock hen, yes? That's what I meant.'

'Oh, shut up,' said Constance, and sat on the end of the bed beside him. She was wearing the skirt she had worn yesterday but had managed to find herself a clean T-shirt with BOTTICELLI'S PROSCIUTTO printed on it, and a picture of a smiling Italian butcher. Her hair was wrapped up in a towel. 'Did you find him yet?'

John leaned back in his chair and pointed to the screen. 'Late last night I managed to hack into Lance, Peutus & Evangeline's confidential files. It wasn't that difficult: they should fire whoever's in charge of their computer security.'

'And?'

'And you should have seen some of the stuff I came up with. We could blackmail every man jack in Central Florida and given ourselves a ten-week vacation on sunny Oahu. But there was no trace of the name Cicero and no trace of the name Lügner; nor any of those other names he used when he was writing his books, like Walter Cera. We looked for any client who had registered a patent in the past ten years; or any client who had published a book; or been involved with a movie. Anything that showed any signs of inventive or creative rights.'

'So? What?'

'We have five registered golf-course designs – well, what would you expect in Central Florida? We have two patents on gym equipment and three patents on air conditioning. We have a patent on curing alligator skin. Somebody called Warwick Bellows wrote a book about how to make money in your old age – *Sunset Stocks*. Somebody else wrote *Success in Life and How to Find It*. But nothing that sounds like genius. If Lance, Peutus & Evangeline have any computer records on Cicero, I'm sure as hell that *I* can't find them. But there's a persistent little jingle, jingle, jingle in the back of my head. I feel like it's here. I feel like I'm looking at it. But I simply can't see for looking.'

'He's hiding himself,' said Micky. 'He's good at hiding. He's been doing it for years.'

Constance said, 'In my experience, people who like to hide also like to leave clues. There's no excitement in hiding if there isn't any risk of your being discovered.'

'Oh, yes?' said John.

Constance gave him a quick, embarrassed smile. 'My first husband, I always believed that he *wanted* me to find out that he was having an affair, so that I would lose my temper and throw him out. He wanted me to take the responsibility for ending our marriage. He wasn't brave enough to do it himself. If you ask me, you won't have any trouble finding William Cicero if you use your wits.'

Micky went up to the computer and peered at the screen. 'Take me back to the list of inventions,' he asked; and John brought up the index headed PATENTS. There were all kinds of patented devices, from reversible golf clubs to weather-sensitive lawn sprinklers, but he couldn't see anything that would have interested Dr Lügner.

'Let me see the books and stuff,' he said.

John brought up COPYRIGHTS. There was *Sunset Stocks*; and a novel called *Wild September*; as well as a teleplay entitled *Orlando Blues*; and *Success in Life and How to Find It* by Bert Singlestone.

'Success in life,' said Micky. 'What was that message that Dr Lügner left on his computer?'

'If A is success in life, then A equals x plus y plus z.'

'And Singlestone,' put in Constance. 'That's the English for Einstein.'

'Bert Singlestone, Albert Einstein – it must be,' said John.

Micky reached across and punched up the details of Bert Singlestone's book deal. It was a straightforward publishing contract with a small specialist company in Tallahassee. But it did include the author's address: Kissimmee Acres Country Club.

'Brilliant,' said John, sitting back in his chair. 'Let's go see if we can find him.'

'We can't,' said Micky.

'Oh no? What's to stop us?'

'Kissimmee Acres Country Club hasn't been built yet. They haven't even cleared the site.'

'So how on earth can he live there?' asked Constance.

John sat frowning for a moment. Then he tapped quickly at the keyboard and brought up REAL ESTATE DEVELOPMENT. There were scores of 'superior residential enclaves' and 'one-of-a-kind estate homes'. There were also seven 'living golf communities'.

'Hate to see a *dead* golf community,' Micky remarked.

John scrolled through another list of properties, and up it came: KISSIMMEE ACRES COUNTRY CLUB. Next to it was the annotation (FULL SIMU-LATION.)

'*That's* how he can live here,' said John. He punched more keys and there, on the screen, in brilliant color, was the entrance to Kissimmee Acres Country Club, with a brick archway and vivid green lawns, and even a pair of ornamental fountains playing on either side of the driveway. Up above, the sky was a flawless, improbable blue.

There was a flourish of trumpets. Then, '*Kissimmee Acres . . .*' said a warm, oleaginous voice. '*If you've dreamed of calling an elegant country club community home, but thought you would have to pay a fortune for the privilege, think again. At Kissimmee Acres Country Club, Central Florida's premier lifestyle awaits. With championship golf, an elegant clubhouse featuring gourmet dining, a pro shop, swimming, tennis and racquetball, your dreams of country club living all come true.*'

'Are you sure we're on the right track?' asked Constance.

'Just watch,' said John, as they were taken in through the archway, along the drive, and up to the clubhouse. Inside, the simulation was so detailed that it was difficult to believe that the club didn't yet exist. There were golf trophies in glass cases and vases of flowers on the tables. There was even a background murmur of conversation.

Their liquid-voiced host guided them across the marble-floored lobby and into the 'bright, congenial bar, where members and their guests can enjoy world-class cocktails and internationally acclaimed appetizers'.

As they came around the curved, chrome-edged bar, they saw a man sitting on a barstool. He was nursing a martini as if he had been waiting for a date from a 'romantic contacts' agency who had failed to show up. He raised his glass and grinned at them, and said, 'Well, then. You got here. Better late than never.'

'It's him,' said Micky. 'Jesus, I can't believe it. It's him.'

There was no question about it. The computerized image was unmistakably that of Dr Lügner, or William Cicero, or Walter Cera, or any one of his hundreds of aliases and *noms de plume*. The simulation had been kind to him. It hadn't reproduced any of his wrinkles. He looked more like a mastermind character out of *X-Men* than the dried, lean, active man that he really was. All the same, he looked unnervingly real.

'Wasn't that hard to find me, was it, Micky?' he said. 'I'm saying that because if you've managed to find me at all, you've done what I wanted you to do, and taken the drug. But first of all, I'm going to have to give you a little security test, just to make sure that I'm talking to the right person. If you don't answer my question within fifteen seconds, this program will automatically revert to a long and very banal sales pitch for Kissimmee Acres, and you and I can amicably part company.

'The question is: what is the speed of rotation of the galaxy multiplied by the height of the famous dome of the church of St Ignazio in Rome?'

John turned to Micky and lifted both hands in a gesture of hopelessness. 'What the hell kind of a question is that?'

Micky covered his face with his hands. He knew the answer. He was sure he knew the answer. Yet he couldn't believe that he knew it. He had read yesterday that the Milky Way rotates around its center at 793,000 k.p.h. – but the height of the dome of the church of St Ignazio in Rome?

'Come on, Micky,' John urged him. 'Only five seconds left to go.'

Micky took his hands away from his face, leaned over the keyboard, and typed out O.

There was a moment's pause, and then Dr Lügner smiled and said, 'Well done. Now we can continue.'

John blew out a long *fewfff*! of relief. Micky smiled at him and said, 'Trick question. The Jesuits who built the church of St Ignazio in Rome ran out of money before they could build a dome. So they got this guy Andrea Pozzo to paint the ceiling so that it looked like a dome. He was a genius at perspective, so when you look at it, you think it's real.'

John could do nothing but shake his head.

On the screen, Dr Lügner took a sip from his martini and then he climbed off his barstool. 'Let's take a walk. You should see some of the greens they're going to lay out here. Beautiful – all designed by Tom Fazio. I love Tom Fazio's courses. So much more naturalistic than Gary Player's. He makes you feel like you're at one with nature.'

He led them through the hallway and out through a large conservatory at the back of the club-house. They went down a wide flight of brick steps and out onto the course. They could hear the breeze and the twitter of birds.

Dr Lügner said, 'Now you've taken the drug, Micky, you'll be able to understand what it's actu-ally done for you. What it's done for your brain.'

Suddenly, he wasn't walking across a golf course at all, but cutting his way through dense tropical jungle, with parrots screeching and insects chirruping. 'You know something – if you could take your brain to pieces, you would end up with a hundred billion separate neurones, which is about how many trees there are in the Amazon rain forest, and *that* covers 2.7 million square miles. And there are billions more connections between each of these brain cells – anywhere between 10,000 to 100,000 inputs from other neurones come converging onto every one of them.'

'What's this, a science lecture?' John demanded; but Constance laid a hand on his shoulder and said, 'Ssh.'

Dr Lügner came out of the jungle and onto the first tee. 'These neurones are in constant com-munication with each other. That's how you think. But to keep on sending signals, your neurones need *power*, so your brain is generating electricity all the time. I'll tell you how much: it only weighs 2 percent of your total body weight, but it uses up 20 percent of your oxygen consumption. All these billions of neurones keep sending out a constant voltage, and the way they send signals one to the other is by tiny little changes in this voltage, that don't last longer than one to two thousandths of a second.'

He paused, and said, 'Don't you just love the way this hole's been laid out? The way you have to drive so close to the trees.'

He walked on, and then he said, 'Most people think of their brain as some kind of supercomputer, or a telephone exchange. Okay – they're not completely wrong – because there are all of these electrical impulses whizzing around from neurone to neurone. But there's a whole lot more to it than that. If your thinking is purely electrical, how come your brain can be affected by chemicals like anti-depressants or anti-anxiety drugs or LSD or Prozac?'

Suddenly, strange red alien-like creatures with waving tentacles began to float across the golf course behind him. Dr Lügner caught hold of one of them and held it close to the screen. 'The reason is, there's a gap between one neurone and another, called a *synapse*. You can only see it when you magnify it 10,000 times with an electron microscope. A neurone sends an electrical signal hurtling along this kind of long tentacle called an axon, on its way to the next neurone, but what happens when the signal reaches a synapse? How does it make the leap to the target neurone on the other side?'

Now the scene changed again, and Dr Lügner

was driving along a broad sunny highway in a stylized car that looked like a 1950s Oldsmobile Fiesta. 'The answer is: the electrical signal is changed into a *chemical* signal.'

He stopped his car at a jetty, and climbed out. A small ferry was waiting on a bright blue river. 'It's like reaching a river, leaving your car behind, and crossing by boat. There are more than fifty types of chemicals in your brain which carry messages across the synapses to the other side, where they're changed right back into electrical signals. Out of the boat, and back into another car.'

'Boats, cars, what the hell is he talking about?' John grumbled.

'*Ssh*,' Constance insisted.

Dr Lügner drove back into the golf club. 'Isn't this gorgeous?' he said, turning around. 'I just can't wait to play on this course. I really can't.'

He started walking toward the second hole. A simulated golf cart drove by, driven by smiling, simulated golfers, complete with checkered pants.

'When the signal is crossing the synapse,' he said, 'when it's being carried by chemicals rather than electricity, that's the time when it's vulnerable to the effect of any other chemical which may be injected into your system.

'Have you heard of curare? That's the poison that South American Indians used to dip their arrows in, when they went hunting. Curare blocks the effect of acetylcholine, which is one of the chemicals that neurones use to communicate with each other.'

They had reached an array of deep, sandy bunkers. The image of Dr Lügner turned around and smiled. 'Some people appear to have natural genius, don't they? Take Mozart. He was composing and performing music in public before he was six years old. He could go to a concert, come home, and write down every single note that he had heard, from memory. Once he wrote a minuet, threw its different parts into a hat and shuffled them around. Whichever way they came out, they still played perfectly. He wrote *Don Giovanni*, *The Marriage of Figaro*, *The Magic Flute*. He wrote chamber music and symphonies, 600 compositions altogether. Yes, he was a genius. But he wasn't *born* a genius. Mozart's a genius was nothing to do with genetics, it was a chemical accident. The rest of us shrug our shoulders and say, that's life, this guy was born brighter than me. But nobody is born brighter than anybody else. The whole damn thing is a biological myth. I've been working for fifty-two years on brain chemistry, Micky, and I can tell you here and now: except for the irrevocably brain-damaged, *every single man and woman on this planet is potentially capable of being a genius. Everybody.*

'Were you bright, before you took my drug? What kind of an Einstein were you? Or should I say Singlestone? You were average-dumb, weren't you? No offense meant. It wasn't your fault. But it wasn't genetic. Some of the world's most brilliant people had the world's most stupid parents; and vice versa. Genius isn't hereditary. It's *chemical*.

'That's right, Micky. You've got it. Because it's chemical, you can enhance it artificially. In theory, you could synthesize a chemical transmitter which enables your neurones to send messages over your synapses at more than a thousand times the normal speed – 2,200 m.p.h. In theory, you could open up whole areas of the human brain which haven't yet developed. If I released my drug onto the open market, then every damn housewife in the US of A would be doing differential calculus in her head at the same time she was pressing her husband's shorts.'

Dr Lügner was walking toward the second green now. In the background, they could hear laughter and the sharp tongue-click of somebody hitting a ball. The realism was extraordinary, but Dr Lügner cast no shadow on the grass.

'Of course,' he said, 'it isn't a theory. It's real. You've taken two or three shots of the drug by now, and you know what it can do for you. The trouble is, like most life-enhancing inventions, who decides who gets to be injected, and who doesn't?

'Why do you think I use so many pseudonyms? Why do you think I'm running? I've got the formula, and it works. I've tried it. Two other scientists have tried it. Now *you've* tried it. It's simple, it's brilliant, and it works.

'At the moment, I can only produce it in very limited quantities. But it won't be long before we can mass-produce it. The trouble is, what's going to happen if I give it to the government? Don't tell me they're going to distribute it equally and freely to every US citizen, like they should. They don't want an intellectual population – a population that switches off *Oprah* and starts to think for itself.

A population that stops boozing and watching base-ball and starts to ask awkward questions. They don't want a population that *knows* that cheeseburgers are crap; and that soaps are nothing but stories; and that Elvis is actually dead, after all.'

John was quiet now. He had worked for so many commercial enterprises that he knew that Dr Lügner was speaking the truth. Even Old Mother Brown's 'kitchen-cooked' mixes were nothing more than flour, cocoa powder, and a whole collection of phosphates.

Dr Lügner said, 'We talk about the American Dream; but Americans shouldn't be dreaming. We should be awake. *All* of us – from the inner cities to the country clubs. When it comes to genius, there shouldn't be any hierarchy, there shouldn't be any privileged few. Genius should either belong to all of us, or none of us.'

He had reached a startling blue lake, with ducks swimming across it. He said, 'Now I know that you've taken the drug, I think we ought to meet. There are one or two things that I want you to do for me – things that are far too risky for me to do myself. I'll tell you how to synthesize the drug, too, so that if anything happens to me, the formula isn't lost for ever – and so that you can help me to work on ways to produce it in commercial quantities. I call it Synaptine, by the way, although I haven't registered it yet.

'You'll be hearing from me soon. Meanwhile, I hope you've enjoyed our stroll. I could get used to living in a place like this.'

He raised his hand in salute, and started to walk

away. They watched him cross the green and disappear between the trees.

'That's that,' said John, and switched off the PC. 'At least we know that he's probably still alive. And if he wants to meet you, we won't have to go on hunting.'

'What are you going to do?' asked Micky. 'You're not going to try to kidnap him, are you?'

'Of course not. But if I can just *persuade* him to come to Broussard with me and show those poor benighted people how to make their missiles work, then everybody will end up happy.'

'Can I believe you?'

'It's up to you. I hope you do, because all I want is to finish this job, get paid and go back to San Francisco.'

'Well, let me make a deal with you. When Dr Lügner calls me, I'll arrange a meet. I'll ask him if he'll consider going to Broussard with you, and if he says okay – then okay.'

'What if he says no?'

'Then it's no.'

'You realize I'll find him anyhow. That's my job. It's just that it's going to take longer.'

'I'll *ask* him, all right? Then we'll take it from there.'

'All right,' John shrugged. 'You're the genius.'

Micky went to get more coffee from the restaurant, and then switched on the PC to watch the simulation again. Again they found themselves at the gates of Kissimmee Acres. Again they glided up the stairs, across the lobby, and into the bar.

229

This time, however, Dr Lügner wasn't there. His glass was empty and his barstool was abandoned. The simulation took them out onto the greens again, but there was no sign of him anywhere. He had obviously arranged it so that a single access would erase his presence altogether.

'We're dealing with a real lateral thinker here,' said John, shaking his head.

'Well, he's managed to stay hidden for God knows how many years, even though he's published all those articles and all those books and written all that music. Did you know that he wrote that Doris Day song, "Sunshine Serenade"?'

At that moment, the telephone rang. John reached out for it but Constance picked it up first.

'Hallo?' she said. 'Elspeth?'

There was obviously no reply. She jiggled the handset and said, 'Hallo? Hallo?' but all they could hear was a dial tone.

'Were you expecting that call?' said John, sitting up in his chair in alarm.

'Yes, I was. I thought it was my sister. I asked her to take a look at the shop while I was away. Why? What's wrong?'

'*You phoned your sister?*'

'That's right. How else was she supposed to—'

'Out!' John shouted. 'Just grab your stuff and get out! Micky – tell your friend Guido to get out, too! And I mean *now*!'

'What have I done?' asked Constance, flustering.

John was ramming his billfold into his back pants pocket and looking around to see if he needed to take anything else. 'If *I* were looking for us, Constance, the very first thing I would have done was check to see if we had any relatives or close friends who we might try to get in touch with. Now, let's go.'

Micky was already in the restaurant, arguing with Guido. 'You have to leave, just for a while. There could be some pretty nasty people on their way here, with guns.'

'What are you talking about? What people?'

'We don't know for sure. But they don't care what kind of mess they make.'

Mario came out of the kitchen wiping his hands. 'What's the matter? What's all the shouting?'

'Mario, we have to leave. It probably won't be for long. But there are some guys coming after us with guns.'

'How can I leave? I'm right in the middle of a *passatelli*.'

'This is a ha-madness!' Guido fumed. 'I can't close the restaurant now! And anyhow, what do these people want?'

'I'm sorry, but they're looking for my friends here.'

'You knew this, when you brought them here?'

'Yes, I'm sorry; but I didn't think that they would ever find them. And it could be that they *haven't* found them at all. But the phone rang a moment ago and there was nobody there and John thinks there could be a risk.'

'You are John?' Guido challenged him, as John came in.

'Listen, we should really leave,' John told him. 'I know it's a problem, and I'm sorry, but these guys are very, very unpleasant.'

'I know how to deal with very, very unpleasant guys,' said Guido. He went around the counter and came back wielding a pump-action shotgun. 'This is how I deal with very, very unpleasant guys!'

'I don't think you understand,' said John. 'These guys will kill you as soon as look at you.'

'Then maybe we should call the cops.'

'I'd prefer it if you didn't.'

'Oh, no? Why not? Don't ha-tell me that the *cops* want you too?'

'Not exactly. But it wouldn't help.'

'Mister John, this is my property, and this is America, and I don't leave my property for nobody.'

He had scarcely spoken when they heard the tortured sliding of tires in the side street, next to the rear of the building, where John and Constance's bedrooms were located. John said, 'Out! Come on, that could be them!'

Guido pumped a shell into his shotgun. His cheeks were white with tension and aggression. 'I don't leave my property for nobody,' he repeated. Mario went back into the kitchen and came back brandishing a meat mallet. 'We had them before, these scum. They wanted to fix our roof, after the hurricane. Eight thousand dollars, for tarpaper! I told them, you touch my roof, you die!'

'Mario, you don't get it,' said John. 'These aren't two-bit roofing contractors, these are—'

There was a bang like a huge door slamming, and

the whole restaurant shook. Empty Chianti bottles dropped off the walls; windows cracked; and a huge trellis covered with plastic vines collapsed sideways behind the bar. Smoke billowed out from under the door and dust sifted down from the ceiling.

John snatched hold of Constance's sleeve and dragged her to the floor. Through the windows at the back of the restaurant, he saw sheets of bright orange flame and whirling black ashes.

'*Down!*' he shouted at Guido and Mario. Micky had already ducked behind the counter, and was scrabbling about for something to use as a weapon.

'My God, what's happening?' asked Constance.

'They've bombed us,' said John. 'Keep your head down, whatever you do!'

Guido shrieked, '*What are they doing? What are they doing? This is my life! This is my business!*' He stalked toward the back door, his shotgun lifted high. '*Bastards! What have you done? I kill you for this! I kill your mothers for this! I kill all of your family!*'

'Guido, for Christ's sake, get down!' Micky shouted at him.

But Guido walked through the smoke, and the diagonal bars of sunshine that shone through the smoke, and threw back the door. The roaring of flame from the buildings at the back of the restaurant sounded like a train coming.

'*Bastards! Do you know how hard I had to work, to build up this business? It's not for you to take it away!*'

'Guido, get down!' John yelled at him, his throat sore with smoke.

Even Mario called out, 'Guido! Guido! Come back here!'

John helped Constance to shuffle on her hands and knees further along the bar until they were crouching next to Micky. 'Okay, genius,' John asked him. 'What do you think we ought to do now?'

'I don't know,' said Micky. 'We could try making a break for it.'

'Out front? Are you serious? That's just where they'll be waiting for us.'

'Out *back*. Right through the flames.'

'Great,' said John. 'Three well-grilled fugitives, to go.'

'They have fire blankets here – don't you, Mario? Are you listening to me, Mario? Fire blankets?'

'*Si, si*, fire blankets,' said Mario, distractedly, trying to make out where Guido had gone. The restaurant was now so thick with smoke that they could see only two or three tables away. And still it billowed in, thicker and thicker.

'Jesus, we have to get out of here,' said John, coughing.

'Guido!' called Mario, his eyes watering, his hand cupped over his face. 'Guido, where are you?'

'Mario – for Christ's sake, stay where you are!' Micky shouted.

John said, 'Constance, wait here,' and crouched his way into the smoke-filled kitchen. Up above him, on the range, the huge stainless-steel pots were still simmering, and there was a pungent aroma of frying meatballs and fresh-torn basil leaves. All of Mario's knives and cooking utensils were still neatly arranged on a huge redwood chopping-board. Next to the range, on the wall, hung a carbon dioxide fire extinguisher and a hook marked FIRE BLANKET. The hook was empty except for three elastic bands.

He crouched his way back. 'No goddamned fire blankets. What do we do now? Report him to the fire department?'

'We could pray,' said Constance, with a handkerchief held to her mouth.

'No, better than that, we could soak some tablecloths in water,' Micky suggested. 'I saw some people do that once, in Tokyo. They wrapped themselves up in wet sheets, and they walked right through a firestorm, and they weren't even singed.'

'Well, I guess we could try it. Anything's better than sitting here, waiting to be picked off like a sitting quail.'

John elbowed his way across the floor of the restaurant and dragged down as many tablecloths as he could. Outside, he heard another earsplitting explosion, much sharper this time – an explosion that echoed and echoed from one side of Vine Street to the other, like a butane gas cylinder exploding. Then he heard shouting, and the fierce crackling of gunfire.

Then one dull boom, which must have been Guido's shotgun.

'My God, this is just like a Western,' said Constance.

John coughed, nodded. 'You could still go home if you wanted to. We could try to get you out of here – raise a white flag, you know.'

Constance looked fierce. 'How many times have I told you, I don't want to go. If I die doing this,

235

then at least I'll have died doing *something*, instead of staring out of the window at the Barbara Frietchie Home for the Old Gray Heads.'

John nodded again. 'Okay,' he croaked. 'Your funeral.' His throat was too sore to say anything more.

'Come on, the tablecloths,' urged Micky, crawling into the kitchen with six or seven of them; and then reaching up and turning on the faucets in the sink.

There was another boom, followed by a moment's pause. Suddenly, the whole restaurant was turned into a hornets' nest of flying bullets. The front windows shattered; the mirrors exploded into thousands of fragments of tumbling glass; the curtains danced in a red-checkered frenzy. Behind the bar, bottles of Campari and Punt E Mes and Galliano were smashed, and dozens of wineglasses dropped from their stems.

Mario was still making his way to the back of the restaurant, flapping at the smoke with his hands. 'Guido! Guido! Where are you, Guido? Are you okay? Just speak to me, Guido!'

John and Micky tamped down the tablecloths into the sink, until they were all soaking.

'Mario!' John shouted. 'Come back here and get yourself wrapped up! We're going to make a run for it!'

The fire at the back of the building was out of control. It made a roaring, funneling sound, punctuated by the ringing of windows, breaking in the heat. John shouted to Mario again, but he didn't answer, and the smoke was so thick that he couldn't see him anywhere. 'Let's go!' he said, wrapping a wet tablecloth over Constance's head, and then draping another one over his own. 'Micky – you know the way, you go first. But stick close together!'

Huddled in their dripping red-and-white tablecloths, they stumbled out to the back of the restaurant. As soon as Micky pushed open the swing door, there was a deep, soft *whoommmppph!* and a ball of flame rolled out of the corridor and almost engulfed him.

'We can't go this way!' he shouted. 'It's all on fire, all of it!'

Behind them, they heard the understated *brrrrrp, brrrrrp,* of Ingram machine-pistols, and they were caught in a minor blizzard of plaster and plastic and splinters of ripped-apart chairbacks.

'Go!' John yelled; and they went.

For the first few seconds, they felt as if they had stepped directly into hell, or the mouth of an open furnace. The heat was so intense that the water in their tablecloths *boiled* on their backs, and they were scalded by steam. But they managed to dodge along the corridor to the rear door of the restaurant, and out into the open, next to the blazing outbuildings where John and Constance had been staying. There was a narrow alleyway that would take them out onto the side street, but it was swept by banners of flame and smoke, and they could see only a quarter of the way down it.

'You think they're out there?' asked Micky.

'We'll just have to take that chance,' said John.

'Whatever,' put in Constance. 'We can't stay here and roast, can we?'

They cautiously inched their way along the alley. The flames were coming from the broken windows of Constance's room, and the wind kept sweeping them right across their path. Inside the room, the bed had been reduced to a black skeleton glowing with tiny fireflies, and the plastic lampshade hung down in a long blazing loop.

Micky took two or three steps forward. Only his fingers were directly exposed to the heat, where he was clutching the tablecloth that was draped over his head, but the pain was almost more than he could bear. He would just have to be quick, and hope to God that there were no gunmen waiting for them in the street. He took a deep breath, and shouted '*Geronimo!*' and ran.

He felt the flames dip and lick against him. He was sure that his shoulder was on fire. He kept on running but then he stumbled over something soft and heavy that was lying in the alleyway. He lost his balance and fell against the wall. For a moment he was blinded by his tablecloth, but when he managed to tug it away from his face, he found himself staring face to face at Guido.

Except that Guido wasn't staring back at him. Guido's eyes were milky-white, and blind. Guido's cheeks were charred, and his neatly clipped mustache had been reduced to ash. There were two bullet holes in Guido's forehead, only two inches apart.

Micky, panicking, scrambled back onto his feet. At that moment Constance came hurrying along the alleyway, and she tripped on Guido's body, too, but Micky managed to catch her. 'Be careful!' he shouted back at John. 'They shot Guido, he's lying right down here!'

John came running through the smoke with one of his tablecloths blazing. Micky and Constance wrenched it off him and stamped on it. They were almost out of the alleyway now; the smoke still made it difficult to see if any of the gunmen were waiting for them.

Then they heard the wailing of a fire siren; and another. They heard police sirens, too, making a high-pitched scribbling sound as they weaved their way through the slow-moving Vine Street traffic.

'We're okay,' said John. 'They won't wait around for us now.'

They dropped their remaining tablecloths and stepped cautiously out of the smoke and into the street. Already there were crowds of people on the opposite sidewalk, watching the restaurant burn. Micky and John and Constance joined them, trying to look as inconspicuous as possible, although one or two people gave them a curious stare.

'Just mingle,' said John, edging backward into the crowd.

As he did so, however, a black Lincoln Continental Mk IX with dark-tinted windows came gliding slowly past the sightseers. It paused momentarily beside Micky and John and Constance, and the passenger window slid down. Inside sat a stone-faced man in tiny black sunglasses. He made a pistol out of his finger and pretended to fire at them, one by one. Then the window slid up again, and the Lincoln drove away.

Its rear window caught the sunlight as it turned the corner on the next block, and then it was gone.

For the first time since they had escaped from the blaze, Micky and John and Constance turned and looked at each other. Each of them had a heavy black mustache under their nostrils, so that they looked like three Charlie Chaplins.

Constance handed round tissues, and they stood wiping their noses and watching while the Kissimmee Fire Department drenched the ruins of Guido's hopes and dreams.

9

Bog the shadow of a buzzard (v.ph.r) to mire down even the slightest thing – Dictionary of American Regional English

The crow-black Cadillac that had carried Sara Lake from Logan International arrived at Twisted River just as the sun went down, so that she could see the photosensitive lights come twinkling on, all across the immaculate lawns and the terraced flower gardens. The lanterns on the gates spontaneously lit up, and the empty tennis courts were suddenly floodlit. The pool became a bright turquoise casket. The limousine swept almost silently up the curving driveway, and behind the trees Sara could see the dark Gothic rooftops and the clusters of decorative chimney-stacks.

The car came to a halt in front of a wide flight of stone steps, flanked on each side by a ferocious stone gryphon. A lean, smooth Italian-looking man came down the steps and opened the door for her. He wore black linen pants and a cream silk shirt and he smelled of 1881. He said, 'Hello, Ms Lake,' but there was nothing subservient in the way he said it. His voice was slightly gravelly, slightly amused.

'Hello, Victor.' Sara climbed out of the car. Even though it was July, it was distinctly colder here in Boston than it was in Florida, and she was wearing a long white summer coat. She had swept her bob to one side, and lacquered it, which gave her a very Paris catwalk look.

'I hope you didn't eat on the plane,' Victor smiled. 'He's ordered your favorite.'

Sara said nothing, but began to climb the steps toward the house. The chauffeur followed, carrying her single Vuitton bag. The sky was the color of bruises on a woman's cheek.

'He's not very happy,' said Victor.

'He's never very happy,' Sara retorted. All the same, she wasn't looking forward to this encounter. On her way to Orlando Airport, Roland had called her to say that John Huntley and his companions were still at large, in spite of 'what can I call it, unh, mayhem', right in the middle of Kissimmee. What was worse, two civilians had been accidentally killed, and that would mean the police department would want more than excuses and ten first-class tickets to Barbados.

The massive carved-oak front doors had been left wide open, so Sara walked directly into the hall, her strappy shoes rapping on the highly polished red-and-white marble floor. All around the hall were softly lit alcoves harboring reproductions of classical nudes that were just on the other side of being tasteful: the pouts too pouty, the breasts too big, the poses too suggestive. In the middle of the hall

242

stood a massive gilded table, on which a polished brass urn the size of somebody's bathtub overflowed with the largest single flower display that Sara had ever seen – orchids, sweet peas, lilies, and roses. As she went past it, Sara paused, and took out a single stem of sweet peas, and breathed in. She thought to herself that an average family could comfortably live for a month on the price of this display.

'You want to wash up first?' Victor asked her. 'He's waiting for you in the library.'

'No, no. I'll go right in. God forbid I should keep him waiting.'

Victor led her across the hallway to a pair of double doors, and knocked. Without waiting for a reply, he opened them and ushered Sara inside.

The library was gloomy, with five green-shaded glass lamps illuminating nothing more than five small islands of brown leather couches and antique side tables and faded Turkish carpets. There was a huge oak fireplace carved with imps and demons and bunches of grapes, but now it was filled with nothing but flowers. There was a distinctive smell in the library – a smell of musty books, and gradually decaying leather, and Vick's medicated rub – as well as the smell of a man who was well past his prime.

Titan Blight was standing by the French windows in a black-and-purple Hawaiian shirt and a voluminous pair of black shorts. He was watching the last S-shaped glimmer of evening light reflected on the Charles River. As usual, he was smoking a cigarette.

'Titan,' said Victor, as if he didn't know. 'Sara's just arrived.'

Titan turned around. Even at the age of 78, he was one of the tallest men that Sara had ever known. In his youth, at Yale, he had stood 6 feet 7½ inches and weighed 288 pounds. His head was enormous. Once it had been crowned with wiry chestnut curls, and his hair was still curly now, but white as silk, and thinner. He had a face that would have suited a biblical epic, such as *The Robe* or *The Ten Commandments*: slabby, with an overhanging forehead and cheeks like cliffs. His eyes, once blue, were colorless now, like impending death. His mouth was thin and pinched, as if it begrudged every word it uttered; but in reality it had been sucked in by a lifetime of chain-smoking and the painful removal of all of his teeth. One of the reasons he had moved to Boston was because of its superior dentists.

'Hello, Sara,' he said. He spoke in a haunted whisper, punctuated by Xhosa-like clicks. 'I'm sorry to drag you away from the Sunshine State. But I hear that you haven't been doing very well down there. One of our people dead; two of them badly injured.'

'I'm sorry,' said Sara. Her voice was as soft as tissue paper.

Titan came up to her and kissed her. His breath and his clothes reeked so strongly of tobacco that Sara's eyes watered. 'You grow more delectable every day,' he told her, tilting up her chin with his nicotine-stained fingers. 'If I have one complaint to make against God, it's this: that he should have made us contemporaries. I would have fucked you, Sara. I would have fucked you until you cried.'

Sara slid off her coat. Underneath she was wearing a severe khaki-colored Armani suit with a very short skirt. Victor came forward with a secretive smile and folded her coat over his arm.

Titan said, 'I thought you could handle a man like Gene Broussard. He's bright, yes. He's almost *likable*, from what I've heard. But he's an engineer, my dear. An engineer! And a patriot, too, in the very worst sense of the word.'

'Gene isn't the problem, Titan. It's the man he brought in.'

'Oh, the catfood man. Hunter, isn't it? I thought *you* brought him in.'

'Huntley. John Huntley. But I didn't have a choice. I tried to persuade Gene that he was a has-been, but Gene wouldn't listen. Gene's panicking, that's the trouble. If he doesn't win this contract, then Broussard could well be out of business.'

'So tell me, sweetness . . . what's the specific problem with John Huntley?'

'He's persistent, that's what's wrong with him. He doesn't have very much imagination, but he's persistent. More than that, he's a survivor.'

Titan gave her a thin, evanescent smile. 'Maybe all that cat food gave him nine lives.'

'He was lucky, that's all. If Roland had done his job, we could have nailed him on the first day, along with Kevin and Jesus.'

'Roland was *very* contrite, as I'm sure you are,' said Titan, opening a large silver box and taking out another cigarette. He held it under his nose and sniffed it. 'Anticipation,' he said. 'That's what makes everything so sweet. Possessing it, but holding back. It's like the male climax. Can you imagine the excitement of having my penis in your mouth, and knowing that I was just about to ejaculate, yet minute after minute I was holding back. Perhaps I had changed my mind, and didn't want to climax after all. Perhaps I didn't think you worthy to swallow my sperm. Perhaps I wanted to save it for another woman . . . waiting like the Naked Maja in another room.'

Sara said, 'Titan . . . please.'

But Titan came up close to her and his face was like a limestone cliff with a grimace hewn into it. 'You don't like it when I talk like that, do you? But don't forget that I rescued you from hell. If it hadn't been for me, what would you be doing now, supposing you were still alive, and not dead in some alley from an overdose? But, no, here you are, dressed better than Ivana Trump, with a smart apartment in Florida, and a new BMW, and the kind of job that most women would die for, even if they had to swallow a quart of sperm every morning for breakfast.'

'I promise you, John Huntley is history,' said Sara, with unsteadily controlled fierceness. It made her tremble whenever Titan reminded her of what she had once been; and how much she owed him. 'I'll deal with him: I promise.'

'Oh, yes, you'll deal with him,' said Titan. 'You'll deal with him because you *have* to deal with him. I don't want anybody coming within sniffing distance of Mr William Cicero. Except for Roland,

246

of course, and Roland is paid to turn people into ground beef first and leave the whys and the wherefores till later.'

'I think John still trusts me,' said Sara. 'He's very, very cautious, but I think he still believes in his original assignment. Why doesn't Roland give him some space and see if he gets back to me?'

'And, in the meantime, while we're "giving him some space", what if he *finds* William Cicero? And what if William Cicero decides to open his mouth?'

'I think that's a risk we're just going to have to accept.'

'Oh, *you* can accept it, for sure! The worst thing that can happen to you is that you tumble back into the shitpile. Good goddamned riddance. But *I* can't accept it, and neither can Roger. Roger is going to be launching Creative Software this October 9, and I'm the one who's putting up the finance.'

'I still don't understand why you want William Cicero so badly. He's a scientist. What's he ever done to you?'

Titan lit his cigarette, and blew twists of smoke out of his nostrils. 'It's not what he's done to me, sweet thing. It's what I've done to him.'

Sara waited for him to elaborate, but all he did was smoke and nod.

'Huntley's been given his security clearance from the Pentagon,' she said, at last.

'What difference does that make, if he hasn't called you, and he doesn't know?'

'He'll call me. I'm sure of it.'

'You're such a reader of minds?'

'No . . . but he's still on the case, isn't he? And if he's still looking for Cicero then he's still interested in what this case is all about, and he's still interested in earning his fee. Poverty and curiosity are both pretty powerful incentives, wouldn't you say?'

'Pain and fear are even more powerful,' said Titan, watching her.

There was another uncomfortable silence. Titan had a way of saying things that stopped conversations in their tracks. It was a mannerism that came with wealth, and self-isolation, and contempt for the feelings of others.

Sara said, 'I don't know why you don't allow Huntley to find William Cicero for you, and then sanction them both. It would save a whole lot of time and money . . . not to mention the risk that Roland is running by stampeding around Kissimmee shooting up the place like *Reservoir Dogs*.'

'Roland is doing what I want him to do.'

'I know he is. But it would make his job and mine a whole lot easier if you just let John find William Cicero first.'

Titan's dead-white face was reflected in the darkened window like the moon. 'You're right, sweet thing, it would be easier. But I don't want anybody finding William Cicero first. Especially a survivor like Huntley. That's the whole reason I planted you at Broussard, and that's one of the reasons you're here tonight. You're also here to meet Roger. You're here to eat lobster.'

His intonation made it quite clear that she was here for one more reason, but he wasn't going to say what it was, not yet. He looked at his watch. 'Listen,' he said, 'I'd better go take a shower, and change. Why don't you go to your room and unpack your underwear? All those soft and silky things you wear between your legs.'

'Yes,' she said, trying not to show her disgust.

He laughed, and then his laughter turned into a coughing fit. 'I love it when you shiver,' he said. 'Why don't you forget about your underwear, and come upstairs to help me shower?'

She said nothing, but lowered her eyes.

He came up to her and grasped her lapel, twisting it around so that she was forced to look him directly in the face. 'I'll tell you what. You come upstairs to help me shower and I'll continue to pay your rent and your expenses and your monthly allowance, and I won't go too hard on you when it comes to discussing the matter of John Huntley and William Cicero.'

Defiantly, she wrenched her head back and tried to pull herself free. But Titan said, 'It's a long way down, Sara. There isn't any future in being brave.'

She heard a cough behind her and turned around. Victor was standing in the doorway smiling at her. It was a kind smile, not at all patronizing, because he, too, had been 'rescued' by Titan from drugs and degradation, and he, too, had just as far to fall. If Titan had told him to walk bareass-naked along Commercial Street, flagellating himself with a leather strap, he would have done it. The alternative was far too frightening even to think about. In one form or another, the alternative was death.

'All right,' she said; but as she did so, she closed

249

her eyes, so that she communicated nothing except subservience. She was blind. She was a slave. She wasn't going to show him what she felt.

John came out of the shower toweling his hair. A local news report on television was telling for the twentieth time how Guido's Italian Restaurant had been firebombed and sprayed with bullets, and how Guido and Mario had been found dead in the burned-out extension in back.

'*Police so far have no leads on the possible identity of the bombers, although they do harbor suspicions that other Italian-Americans may be involved. Competition among ethnic restaurants along Kissimmee's Vine Street has become intense since the recent fall-off in the tourist trade, and Guido's is the second restaurant to be torched in three weeks.*'

'They haven't tied it in with all that shooting at Dr Lügner's house?' said Micky, shaking his head. 'They must be brain dead.'

'Hey, come on, Micky,' said John, sitting on the bed beside him. 'We're not all geniuses.'

'We could be, though, couldn't we? I mean, if we *all* took Synaptine.'

John said, 'Doesn't bear thinking about. The world needs its stupid people just like it needs its clever people. If everybody understood quantum mechanics, who's going to clean the toilets?'

'I don't know . . . if we've discovered the means of doing it, I think we ought to do it.'

They sat and watched baseball for a while. They were both exhausted by what had happened during the day, and they needed to rest and to reassemble

250

their minds. Constance had already gone to bed; and when Micky had looked in on her, to see if there was anything she wanted, he had found that she was deeply asleep, and tunefully snoring. Micky thought that she looked almost beautiful, as if she were dreaming of being young again, and it showed on her face.

They had booked two rooms at the Royal Tudor Motel, a rectangular concrete building painted with pretense oak beams and topped with an artificial fireproof thatch, in a grotesque effort to appeal to British tourists. There was a British-style pub which sold Worthington bitter and a ferociously air-conditioned restaurant which served up fish 'n' chips and bangers 'n' mash.

Micky hadn't taken the risk of going back home. They didn't know for sure whether their pursuers knew who Micky was and where he lived. But Micky had called Roxanne at Sav-Mart and told her not to go back to his house tonight; and he had also called his neighbor Rhett and asked him to feed Orbison for him.

'Does he eat pizza?'

'So long as you pick off the chilies. You can take him walkies, too, if you want to.'

'You think I'm taking that fleabitten mutt of yours out for a shit you got rocks in your head.'

'Sorry, Rhett. It was only a suggestion.'

'How long you planning to stay away?'

'I don't know, Rhett. Not long. I'll call you tomorrow. And thanks.'

John said, 'How about something to eat? We could call room service.'

Micky shook his head. 'I'm a little tired is all. Ever since I took that drug, my brain feels like it's running a hundred times faster than the rest of me.'

'Well, you heard what Dr Lügner said. Your brain uses up 20 percent of your body's oxygen.'

'Do you think we'll be able to find him?' asked Micky. 'I mean, he's not going to be able to find *us* now, is he?'

John shrugged one shoulder. 'Depends. He's left a whole lot of clues, all of his life. Books, articles, paintings. God knows how many false identities. We'll just have to cross-reference all of the known facts until we come up with something that clicks. If he was just your common-or-garden industrial spy, I'd say that it wouldn't take more than a few days to track him down. But this guy isn't a common-or-garden anything. He only lets people know what he wants them to know. He's a genius, after all.'

'An Einstein, for sure,' said Micky. But something was troubling him; and when he mentioned Einstein it troubled him even more.

'What's wrong?' John asked him. He was not usually so sensitive to other men's feelings, or to anybody else's feelings. But in the few hours since he had met Micky he had found, to his surprise, that he was beginning to enjoy his company. Maybe there was something about Micky that reminded him of the way that *he* used to be, at that age: over-confident, ambitious, wacky and scared. He had grown out of the teenage years of total fearlessness, but he hadn't yet become fudsy and over-cautious.

Of course Micky had something else to worry

252

about, apart from his normal growing-up. His brain was ballooning with ever-increasing intellect, and his personality was having a difficult time catching up. It wasn't easy, having a complete understanding of the musical construction of a Bach fugue when his natural preference was for Beck or ZZ Top.

Micky said, 'I don't know what's wrong. I feel, like, fine. But I don't feel fine. I feel, like, *different*. I never read anything about Einstein, you know? But I knew that quotation about success. You know, A equals x plus y plus z. How did I *know* that?'

John leaned back on the bed. 'Your memory's improved, that's all. You must have heard it at school.'

Micky shook his head as fiercely as a wet dog. 'I didn't hear it at school. I didn't hear it anyplace at all. It was *there*, John, it was right inside my head, as if I knew it already. I can't explain it. I feel like I know things that I never learned. I feel like I know things that I don't even understand. I know all about *insecticides*, for Christ's sake.'

'Insecticides? What the hell are you talking about?'

'You want me to give you chapter and verse? You want to know all about DDT, and BHC, and tetraethylpyrophosphate? They developed them from wartime experiments on nerve gas. But how do I *know* that?'

John reached for the remote and turned down the sound on the television. 'Come to think of it, you said something when we were trying to get out of

253

the restaurant – something which surprised me. You said, "Let's wrap some wet sheets around us, I saw that in Tokyo after it was firebombed, and the people weren't even singed."'

Micky stared at him. 'Did I say that? I never went to Tokyo in my life. The furthest I ever went was to New Orleans, with Mingus, for the Mardi Gras. I was mugged for thirty-seven bucks.'

'Even if you *had* been to Tokyo, you certainly wouldn't have been there when it was firebombed. That was back in 1945.'

There was a long silence between them. Then, simultaneously, they both said, 'Do you think that – ?' and stopped.

'Do I think that Dr Lügner could have passed on his *memories* as well as improving your intellect?' asked John.

Micky nodded. 'There's no other way, is there? I read a whole lot of stuff yesterday morning but I didn't read half of what I know. Listen,' he said, and hummed a snatch from Sugar's song 'Changes'. He picked up a postcard of the Royal Tudor Motel, sketched out a musical staff and a treble clef, and jotted down the melody that he had just hummed.

'So?' said John.

'So I can play the guitar but I can't read or write music. Well, the day before yesterday I couldn't.'

'What else can you do now that you couldn't do before?'

'I don't know . . . but I'm beginning to feel that I can do just about *anything*.'

'But how the hell did Dr Lügner get memories into a liquid?'

'I guess there's only one way to find out, and that's to ask him.'

'Jesus . . . do you know what this is going to *mean* – if we can pass on memories from one person to another? Well, stupid question. I guess you must do.'

'It could change everything, couldn't it?' said Micky. 'I mean, we'll be able to communicate *everything*. Not just information, like computers do, but *understanding*. Kids wouldn't have to spend hours and hours in school, learning stuff by rote, would they? A couple of shots in the butt and that's it, man, you've graduated *summa cum laude*.'

'A college education for *everybody*, regardless of what abilities they were born with, whether they were willing to work at their schooling or not,' John put in. 'That would hit the inner cities like a bomb-shell, wouldn't it? Can you imagine the Bloods and the Crips with PhDs?'

'And science, and science,' Micky enthused. 'A scientist won't have to prove his work on paper, he'll be able to share his thinking directly, brain to brain. One shot of Stephen Hawking chemical and you'll know exactly what he's talking about. You'll have the knowledge *and* the IQ, both. And singers, and writers, and painters, and athletes. You won't just *watch* your favorite baseball player, you'll know what it's like to *be* your favorite baseball player.'

John said, 'If this works, think about it, people will never really die. You could have your father's memories, your mother's memories, right there inside of your head, clear as if you'd lived their lives yourself. It's sure going to put Kodak out of business.'

'I don't know . . .' Micky frowned, and thought for a moment. Then he said, 'It seems like I have plenty of *scientific* stuff in my head . . . music, too, and how to draw. But there's nothing really *personal*. I have this kind of peripheral vision . . . like, I can see places and people out of the corner of my mind's eye . . . but I can't seem to focus on them.'

'Maybe Dr Lügner found a way of being selective about what memories he passed on,' John suggested. 'After all, what did he say, there are more than fifty different transmitter chemicals. Maybe it's possible to pick and choose what you want people to know.'

'I'm trying to remember Tokyo. You know, the firebombs and the wet sheets, but I can't. I can remember someplace that looks like Japan, but it's in the country. There's a girl, and some ducks. But that could be one of *my* memories, from when I was a little tiny kid. I'm starting to remember all kinds of things I never even knew I knew.'

John looked at his watch. 'When are you supposed to take your next shot?'

'About a couple of hours ago.'

'You're going to carry on, aren't you? You're going to take the whole course?'

Micky hesitated. 'I don't know. I just seem to be getting into deeper and deeper doo-doo.'

'Listen – Dr Lügner invited you to take his drug for a reason. We don't yet know what that reason was, but until we do we're never going to find out why these guys in suits are so hot to nail our asses to the wall.'

'The stuff's in my icebox at home. I guess my friend Mingus could go get it for me.'

'Good. Why don't you go to the payphone across the street and give him a call?'

Micky nodded, but without much enthusiasm. All of a sudden he felt tired and depressed, as if he had run a very hard race and ended up way behind the field. John put his arm round his shoulders. 'Listen,' he said, 'I've been looking for people and running away from people for as long as I can remember. It's always confusing and it's always frustrating and it never ends up the way you think it's going to end up. So what you have to do is, think about yourself and the people you care about. Nothing else matters.'

'I know. I cared about Guido, and I cared about Mario. I can't believe they're dead.'

John didn't know what to say. He supposed that he should have felt responsible for what had happened at the restaurant, but he felt responsible for Jamie, too, and Maggie, and Constance, and even Molière, and in the end you couldn't blame yourself for everything, or else there was nothing left but whiskey and too much Valium, or a .38 SAA ball in the palate. He gave Micky a slap on the back and said, 'Go on. Go call your friend.'

The huge glass shower cubicle was filled with steam, like a stage magician's cabinet. Titan was already in there, washing his hair. The hammered panels made it look as if he were melting. He was singing, too, in a deep, deadly baritone – 'Aquellos Cuos Verdes', a hit song from the 1940s. 'Green Eyes', they called it in English.

Sara came into the bathroom wearing a robe of aquamarine satin. She closed the door as quietly as she could, but all the same Titan immediately stopped singing and called out, 'Sara? Is that you?'

She stood still for a moment, not responding. She was strongly tempted to turn around and leave. Her hand, after all, was still on the door-handle. She could see herself in the mirror over the wash-basin, and she thought that she looked ghostly and very dark-eyed.

'Sara!' Titan repeated. 'Come and join me, before I get bored! I'm bored, Sara! I'm alone, and I'm bored!'

'You're a big, evil bastard,' said Sara, under her breath. 'I hope you bore yourself to death.'

Titan was silent for less than five seconds. Then he said, 'You shouldn't be so discourteous, my dear. You know what they say about biting the hand that feeds you.'

Sara relinquished her grip on the door-handle and walked toward the shower cubicle. Her heart was beating so furiously that she thought she might faint. The bathroom was vast: It was tiled all over, floor and walls with ripple-glazed tiles in a vivid shade of green. The basins were green; the towels were green. Even the soaps were green, like lozenges of polished onyx, and lime jellies.

'Come on, Sara!' Titan demanded.

She hesitated for two more heartbeats. Then she

let her satin robe slip to the floor. Underneath she was completely naked. Her skin was so pale that it was almost silver. The only color was the faint pale pink of her hardened nipples and the blue tracery of the veins in her breasts. There was a single mole a few inches above her navel, slightly off to the left. Her pubic hair was as dark as the hair on her head, and just as silky.

She opened the door of the shower cubicle, closed her eyes, and stepped inside. She stood for a while in the hot, cascading water, her face slightly lifted. She could feel Titan's heavy belly sway against her like a sea lion. 'Open your eyes, why don't you?' he asked her. 'Afraid you might like what you see?'

The water was several degrees hotter than any shower that Sara was used to, and she found it hard to breathe. 'Open your eyes, talk to me,' Titan urged her. 'This is like taking a shower with a fucking statue.'

But Sara kept thinking; *so long as I keep my eyes closed, he can't see me. I'm just nothing. I'm invisible.*

Titan took hold of her hips, and drew her closer. She kept her arms limply by her sides. 'Do you remember the day we met?' he asked her. 'You came right up to me in Clarke's and asked me what I wanted you to do. And I said to you, "What do you have in mind?" And you said, "Anything. Absolutely anything." And do you know what? You *smelled*. You were pretty as all hell, but you smelled. You smelled like dope and alcohol and no panties, that's what you smelled like. And you smelled like something else, too, like some part of you was dying already. Emotional gangrene. Open your damned eyes.'

Sara did what she was told. Titan's face was right in front of her, with a ludicrous bathing cap of white bubbles, like a giant baby in the bath. Nude, he seemed even bulkier than he did when he was dressed. His tailor could give an edge to those fat, rounded shoulders, reddened with heat. He could trim those sagging udders with their dripping, downturned nipples, and all those creases and folds and cellulite-rippled bulges. But without his tailor, Titan was shapeless.

'Here,' he said, and took down a cake of soap-on-a-rope, camomile and burdock. 'You can soap my back for me.'

He turned around, and Sara found herself facing a great reddened wall, speckled with moles and angry little scarlet spots. Hesitantly, she lathered her hands with the soap, and began to smooth it onto Titan's shoulders. She had expected his skin to be soft, and it was certainly yielding, but it had a harshness to it, like a cat's tongue. She kept on soaping, further and further down his back, while he hummed to himself, and occasionally sang a few words, some dated 1940s song like 'He Wears a Pair of Silver Wings'. 'That's great,' he kept interjecting. 'That's wonderful. A little lower. That's it. A little lower. That's heaven, yes.'

She soaped the heavy, hanging cheeks of his ass, which felt like two muslin bags overloaded with cottage cheese. He stopped humming for a moment while she did so. 'Be thorough,' he said, after a while, and she was, although she hated it. He was right. She had walked right up to him in Clarke's Saloon and offered him anything, anything at all. If she didn't want to give him what he wanted, she could always turn around and walk away.

'Now I want you to hold me close,' said Titan, still with his back to her. 'I want you to hold me close and put your arms around me and squeeze your hands into my stomach. A deep, deep massage. Plenty of soap.'

Sara hesitated for a moment, but then she inched closer, and wrapped her arms round him, her breasts squashed against his back. Water sprayed off his shoulders and into her face, and she kept having to turn her face sideways so that she could breathe.

'Now, squeeze me,' he told her. 'Squeeze me deep. I want you to feel my insides. I want you to feel the very guts of me.'

Sara pressed the thick blubbery flesh of his belly. It felt to her as if he were *all* guts, lumpy and bulging, a Santa Claus sack crammed with liver and pancreas and piles of intestine.

'Do you know what you're doing?' Titan asked, turning his head so that he could see her out of the corner of his eye. 'You're feeling a miracle.'

Sara slowly took her arms away and stepped back. Titan turned around, smiling. A long stream of water ran from his penis as if he were endlessly urinating. 'I should have been twins, do you know that? It happens sometimes – very, very rarely. One chance in twenty million, something like that. My father was a schoolteacher. A soft man; kind to animals; kind to his fellow man. He was so kind that he married my mother, who came from a very poor family who lived up near Billerica. She was pretty and willing but she had no intelligence. She was so stupid that she drove my father crazy, in the end. Him being a schoolteacher, you see, and very well educated.

'There was something else wrong with her, too. Something genetic. She was supposed to give birth to twins, but she didn't give birth to twins, she gave birth to me. Except that I have four kidneys, and two stomachs, and two extra lungs. When you're looking at me, my darling, you're looking at two people in one.'

Sara didn't know what to say. She didn't understand what he was trying to tell her. Was this a metaphor? Or was it a joke? She began to feel breathless and panicky and all she wanted to do was get out.

Titan took the soap away from her and lathered it between his own hands. Smiling a terrible benign smile, he began to soap her shoulders and her upper arms.

'I was always more than my mother could cope with. She used to fluster and dither and burst into tears. My father tried to teach her how to bring up a child. He used to try to teach her all kinds of things – but she couldn't learn, or else she simply wouldn't. Some people never see the need for knowledge. They go through the whole of their life from uterus to sarcophagus and they never learn anything; and they never want to.'

Titan soaped her neck and for a moment his

262

hands encircled her windpipe. She stared into his eyes, searching for the smallest indication that he wanted to hurt her, but he kept on smiling, and then he took his hands away from her neck and started soaping her breasts. This time she refused to close her eyes. In fact she couldn't. She was too fascinated by the look on Titan's face; and even though she hated him – even though he disgusted her so much – his slow, circular soaping began to arouse her, particularly the way he kept rhythmically tugging at her nipples.

'In the end, my father couldn't take any more of my mother's stupidity. I don't exactly know what happened, but there was a fight, and my mother fell downstairs. Coma, then death. Never recovered. Neither did my father. He had a friend who ran a wallpaper business in Brookline. He went out there one day and put his head under a wallpaper cutter. They didn't tell me what had happened until I was 16 years old.

'But cutting his head off wasn't a random choice. He left a letter, you know, and in this letter he said that his head had never been any damned good to him, all of his life. His head had brought him nothing but grief and misery. He said there was no greater suffering than to be educated, in a world of wilful ignoramuses.'

Titan's hands smoothed their way around Sara's back and around her hips. His huge stomach with its double load of vital organs slid against hers. He kissed her on the forehead with water streaming down both their faces. As he did so, his hands cupped her buttocks and the very tips of his fingers tugged her ever so slightly open.

Their eyes were no more than inches apart. He kept on smiling but when she looked into his pupils it was just like looking into outer space: millions of light-years of nothing at all.

He took his hands away. 'How about dinner?' he said. 'I've ordered your favorite. And I just can't wait for you to meet Roger.'

God, she thought. He's done it again. I detest him and he nearly made me want him and now he's just dismissed me. She swung back her arm as if to slap his face but he was far too quick for her and caught hold of her wrist. Almost immediately, however, he released it, as if daring her to try again.

'You smell better now,' he said, as she stepped out of the shower and picked up her towel. 'No dope, no alcohol. But still no panties.'

Mingus was about to leave home when Roxanne called him.

'Mingus? Did you hear from Micky?'

'Sure, about a couple of minutes ago. He wants me to go back to the house and pick up that brain drug stuff.'

'How are you going to get in?'

'That guy next door, Rhett. He has a spare key.'

'And then what? You're going to meet him?'

'Listen, Roxanne, he asked me to keep you out of this. You know Guido's was burned down. It was something to do with that.'

'So what am I supposed to do? Sit on my thumbs? Mingus, I'm going crazy here. Please.'

'He'll kill me if I take you with me.'

'And I'll kill you if you don't. So take your pick.'

Mingus pinched the bridge of his nose like a man with sinus trouble. Then he said, 'Okay. Where are you – over at your mom's?'

He collected her from the small yellow-painted house on Tohopekaliga Street just after 10 p.m. He could see her mom watching them from the starkly lit living-room. Roxanne and her mom were strikingly alike, except that her mom had blonde-highlighted hair and the expression on her face bore permanent witness to living with an ignorant, violent man.

Roxanne was wearing a cerise satin blouson and a short black tube. She had used so much hairspray that she was a fire hazard. She said, 'Micky wouldn't tell me anything, just that he had to stay away from home for a while, and that I couldn't go there, either.'

Mingus U-turned and headed back toward the post office. Then he turned right toward 10th Street. 'He didn't tell me too much, neither. But it seems like some guys in suits are looking for him.'

'Because of the drug?'

'I guess. Why else? They didn't shoot up Guido's because they weren't satisfied with the way he washed the dishes.'

They reached Micky's house on Canoe Creek Road. Mingus U-turned again, and parked on the opposite side of the road, so that – if necessary – he could make a quick tire-burning getaway directly back to St Cloud. He killed his lights, opened the windows, and listened.

'What are you doing?' asked Roxanne. 'I've got

my own key here – we can go right in and get the stuff now.'

Mingus raised a hand in caution. 'I just want to wait and see if we were being followed; or if there's anybody else around.'

But minutes went by, and only two vehicles passed them on the road: a tow-truck from Jessy's Breakdown and a twenty-year-old Buick with four elderly women in it. They heard nothing else except the insistent chirping of the cicadas and the distant swish of traffic on 10th Street. Behind the net curtains in Rhett's front window, the television flickered like summer lightning behind the clouds.

'Okay, come on,' said Mingus, and together they climbed out of the car. They crossed the road and went up to Micky's front door. Roxanne took out her keys, and opened it up.

'Don't switch the lights on,' Mingus warned her. 'Let's just take the stuff and get out of here.'

'I want to collect some of my clothes,' said Roxanne. 'My cosmetics, too. There's a brand-new eyeliner here someplace.'

'Come on, we don't have time for that.'

'But three of my best dresses are here, Mingus; and my best shorts.'

'For Christ's sake, if I knew you were here to pick up your entire wardrobe I wouldn't have brought you with me.'

'It won't take long . . . all I have to do is stuff it all into a bag.'

They crossed the darkened living-room. Roxanne went toward the bedroom while Mingus made his way to the kitchen. He opened the icebox, cleared aside the plate of leftover pepperoni pizza and the almost-empty carton of Land o'Lakes butter, and took out the ampoules of Synaptine. He also rummaged in the kitchen drawer and found three more fresh syringes that Micky had bought. He was searching for a fourth syringe when he felt a tap on the shoulder.

'I'm coming,' he said. 'Micky said there were four syringes, that's all.'

He turned around, and shouted '*Wah!*' in surprise. It wasn't Roxanne but a white-haired, white-faced man, his glasses reflecting the light from the half-open icebox. 'Please – it's all right,' the man told him.

'Who the hell are you?' Mingus burst out. 'What the hell do you mean – tapping me like that, practically scaring the living shit out of me?'

Roxanne came in, holding an armful of clothes. 'What's going on? Who's this?'

The white-haired man lifted his hands to show that he wasn't armed and that he was trying to be conciliatory. 'I'm sorry, I didn't intend to frighten you.' He turned around, and said, 'You must be Roxanne. Micky told me a lot about you, how pretty you were.'

Roxanne blushed and shuffled her feet. 'He's a flatterer when he wants to be.'

The white-haired man smiled. 'And you must be Mingus, the musician.'

'Aspiring musician,' Mingus corrected him, still grumpy for having been surprised.

'Well,' said the white-haired man, 'when this is

all over, maybe we can do something to help you fulfil your aspirations.'

Roxanne said, 'You're Dr Lügner, aren't you? That's who you are. You're Dr Lügner. What are you doing here?'

Dr Lügner said, 'Yes, Roxanne, I'm Dr Lügner – smart guess. I'm looking for Micky, as a matter of fact. I gather that he's been having a little trouble.'

'A little *trouble*?' said Mingus. 'Are you putting me on?'

Dr Lügner was unfazed. 'He has the intellect to look after himself. The same people have been looking for me for nearly fifty years and they haven't caught up with me yet.'

'But who are they?' asked Roxanne. 'And what do they want?'

Dr Lügner shook his head. 'I can only tell you what I told Micky. It's better for you if you don't know who they are. Even if you did, you wouldn't be any the wiser. And as for what they want – well, only they know that for sure. But it seems to involve my being dead.'

'This brain drug of yours,' said Mingus. 'Is this what they're after?'

'No. They know about it, I suspect, but it isn't their first priority. Their first priority is covering their asses, if you'll pardon the expression, and covering up one very important ass in particular. That's why they're so determined; and that's why they're so violent. You thought that Watergate was a scandal? That was nothing, compared to this.'

'Actually, I was kind of young to understand Watergate,' Mingus admitted.

'That was when President Carter had to quit,' said Roxanne.

A car went past, its lights swiveling across the ceiling, and Dr Lügner glanced anxiously toward the front of the house. 'Listen,' he said, 'I have to meet with Micky – now, if possible, but soon. So long as you can give me a contact number.'

'I think I'd better ask him first,' said Mingus. 'You may want to meet him, but supposing he doesn't want to meet *you*?'

'Well, fine. Ask him. I didn't coerce him into taking the drug. I only invited him to try it out. If he wants to stop taking it now, that's okay by me. But I presume by the fact that you're here to collect it that he *doesn't* want to stop.'

Roxanne said, 'I want to know why you asked him in the first place. Like, why *him*? He's just a regular decent guy, that's all. Not too bright, I'll admit it. But some people are born bright and some aren't, and he was happy. That was the whole thing about Micky. He was always happy. Now he can't even come home.'

Dr Lügner said, 'I'm sorry for that. But he's involved in this now, whether you like it or not, and right now he's going to need some further guidance. That's why we have to meet.'

'But you used him like a rat in some laboratory.'

Dr Lügner shook his head. 'All I did was offer him the opportunity to develop his mind. Whether he did it or not, that was entirely up to him. Laboratory rats don't get that kind of choice. Now – how can we arrange for me to meet him?'

269

Mingus said, 'How well do you know Disney World?'

Roxanne finished stuffing her clothes into a pink sport bag. Then the three of them made their way toward the door. Dr Lügner opened it slowly, and took a cautious look outside. He waited for a moment, and then he stepped out onto the stoop, and immediately ducked into the shadows at the side of the house.

'What's the matter?' Mingus stage-whispered. 'What's wrong?'

'I don't know,' hissed Dr Lügner. 'There's a car parked down the road a way that wasn't there before.'

'I don't see it.'

'It's black . . . right beside that fence there, under those trees.'

'I still don't see it. Oh, yes I do. What are we going to do?'

'There's nothing much we can do except walk out and hope for the best. My car's right over there, that Ford.'

'I don't see that, either.'

'Next to the gate there, see it? You go first – you've got the Synaptine. I'll shout if I see anything suspicious.'

'Maybe you should go first,' Mingus suggested. 'I mean, what if they're armed?'

'Whether they're armed or not, we can't stay here all night.'

'Then maybe we should all go together.'

'All right, then, whatever you want.'

Mingus and Roxanne edged out of the front door and closed it behind them. They waited on the stoop for a while, peering all around them, and everywhere they looked they could see grotesque shadows under the trees, and hunched-up figures in the bushes, any one of which might have been a troll or a demon or a man in a suit.

'I don't think there's anybody here,' said Mingus. 'Let's go for it.'

They hadn't even taken three steps when two men appeared from the other side of the house, with all the swiftness of sharks. They were dressed in dark suits, so that at first they appeared to be nothing more than angular white faces and white V-shaped shirt fronts. A thick voice said, 'Let's play statues, shall we?'

Mingus and Roxanne put up their hands, still holding their bags, but the voice said, 'Put them down, for fucksake, this isn't a Western.' Out of the corner of his eye, Mingus could see Dr Lügner edging his way back toward the shadows, but the second man walked around and pointed a blue-steel automatic directly at his head. 'You were told to play statues, isn't that right?'

'Want to tell us who you are and what you're doing here?' the first man asked Mingus and Roxanne.

'Who wants to know?' Mingus challenged him, even though his heart was beating like somebody tumbling downhill.

'Mr Smith and Mr Wesson want to know, that's who. You got three seconds. It doesn't make any difference to me whether you live or die. I don't know: it might make a difference to you.'

'This lady here came to collect some clothes,' said Mingus.

'Clothes, what clothes?'

'These,' said Roxanne, pulling some out of her sport bag so that the man could take a look. He dragged out a lacy bra and held it up in his left hand like a cat's cradle, turning it this way and that.

'She split up with her boyfriend, that's all,' Mingus improvised. 'I brought her here to pick up the rest of her belongings.'

'And who are you, boy? The new man in her life?'

'No, sir. I'm just a friend from work. She asked me to drive her.'

The first man stared at him for a while with foxy, narrow-eyed hostility. Then he turned to Dr Lügner and said, 'How about you? Where do *you* fit in?'

Dr Lügner kept his face well hidden in the shadow. 'I'm just a neighbor, mister,' he said, in a strong Cracker accent. 'I opened up the door for them, and he'ped them to carry their bags. No harm done to nobody.'

'Step out here, let's take a look at you,' the first man ordered him.

'I ain't done no harm to nobody, mister. All's I want to do is to go on home.'

'I said step out here you old shit where I can take a good look at you.'

Dr Lügner appeared to step forward for a split second, but his movement was more like Michael Jackson's moonwalk, backward instead of forward, and he vanished into the shadows at the side of the house. The second man had a gun pointed right at him, but he made no attempt to shoot – not until the first man bounded across the stoop and yelled, 'Stop him for fucksake, what are you doing? That's Cicero!'

The second man fired. There was an earsplitting bang, and the front yard was lit up with the flash.

The first man ran at full tilt down the side of the house, and the second man went after him.

'Oh, God, there's no way out of there!' screamed Roxanne. 'They've trapped him, they'll kill him!'

10

Abiit, excessit, evasit, erupit [He departed, with-drew, broke away, rushed off] – Cicero

Dr Lügner reached the whitewashed picket fence that surrounded Micky's back yard and made a pathetic attempt to jump up and grasp the top of it. He kicked over a tub of flowers and tried to climb onto that, and then to the roof of Orbison's kennel, but all he succeeded in doing was sliding back down again and grazing both wrists.

In the end, he stood where he was, panting, his head slightly bowed, as if he knew that any further attempt to escape was hopeless.

The first man came into the yard and pushed his automatic back into his shoulder holster. 'Turn around,' he told Dr Lügner. 'Let's take a look at the famous William Cicero. The Lord only knows how long I've been looking for you, Mr Cicero.'

Dr Lügner slowly turned around, and took off his glasses. 'I'm sorry to have wasted so much of your valuable time,' he said, and his expression was utterly calm, almost amused. 'I hope you're not disappointed by what you find.'

'Oh, no, not at all,' the first man told him. He was a lean, Slavic-looking man who could have been handsome if his eyes hadn't been set quite so close together and his lips hadn't been quite so livid. His hair was dyed, too, although his age was betrayed by the wriggly blue veins on the sides of his forehead. His dark blue suit was immaculately tailored and he was wearing a discreet gold wrist-watch, but there was still something shabby about him. A cheap personality dressed in classy clothes.

'I hope you're going to make this easy for us,' he said. 'We'll walk together, over to our car, and we'll all look like buddies, shall we? Don't give me any problems, Mr Cicero, because it's immaterial to me whether I bring you back alive or whether I bring you back dead.'

At that moment, an unearthly noise came out of Orbison's kennel – a long, alien yowl. It was Orbison yawning, his sleep disturbed by the second man's shot, and by Dr Lügner scrambling on top of his kennel. He whuffled, and shook his head, and then he gradually inched his way out into the yard, staring up at the first man with amber-eyed hostility.

'Nice dog, just sit, will you?' the first man said, dismissively. 'Now, come on, Mr Cicero, let's go.' He reached out his arm to take hold of Dr Lügner's elbow, but Orbison growled at him, and rolled back his lips to reveal his teeth. The first man said, 'Nice dog, just go back to sleep, for fucksake. Come on, Mr Cicero, let's get out of here.'

But Dr Lügner pressed two fingertips hard against his lower teeth, and blew out his cheeks, as if he were whistling for a taxi, although no sound came out at all. At least no sound came out that any human could have heard; but Orbison's ears leapt up, and his fur ruffled as if he had been given an electric shock.

'What the fuck?' the first man demanded, impatiently, just as Dr Lügner added the ring finger of his left hand to the other fingers pressed against his teeth. He blew even harder, and without any hesitation Orbison launched himself at the first man in a frenzy of barking and snapping and biting. He was a big, heavy dog, even if Micky forgot to feed him now and again, and his second jump toppled the man backward, so that his head audibly knocked against the redbrick paving.

The man tried to protect himself, but Orbison tore at his sleeves and raged against his necktie, and in seconds his shirtfront was splattered with blood.

The second man had come running up, but all he could do was stand with his gun in his hand looking indecisive.

'For fucksake kill it!' the first man screamed. 'It's ripping my fucking face off! Kill it!'

His screaming roused Orbison to an even greater frenzy. He sank his teeth into the man's hand and furiously worried it from side to side as if it were a rabbit.

'*Kill it, you asshole!*' the first man shrieked. His blood was flying up the windows of Micky's kitchen now, and all around the yard.

The second man dodged and ducked from side to side, trying to get a clear shot. Orbison tore a long shred of sleeve from the first man's coat; and as he did so he lifted himself up a little, and that was all the second man needed. Steadying his automatic in both hands, he fired at Orbison at almost point-blank range.

Orbison was flung back against the fence, with smoke billowing out of his fur, but he twisted around and came jumping up at the second man with just as much fury as he had attacked the first. The man turned and ran, pushing past Mingus and Roxanne; and disappeared into the darkness with Orbison chasing after him.

The first man climbed to his feet, and stood swaying and bloody in the yard. His coat was in shreds, his face was like a wet scarlet mask, and his dyed hair was standing up on end.

Dr Lügner walked up to him, reached inside the remains of his coat, and took out his automatic. 'In case you're tempted,' he said. He took out the magazine, pocketed it, and tossed the gun over the fence.

'I swear to Almighty God that I'll get you for this,' the first man warned him. 'I swear to God that you are going to burn in every circle in hell.'

'Well, I look forward to a rematch,' said Dr Lügner.

The man limped off, still dripping blood. He crossed the road to his black Caprice, and in a moment the doors slammed and it was speeding back to Kissimmee with its lights blazing and its tires howling on the blacktop.

'What the hell happened?' said Mingus. 'I never saw Orbison do no guard-dogging before. Not like that.'

'It's something I learned years and years ago from the Austrian police in Salzburg,' Dr Lügner told him. 'They teach their dog-handlers how to whistle commands in ultrasound, so that only the dogs can hear them. I learned it out of interest, that's all. I never thought it would save my life.'

'You learned it out of interest,' said Mingus, in disbelief. 'That's like learning how to spin plates, you know, just in case you might need it someday.'

Roxanne said, 'Where's Orbison? He hasn't come back yet.'

'I think he was injured,' said Dr Lügner. 'I'm not sure how badly . . . it didn't seem to slow him down.'

Rhett came out from next door. He was wearing an undershirt and shorts and carrying a can of Coors. 'Hey, you guys, what was all the noise about? Was that a backfire, or was that shots?' His front door was open and his television was so loud that they could quite distinctly hear the dialog of *The X Files* even out here. Obviously it was a no-homework night for Rhett Jr.

'We think that Orbison may have been hurt. You want to give us some help to look for him?'

'For sure. Which way did he go?'

Dr Lügner said, 'I'm sorry . . . I'll have to leave now. I can't risk staying around here any longer. I'm sorry about the dog, I hope he's okay. Mingus, I'll meet you tomorrow noon at Disney World. Roxanne, goodnight, take care of yourself. Give my best to Micky.'

He gave her a light kiss on the cheek and then he was gone. Roxanne watched his car lights disappear, and then she said, 'You know . . . he may be old, but there's something about him.'

They whistled and searched for Orbison for almost a half-hour. Then, just as they were about to give up, Rhett came walking up the road with a heavy burden in his arms. There was blood all over Rhett's undershirt and running down his legs. Orbison lolled with his eyes closed and his tongue hanging out.

'Found him in the long grass,' said Rhett. 'Looks like he took a bullet right in the breadbasket.'

'Is he dead?' asked Roxanne, tearfully.

'He's still breathing, but only just. Let's get him into my place, and you can call for a vet.'

Rhett opened his garage door. He spread out an old blue blanket on the concrete floor and carefully laid Orbison on top of it, and wrapped him up. Mingus went into the house and dialled the emergency veterinary service. When he came back, he found Rhett cradling Orbison's head in his lap.

'There, boy. You rest easy. We're going to get you fixed up just as soon as we can.' He sounded like a Western hero talking to his wounded partner. He looked up, sweaty, at Mingus and Roxanne, and said, 'You know that the cops are going to want to know who shot him, don't you? What are you going to say?'

'Well, you've been looking after him,' said Roxanne. 'We were kind of hoping that *you* would talk to the cops. Something like, some wacko shot him from a passing car, you didn't see who it was. You know, being night, and all, and dark.'

'You want me to lie?'

'Listen,' said Roxanne, 'Micky's in real bad trouble. If the cops get involved . . . well, it's going to get so much worse.'

'Has he broken the law?'

'No. Definitely not. No.'

'So you want me to say that it was a drive-by shooting?'

'For now, yes. For Micky's sake. And for Orbison's sake, too.'

Rhett thought for a while, and then he said, 'The furthest I'll go is, I heard a shot and then I found him in the road. Those two things are true. I won't mention nothing else.'

They heard a car arriving. 'The vet,' said Mingus. 'It's time that me and Roxanne weren't here.'

Dinner was always held late at Twisted River. Titan preferred the night, and commonly stayed up until three or four in the morning, smoking and playing bridge and listening to opera and smoking. Tonight, because there were only three of them, dinner was laid in the card room – an intimate side salon with a fine Persian carpet and thick brown velvet drapes that deadened every sound. The polished mahogany table gleamed with good crystal and English cutlery. The plates were Dresden – a delicate red-and-white pattern with flowers and leaves.

'You like them?' Titan asked Sara. 'They're genuine, one of the largest surviving complete dinner sets from the heyday of the Meissen factory, 1729.'

'They're beautiful. They must have cost you a fortune.'

Titan dragged on his cigarette and shook his head. 'They were a gift. I used to have a good friend in Germany, once upon a time.'

Sara was looking pretty but pale. She had pinned her hair with a jeweled barrette, and she was wearing a low-cut evening dress of watered blue silk. Titan wore a huge tuxedo like a bedouin tent, and a wide black cummerbund to keep his stomach under control. Roger Menotsky hadn't yet arrived: his Lear Jet had been delayed leaving Washington. But Titan had already asked Victor to open a bottle of Sauvignon, and pour them each a large chilled glass.

'I've been looking for a man like Roger for years,' said Titan. 'Men like him . . . they're unique. One-off. Half of the time they don't even understand the implications of what they're doing. You know where we found him? University of Montana, in Missoula, working all alone in a rundown shed right on the edge of the campus that nobody else ever used any more. The faculty were just about to throw him out but one of our people got to hear about it and flew to Missoula to see what he was doing.'

'And?'

'He was writing programs to help farmers to make the best use of their buildings and their acreage. What he didn't realize was that he was changing the face of the world as we know it. He was writing programs that could take a basic idea and turn it into any number of brilliant finished

281

projects. You want to design a house? You punch in your site details and your basic requisites and Creative Software comes up with ten, twenty different designs, all based on optimum efficiency and minimum cost.

'You want to reorganize your business? Reorganize an army? Design a dress? Design an automobile? Build a suspension bridge? Irrigate the whole of Kazakhstan? Creative Software does it in *seconds*. It takes the whole sum of human creativity and puts it at anybody's disposal. And do you know what? I've invested more than $280 million into this project, Sara. But in five years, nobody on this planet will be able to live without it. Windows? This makes Windows look like Donkey Kong.

'And the ultimate beauty of it is that *we'll* be writing the programs. Not the government. Not the Pentagon. Us. We won't need elections to get into power. We won't need to lobby on Capitol Hill. Creative Software bypasses the whole democratic process.'

He blew a steady stream of smoke into her face. 'Do you know something, Sara? I always dreamed of international co-operation, above and beyond nationalities and nations, and Creative Software can bring it about. A global community, with the people in charge of their own money and their own destiny.'

'And you in charge of the people, I suppose?'

Titan shrugged and smiled and blew out more smoke. 'You always sailed a little too close to the wind, didn't you? So you be careful. You wouldn't want that wind to blow you away.'

At that moment, a short black-bearded man came into the room. He was wearing a new black mohair suit and a necktie that looked like a full American breakfast. He couldn't have been older than 35 or 36, and even though he wore heavy-rimmed eyeglasses, he was quite handsome in a boyish way.

'Roger!' said Titan. 'So glad you could make it.'

Roger went straight across to Sara, took hold of her hand and kissed it. 'Old Polish custom,' he said. 'My father always used to do it when he met any woman he really liked the look of. You must be Sara, the woman of Titan's dreams.'

'And you must be Roger, the man of Titan's dreams.'

'What have you been telling her, Titan?' Roger laughed. Actually it was more of a high, jack-hammer sound. He went across to Titan and shook his hand and jack-hammered some more. 'We've made some terrific progress today. That glitch we had with the finance program . . . that's all sorted out. We can get disgustingly rich on that program alone. Creative 24-hour investment in every market around the globe.'

He turned to Sara and said, 'Your PC can make continuing investment decisions for you while you're *asleep* . . . think of that!'

He seemed unusually humorous and self-confident for a computer nerd. In fact, almost *too* humorous and self-confident, like one of those hyperactive children who starts off being amusing and ends up being a pest. He sat at the table between Titan and Sara, and Victor poured him a

283

glass of wine. He raised his glass to Sara and said, 'It's really good to meet you at last. Titan's told me some pretty interesting things about you.'

'Titan's an incurable liar,' said Sara. 'Did he tell you I was a dope addict and a hooker, and that he rescued me from desperation, degradation, and a premature death?'

Roger turned to Titan and raised his eyebrows. Titan drank wine and smiled benignly and said nothing.

Sara said, 'Titan likes people to believe that he's the center of the known universe, and that nobody could possibly live their lives without him. That's why he makes up these stories about saving girls from the gutter. Tell me, Mr Menotsky, do I look like a girl who's been saved from the gutter?'

Roger took off his glasses. 'If you are, Sara, then somebody made a darn good job of it.'

Victor brought in little pastry nests filled with pâté de foie gras and quails' eggs. Titan parked his cigarette in a silver ashtray next to his plate and attacked his pastry with messy ferocity.

Roger said to Sara, 'Titan tells me you're doing some pretty important research work for us.'

'I suppose you could call it that.'

'It's not just important, it's critical,' put in Titan, with his mouth full. 'It could make or break our entire launch.'

'You want to *share* it with me?' said Roger. He was obviously irritated that something critical had been going on without his knowledge.

'No,' said Titan.

'Well, pardon me for asking, but Creative

Software is my baby. Don't you think I have a right to know?'

'Let's just say that Sara is in charge of ass-covering.'

Roger took a sip of wine and coughed. 'I wasn't aware that our asses needed covering. Why do our asses need covering?'

'You know what they say about monkeys who climb up trees.'

'Oh come on, Titan. What's going on?'

Titan leaned forward, taking out another cigarette. 'Roger . . . there is such a thing as knowing too much. Let's just say that we have a few local difficulties, and that they're all being taken care of. And by the way, when you say that Creative Software is your baby, just remember who's financing it.'

Roger didn't look at all happy at this. He turned to Sara and said, 'Down in Florida. You're working down in Florida, aren't you?'

'The climate suits her,' said Titan. He paused, and stared at her lasciviously. 'All-over tan.'

'So Florida – ' said Roger, thrown off his stroke ' – is that where we're having these local difficulties?'

Sara shrugged. 'I'm just doing some pretty routine research, that's all. I should be back up in Boston in a month or two.'

'Don't start fretting, Roger,' Titan reassured him. 'We've had some background problems but I'm expecting to hear any day now that they're all cleared up. Let's put it this way – we don't want to launch Creative Software to find that somebody else has already thought up a better technology, do we?'

'What do you mean? There *is* no better technology.'

'There's always a better technology, Roger. You should know that, of all people.'

'Is that the only problem?'

'Well . . . we just want to make sure that we've dealt with anyone who might have a grudge against us. Anybody who might be tempted to spoil our launch with totally unjustified allegations.'

'What allegations? What are you talking about, allegations?'

'Well . . . you don't know what people are going to say until they say it, do you? It could be an allegation of unpaid taxes; or property deals that were slightly off-center; or underage girls who can identify the teddy-bear-shaped mole on the side of your schlong.'

'Hey, wait a minute – ' said Roger. 'I've spent the past four and a half years in a shed in Missoula. I've been a goddamned *monk*.'

'Then you don't have anything to worry about, do you?'

'No,' said Roger. He paused, and blinked, and then he said, 'Do *you*?'

Sara took hold of his arm. 'Don't worry. Everything's going to work out fine.'

'Are you going to be working for Creative Software?' asked Roger.

'It depends what Titan wants me to do.'

'Can't you do what *you* want to do?'

She smiled and laid her hand on top of his. A pale

honey-colored hand on top of a darkly tanned mahogany hand, with a heavy gold signet ring. 'I was never the kind of woman to determine my own destiny. I see the stars, but they just drift by. I don't know how to steer toward them.'

'I can't believe that. You seem so together.'

'You think so? Maybe Titan wasn't lying after all.'

'What do you mean?'

'Have you ever been so low that you have to think twice about accepting $50 to have somebody piss in your mouth?'

Roger stared at her and his smile emptied out like warm water through the bottom of a brown paper bag. He searched her eyes for some inkling of understanding, some grain of reassurance. Deliberately, she didn't give him any. But after a moment, his smile began to fill up again, and he arched his neck back, and he let out another jack-hammer laugh.

'You're some kind of woman, Sara! I'll grant you that! You give as good as you get! If Titan doesn't let you work for Creative Software, I'm going to want to know why! Do you hear that, Titan? I'm going to want to know why!'

All the same, Sara knew that she had deeply shaken him, and she was inwardly pleased. She wondered how shocked he would have been if she had told him that she had taken the $50, and spent it on smack.

Victor was serving a dessert of poached pears when the telephone rang. He picked it up, listened for a

287

while in silence, and then handed it to Sara.

'Who is it?' Titan growled.

Sara said, 'All right, then,' and handed the phone back to Victor. 'That was Roland. He caught up with Cicero at Frasier's house.'

'And?'

Sara gave him the slightest shake of her head.

Titan slowly dragged his napkin out of his collar. Then he lifted his fist and smashed it down on his dessert plate, splattering his pear all over the table-cloth, and Roger's necktie, too.

Mingus parked his car on the rough grass in front of the Cracker House saloon. The Cracker House was a turn-of-the-century shack that had once been typical of pioneer dwellings all through Central Florida, but now it stood on its own, dwarfed by the concrete overpass of Florida's Turnpike.

Mingus climbed out. Traffic whooshed over the turnpike, and close behind him, along Route 92, almost drowning out the sound of country-and-western that scraped and wheezed its way out of the Cracker House doors. It was late, but the saloon was crowded, and the parking lot was crammed with pick-ups and motorcycles and beaten-up Thunderbirds.

'Are you coming?' said Mingus, leaning back into the car.

'Just make sure that he's there first,' Roxanne asked him. She looked pale and nervous.

Mingus went up the wooden steps, and walked around the veranda until he reached the back of the saloon, where there was a pool table and a greasy barbecue. In the darkest corner, wearing a shapeless black Stetson with the brim pulled low over his forehead, sat Micky, his boots parked on the table, drinking Coors out of the bottle. In other words, he was indistinguishable from every other man in the Cracker House.

Inside, in the barn-like bar, a lot of whooping and laughing was going on, and a band called Rex McShane and the Alligator Five was tuning up ready for a late-night session. The jukebox was playing 'A Lot about Livin' and a Little 'bout Love'.

Mingus sat down opposite Micky and carefully placed the ampoules of Synaptine on the table.

'Nobody followed you here, did they?' asked Micky, still keeping his face hidden.

'Not so far as I know.'

'Thanks. And, hey – thanks for bringing the stuff.'

'Listen,' said Mingus, 'there was a fight, back at your house. Orbison's hurt.'

'Hurt? What do you mean he's hurt?'

Mingus told him what had happened at Canoe Creek Road. 'But Rhett's promised to take care of Orbison like he's his own son.'

'Jesus, I should go see him,' said Micky. 'He's going to think I abandoned him. He's never going to trust me again.'

'He won't, Micky. Dogs don't think like that.'

'But come on, Mingus, what if he dies, and I never even get to say goodbye?'

'It's too risky. Those guys are watching out for you like buzzards.'

'I still think I should go see him. I could wear a disguise.'

'For God's sake, I'll visit him every day, and I'll call you if there's any change.'

'The guys who shot him – do you have any idea who they were?'

'Not a clue, man. But they definitely wanted Dr Lügner. If it hadn't have been for Orbison—'

'Shit,' said Micky, banging down his bottle. 'If I hadn't tried to save him . . . if I hadn't been such a goddamned hero.'

Mingus shook his head. 'You can't turn back the hands of time, man. What's happened is happened. Besides, think of what you've got to look forward to.'

'Give me a f'rinstance.'

Mingus turned around in his chair. 'Here's a f'rinstance.'

Micky frowned, and then turned around, too. Under the lanterns, where the moths flapped and pinged, stood Roxanne. Her hair was curly and her lips were painted bright red and her eyes sparkled like a Barbie doll. Micky stood up, and took off his hat, and walked toward her with such a smile on his face. He held her close and they kissed for so long that Mingus reached over and finished the rest of Micky's beer.

Micky and Roxanne sat down close together, hand in hand. Mingus said, 'I think it's time for you to make some decisions, man. I think it's time for you to face up to what you've done; and what you're going to do next. All of your friends are frightened for their lives, me included, and two of your friends have died. You can't just go on running, and neither can we.'

'I know,' said Micky. 'But what do you suggest? You can't *talk* to these guys. They just want to waste us, and that's it.'

Roxanne said, 'Maybe we should go away for a while. You know, until it's all blown over.'

'That's not a bad idea,' said Mingus. 'We got cousins in Mobile, you could stay with them.'

'But what about Dr Lügner? What about the drug?'

'What about it? You stumbled into this by sheer accident. You can stumble right out of it again.'

Micky sat back. Roxanne took hold of his arm and said, 'Mingus is right, honey. This is nothing to do with you, any of this. And you could get yourself killed at any minute, without ever knowing why.'

Inside the Cracker House, the Alligator Five were beginning to play the opening chords of 'Back Door Man', and over the distorted sound system the singer was saying, 'Testin' . . . testin' . . . one – two – three . . .'

Micky was frightened and he hurt inside. But he knew that he couldn't just turn his back on Dr Lügner and Synaptine and walk away. Dr Lügner had affected his life like an earthquake. He wasn't Micky the happy-go-lucky moron any more. His brain was developing exponentially, and even while he was talking to Roxanne and Mingus, he was thinking about time and space and distance and probability. He was thinking about words and music and numbers and equations. He was wondering whether less intelligent people perceived time in a different way from more intelligent people – if their body clock ran at a different speed. He guessed that you could work it out by testing the suprachiasmatic nucleus in their brain, and then by—

'No,' he said. 'I can't run away.'

'But why?' asked Roxanne. 'You don't owe this Dr Lügner anything. All he's done for you is get you into trouble.'

'Let me show you,' he said. He finished his beer and got up from the table. He opened the door to the bar, and led them inside. The bar was crowded and smoky, and the Alligator Five's guitars were weeping and moaning so loudly that they had to shout to make themselves heard. Men in hats and checkered shirts and middle-aged women in over-tight dresses were swaying from side to side and joining in, 'If the world had a front porch like we had then, we'd still have our problems, but we'd all still be friends.'

When the song had finished, Micky went up to the leader of the group and said something in his ear. After a moment of frowning and nodding, the leader took off his guitar and handed it over. Micky briefly tuned it, and then he started to play.

He didn't like country music, and he didn't know any country songs, either. But he didn't have to know any. A wry, sad melody flowed out of his fingers as if he had been practising it for weeks, even though he was composing it as he went along. He stepped confidently up to the microphone and started to sing, and by the end of the first chorus he had the whole saloon whistling and whooping and clapping their hands.

> *'I can't offer you a mansion, with rooms all*
> *painted gold*
> *I can't offer you a trailer, my trailer's long been*
> *sold.*
> *I can't offer you a hotel room; my credit's no good*
> *there*
> *All that I can give you is a castle in the air.'*

By the time that Micky had sung the last line, '*All – that – I – can – offah – yeeewww – is – a – cassul – in – thuh – ayuhhhhhh –* ' the audience were ecstatic, yipping and stamping and shouting for more. But Micky handed back his guitar, and lifted his hands in surrender, to show them that he wasn't going to play any more.

'That was something else, you know that?' the leader of the group told him. He had twinkly gray eyes and a droopy mustache.

Micky shook his head. 'It's just a party piece, is all.'

'You haven't thought of playing perfessional? I could offer you six weeks of regular gigs all around Tampa and Sarasota and St Pete. Two hundert the night, all found.'

'I'm sorry. Country's not really my thing.'

'You're kidding me. That was the sweetest country I ever heard in my life. But listen . . . even if you don't want to play, just tell me who wrote that song of yours. I could use that in my repertwah.'

'I made it up, just now.'

The leader of the group gave him a long, peculiar look.

'Listen,' said Micky. 'I'll write it down for you. You're welcome to play it any time you like.'

Roxanne came over and held him possessively close. 'That was incredible,' she said. She kissed him, and then she whispered in his ear, 'I understand, sweetheart. I really understand.'

Mingus shuffled up and shook his hand. 'I should have taken that brain drug myself, man. You were great. And I *hate* country. I mean, country—' and he stuck his finger down his throat in imitation of Bart Simpson.

Micky put his arm around Mingus' shoulders and gave him an affectionate squeeze. 'There's going to come a day when you can buy Synaptine over the counter. Then you'll be able to play that way, too.'

Mingus didn't look impressed. 'Sure, but so will everybody else. No good being Lenny Kravitz in a roomful of Lenny Kravitzes.'

It was almost two o'clock in the morning when Sara got up from the table and said, 'Thanks for the dinner, Titan. I think I'm going to call it a night.'

Titan leaned back in his chair, one eye closed against his trailing cigarette smoke. 'I was going to ask you if you were interested in a game of slippery sam.'

'No, thanks. I want to catch the early flight back to Miami.'

'*Strip* slippery sam, just to make it interesting? No? You're such a modest girl, Sara. Mind you, I like that, modesty. I think I like modesty even more than I like servility. I'll talk to you over breakfast, yes?'

Sara kissed Titan's cheek, and then went over and kissed Roger, too. 'Sleep well,' he told her, without taking his eyes away from hers. After she had left, he said, 'Now *there's* an interesting girl. Very attractive, too.'

'She's the kind of girl that all men dream about,' Titan replied. 'She has beauty, brains, and the kind of body that has cardinals creaming their vestments, and yet she has absolutely no character. Ideal for what I've asked her to do.'

'I'm still a little worried about these "local difficulties",' said Roger.

Titan lit one cigarette from the butt of another, blew out smoke, and shook his head. 'Don't be. We nearly had everything neatly squared away when somebody fumbled the ball, that's all. Sara will sort it out.'

'I hope I can trust you.'

Titan looked hostile. 'Listen, Roger, we may be talking about your future as Bill Gates the Second, but your future is entirely dependent on *my* money. I want this situation shut down and I want to shut it down fast.'

'All right,' said Roger, backing down. 'You know how much I appreciate everything you've done for me.'

Titan glanced at his heavy gold Jaeger-le-Coultre wristwatch. 'Five minutes,' he said. 'That should have given her enough time.' He heaved his bulk out of his chair and beckoned Roger to follow him.

'Come on, and bring your wine with you. We should have a little entertainment in store for us, before we hit the sack.'

He led Roger through the darkened corridors of Twisted River until they reached the stairs. By the first landing Titan was perspiring and he had to pat the back of his neck with a large folded handkerchief. 'There's an elevator at the far end of the house, but my doctor said I should exercise. Stop smoking, that's what he said, and exercise, especially sex. I asked him if I could have a prescription for six hookers a week.'

Roger tried to smile. Every time he visited Titan he felt increasingly uneasy. He knew that Titan was passionate about global co-operation, just as he was. He knew that Titan wanted an end to trade tariffs and travel restrictions, and an opening up of international co-operation in science and medicine and aid for underdeveloped countries. Titan talked about 'an Internet of human emotion' and 'a worldwide web of love and understanding'. But, face to face, Roger found Titan's coarseness difficult to stomach, and he couldn't help suspecting that Titan had a hidden agenda, which would only become clear once Creative Software was up and running.

Roger wanted so much to see Creative Software become a worldwide success that he could never sleep at night. But he was beginning to suspect that – in order to achieve it – he might have made an irrevocable deal with the devil.

Titan led Roger through to a third-story bedroom suite. It was dark, but he didn't switch on the lights. Instead, he drew back the drapes, so that the room was suffused with moonlight and the dim radiance of other windows.

Titan dragged one armchair up to the window, and then another. 'Have a seat,' he said. 'How about a glass of champagne?'

Roger said, 'Thanks, I'm fine. I have to do some more work on that finance program tomorrow.'

Titan eased himself into his armchair. 'All work and no voyeurism makes Roger a dull boy.' He leaned forward and flicked cigarette ash onto the carpet. After all, it was *his* carpet. 'Now, look . . . there she is. Same as always. Isn't she something?'

Roger hesitated. He had a feeling that he already knew what he was going to see; and he wasn't at all sure that he wanted to see it. But Titan was already leaning forward in his chair, his thick neck extended, his face lit up with lust and reflected light. 'God, she's an angel . . . did you ever see a woman like that before?'

Roger said, 'I'd just as soon forget it, Titan. Everybody's entitled to their privacy.'

'Privacy? Sara gave up her privacy when she was 14 years old. She doesn't know the meaning of the word. Her privacy belongs to the man who keeps her in designer clothes and fancy food and German cars. She's a whore, Roger. You know that. What did she tell you at the table?'

Roger looked down at his wineglass. Titan glanced at him, and laughed. 'Go on, look,' Titan urged him. 'She wouldn't mind, even if she knew you were there.'

The more Titan encouraged him, the more

reluctant Roger felt. Eventually, however, he shifted a little higher in his armchair and peered out of the window. He found himself looking into the central courtyard around which Twisted River had been built. On the left-hand side of the courtyard, on the floor below, he could see a large lighted window, with the drapes drawn back. He could see pink carpet and pink-and-yellow furnishings, and a large pink-and-white bed. Lying on the bed was Sara Lake, naked except for her pantyhose, which she was just in the process of tugging over her ankles.

'Now look away,' Titan teased. 'But you can't, can you? You can't take your eyes off a body like that.'

Sara's forehead was encircled with a pink-and-white sweatband. Her body gleamed white in the light from the bedside lamp. She smoothed her hands around her hips, and then grasped her breasts and slowly began to squeeze them until the flesh bulged out between her fingers, and her nipples crinkled. She closed her eyes and massaged her breasts around and around. Roger looked quickly at Titan, but Titan was completely engrossed, his cigarette burning right down to his fingertips.

Sara climbed off the bed and stood in front of the closet mirror. From where he was sitting, Roger could see her bare back, and most of her front from the neck down. She performed a number of basic ballet positions, her arms held high so that her breasts rose firm and round; her thighs parted so that Roger could glimpse the pinkness of her vulva.

He felt hot and aroused and very ashamed: but he couldn't look away.

Sara's physical flexibility was extraordinary. She lay on the floor and arched her back, so that she formed a bridge. She folded herself into a ball, arms and legs interlocked, and then she stretched herself out so that her heels touched her back.

Titan lit another cigarette, cupping his hand to mask the flare of the match. 'What did I tell you? An angel? She's mesmerizing, isn't she?'

Roger didn't know what to say. But he couldn't stop himself from watching as Sara flexed and stretched, sometimes concealing her nakedness in a geometric arrangement of arms and legs; at other times exposing herself so blatantly that his lips opened in accord with hers, and his fists tightened.

'What do you think?' asked Titan. 'Do you think she knows we're watching her, or not?'

'Does she always do this when she comes here?'

Titan smoked and nodded. 'She does it every night, wherever she is. She wanted to be a dancer, once, before she met the wrong man and started to slide. She could have been great. She could have danced on Broadway. But you have to give your soul to dance on Broadway; and she never had a soul, any more than she ever had a character. She's nothing, Roger. A beautiful tantalizing nothing.'

Sara sat on the bright pink carpet and placed her hands flat on either side of her. Then she closed her ankles together and pointed her toes. Roger watched in awe as she lifted herself up off the floor, using her arms alone, her legs totally horizontal, her toes still pointed.

'Christ, that takes some strength,' he said. But Titan pressed his finger against his lips to shush him. 'You ain't seen nothing yet.'

Gradually, her face completely calm, Sara parted her feet until there was almost a yard between them. She was still balancing entirely on her hands, and Roger could see her elbows quivering. The effort must have been enormous, but she scarcely wavered. Slowly, she lifted both legs until they passed right behind her ears, and her body was doubled over to form the shape of a lower-case 'e'. Now she was able to lower her head between her thighs so that she was confronted with her own vulva, half-open and visibly glistening.

She almost lost her balance, but then she re-adjusted the position of her hands, and bent her head forward even more. Out of her scarlet-painted lips her tongue stretched like a long tawny snake and flicked at her pubic hair. She strained her neck downward: Roger could see her sinews stretching with effort. Then her tongue came stretching out again, and licked the pale pink beak of her clitoris, again and again and again.

She was quivering now, with effort and excitement. This couldn't last much longer. Roger could tell by the muscles around her shoulders that she was almost about to give up. But her tongue flicked faster and faster, and he could see that she was desperate to make it stretch even further. Her head kept on bobbing up and down. Her face was flushed now, and there was a look of riveting intensity in her eyes as she tried to reach her open vagina.

She made one more lunge; but then her right

elbow folded, and she fell sideways onto the carpet like a wounded flamingo, all arms and legs. She lay there panting for a long time, one hand held between her legs, but at last she stood up and did a few simple warming-down exercises, and picked up her robe.

'Show's over,' said Titan. Roger stood up and pushed his chair away from the window. He felt ashamed of himself.

'You don't understand why I showed you that, do you?' said Titan. 'You think that was some kind of burlesque, don't you?'

Still Roger said nothing. He had nothing to say.

Titan stood up, too, and laid his heavy arm on Roger's shoulders. 'I wanted to show you how far people are prepared to go to get a little gratification. They'll wade waist-deep through shit, believe me. It's a boring, boring world, Roger, with very few pleasures in it and a whole lot of taxes. Even the pleasures are boring, and they're taxed, too. But if you can offer them something new . . . If you can offer them excitement, for free . . .'

Roger finished his drink. 'You want me to write a program on sixty creative ways to lick your own ass?'

'You're a funny man, Roger,' Titan told him, without a trace of amusement in his voice. 'You just go out there and remember what you saw tonight. It's a metaphor, Roger. Think about it. It's a clue.'

Roger said goodnight and went to his room. He was exhausted, and drunk, but he found it impossible to get those images of Sara out of his head. He stood in front of the bathroom mirror staring at himself. If he went down and knocked at her door, would she find him attractive? Would she ask him inside, and show him those pink shining lips that he had already seen, covertly, with a glass of wine in his hand and his tailored pants rearing?

No, he decided. She probably wouldn't.

He sat on the bed, picked up the phone and called his mother. He wasn't quite sure why, but he felt that he needed to. Then he realized it was nearly three in the morning and put down the receiver before she could answer.

He took a long hot shower. He had felt lonely in that shed in Missoula, but he had never felt so lonely as he did tonight.

11

Unless one is a genius, it is best to aim at being intelligible – Sir Anthony Hope Hawkins

The next morning, at eleven o'clock, Pluto was shuffling up and down in front of Mickey Mouse's house, followed by a squealing crowd of little children and their loud, sun-scorched parents. It was a clear day, intensely hot, and the temperature inside Pluto's outer skin was close to 105 degrees, with 87 percent humidity.

'Hey, Jack – do you want to hold still for a second?' one father demanded, trying to focus his Polaroid. 'I just want a shot of you and my Lee-Marie.'

Pluto crouched down for a moment so that Lee-Marie could sit on his knee. She was pigtailed and sticky and her diaper was soaked through. He tried to resist the temptation to nudge her off, nose-first onto the tarmac path. He pretended to cuddle her while the father fiddled interminably with a camera that was far too complicated for him. Lee-Marie's mother stood behind him, with frizzy blonde hair and stretch turquoise leggings, staring into the middle distance and eating toffee popcorn like a ruminating cow.

'Pluto! Pluto! Would you pose with my little girl, please?' begged another mother. But it was then that Pluto saw Dr Lügner walking down the path. Dr Lügner wasn't disguised, but he was wearing a white straw hat and heavy dark sunglasses, and Pluto wouldn't have recognized him if he hadn't been expecting him.

'Pluto! Do you *mind*?' the mother complained, as Pluto brushed her little girl aside.

'Sorry,' said Pluto, in a muffled voice. 'Call of nature. Got to find myself a tree.'

Dr Lügner went up to Mickey Mouse's house and stood outside for a moment, looking this way and that. Then he went inside. Pluto followed him through the hallway into the bedroom, where there were mouse-ear motifs everywhere.

'Dr Lügner?'

Dr Lügner turned around, saw Pluto looming over him, and clapped his hand against his chest. 'Jesus, you frightened me!'

'I'm sorry. This is my job. Listen, I talked to Micky yesterday night and he wants to meet you. He's been taking that brain stuff every day, and he really wants to carry on with it.'

'Well, I thought he would. Once you've had a taste of genius . . . well, it's much more difficult to turn your back on it than any narcotic you could think of.'

'It's not addictive, that stuff, is it?'

'Synaptine? Not physiologically. But knowledge is addictive. Spatial reasoning is addictive. Being the best at everything you do, that's *very* addictive.'

'It's just that Micky's been in trouble ever since he met you. He's my friend, Dr Lügner, and I don't want to see him hurt.'

Dr Lügner took off his sunglasses. 'That's the first time I've been verbally cautioned by a six-foot yellow dog. But, believe me, I don't want to see him hurt either. He has something very important to do.'

'Okay, then,' said Pluto. 'Just follow me round to the staff quarters, so that I can change my clothes and clock out. I'll take you to meet him.'

Dr Lügner glanced toward Mickey's front door. 'My God, there are more animals outside. Who are those two?'

'Chip 'n' Dale,' he remarked, waving his paw in greeting. 'Actually their names are Terry and Vance. Business students, both of them.'

'I never came here before,' said Dr Lügner. 'It's definitely a gap in my cultural education. I find it difficult to understand why all these people are *here*, and what they think they're going to find.'

'Simplicity,' Pluto told him. 'Fun, and furry animals, and a happy childhood that they never had.'

'You sound a little disillusioned,' said Dr Lügner.

'You want to walk around wearing this suit. By the end of the afternoon you won't just be disillusioned, you'll be homicidal.'

Chip 'n' Dale skirted a crowd of children and began to approach Mickey Mouse's house. Pluto noticed something odd in the way they were walking. Not the friendly little chipmunk-shuffle which they usually adopted, but long, determined strides. And instead of stopping to pat children on the head, and shake paws with their parents, they were weaving away from every proffered hand, and ignoring the children who tried to catch at their fur.

Think about it, Pluto said to himself. *If two guys came toward you in the same way that these two guys are coming toward you, and they didn't happen to be wearing those stupid chipmunk suits, what would you do?*

It was when Dale's paw dived down into the furry pouch at the front of his suit that Pluto seized Dr Lügner's arm and said, 'Come on – we gotta get out of here.'

They jostled through the crowds of tourists who were admiring Mickey Mouse's clumpy cartoon-like furniture and all the pictures of his mouse-relations on the walls. The rear door was blocked by a grossly fat man in a pink Hawaiian shirt, sucking two orange ice-pops, one in each hand. Dr Lügner couldn't force his way past him, but Pluto gave him a hefty shoulder-tackle and he staggered sideways, lost his balance, and collapsed over the rope which kept the public from invading Mickey's kitchen. There were cries of 'hey!' and 'watch what the hell you're doing, mister!' and a woman started thrashing the man in the pink Hawaiian shirt with her bag of Disney souvenirs. 'You almost flattened my kid, lardass!' Nobody thought to blame Pluto.

Pluto and Dr Lügner escaped out of the rear of Mickey's house, crossed the grass, stepped over the fence, and made their way back through the milling crowds toward Main Street. Tourists kept calling out, 'Hi, Pluto!' and trying to grab hold of him, but he pushed them away and kept on running as fast as his oversized feet would allow. He twisted his head around now and again to make sure that Dr Lügner was keeping up with him, but he soon realized that Dr Lügner was just as fit as he was, and he wasn't wearing a dog suit, either.

'Are they following us?' he panted. 'I can't see a goddamned thing inside of this head.'

'They're three or four hundred feet away. I don't know whether they can – no, they've spotted us.'

'Not difficult, when I'm dressed like this,' Pluto complained. He was bursting with sweat and his head made a deafening jostling sound as he ran.

They reached Main Street, but Chip 'n' Dale were catching up on them now. Pluto kept stumbling over his feet, and he felt as if he were close to having a heatstroke. Dr Lügner took hold of his elbow and tried to help him along, but both of them knew it was hopeless.

It was then that they heard the *boom-boom-boom!* of a drum and the sudden blaring of trumpets, and a Disney Parade appeared at the lower end of Main Street, led by a baton-twirling Mickey Mouse, complete with band and balloons and decorated floats. Snow White and the Seven Dwarfs, Winnie the Pooh, and all the characters from *The Lion King* and *Aladdin*. The sidewalks were crowded with tourists, their children perched on their shoulders and their camcorders growing out of their heads.

Hoarsely, Pluto shouted, '*Follow me!*' and with

307

Dr Lügner clinging onto his loose yellow fur, he dodged around Mickey Mouse, who tried to side-step and dropped his baton. Two Disney employees made a half-hearted attempt to go after them, but he was Pluto, after all, and they weren't at all sure that this wasn't a prearranged stunt. Pluto plunged right into the band, dragging Dr Lügner after him. For a few chaotic seconds, all he could hear was 'When the Saints Go Marching In' blaring in his ears, punctuated by some very un-Disneylike expletives as he collided with two trombone players and stepped on a cymbal-clasher's foot. He turned around to see how close Chip 'n' Dale were, and his nose sideswiped a cornet player and knocked his music off his instrument. The chipmunks had split up. One of them was following Pluto and Dr Lügner between the wavering ranks of the band. The other must have skirted around to try to cut them off.

Pluto and Dr Lügner pushed their way clear through the band, and found themselves colliding with a group of pirouetting, pom-pom-shaking cheerleaders. Pluto knocked two of them over, and heard screams and shouts; but he heard laughter, too. 'Look at Pluto, Dad! He's messing up the whole parade!'

Pluto stumbled again, and just managed to avoid being struck by the front of Snow White's float. He pulled Dr Lügner along the side of it, and then ducked in behind it. 'What are we going to do?' he shouted.

'How should I know?' Dr Lügner retorted. 'I've never been chased by chipmunks before.'

Pluto stayed close behind the Seven Dwarfs float. At first he thought that the chipmunk must have given up, and stopped following them, but then he abruptly appeared around the back of the float, one hand still deep in his pocket, his cheeky, cheery face completely belying his intentions. He let out a muffled blurt, but then Pluto punched him in the nose, as hard as he could, and the chipmunk rolled over backward onto the tram-tracks. His mask must have protected him, because he was up on his feet instantly. He tried to drag out a gun – Pluto could see the hammer and the chamber – but the sights must have snagged on the inside of his pocket, and he was still frantically pulling at it when Pluto hit him again.

'Mom! Pluto and Chip, they're *fighting*! They're really fighting!'

The chipmunk tried to get up again; and Pluto hit him again – a deep, upward stomach punch that left him staggering from side to side and whining for breath. Pluto was just about to give him the *coup de grâce* – a rabbit punch to the back of the neck – when he was suddenly pushed to one side. He swung around, his long black ears flying, to see the second chipmunk with his arms raised. His paws half concealed a black, silenced handgun, which he was pointing directly at Dr Lügner.

Before Pluto could think what to do, the chipmunk fired. Inside his mask, Pluto couldn't hear the sound of the shot, especially with all the shouting and cheering and band music – but he saw a tiny white puff of smoke, like a little ball of cotton. He saw something else, too. He saw Dr Lügner flinch, as if he had been hit. He was already stepping toward him with his arms held out to catch him when Dr Lügner turned to look at him. Goddammit, he was *smiling*.

A woman started screaming. There was a moment when Pluto thought that the chipmunk might try another shot, but the next float rolled forward and blocked his line of fire, and two security guards were pushing their way through the crowds toward him. He hesitated, and then forced his way between the tightly packed ranks of frightened children and protesting parents and disappeared.

Pluto turned to see what had happened to the other chipmunk. He lay flat on his back in the roadway, his arms outstretched, still cheekily smiling. But there was a bright red stain on his chest, like a lobster-bib, and it kept growing larger and larger.

'Come on,' said Dr Lügner. 'I think it's time we were someplace else.'

'What the hell happened?' Pluto demanded.

'I'll tell you later. Right now let's get out of here, before the police turn up.'

They jostled their way out of the crowds and nobody tried to stop them because nobody really understood what had happened. Pluto took off his head as he jogged toward the staff parking lot, leaving a school group of five-year-old children staring at him in shock. Three of them burst into tears. In Disney World, taking your head off in public view was a sacking offense. But Mingus didn't care. He wasn't going back there. His dog days were over for good.

310

*   *   *

'I learned it in Japan, from a *t'ai chi* master. He taught me how to read my opponent's body movements. It wasn't easy when my opponent was wearing a chipmunk suit. But he lifted his shoulders slightly before he fired, and lowered his head, because he couldn't see me very well. It wasn't difficult to get out of the way.'

'Did you know that he was going to hit the other guy?'

Dr Lügner shook his head. 'That was just bad luck. For him, anyhow.'

They reached the Royal Tudor Motel, but Mingus drove right past it, hung a right, and parked outside Rayz T-Shirts and the Klassik Komik Kompany. He climbed out of the car, put on his Stevie Wonder sunglasses, and took a good look left and right before he beckoned Dr Lügner out of the car. The sun was beating down so hot that the parking lot was rippling with distorted reflections. They crossed it like two explorers crossing the desert.

Micky and John were waiting for him in the Henry VIII Restaurant, in a mock-Tudor booth right at the very back, under dim red lights. A chipped plaster sucking-pig rotated on a spit in front of dancing tissue-paper flames, in a hearth that gave out nothing but a rustling noise and a steady stream of cold air. The restaurant floor was strewn with straw, and guests were encouraged to throw their gnawed chicken-legs over their shoulders 'except when occupying adjacent booths'.

311

Micky stood up and shook Dr Lügner by the hand. John remained seated, and gave him a salute.

'Well, well,' he said. 'You've saved me a whole lot of trouble, believe me. You've also earned me $300,000.'

Dr Lügner took off his glasses and tucked them into his shirt pocket. 'Who's paying you that, then? Gene Broussard?'

'Who else?' asked John.

'Well . . . there are quite a number of people who would like to know where I am, and quite a number of people who would like to see me in the gardens of remembrance.'

'Gene Broussard doesn't want to see you in the gardens of remembrance. Gene Broussard wants to see you connecting up his missile-guidance system for him, that's all.'

'With regret, Mr Huntley, I can't. If those men can find me in Disney World they can find me anywhere.'

'They *found* you?'

Dr Lügner turned to Mingus and said, 'Go on. Tell them.' And when Mingus had finished, he said, 'You see? I can't afford to take the risk.'

'Listen, if you come to work on the missile, I can give you 100 percent, round-the-clock protection.'

'From these people, there's no such thing as 100 percent, round-the-clock protection.'

'So who are they? I think we have a right to know, don't you?'

Dr Lügner said, 'Yes, I guess you do. But the first thing I want to do is to apologize to all of you who have been dragged into this business against your will. You don't deserve any of this trouble, but sometimes there are greater currents running through the world we live in, and we *have* to get involved.'

'Seems like we didn't have much of a choice,' said John, signaling for the waitress.

'Just hear me out first,' said Dr Lügner. 'Over fifty years ago, I was part of a major scientific program to improve the capacity of the human brain. And I mean major. This wasn't two crackpots in a basement. I had a staff of more than a hundred, and four laboratories. It was wartime, of course, so many of the usual restrictions on budgets and scientific ethics didn't apply. We had so much money and so much freedom that we made incredible strides in under three years. By the time the war was coming to a close, we were right on the verge of producing the first samples of what later became Synaptine.

'Unfortunately, once the war was over, funding was discontinued and the whole program was broken up. There were several reasons why. There was a strong public reaction against elitism in those days, and I think that some of our more liberal politicians thought it smacked too much of creating a "master race".

'However, I continued the work on my own, in secret, and in 1954 I managed to produce a viable quantity of a synaptic accelerator. The trouble was, I couldn't go any further without asking somebody else to verify my work. Very reluctantly, I confided in two other research chemists – Dr Charles Bron at the University of Minnesota and Dr Nathan

Schoenman at Brigham & Women's Hospital in Massachusetts. They both independently checked through my work on Synaptine, and both of them took a limited dosage, with the same kind of results that Micky has been experiencing. Enhanced reasoning, highly comprehensive long- and short-term memory, greatly developed creative skills.

'Both Bron and Schoenman were very excited about Synaptine and urged me to publish, but I wasn't ready for that yet. I still had a lot more research to do. Besides, I was worried about who was going to take control of this drug, once it was manufactured. It's difficult enough to make decisions about heart surgery and cancer treatments – who's worth saving, and who isn't. What would happen if the government restricted the use of Synaptine to certain sociological groups? What if nobody was allowed to have it except the administration and the military? It would totally unbalance the whole of society. You could have a black market in Synaptine that would make today's crack trafficking look like a Girl Scout brownie sale.'

'You didn't think about any of this before you went ahead and developed it?' asked John.

'Of course I thought about it. But no scientist is going to stop work on a critical project just because of its socioeconomic implications. If they did that, we wouldn't have the MR angiogram, or radio frequency catheter ablation, or stem-cell transplants, or you name it. Think of the effect of penicillin, or birth-control pills. Miraculous, on a worldwide scale, but socially catastrophic, too.'

'All the same, you didn't publish?'

Dr Lügner shook his head. 'I simply wasn't ready. To begin with, I could only produce Synaptine in very limited quantities; and for another thing, I knew that as soon as I published I would have the newspapers and the TV people chasing after me, and every science magazine on the planet asking me for further proof and test results. I wanted to keep the whole thing under wraps until it was totally proven. Besides that, I began to understand that I'd invented something very dangerous – to me, that is – and, as it's turned out, to you, too. I came back to my house in Escondido after a trip east and found that it had been ransacked . . . my furniture vandalized, my files broken into, my books ripped apart. Two days later, my car was forced off the road when I was driving to San Diego. I went down a 200-foot slope and my car caught fire. I only managed to get out of it by a miracle.'

He lifted his shirtsleeve and showed them a red, W-shaped scar on his upper arm. 'The door-handle. It nearly took my whole arm off.'

'So that was when you decided to keep yourself to yourself?' John asked him.

'Wouldn't you? I'd spent twenty-five years developing Synaptine. I wasn't going to let myself be bumped off by some faceless hireling before I had the chance to enjoy the fruits of all that work.'

'So what did you do?'

'I disappeared. I had a few influential friends in the Far East, and they helped me to re-establish myself and set up a new laboratory. I produced a new batch of Synaptine, and tested it on myself.

The rest I guess you know. I became a writer, a painter, a musician, a sportsman, a physicist, an astronomer, a mathematician, a surgeon – anything I wanted to be. I worked in Seoul and Tokyo for a while. Then I moved to Hoshi's factory in Seattle. Eventually I came back here to Florida.'

'And you never once thought of sharing this secret with nobody else?' asked Mingus.

'I've been considering it for years. I've passed on as much of my genius as possible, by writing books and composing music and co-operating on scientific projects. Hoshi wasn't the only company I worked with. I also developed a new fuel-economy system for the Ford Motor Company; and a digital color-scanner with Rockwell. But in the end I always held back from releasing the details of Synaptine. I guess I didn't want to be responsible for the implications. But then the men in suits finally found me, and changed my mind. I just had to pass it on to somebody else, although I didn't know who.'

He turned to Micky and gave him a smile that was almost apologetic. 'I didn't want anybody with any preconceived academic ideas. I wanted somebody to whom mathematical and scientific understanding would come like a great burst of light. I wanted to find somebody who couldn't usually remember what they had for breakfast . . . so that I could show them what it's like to be able to learn the Bible by heart from "In the beginning . . ." to "Come, Lord Jesus", in no more time than it takes to read it. I wanted somebody who had the urge to learn, the urge to create, but couldn't.

'I wanted somebody like those Catholic Penitentes in the Sangre de Cristo Mountains who try to knock understanding into their heads with blocks of wood.

'The trouble was, I didn't know anybody like that. The few people with whom I *do* have contact are all eggheads in their own right. Intellectual, yes, but prejudiced and opinionated and narrow-minded; and the whole point of Synaptine is that it expands your *whole* consciousness. It makes you Renaissance Man to the zillionth power.'

John said, 'Those first two guys who tried to kidnap you were sent by Broussard Guidance Systems . . . the same people that I'm working for. I know they roughed you up some, but they weren't out to do you any harm.'

'I had no way of knowing who they were. They were very violent.'

'Not half as violent as these other guys who are coming after you. You should see what they did to your house. Come on, Dr Lügner, or William Cicero, or whatever your name is, I think it's time you told us who they are. Then maybe we can arrange a little counter-attack.'

Their drinks arrived, and Dr Lügner drank half his glass of mineral water in three noisy gulps. Then he said, 'As far as I know, they work for an independent federal agency called OGRE – the Office of Global Research and Experimentation. It was set up in the mid-1930s to exchange scientific research between different countries around the world. Actually the idea wasn't as philanthropic as it sounds. The government and the military were

317

worried that a whole lot of potentially devastating inventions were being developed in foreign universities and research institutes, but our usual run-of-the-mill intelligence agents weren't intelligent enough to understand their significance.

'Several distinguished scientists worked for OGRE, analyzing state-of-the-art research from England, from France, from Sweden . . . even Japan. I did a little work for it, too – nothing special. Albert Einstein was attached to OGRE for a while. It was then that he warned the government that the Germans were producing heavy water, which meant that they were working on a nuclear bomb.'

'You'll forgive me for sounding like less than a genius,' said John. 'But why should OGRE be so goddamned set on giving you an early funeral? If they've gotten wind of Synaptine, surely they'd be doing everything they could to keep you alive and well? Commercially, it must be worth billions.'

'Don't you understand? Synaptine is the single greatest threat that the American establishment has ever known. How do you think that the government is going to control a population who can see through everything they say – who won't be duped by media hype or specious arguments or false statistics? How long do you think our present politicians could stay in power once Americans switch off their televisions and open their eyes to what's *really* happening in the world around them?

'Synaptine will give a power to ordinary people such as they've never had before. It's a social and cultural revolution in a bottle. That's why OGRE and the federal government want me dead before I discover how to mass-produce it.'

'But surely they want to find out how to make it, even if they're going to keep it to themselves.'

Dr Lügner shook his head. 'They know that I would never tell them, and even if they got hold of a sample for analysis they could never work out how to produce it. So the only course of action open to them is to kill me.'

'Do you mind if I ask you just one more question?'

Dr Lügner shrugged. It was neither a yes nor a no.

'Your maid – was she your maid? That was the way Micky described her. An Oriental girl called Suna. What happened to her? When our people broke into your house, they found her dead.'

'I heard,' said Dr Lügner.

'Do you know how that could have happened? Who could have done it?'

'I expect your people did it themselves. Why don't you ask *them* a few questions?'

'That wouldn't be easy. They're dead. Some of your OGRE friends got to them first.' He pointed two gun-fingers to the side of his head and released his thumb-hammer.

'In that case, I don't have any idea. And, listen, it upsets me to talk about it.'

'All right,' said John. He stirred his Bloody Mary with his stick of celery, then bit an inch off and noisily crunched it. 'But let me make a suggestion. How about you try to forgive Gene Broussard for trying to have you kidnapped? Okay, you took a knock on the nose, but there was no serious harm done, was there? How about you come over to Cocoa Beach and talk to Mr Broussard about connecting up his guidance system? I'll give you my personal protection. That way, we'll all win out. Mr Broussard will get his missile contract. You'll wind up with a trunkful of cash, and I'm sure that once you've done the business, Mr Broussard will assist you to vanish to wherever you want to vanish to.'

'Not a chance,' said Dr Lügner.

'Hey – I'm not blowing any trumpets for Broussard, Dr Lügner. They dragged me into this against my will. All I want to do is finish my job, collect my money and go home.'

'Still not a chance. I don't want to sound paranoid, but I'm convinced that there's an OGRE informer working for Broussard.'

'An *informer*?'

'Why do you think I left the MiGR8 program so abruptly? I found out that something was wrong right after Hoshi sold out to Broussard. Everything was in turmoil – you know, moving offices, transferring files. Somebody called up Broussard to ask where they could send my mail, and one of Broussard's secretaries gave them my postal box number. Human error, she meant well. But when I went to pick up my mail two days later, three shots were fired at my car. Lucky for me, they all missed. But it wasn't a mistake, and it wasn't a coincidence. When I got back to my apartment, my front door had been forced open. I didn't go in. In fact, I never went back to that apartment again. I never went back to Seattle again. Not that I miss it. All that damp seeps into the bones.'

John said, 'Listen – if you come back to Broussard, I can give you a guarantee that I can locate that informant, and take him out. I'm very good at that kind of operation. It's what I do.'

'No, Mr Huntley. The answer's still no.'

'I have three hundred grand riding on your return, Dr Lügner. That's a lot of money to a guy like me.'

'So what? You get three hundred grand and I get to see the inside of a $300 casket. That doesn't sound like much of a deal to me.'

'Then why the hell did you come here today? If you're not prepared to come to Broussard, then what?'

'Mr Huntley, I want to see my work on MiGR8 completed even more than you do. I can't finish it myself, but I can send a replacement.'

'What replacement? What are you talking about?'

'A replacement for *me*, don't you get it?'

John stared at Dr Lügner and then the coin dropped. They both turned their heads toward Micky, who was jabbing the ice in the bottom of his glass with his cocktail stick and jabbering to Mingus about writing a rock opera.

Micky was suddenly aware that he was being stared at. 'What?' he wanted to know.

'What do you know about cruise missiles?' John asked him. 'Dr Lügner's suggesting that you fit in the MiGR8 guidance system instead of him.'

Dr Lügner said, 'You don't have to do this, Micky – any more than you had to take Synaptine in the first place. But I don't believe that you'll be in any kind of personal danger. I'll be gone. I'll be out of the picture. And once I'm gone, you won't represent any kind of a threat to them, will you? You might have taken Synaptine, but without my research notes you'll never know how to formulate it – even if you *are* a genius. No, they're only chasing you to get to me.

'Besides – if you can get MiGR8 to function, the Department of Defense will be very happy indeed. Think about it. The US Navy could anchor off Somalia and send a single low-flying projectile looking for one particular rebel leader – across the desert, into the town, round the corner, there he is, and *boofff*! No, they're all in favor of that. The only person the bastards want to eliminate is *me*.'

John couldn't help thinking that there was something about Dr Lügner's story which didn't quite ring true. He was aware that Dr Lügner could out-think him in every conceivable discipline; but all the same he was watching for the signs that he always watched for when he was talking to men who stole stove-top stuffing recipes, and toilet-spray formulas, and cereal premiums. They always thought that they were ten times smarter than anybody else, and they always believed that they were under-appreciated and under-rewarded. But they always had some kind of serious character flaw, which you never usually discovered until it was far too late.

John held his stare for a moment and then turned to Micky. 'How about it, Micky? Do you think that you could put this goddamned missile together?'

Micky said, 'You're not going to believe this . . .

but I think I have kind of a rough grasp of how to connect it up already.'

Dr Lügner smiled at him, and nodded.

'I was right, then,' said Micky. 'You've given me some of your memories.'

'You've remembered things that never happened to you? Books you've never read? Places you've never visited? The height of the dome of the church of St Ignazio in Rome?'

'That's right. I remember someplace in China . . . I remember talking to somebody in Japan.'

'Micky – all of that happened before you were even born. You're remembering some of the things that I remember. I tried to give you a new set of specific memories with every new dose of Synaptine . . . and the second dose contained the basic information for connecting MiGR8.'

'But how can you *do* that?' asked John. 'How can you pass on a memory with an injection?'

'Scientifically, it's comparatively simple. I used only equipment which was already commonplace. Synaptine contains acetylcholine, which boosts the memory signals between your brain cells. While I was synthesizing Micky's particular batch of Synaptine, I subjected the acetylcholine to electrical impulses straight out of my temporal cortex, using a standard hospital-type electroencephalograph.

'I made a conscious effort to concentrate my thoughts on MiGR8, see? And higher math; and a few other memories which might be useful. The electrical impulses out of my brain caused a pattern of chemical changes in the acetylcholine – the same

323

changes that happen naturally, whenever we're thinking. So – once Micky had injected it, the chemical information was changed back into electrical impulses and into *his* memory.

'I haven't yet completely perfected the memory-transference process, not by a long way. It's like the early days of photography, compared with the digital cameras we have today. So Micky obviously picked up quite a few random memories as well, like the time I spent in China and Japan. But I'm working to make it more accurate. You know, edit out the mental clutter.'

John said, 'What do you think Micky? If I call Broussard, and tell them that *you* can set up their guidance system – what would you say?'

Micky looked at Mingus. All Mingus could do was pull one of his Pluto faces.

'I really believe it would cool things off,' said Dr Lügner. 'I could disappear. You could collect your money, Mr Huntley. And you, Micky, would probably be so well rewarded by Gene Broussard that you could do whatever you liked for the rest of your natural life. Read, paint, fish, sail, tinker with quantum mechanics. Maybe you could work on some more missiles. There's a whole lot of satisfaction to be had from working on missiles.'

Micky said, 'I don't know. I'm not too sure I'm up to this.'

'Are you joking?' said Dr Lügner. 'With your mental capacity, I can teach you how MiGR8 works in less than an hour.'

John leaned forward, intent. 'Seriously, Micky, this could really take the heat off. If these guys in suits discover that Dr Lügner has left Florida for parts unknown, and that Broussard aren't looking for him any longer – well, there's a good chance that they'd leave *us* alone.'

Micky thought for a long time. Nobody had ever depended on him before, apart from Roxanne, and he was unused to making decisions. This morning, he had thought of taking Roxanne and driving west, to New Mexico, maybe, or Arizona. But he was intelligent enough now to realize that if he did that, he would end up just like Dr Lügner, an intellectual refugee in a world that was determined to be dumb. And what would they really do? Hide in motel rooms with the blinds drawn, waiting for the men in suits to pull up outside in the wavering summer heat?

He was still thinking when Constance came in. She had bought herself a pale lilac cotton dress from the shopping mall on the other side of Vine Street; as well as a new pair of sandals, and a matching purse. She had washed and blow-dried her hair, and sprayed herself with Femme, and she looked ten years younger.

'Hi, gentlemen,' she said. 'Mind if I join you?' She sat down, and then she beamed at Dr Lügner. 'You must be that Dr Lügner I keep hearing so much about. You're a Capricorn, aren't you?'

Dr Lügner glanced worriedly at John; but all John could do was shrug in the same noncommittal way that Dr Lügner himself had shrugged, and look away.

Constance planted her elbows on the table and stared into Dr Lügner's glasses. 'I can tell you're a

Capricorn because you have such a muddy aura. Maybe you've been living in Central Florida too long.

'What else? Oh yes, typical Capricorn. You're very ambitious but you're always questioning your ability to succeed. You have two personalities who keep saying, "I'm brilliant!" "No, I'm not!" "I'm a genius!" "No, I'm not!" But in reality you're good; you *are* brilliant, and you know you are. But you keep it deeply hidden, just in case you have to share it with anybody else. You can be very caring and very loving, but you can also be very selfish and over-opinionated, and your brilliance has made you very impatient with people who aren't as intelligent as you are.'

There was a long moment of embarrassed silence. John stared at Constance with his mouth open. Mingus pressed the heel of his hand against his forehead in despair; and Micky looked way, tugging at his nose as if somebody had just silently broken wind.

But gradually, a smile leaked its way across Dr Lügner's lips, and he began to nod. Constance smiled back, with her eyes twinkling.

'Well, you're right, I *am* a Capricorn,' he told her. 'I do have arguments about my brilliance, too. And I *do* try to hide it. I'm not so sure about the *muddy* bit.'

'I only said that to annoy, because I know it teases,' said Constance – and Micky, to his own silent surprise, recognized that she was quoting *Alice in Wonderland*. 'I'm Constance Carden. I seem to have gotten myself inextricably mixed up

326

with whatever this is; and I seem to find that I'm scared half to death most of the time, but I wouldn't have missed it for the world.'

'Ms Carden helped me to escape from your OGRE people,' John explained. 'She, uh, runs an art gallery. Paintings, sculpture and stuff. You know. That's when she's not telling fortunes.'

'I've sold some of your paintings,' said Constance. 'I love you when you're Charles Babson. I'm not so sure about your Davis Watkins. A bit *desolate*, I thought.'

'I was going through a desolate time, just about then. I didn't realize it showed so much.'

Constance laid her hand on top of his. Her sun-mottled fingers; and all her gold and silver and amethyst rings. He didn't make any move to draw it away. 'A painter gives himself away more than a writer,' he said. 'A writer can disguise his feelings with tricks and jokes, but a painter can't do that. A painting is a human soul, laid out bare, like an autopsy; no matter how prissy or particular that painting may be.'

'Why do you hide?' Constance asked him.

'Because they want to kill me, that's why.'

'It's more than that. You're hiding from very much more than that.'

'Is that something else you can divine from my star-sign? Or do you see it in my paintings?'

'Now you're being defensive,' Constance chided him.

'Ms Carden, I hardly know you. Why should I be defensive?'

Constance took her hand away, and smiled; but

when she did, the expression on Dr Lügner's face betrayed a sudden sense of loss.

'I'm sorry,' he said. 'Maybe I didn't quite understand you.'

'Oh, I can't believe *that*,' she teased him. 'You're a genius.'

12

Quand la populace se mêle de raisonner, tout est perdu – Voltaire

Roland checked his watch. Then he switched off the Lincoln's engine and climbed out, shooting his cuffs and adjusting his Versace necktie. Three other men climbed out, too, and shot *their* cuffs, and adjusted *their* neckties. All four of them wore dark wraparound sunglasses and their hair shone in the midday sun.

'There are times when God smiles on me,' said Roland.

'There are times when you're one lucky s.o.b., more like,' Sebastian corrected him.

If Sebastian had been able to see through Roland's impenetrable sunglasses, he would have seen that Roland was giving him a look that would have aged him eleven years right where he stood.

Roland was in a seriously violent mood. In fifteen years of security work, he had never suffered a single casualty, until now. Yet in 48 hours he had lost one killed (Kaminski, his head crushed by Dr Lügner's Steinway); two badly injured (Venn and

Spinetti, both piano victims, too); and now his right-hand man Brogan was lying under guard in the Osceola County Hospital with a near-fatal chest wound.

The Orlando police department and the Osceola County sheriff's office were already beginning to make uncooperative noises, and if anything else went wrong Roland knew that he would have to pull his people out of Central Florida, and fast. There was only so much Quentin Tarantino stuff that the local forces would tolerate, even if he *had* been able to convince them that it was all in the interests of 'national security'.

Still, there was no reason why anything else should go wrong, not today. He had discovered earlier this morning that John Huntley and Micky Frasier and Constance Carden were staying here at the Royal Tudor Motel. Last night, Sebastian and Matthew had seen Mingus' car parked outside Rayz T-Shirts, and Roland had sent them to every hotel and motel within two miles in either direction, checking the register for new arrivals (not difficult, with occasional $10 bills to facilitate matters). Only two hotels had reported the arrival of a party of three people – one young man in his mid-twenties, one sixtyish woman and an elderly gent with white hair and glasses. One of the parties was a husband and wife from Omaha, Nebraska, taking their mentally challenged son for a trip to Disney World. The other party claimed they came from Madison, Wisconsin. Roland prided himself on being cultured enough to identify the false names which they had picked out for themselves. It always amazed him how many fugitives were too clever for their own good. They could have chosen Goin and Prizer and Loing, or Carroll and McComas and Pyle, and it would have taken him hours to check their identity – if not days. Instead, they had registered themselves as Serre, Werner and Moreau, and anybody who knew his French cinema of the 1960s knew that these were the stars of *Jules et Jim*.

'What the hell is *Jules et Jim*?' Sebastian had asked him.

'It's a tragic story about two guys and a woman. It's all in French so you wouldn't understand it anyway. In the end they all fucking die. That's all you need to know.'

Roland was trying hard to be pleasant, but he never found it easy. This morning he had sent Brogan and Harkins to follow Mingus to work, and to watch for any reappearance of 'William Cicero'. 'Disguise yourselves, blend in,' he had told them. 'Don't arouse his suspicions, okay?' He still couldn't believe that they had followed Mingus to the staff quarters and hijacked two chipmunk outfits. He had been too stupefied to be really angry. He couldn't believe how anybody could act so totally dumb – while being convinced, at the same time, that they were being so ingenious.

'You thought you saw William Cicero?' Roland had asked Harkins.

'It must have been William Cicero.'

'So – instead of watching him, and following him – you chased him?'

331

'Come on, Roland. We could have whacked him, there and then.'

'In a fucking chipmunk outfit?'

'What difference does it make? I could have been nude. If I'd have whacked him, you wouldn't have turned a hair.'

'Yes, but you didn't whack him, did you? You near-as-dammit whacked Brogan. Blew half his fucking lung away. He's never going to smoke again.'

For all that Brogan and Harkins had screwed up, they had given Roland the reassurance that he had been looking for: that William Cicero was still in the Kissimmee area. They were all tied in together, this ragbag collection of John Huntley and Micky Frasier and Constance Carden, as well as Mingus and that long-legged, big-chested chick with the hair like a dynamited hayride. Amateurs, all of them – but Roland knew from experience that amateurs were often the hardest to deal with. They didn't follow the rules. They did things that you didn't expect, like dropping grand pianos from the ceiling.

'Let's hope and pray we don't walk into some goddamned flying harmonium,' said Roland, as they walked across the hot concrete parking lot. A lizard scuttled out of Roland's way. It recognized a superior reptile when it saw one.

The Royal Tudor Motel was much easier to cover than Guido's. There were only two rear exits, both of which could be watched by one man, and a small separate side entrance giving street access to the Olde Englishe Souvenir Shoppe, which was crammed with models of red double-deck buses and gilt-edge plates with pictures of Princess Di printed on them.

Roland walked up to the main entrance and in through the tinted, automatic doors. The air conditioning was so cold that he gave an involuntary shiver, as if somebody had stepped on his grave. A whiskery Beefeater with whiskey on his breath said, 'Welcome, folks, to the Royal Tudor! A taste of Olde Englande in downtown Kissimmee! Eat, drink and be merry!'

'Eat, drink and kiss my ass,' Sebastian told him.

They walked through to the restaurant. The plaster sucking-pig was still rotating, but all of the booths were empty. Sebastian stalked up and down, and finally had to stop and spread his arms in defeat. 'They were supposed to be here. They ain't.'

Roland went up to the waitress. She was white-faced, with blobby black lashes and henna-dyed hair, trailer-trash trying to make good. Roland immediately tucked a sharp-folded $50 bill into the front of her dress. 'There were some people here, yes? Two white guys, and a black guy, and an old woman and an old man.'

'What if there was?' the waitress retorted.

'Listen, sweetheart,' said Roland. 'Tell me yes or tell me no. We're government security agents. We have to know.'

'They was here, yes,' the waitress told him. 'But they left about five minutes ago.'

'Any idea where they went?'

'They was guests, sir. I'm not permitted to tell

you nothing like that. I mean, that's a confidence.'

'Listen to me, miss. It's not a confidence when it comes to national security. Don't you watch television? Those people are *bad* people, got it? They're trying to undermine the Constitution. You know what the Constitution is?'

'Of course I do. But I'm not supposed to give out information like that.'

Roland grasped her Union Jack cravat and glared at her from only two inches away. 'Do – you – know – where – they – went?' he demanded.

She said nothing, but simply stared at him, tight-lipped. In the end, he released her, and said to Sebastian, 'Check out their rooms. Third story, 323 and 325. And as for you – ' he said to the waitress ' – I'm going to make it my business to find out where you live. You've made my life a misery . . . I'm going to do the same to you.'

'I'm a single mother, trying to make a living,' she said. 'What kind of animal are you?'

Roland gave her a feral grin. 'You don't even want to know, sweetheart. Or maybe you do.'

At that moment, Sebastian reappeared. 'They're gone,' he said. 'Their rooms are totally empty. Not even a cigarette butt or a candy wrapper. Oh . . .' he added, and held up a hair-grip. 'If this means anything.'

'Shit, they knew we were coming,' said Roland. He smacked his fist into the palm of his hand, and bruised himself, because he was wearing so many heavy gold rings. 'How the hell did they know that we were coming?'

★   ★   ★

They were squashed together in Mingus' pick-up, watching the Royal Tudor Motel from the parking lot across the street. Their few belongings had been tossed into the back – shirts, pants, underwear, dresses, and everything else they had managed to clear out of their rooms in the five minutes since Roxanne had warned them that Roland had arrived.

'I think we owe you one,' said Dr Lügner, awkwardly turning his head and giving Roxanne an approving smile.

Roxanne was sitting on Micky's lap. 'I recognized him from yesterday. What a *grotesque*.'

Micky kissed her. 'You did good. I couldn't believe it when the waitress came up and said there was a phone call for me.'

Roland hadn't reckoned with Roxanne – that she might be approaching the Royal Tudor Hotel while he and his team were waiting outside. Roland wouldn't have been able to imagine having that much shitty luck, all in the same morning.

'Right, we'd better get out of here,' said John. 'Let's find ourselves another motel while Dr Lügner tells Micky how to get this missile working. Then we can decide what we're going to do next.'

'Can't we wait and see what happens with the pineapple?' asked Roxanne.

'No, too dangerous. Let's just get going.'

Mingus started the engine and swung the pick-up around. As he did so, however, the traffic signals changed, and a large, toiling truck came past, with a long line of vehicles creeping along behind it. Mingus waited for a break in the traffic, his fingers drumming on the steering-wheel. Even when the signals changed back to red, their way out of the parking lot was still obstructed. 'Come on, come on, come on,' he muttered, under his breath. 'What the hell is this, a funeral procession?'

They were still trapped when Roland appeared at the front of the Royal Tudor Motel, followed by Sebastian and another member of his team. Roland took off his sunglasses and looked left and right. He paused for a moment, as if he had seen something; but then he gave a cursory wave of his arm and the three of them started walking toward the parking lot.

'For Christ's sake, don't look this way,' said Micky, under his breath. Mingus kept gunning his engine, but they were still penned in by a green Ford Galaxy crowded with a dozy-looking family in white Jack Lemmon sunhats, and there was no way in the world that Ford Galaxy daddy was going to move his vee-hickle three inches forward so that Mingus could get out. Mingus blipped his horn, but Ford Galaxy daddy did nothing but dismissively wave one fat freckled arm. Like, what's your hurry, fellah? I'm on vacation here.

Then two things happened at the same time. The traffic shifted forward, so that Mingus could nudge his pick-up into the stream of traffic. His tires squealed, and Sebastian turned around and saw them. He caught Roland's arm and pointed, and the three of them wrenched open the Lincoln's doors and jumped inside.

'*Go!*' said John, slapping the pick-up's instrument panel.

Mingus swung into the outside lane, and began to head eastward toward St Cloud, his lights flashing and his horn blaring. Miraculously, the traffic moved out of his way. Most drivers were too comatose to tell the difference between a genuine emergency vehicle and a pick-up truck full of panicky fugitives. 'I'll take you back to my place,' said Mingus, overtaking an overloaded Winnebago in the inside lane. 'They won't find us there.'

Roxanne craned her head around and said, 'Mingus! The pineapple! It hasn't worked!'

Roland swerved out of the parking lot of the Royal Tudor Motel. The Lincoln jounced across Vine Street, right in front of the oncoming traffic, and there was a salvo of horns and a hallelujah chorus of squealing tires. A red-faced van driver drew up alongside, and yelled at Roland, 'You! Yes, you! What the fuck you doing, friend?'

Roland gave him the finger and kicked hard down on the Lincoln's gas pedal. At that moment there was a deafening bang, and the Lincoln's hood flew up in the air and clattered into the road. The car came to a halt, with a grinding, clashing, screeching sound, and stayed where it was, right in the middle of Vine Street, with black smoke billowing out of it.

Roland kicked open his door and climbed out. He stalked around to the front of the car and stared in fury at the engine. The cylinder head had blown off, as well as the oil filter and the air-conditioning unit. There were wild wires and burst hoses everywhere, and a cacophony of boiling coolant and sizzling brake fluid. He stood and stared at it, and roared, 'What? *What?*'

Sebastian climbed out. He didn't have to look at the engine. He went around to the back of the car with a tired lack of surprise; and nodded.

'They didn't just know you were coming, Roland. They murphied you, good and proper.'

'What are you talking about for fucksake murphied?' Roland raged at him.

'Look for yourself. Most of the time, they use a potato. Murphy, potato, you get it. They ram it up your tailpipe, the exhaust pressure builds up. One good slam on the gas and you get one of two results. A potato that flies for two miles and kills anything that happens to be standing in its way; or else your cylinder head goes into orbit.'

Trembling with fury, Roland joined Sebastian at the back of the car. Somebody had forced a whole pineapple over his exhaust – hammered it, probably, by the look of it. He was so sick and angry that he kicked the pineapple, and missed, and then he turned around and stared at nothing at all, his mouth tight, his teeth grinding together, hyperventilating and hating everything, especially William Cicero and all of his amateur ensemble, and Sara Lake, too, that over-opinionated whore, with her snotty Vassar accent and her nipples that showed through her blouses.

He was still fulminating when the red-faced van driver appeared, the sleeves of his checkered shirt rolled up tight, his forehead decorated with a coronet of perspiration. His eyes were blue and very close together and his nose was twisted.

'Hey, friend,' he said, giving Roland a flat-

338

handed push on the shoulder. 'You just made some kind of gesture at me.'

'Gesture? What are you talking about, gesture?'

'Well, either you was trying to tell me that you only had one sausage for breakfast, or else you was being offensive.'

Roland was furious. This was all so goddamned irrelevant. This was all so goddamned frustrating. He was trying to redeem his entire career, and here was this meathead accusing him of being impolite. He swung around, his left fist raised, and it was then that the meathead hit him a short, hard punch on the jaw, so that he fell back onto the blacktop with his arms stretched wide, knocking the back of his head, concussed and crucified.

He dreamed momentarily of his mother, in the sunlit kitchen of his grade school days. He believed that she was still alive. He touched her apron, and it was real. He touched her face, and it was real. 'Mom?' he said, and then he opened his eyes and found that he was stroking Sebastian's well-shaved cheek, and twiddling with Sebastian's repulsive red-and-purple necktie.

'Come on,' said Sebastian. 'We have to vamoose before the cops show up.'

'What about the tools?' said Roland. His mouth was filled with blood, and one of his teeth was waggling.

'The tools are okay, Leon has them. We've flagged down a taxi. Come on. See if you can stand.'

Roland rolled sideways, and managed to lift himself up on one arm. A crowd had gathered, and people were staring at him, like goldfish staring out of their aquarium at a world that they couldn't conceivably understand. A fat boy in a Sea World T-shirt was steadfastly chewing gum and watching every move he made without blinking. Roland would have given a month off his life to go to the taxi, open the gray canvas sack in which they carried their guns, untangle an Ingram, and reduce that boy to tomato *concassée*.

They heard sirens scribbling in the distance. Sebastian helped Roland to his feet, and into the back of the taxi. 'You don't want to stay for the cops?' the taxi driver asked them.

'No, Fidel, and neither do you,' said Sebastian. The taxi driver shrugged, and turned his steering-wheel flat-handed, so that they swerved out into the traffic flow, regardless of the horns and the squealing brakes. 'Your friend okay?' he wanted to know, his eyes floating in the rearview mirror, complete with black bushy eyebrows.

'Just mind your own fucking business and drive.'

'Hokay. I only asked.'

'Did I ask you to ask? When I want you to ask, I'll ask. Okay?'

'Hokay.'

Roland had been pressing his padded-up hand-kerchief against his mouth. It was wet with saliva and stained with blood. 'They won't go far. We've surprised them, they won't have planned anything yet. They won't go back to Canoe Creek Road. What's the betting they go back to the black guy's house?'

'We could go see. Let's go pick up my car first.'

'Since when did you give the fucking orders?'

The taxi driver took them to the Whispering Palms Motel, where they were staying – a yellow-painted brick building without a single palm in sight. Sebastian paid the taxi driver off while Leon tugged the gray canvas sack over to the silver Buick, opened the trunk, and carefully lowered it in.

'You sure you don't want to splash some cold water on that mouth?' Sebastian asked Roland, trying to be solicitous.

'Who are you, Dr Kildare? All I want to do is to lay my hands on those clowns and do the same thing to them as they did to my car.'

They drove out of the Whispering Palms with a shriek of tires, leaving a crescent-shaped black mark on the concrete. 'You can remember where his house is?' asked Roland.

'I remember.'

Roland leaned forward, his face grimmer than any of them could remember it. The only thing that betrayed his agitation was the way in which he kept swallowing and tugging at his collar, as if he felt that he were being strangled.

Mingus' mother was out in the yard when they arrived, watering her pot-plants. She was wearing a cheerful pink-and-yellow dress that her neighbor had brought her back from Cuba, and a bright pink headscarf. Mingus' eleven-year-old sister Dauphine was playing with her Baywatch Barbie on the step.

'Mom . . . there's some people I'd like you to

341

meet. This is Dr Lügner . . . this is Mr Huntley . . . and this is Ms Carden.'

Mrs Wells shut off the hose and came across the yard, wiping her wet hands on the side of her dress. 'Pleased to make your acquaintance,' she said, one eye closed against the sunshine. Then, 'Hallo, Micky; hallo, Roxanne. How are things with you?'

'Well, so-so, just at the moment, Mrs Wells,' said Micky. 'We were wondering if we could stop here for a half-hour or so, just to freshen up.'

'Are you in some kind of trouble?' asked Mingus' mother. 'Dexter? What's going on here?'

'It's nothing, Mom. Just a misunderstanding, that's all.'

'Well, begging your pardon, it looks like a whole lot more than a misunderstanding to me.' She turned to John and Dr Lügner and said, 'You'll forgive me, gentlemen, but you and the good lady here are not quite the usual type of friend that my son brings back. I mean, you're not exactly home-boys, are you?'

Dr Lügner gave her a wan smile. 'We don't mean to cause you any trouble, ma'am. It's just that your son very kindly agreed to help us with a little trans-portation problem. We won't be very long, I promise you. Thirty, thirty-five minutes, that's all. Then we'll be out of your hair.'

'Okay, then,' said Mingus' mother. 'I guess you all could use a cup of coffee and some carrot cake.'

John said, 'Thanks. That sounds like the best idea I've heard all morning.'

They all went back toward the house, but Dr Lügner laid a hand on Micky's shoulder. 'Let's stay out here. This won't take long, but you're going to have to concentrate.'

'Don't you want no coffee?' called Mingus' mother.

'Just give us five or ten minutes,' said Dr Lügner, with a wave. Then he sat down on the step and beckoned Micky to sit beside him. He took off his glasses, and said, 'This situation is getting far too dangerous for comfort. The last thing I want is for anybody else to get hurt. As soon as I've finished telling you everything you need to know, I'm leaving, and I won't be back.'

'You won't be back *ever*?'

'Absolutely never. And I won't be getting in touch, either. So if you have any questions after I'm finished – any questions at all – you'd better ask them, because you won't be getting a second chance.'

'Okay,' Micky agreed. But the truth was that – as his intellect grew – he was far less impressed by Dr Lügner than he had been to begin with. After all, if almost everybody were potentially capable of writing and painting and inventing and working out modular functions – if *he* could do it himself – then what was so special about Dr Lügner? Now that he was no longer dazzled by Dr Lügner's wealth and brainpower, Micky was beginning to question whether he really respected him or not – and even whether he really *liked* him.

All the same, he sat down on the step while Dr Lügner took out a sheaf of folded notes.

Dr Lügner said, 'Broussard have three cruise missiles ready for the MiGR8 guidance system,

343

although only one guidance system is oven-ready for installation. The missiles are all BGM-109 Tomahawks, one of which is supposed to be tested for the Navy and two for the USAF Tactical Air Command.

'In their strategic role, Tomahawks are normally guided by Tercom. That's terrain comparison: they use radar to look at the ground below them and compare it with the "map" with which they've been programmed.

'MiGR8 is very much simpler. It works exactly in the same way that a bird's brain works – sensing the earth's geomagnetic field, and judging the position of the sun and the stars.

'Just like a bird, too, it knows where it's going, and who or what it's supposed to head for . . . and when it arrives at its target it recognizes it, the way a bird does. Not only "it", either. It could be him, or her. Once it's been guided to its general target area, it has the ability to find a very specific location, such as a single house in a particular street – and then it uses a facial recognition facility to seek out and recognize a single human being, and kill them. Well, *overkill* them, actually. The Tomahawk can carry a nuclear warhead or 454 kilograms of high explosive.

'But the *real* beauty of MiGR8 is that all its connections are *chemical*, rather than electrical. The guidance platform sends messages to the Tomahawk's controls in the same way that neurones send messages one to the other. This is why those poor idiots at Broussard couldn't work out how to instal it. There are microscopic synapses

344

between all of the electrical connections, and they couldn't understand what they were for or how to bridge them. Even if they *did*, they didn't have Synaptine.'

'What are you saying? MiGR8 uses Synaptine too?'

'Of course. That's why it works so brilliantly. By using a *chemical* transmitter, I could make a computer a thousand times faster and cleverer without taking up any more space or any more weight. MiGR8 isn't a computer, Micky: it's almost a *brain*. It can make judgements. It can even have opinions.

'Look at this schematic – the guidance unit sits here in the Tomahawk's nose. You inject the unit's rear duct with 15 millilitres of Synaptine, and it's ready to go. Simple . . . but I never explained it to anybody at Hoshi, and of course the research team at Broussard are all electronics experts. Not a neurochemist among them.'

'This is amazing,' said Micky, frowning over the drawings. 'But how do you program it to target an individual person?'

Dr Lügner smiled a wide, self-satisfied smile. 'You simply put a picture of your target's face into a scanner. The scanner uploads the picture into the MiGR8 unit, and the MiGR8 unit remembers it. The missile has onboard cameras and infrared detectors, both of which are capable of recognizing a particular human face from half a mile away, even at night – even through walls. The technology isn't even advanced. When I built the prototype, I borrowed Mandrake face-identification cameras from Software & Systems International in Britain and infrareds from the Seattle Fire Department.

'Let's put it this way: if you had a powerful enough telescope, you could recognize your girl-friend from over a mile away. This missile can do the same.'

Micky leafed through the last of the drawings. Less than a week ago, he would have said '*duh?*' and handed them back in bewilderment. But the circuit diagrams seemed as clear as highway maps, and the installation instructions as easy to follow as his well-thumbed Dodge workshop manual.

He had one doubt, though. 'So who is this missile going to hit?'

'The test missile? A specially built dummy, with an artist's impression for a face.'

'I don't know,' said Micky. 'I need some time to think this over.'

'Micky – think about it. If MiGR8 works as well as I expect it to, the United States will have incal-culable superiority over every other military force in the world. People think that it's all peace and friendship now that the Communist bloc has broken up, but the world is a much more dangerous place than it ever was; and MiGR8-guided missiles are exactly the kind of surgical weapons we need.

'Think of it. We could fly a missile right into the front door of the People's Palace and hit the Chinese premier right in the nose.'

Micky said, 'Sure. But what's in it for you?'

'Satisfaction, I guess. The same satisfaction I got when I designed a new girder that would make buildings impervious to earthquakes.'

'Satisfaction? Is that all?'

'No, that's not all. Self-preservation, too. When the government realizes that they have to have Synaptine to fly these missiles, and that I'm the only person who knows how to synthesize it, maybe they'll stop trying to kill me. I'm using MiGR8 to change their minds, Micky. There's nothing that makes the US administration salivate more than a fancy new weapon.'

'When is the test missile supposed to fly?'

Dr Lügner checked his watch. 'The original test date was supposed to be three days from now. It's going to be air-launched from an A-6 Intruder flying from Cape Canaveral Air Force Station.'

Micky wiped his nose with the back of his hand and looked dubious. 'So all I have to do is insert the Synaptine and connect up the guidance systems to the pre-launch computer?'

'It's almost as simple as that, yes. I gave you ten ampoules of Synaptine. Use numbers 7 and 8. Believe me, the MiGR8 system is foolproof. Once that missile is go, then nothing can stop it.'

'Supposing you change your mind?' asked Micky.

Dr Lügner stared at him. 'What do you mean, supposing I change my mind?'

'Well, what if you launch one of these MiGR8 missiles, and it's targeted onto Ali ben Wali, or whoever, and Ali ben Wali calls you up and says, "Hey, I'm sorry, I surrender." You can self-destruct it, right?'

'Sure . . . and you can also change the target image in midflight, and direct it to hit somebody else.'

347

Mingus' mother slid back the patio door and called out, 'Hey! The coffee is getting cold! And we're almost out of cake!'

'We're coming,' said Micky. Then, to Dr Lügner, 'if you're disappearing for good, what happens when I run out of Synaptine?'

Dr Lügner smiled. 'The doses I've given you are enough to keep up your mental abilities for the rest of your life. The tenth dose is a final booster – whatever you do, make sure you don't forget to take it.'

They went inside. In the kitchen, Constance was perking a fresh pot of coffee while Roxanne was helping Mingus' mother with the dishes. John was sitting at the table with Dauphine.

'You want some cake?' Constance asked them.

Micky shook his head, but Dr Lügner said, 'Delighted, Constance. Thanks.'

Then he announced, 'I've just given Micky all the information he needs to activate Broussard's missile. Now I can disappear and let all of you good people get on with your lives. I'll make sure that those men in suits are more than aware that I've gone.'

'Please God I hope you're right,' said Roxanne, taking hold of Micky's hand.

'You want a ride anyplace?' Mingus asked Dr Lügner.

'Well . . . before I go, there's one thing I have to hear. I have to hear Micky saying yes – that he *will* launch the MiGR8 missile.'

Micky looked around the kitchen – at Roxanne, at John, at Mingus and Constance. He knew that he wouldn't be able to say no. Although he had become involved with Dr Lügner by accident, it was clearly up to him to do whatever was necessary to protect his friends. And, who knew, he might even enjoy working with missiles. He liked tinkering with his car, after all.

'Okay,' he nodded. 'I'll do it. John can take me back to Cocoa Beach as soon as he likes.'

Dr Lügner came up to him and grasped his hand between both of his. His eyes were watery with emotion. 'I won't forget you, Micky Frasier. In fact, I probably won't be able to. One day soon you're going to be so famous that all of America will have heard of you. Rock musician, artist, writer, you name it. It's all yours for the taking. I'm just sorry that I've put you and your friends into so much danger, and caused you so much pain.'

He turned to Mingus' mother and thanked her for the coffee. Then he gave Constance a kiss. 'You're a courageous, interesting woman, Ms Carden. I wish we could have met at a happier time.'

'Me too, Dr Lügner, or whatever your name really is.'

Dr Lügner smiled. 'Names don't mean anything, Ms Carden. Mozart would still have been a genius, even if his name had been Katzenjammer.'

To John he said, 'I'm sorry you couldn't take me back to Broussard with you. But I think they'll be pleased with Micky here. It isn't often that a scientist gets the chance to see his experiments turn out so well. Just make sure that they pay you your 300,000.'

John shook his hand. 'Catch you later, Dr Lügner.'

Dr Lügner turned to Mingus. 'How about a ride to the Orange Blossom Trail? Is that too far? I can catch a bus from there.'

'That's no problem,' said Mingus. He kissed his mom, took a playful swipe at his sister, and went to the front door, and opened it. Instantly, they all heard a sharp, descending *tyoo*! like somebody pulling the slide down a penny-whistle. The back of Mingus' head flapped up, and two and a half cupfuls of blood and brains were splattered all over the white hall wallpaper.

Mingus stood in the doorway for a moment as if he had suffered nothing more serious than a mosquito bite on the neck – as if he intended to continue walking out into the sunshine. But then his knees buckled, and he twisted and collapsed.

'*Dexter!*' shrilled his mother, and bustled toward him, her arms spread wide. '*Oh, no, Lord! No, Lord! Dexter!*'

'*No!*' John shouted. He snatched at her dress and pulled her heavily down to the floor. She lay face-down in the hallway, one hand outstretched toward Mingus' blood-spattered sneaker. There was another *tyoo*! and then another, and the wall-mirror shattered and dropped from the wall. Mrs Wells lay with her face pressed against the beige sculptured rug, sobbing and sobbing, and beating her fist as if it were her son's heart.

13

*They change their skies but not their souls who run
across the sea* – Horace

John heaved Mrs Wells up from the floor and
retreated into the kitchen, frantically waving at
everybody to stay well down.

Micky was white and stiff-legged, and Dr Lügner
almost had to drag him onto the floor. '*Mingus!*
That's my best friend, man! They killed my best
friend! They *killed* him!'

'Just stay down, for Christ's sake! We have to find
a way out of here!'

'What about the back yard?' said Roxanne,
almost hysterical. 'Can't we get out that way?'

As if in direct answer, there was an abrupt salvo
of *brrrp! brrrp! brrrp!* from the rear of the house. The
pale-blue venetian blinds danced a jerky, maniacal
rumba, and shattered glass flew everywhere.
Mingus' sister started to scream – such a high-
pitched scream that it sounded more like a whistle.
Roxanne covered her ears with her hands.

'Listen – maybe I should give myself up,' said Dr

Lügner. 'They won't hurt the rest of you, once they have me.'

'No!' Constance protested. 'They'll kill you!' But John turned around and looked at Micky, and even though neither of them said anything, they both knew what the other was thinking. Dr Lügner got us into this – Dr Lügner can get us out.

After the firing from the back yard, there were two or three minutes of silence. Micky lay on his side behind the icebox, his arms around Roxanne. Dr Lügner and Constance were crouched in the niche between the dresser and the wall. Mrs Wells sat behind the back door, still wide-eyed with shock, but stroking and hushing Dauphine to calm her down. Only John remained standing, pressed against the kitchen wall, dipping his head forward now and again to see if anybody was approaching the house from the front.

'I see one,' he said, after a while 'Yes – and there's another one. Two in the front, two in the back, that's my guess.'

'What do we do, then?' said Constance. 'If we try to run away, they'll kill us, won't they? And if we don't, they'll come in and get us.'

Micky said, 'There's one way out – and that's if we're just not here.'

'What do you mean – "just not here"?'

Micky cautiously raised his head. 'I'll show you. But we have to be quick.'

Roland dodged in through the front doorway and pressed himself up against the wall. He glanced down at Mingus to make sure that he was dead.

Then he crossed the hallway and took up a position beside the kitchen door, his Ingram held in both hands.

Sebastian came in next, stepping over Mingus with a complete lack of interest. 'Do you know where they're at?' he asked Roland.

Roland put his finger to his lips. 'Cover me,' he said; and then he ducked into the kitchen with his Ingram pointed stiffly out in front of him. The kitchen was empty.

Sebastian followed him as he darted into the living-room, and then along the corridor to the bedrooms. All of them were empty, and so were the bathroom and the toilet.

'Where the fuck are they?' Roland demanded. He banged open the closet doors, and jabbed the barrel of his Ingram in amongst the clothes, but there was nobody there. He wrenched open the shower, shattering the glass. 'They're not here! They have to be here!'

Sebastian went back to the kitchen and opened the door that led to the garage. He ducked down and looked under Mingus' LTD. He peered into the car's windows to see if anybody was hiding inside, but the car was empty, too.

Roland came in, his face rigid with fury. 'This is insane! This is fucking insane! There was no way those people could have gotten out of here!'

'What about the attic?' Sebastian suggested.

Roland gave him a look that could have killed a turtle at twenty paces. But then he stalked back to the corridor and poked his Ingram up at the trap-door that led to the attic. He pulled down the wooden ladder and said to Sebastian, 'You think they're up there? *You* go look.'

'What if they're armed?'

'They'll blow your fucking head off, what do you think?'

Sebastian cautiously climbed the ladder. Every step creaked. He hesitated for a moment, and then he quickly lifted his arm and whipped it back down again.

Roland said, 'Move it, Sebastian, for Christ's sake.'

Sebastian took two more steps up the ladder, and gingerly poked his head through the trapdoor. He waited for almost half a minute but nothing happened. Then he found a light switch.

'There's nobody up here!' he said. 'Just a couple of old mattresses and loads of books!'

He came back down the ladder again, and wiped the perspiration from his upper lip. 'They've gone, man. I don't know how. But they're gone.'

Roland flew into a rage. 'Did you see them come out of the front? Did you see them come out of the back? They can't be gone!'

He punched the wall and kicked at the living-room door. 'They can't be gone! It's fucking impossible!'

Sebastian whipped open a closet in the hallway and shouted, 'Ha!' but all he discovered was a vacuum-cleaner and a mop and a deflated alligator airbed. Roland went into the living-room and poked his gun into the drapes, but there was nobody hiding there, either. His cheeks rhythmically flexed as he ground his teeth.

'I don't know how they did it, man,' said

Sebastian. 'But they gave us the slip. Maybe they went back to Frasier's place.'

'They can't be gone,' Roland muttered.

Sebastian laid a hand on his shoulder. 'Come on, man,' he said, and gently but firmly pushed him out through the front door. A few neighbors had gathered to see what was going on, but they quickly retreated to their houses when they saw the guns. 'Come on, man. The cops are going to be here in a couple of minutes.'

'They *must* be here,' Roland repeated. 'There's no fucking way that they can't be here.'

'Listen, they found some secret way out. A fucking secret tunnel. How should I know? But the longer we stay here, the further away they're going to be. Besides, you don't want the cops to catch us with another stiff, do you?'

Roland looked back at the house, his nostrils flaring and the veins on his neck bulging. 'Okay,' he said, at last, and threw himself into the Buick's passenger seat. They screeched away from the curb and snaked around the corner, heading for Canoe Creek Road.

Inside the garage, the lid of the washing-machine was cautiously opened. There was a moment's hesitation and Micky climbed out. He went straight over to Mingus' LTD, took out the keys, and unlocked the trunk. Carefully curled up inside lay Constance and Mrs Wells.

'Are you okay? You haven't suffocated yet?'

'We're all right,' said Constance. 'Have they gone now?'

'They're gone.'

Micky helped them out, and then he went through to the house. In the living-room, the seat cushions on the couch rose up, and John emerged from his hiding place. In the main bedroom, Micky pulled out the drawers under Mrs Wells' divan bed, where Roxanne was huddled up in a fetal position.

'It's okay, now, honey. You can come out now.'

He took her hand and lifted her out. Then he pulled open the next drawer, where Dr Lügner was lying.

'I should have read that book on Harry Houdini, too,' said Dr Lügner.

'One more to go,' said Micky. He went into the kitchen and opened up the larder. Doubled up in the vegetable rack, among the onions and the sweet potatoes, was Dauphine.

'Are you okay, sweetheart?' he asked her.

'Squashed,' she said.

'I can't believe they didn't find us,' said Constance.

'It isn't surprising,' said Micky. 'They were panicking, and they were short on time. But apart from that, they looked in all the logical places – like up in the attic or behind the drapes. But Harry Houdini knew that you can fold a reasonably fit human being into a space much smaller than most people would ever think possible.'

'You can say that again,' said Dr Lügner, rubbing his elbows. 'I wouldn't have believed you could have gotten a *dog* into that drawer, let alone an 80-year-old man.'

John went over and put his arm around Mrs

Wells. 'Why don't you come sit down? The cops are coming. I think you've had enough for one day.'

Mrs Wells looked wretchedly toward the hallway, where Mingus was still lying on his back, eyes open, staring at the ceiling.

'That's my only boy,' she said, her lower lip trembling. 'Why did they have to take my only boy?'

Dr Lügner said, 'I think it's time we split up. The police will be here in a minute, and I don't trust the police any more than those characters.'

They heard a warbling siren only two or three streets away. 'I'm staying here,' said Mrs Wells. 'I'm not leaving my Dexter.'

'Of course,' John told her. 'But the rest of us have to go. I can't tell you why . . . but all I can say is that Dexter died doing something really brave.'

The police siren was joined by another, and another. John looked around and Dr Lügner was gone. 'Come on,' he said to Micky and Roxanne, and they ran across the street, dodged between the houses, and jogged across a field of prickly grass jumping with crickets.

'Constance!' John panted. 'Did anybody see where Constance went?'

Micky said, 'No, but don't worry – I think she's old enough to look after herself.'

John looked back, but it was too late now. The police cars had arrived at the Wells house, and the sirens had abruptly stopped. They slid down an embankment, trudged across a short stretch of swampy sawgrass, and at last found themselves back on the main Kissimmee highway.

'*Taxi!*' called Micky, and let out a piercing whistle that had John clapping his hand over his ear.

'I didn't know I could do that,' said Micky, in awe, as a red-and-white cab slewed into the side of the road.

Roxanne wanted to come with them to Cocoa Beach, but John was adamant that she stay at home.

'You'd probably be safe. But – you know – you never know.'

Roxanne gave Micky a long goodbye hug outside her mother's house while her mother pulled a dozen different disapproving faces and John patiently waited in the back of the taxi with his head tilted back and his eyes closed. He knew what it was like to lose people.

He and Micky took the cab to the Southern Sun Hotel on Vine Street and rented a bronze Buick Regal from the Alamo desk, using the last $150 on John's Masterchange. The girl behind the counter had green eyeshadow like a basking lizard and didn't smile once.

'Has somebody died or something?' Micky demanded.

'Excuse me?'

'Oh, I see. You're just being miserable on purpose. What the hell do *you* have to be miserable about?'

John put his arm around his shoulders. 'Come on, Micky, let's have a drink.' He could see that Micky was still fretful and shocked. They found a corner booth and sat down on the sticky brown vinyl under a *faux* Tiffany lamp. They ordered two beers and two Jack Daniel's. Their waitress was a bleached blonde with a short skirt and the blankest expression on her face that John had ever seen.

'It's like *The Day of the Dead* in here,' said Micky.

'Try to relax. You won't do yourself any good getting all worked up.'

'I can't believe they killed Mingus. It's like something I dreamed. I keep thinking I'm going to wake up.'

'What can I say, except that you're not?'

Micky took the remaining Synaptine ampoules out of his shirt pocket.

'That's the stuff?' John asked him.

Micky said, 'Jesus - I wish I'd never taken it. I wish I'd looked the other way and let those guys just take him away.'

'So what are you going to do? Stop taking it?'

Micky miserably shook his head. 'How can I?'

'It's not addictive, is it?'

'Not in itself. Not like smack. But being a genius is addictive. Yesterday morning, when I woke up, I lay in bed and invented a machine that could supply the average house with all of the electricity it needed, for ever. Not totally for free, but as close as you can get.

'You attach a nine-foot steel pole to a vertical shaft from a diesel-powered generator. At one end of the shaft you have a battery-powered propeller. At the other end, you fit a counterweight. You spin the pole until its tips reach 900 m.p.h. Then you switch off the generator, and switch on the propellor, and the gyroscopic effect keeps the pole

359

spinning until you've generated enough electricity to provide all of the energy you need, *and* to recharge your battery.'

John finished his Jack Daniel's. He didn't say a word, but lifted his finger to the waitress for another one.

'There are only two problems,' said Micky. 'If everybody had one, it would slow the rotation of the world by a millionth of a second every year.'

'And what's the other problem?'

'If the pole breaks . . . goodbye house.'

As he talked, Micky's finger drew invisible blue-prints on the tabletop. John watched him sadly and said nothing.

'We were going to be famous, Mingus and me. I never thought that it was going to end up like this.'

'No-one ever does,' said John. 'Give me five minutes. I have to make some phone calls.'

He called Maggie first. She sounded distant, even though she kept assuring him that she was alone.

'I should be back in San Francisco in a couple of days. And rich.'

'I don't know, John. Danny's been hurt so bad.'

'What are you telling me? I need reassurance, that's all. I need some normality.' He could see his face reflected in the small mirror over the tele-phone's coinbox, and he looked wild and strained. He had never seen himself looking that way before.

Maggie said, 'John – I can't give you normality. I never could. I thought that was the whole point.'

John hung up, and immediately wished that he hadn't. But he didn't know what to think about his relationship with Maggie now. So much of its excitement had come from their belief that Danny didn't know.

He called the clinic in Santa Cruz. Jamie was 'stable', and that was all that they could tell him.

'No sign of improvement?'

'None, Mr Huntley. I'm sorry.'

'But no sign of getting worse?'

'No, Mr Huntley. No sign of getting worse.'

He called Lorna but when she answered he couldn't speak and he put the phone down. Finally he dialed Broussard Guidance Systems and asked to speak to Sara Lake.

'John . . . we've been all so worried about you. Are you okay?'

'I've been better.'

'Did you find William Cicero?'

'I didn't find him: he found me. But, let me tell you, that guy's a fatal accident just waiting to happen. We've spent the past couple of days just trying to stay alive.'

'Where is he now?' asked Sara, and there was a hint of panic in her voice.

'I don't know, and even if I did know, I think I'd be pretty cautious about telling you.'

'John – you're being paid to find him! It's urgent! The whole MiGR8 program will just fall apart if you can't get him back here!'

'I'm sorry, Ms Lake, there's absolutely no way that William Cicero will come to work for Broussard, and I think I agree with him. He believes you have an informer working for you, and that as soon as he shows himself he's going to be nailed.'

'He's paranoid.'

'Hey, come on, I think *I'd* be paranoid if I had the same guys chasing me that William Cicero has chasing after *him*. He won't help you, Sara, whatever you do. He wants to stay alive.'

'John – you must bring him back. I don't care what it costs. Just name your price, okay? You have to bring him back even if you have to coldcock him and bring him back in handcuffs.'

'Unh-hunh. You asked me to find him and I found him. If I brought him to Broussard Guidance Systems against his will, I'd be committing a major felony; and I can just imagine who'd take the fall for that, and it wouldn't be you and it wouldn't be Gene Broussard.'

'God, John, don't be so damned obstructive!'

'I'm a private investigator, Ms Lake. I have to think about my license.'

'Who cares about your license? I *have* to have Cicero! You just can't imagine what's going to happen to me if I don't!'

John frowned. This didn't sound like a woman begging for her job. This was a woman who was pleading for her life. There was genuine terror in her voice, an unstable upswing, and she was obviously close to tears.

'Listen,' he said, 'I may be able to help you out.'

He told her about Micky and she listened in silence, although he could still hear her panicky breathing. After he had finished, the silence continued.

'Hallo?' he repeated. 'Hallo?'

'Erm, I don't think that's going to be good

'enough,' said Sara. Her voice still sounded as strained as it had before; like a musical saw.

'Sara, believe me, this guy may be young but Cicero's given him all of the technical detail.'

'I'm not convinced.'

'You're not convinced? I'll tell you what – I'll bet you my entire fee that he can do it!'

'That's no bet. If he couldn't do it, you wouldn't be paid anyway.'

'This is getting ridiculous,' said John. 'I've found what you need. I guarantee it. Let me talk to Mr Broussard.'

'*I must find William Cicero!*' Sara shrilled at him. '*Nobody else is any good at all! I must find William Cicero!*'

John hung up. He had been through enough tension for one day. He didn't need Sara Lake screaming at him like a demented soprano. He went back to the table and swallowed a large mouthful of Jack Daniel's, and shuddered.

'Everything okay?' Micky asked him.

John shook his head. 'In my life, Micky, nothing is ever okay. I went out one night with my son in my car and nothing has been okay ever since. It's like one of those fairy stories where you have to choose which fork to take in the forest. Go the wrong way and you're screwed for ever after.'

Micky said, 'Nobody's screwed for ever, John. Look at me. One minute I was washing dishes, the next I was playing the guitar like Ry Cooder and inventing perpetual-motion machines.'

'Oh, yes, that machine,' said John, looking at Micky over the rim of his glass. 'What would happen if it slowed the earth by a millionth of a second every year?'

Micky shrugged. 'Eventually, the earth would be turning so slow that we'd all fall off.'

'I can believe that. In fact, I think I've fallen off already.'

He called Sara a second time. She still sounded edgy and distraught.

'Listen,' he said, 'I'm sorry if I hung up on you, but the reality of the situation is that you can't have William Cicero, whereas you *can* have somebody who can get your missiles flying for you.'

'You'd better bring him in, then,' said Sara, in a voice like a bouquet of frozen thistles.

'He'll need someplace secure to stay. There's still a chance that somebody may be after him.'

'Don't worry . . . I'll arrange all of that. I'll arrange for bodyguards, too.'

'Have you told Mr Broussard about this?'

'Yes, he's delighted.'

'But *you* don't sound delighted.'

'I promised to bring in William Cicero, and I failed. That's not going to look very good on my CV, is it? Especially if this hero of yours can't get our birds to fly. If our best technicians couldn't do it, how on earth is *he* going to do it?'

'He'll do it, Ms Lake.'

Another long silence. Then, 'All right then, John. You'd better bring him in. But just let me ask you one more time: do you really not have any idea where William Cicero is?'

'My lips are sealed, Ms Lake. I'm sorry.'

'I hope you won't be. And don't keep calling me Ms Lake.'

John hung up, but he stayed in the phone booth for a moment, frowning at the receiver. He thought to himself: why was Sara so panicky about finding Dr Lügner in person? If Gene Broussard was happy, why did it matter so much? Unless she was looking for Dr Lügner on somebody else's behalf . . . somebody who didn't particularly care about MiGR8, but who really cared about keeping Dr Lügner quiet.

Roxanne was sitting in the yard outside her mother's house on Holopaw Road, drinking Dr Pepper, when Micky called to say that he was leaving for Cocoa Beach.

Her mother watched her proprietorially, her sundried face shielded by a huge conical hat of lime-green raffia. Her mother had never approved of Micky. Her mother thought that Roxanne had no taste. Her mother was wearing a purple sleeveless T-shirt with Betty Boop embroidered on it, and variegated orange Bermuda shorts, and shocking-pink socks. Beside her was a Busch ashtray crowded with crushed-out cigarette butts and a copy of *Woman's Own*. One of the coverlines asked: ORGASM, ARE YOU NORMAL?

Roxanne said, 'Do you really have to go?'

'I'm sorry . . . but you know what's been going on inside of my head.'

Roxanne nodded, even though he couldn't see her. 'How long're you going to be away?'

'I don't know. Three or four days maybe. I'll miss

you, sweetheart. I'll call you every day.'

Roxanne turned toward the house. Through the open patio door she could see Mrs Wells sitting on the couch with Dauphine on her lap, staring at *Rug Rats* with the sound turned down. Tears were streaming down Mrs Wells' cheeks.

'Those men *are* going to leave us alone now, aren't they?' she asked.

'I think so. They never wanted us. It was Dr Lügner they were after.'

'Supposing they can't find him? Won't they come back?'

Micky hesitated. Then he said, 'Let's just pray that they don't.'

Roxanne put down the phone. Ever since he had taken that drug, Micky sounded so different. His ideas were different, the words he used were different. Even his *voice* was different. It was like listening to a home video of somebody you once used to know very well, but who had moved away, or died. She wondered if he was finding it difficult to go on loving her, especially since she couldn't add up and she didn't understand Mozart and she could only draw stick people.

Her mother came out. 'What's happening? He's leaving you?'

'He's going away for a few days, that's all.'

'You deserve a better boy than that. All dressed in black. You might as well date a mortician.'

'I love him, Mom.'

'And he loves you?'

'He's a little mixed up, that's all. He hasn't been feeling too good.'

They were still bickering when the doorbell chimed 'You've Lost That Loving Feeling', which was a sardonic tribute to Roxanne's father, who had left her mother for a woman who worked in Dunkin' Donuts. ('No taste, your father.')

Roxanne went to the front window and peered through the slats of the vertical cotton blinds. Outside in the street a large black Lincoln was parked, its windshield reflecting the sun. Two men were standing beside it, both of them dressed in dark-gray suits.

She went into the kitchen, picked up the phone, and quickly punched out the number of the Southern Sun Hotel. She heard a ringing tone, but then there was an agonized squeaking sound outside, like somebody wrenching open a metal door, and almost immediately the phone went dead. The men in suits had opened up the junction box and cut her off.

Her mother came in from the yard, still wearing that ridiculous raffia hat. 'Roxanne? Who was that ringing at the door?'

'Nobody, Mom. Forget it.'

'But there's somebody *out* there! I can see them!'

Roxanne turned. There was a green hammered-glass panel in the center of the front door, and through it she could see a wildly distorted man's face, grinning at her triumphantly. She seized hold of her mother's T-shirt and dragged her back toward the patio door. At the same time, she called out, 'Mrs Wells! Mrs Wells! Come with me, quick!'

Mrs Wells didn't seem to understand at first. She

367

wiped her tears with her fingers and said, 'What? What's happening?'

'Mrs Wells, hurry! We have to go!'

Dauphine jumped off her lap; but it was already too late. Roland was standing out in the yard, his suit dusty, his sleeves rolled up, wearing a pair of borrowed dark glasses that were a size too small for him, but which gave him an even more threatening look than usual, as if he were insane as well as reptilian.

He stepped in through the patio door, flexing his shoulders and shooting his cuffs as if this were some kind of sign language which they would all understand.

'Who the two-toned tonkert are you?' demanded Roxanne's mother. 'You can just turn around and walk right out again, as soon as you like.'

'I'm sorry, I can't do that,' said Roland. 'I need to talk to this young lady, on one or two matters of important business.'

Roxanne's mother came up and pushed him in the chest. 'You just clear off, before I call a cop!'

'Mom—' Roxanne warned her.

At first it seemed as if Roland wasn't going to react. He stood very still with his arms by his sides. But then he took off his sunglasses with his left hand and slapped Roxanne's mother; and Roxanne's mother was thrown over sideways so that she hit her shoulder against the wall, and her head against a large blue Mexican plant-pot.

Roxanne seized Roland's sleeve, but immediately he swung her around and twisted her arm behind her back. Roxanne's mother was trying to lift herself up. She had an angry red bruise on her left temple and her lip was bleeding. Roland pointed his finger at her as if it were a gun and said, 'You stay where you are, Granma.' Then he pointed his finger at Mrs Wells and said, 'The same goes for you, too, Mammy.'

Roxanne tried to wrench herself free. Roland simply crushed her fingers in his left hand until she yelped in pain. 'Come on, sweet thing. Don't make this difficult. We're not going to hurt you. We're going to take you for a little trip, that's all.'

'You let her go!' Roxanne's mother blurted at him, climbing to her feet. 'You let her go or I'm calling the police!'

Roland gave her a stretched, humorless grin. 'If I even *imagine* that I hear a siren, Granma, this little girl won't be coming back home. Not tonight, not tomorrow night. Not ever.'

'Mom,' Roxanne begged her. 'Do like he says. Please.'

Roland said nothing more, but forced Roxanne out of the patio door, into the yard. Then he frog-marched her out into the street. One of his dark-suited colleagues opened the Lincoln's door, and Roxanne was pushed into its frigid, leathery-black interior.

'You and your friends have been causing me pain,' said Roland, climbing in beside her. 'Now we're going to see what we can do to redress the balance, so to speak. An eye for an eye, a pain for a pain. You know where that William Cicero's at?'

Roxanne shook her head. Roland nudged his thigh a little closer and breathed garlic and Big Red

chewing gum all over her. 'If you know where that
William Cicero's at, we could all save ourselves a
whole lot of time and expense. Not to mention
physical discomfort. Have you ever suffered physical discomfort? I was in the Marines, I suffered
physical discomfort. One day, during an exercise, I
jumped off a 30-foot wall into a whole tangle of
razor-wire, and there I was, trapped, and suffering
considerable physical discomfort. I quit the
Marines after that. I decided that if there was going
to be any physical discomfort being meted out in
this world, I wasn't going to do the suffering, I was
going to do the meting.'

'Where are you taking me?' asked Roxanne, as
the Lincoln took the tight turn northward up Route
15 toward Narcoossee.

'If you can tell me where William Cicero is at,
sweet thing, no place at all.'

'I can't. He just went off. He didn't say where he
was going. He said we would never see him again,
ever.'

'You know that I have to find that man at any
price.'

'You've killed people!' retorted Roxanne, and
her voice was clogged up with tears. 'You've
murdered our friend! What did you have to do that
for?'

'I told you. I have to find William Cicero.
Nothing else matters. Besides, none of this was my
fault. Nobody would have gotten hurt if William
Cicero had given himself up.'

'And what would you have done to him?
Murdered him too?'

'What do you care?'

Roxanne stared at Roland in utter horror. She had met brutal men before; and crude men; and men who enjoyed causing distress. But she had never met a man like Roland, to whom other people's suffering was a matter of complete indifference. She shuddered, and it wasn't the Lincoln's air conditioning that caused it.

The bus had just passed Palm Bay on its 201-mile journey southward on Route 1, heading for Miami. It was almost empty, except for a small party of noisy black children on their way to Fort Pierce, four students who were playing poker, and an elderly couple who sat right at the very back and kept themselves to themselves.

The man was wearing a crumpled off-white suit and a dented white hat. The woman was dressed in lilac. There was a small traveling-bag on the floor beneath the woman's feet.

'I hope you're not going to regret this,' the man remarked.

The woman laid her hand on his sleeve. 'My stars tell me that this is my destiny. This is what I was born for.'

'I don't know how you can simply up and leave everything behind. Your friends, your sister, your store.'

'You've done it.'

Dr Lügner gave her a soft, wry snort. 'I was forced to do it. I loved that house. All of my books were there, all of my paintings, all of my research materials. I'm too old to start again.'

'I don't think you're ever too old to start again,' said Constance. 'Ever since John appeared in my life, I've asked myself again and again if I was making a fool of myself. But I think it was fate that brought John into my doorway. Fate said, "You've been living a safe, boring existence for the past forty years, here's a chance to do something dangerous. Here's a chance to *live*."'

'Live? Jesus, you nearly died.'

'That's the whole point. You don't know what it's like to be alive until you face the real risk of death.'

'Don't you think that death is going to come soon enough, in any case?'

'Hey!' she protested. 'I'm not *that* old!'

'I'm sorry,' he said, and went back to looking out of the window.

After a while, Constance said, 'You don't *mind* me coming along with you, do you?'

He looked at her and shook his head. 'I enjoy your company. You're clever, and you make me laugh. Not only that, you're a wonderful part of my disguise. The OGRE people are going to be looking for a single senior male in a rental car; not a retired couple on their way to Miami by bus.'

'May I ask you something?' said Constance. 'May I ask you what your real name is? I mean, your *real* real name?'

Dr Lügner was silent for a while. Then he said, 'I think I've probably forgotten it.'

'But if we're going to be spending so much time together, it would be nice to know who I'm spending so much time with. I can't keep on calling you Dr Lügner or William Cicero or Charles Babson, can I?'

'Well, we're supposed to be married, so you could call me "darling", or "you stupid old goat".'

She reached out and took hold of his hand. She looked into his eyes and suddenly realized that nobody could have held him like this for a long, long time. No words passed between them, but Dr Lügner's eyes moistened and he had to swallow. Constance could only guess how isolated his life must have been.

'My name's . . .' he began, and then he paused.

'Rumpelstiltskin?' she teased him.

He shook his head. This was so painful for him that he couldn't even raise a smile.

'My name's . . .' he began again; and then he told her.

14

We have within our grasp the basic technologies to build machines that might just be capable of some form of free thinking. What is lacking is a sensory system that will match them into our, and other, worlds – Peter Cochrane, Head of Advanced Technology at British Telecom

Sara was standing beside the reception desk when the automatic doors of Broussard Guidance Systems opened with a sharp *pifffff*! and John and Micky came through them like Wyatt Earp and Doc Holliday on their way to the OK Corral. They walked toward her, with Micky's heels clicking on the shiny marble floor. 'Well, John, welcome back!' she said, in a clear, bold tone.

'Hello, Ms Lake,' he replied. She might have sounded upbeat and bold but his years in commercial espionage told him how agitated she was. She was wearing a gray silk blouse that was fastened at the neck with a single pearl brooch, under a plain black coat. Her skirt was black, too, but it was very, very short, worn with glossy black pantyhose.

Sara said, 'You must be Micky Frasier,' and held

out her hand. 'Welcome to Broussard. It seems like you might be able to do us a considerable service.'

'That's company-speak for "pull our rear ends out of the campfire",' John remarked.

'Still no indication where Cicero might be, I suppose?' said Sara, as they walked toward the elevators.

John shook his head.

Gene Broussard was waiting for them in his office when they arrived, sitting at the far end of his huge glass conference table so that his upper body was reflected in it, turning him into a playing-card figure, one head up and one head down. He was wearing a blue shirt with large pointed lapels and a linen suit in firetruck red.

He didn't get up as Sara ushered them into his presence. He sat staring at Micky with undisguised disappointment.

'Micky Frasier,' said Sara. 'He just arrived from St Cloud.'

Gene said, '*You're* William Cicero's protégé?'

'Not exactly his protégé, sir,' said Micky. 'I mean, the way we got together, it was kind of like accidental. But he did teach me how to hook up the MiGR8 guidance system.'

He shrugged and shuffled his feet. John had warned him not to show off too much of his newly acquired intellect; and not to mention Synaptine – not until the missile test was completed, anyhow. If the MiGR8 guidance system really worked, then Gene Broussard would be desperate to know *how* it worked. And when they told him, he would be even more desperate to lay his hands on a regular supply of Synaptine. If John and Micky could act as go-betweens for Broussard and Dr Lügner, they had a fair chance of making millions of dollars of commission. He could give up industrial espionage for life, and take Maggie away with him to someplace like Maui. Even Mill Valley would do.

'So . . . what were you doing before you met William Cicero?' Gene asked Micky.

Micky pulled a face. 'I was trying to form a rock band, but during the day I was depastarizing.'

'Depastarizing? What's that?'

'Well, like, washing dishes at this Italian restaurant. Depastarizing, scraping off the pasta.'

'Is this a joke?' Gene demanded.

'No, Mr Broussard, it's not a joke,' said John, stepping forward. 'Micky was doing some menial work when he met up with William Cicero, but he still had a brain that was capable of understanding MiGR8. You can call it a fluke of nature, if you like. But William Cicero recognized Micky's abilities, and decided that Micky was capable of connecting up your guidance system, and here he is.'

Gene stood up for the first time and walked around the table. He approached Micky and stared at him face to face, pouting like Mussolini. 'You don't *look* like a guidance technologist.'

Micky said, 'Phew.'

'So what do you mean, "phew"?'

'You think I *want* to look like a guidance technologist? I'm trying to look like a rock singer. Besides, you don't need a guidance technologist to connect up MiGR8. That's been your problem all along. MiGR8 isn't the same as any other system.'

376

'Meaning what?'

'Meaning that it works differently from any other guidance system ever invented. It's much more *organic*, you know? It *thinks* where it's going.'

'So, tell me,' said Gene, 'how does it actually work?'

Micky shook his head, just as John had told him to. 'I'm sorry, Mr Broussard. I can come here and I can connect up your MiGR8 system, so that your missile can be tested on schedule. But just at the moment, that's all I'm going to do.'

Gene walked around and around. He stood by the window staring out at A1A and the gray-blue Atlantic beyond. 'I can't believe this situation. I have a billion-dollar cruise-missile guidance system, and the only person who can make it work is a dishwasher who wants to be a rock star. Tell me, Sara, what happens if I close my eyes and say "there's no place like home"?'

'Maybe Micky should talk to our technicians,' Sara suggested. 'They could soon find out if he can really do what he says he can do.'

'I can do it,' said Micky. He tapped his forehead. 'It's all in here. Geomagnetic guidance responses, human recognition targeting. If the missile's ready and the guidance systems are ready for installation, I can have it connected up in 48 hours. Ready for firing by Wednesday.'

Gene shook his head and grinned and kept on walking around. 'I don't believe this, you know? I just don't believe it. This is a scam, right, so that John can collect his $300,000 and leave us in the shit? No, it isn't. It can't be a scam. If this was a scam, you wouldn't bring me a guy who looked like he fell off the back of a Fat Boy. Or maybe you would. Maybe it's a double scam. Maybe you think it's so unbelievable that I have to believe it.'

John said, 'This isn't like you, Mr Broussard. What about that secretary of yours, Velma, the one you rescued from the strip club? She may have looked like a tramp, but she hasn't got a tramp's brain, does she? If *she* had it in her, who's to say that Micky hasn't, too? You're judging him by his appearance, aren't you? Why don't you ask him a question – go on, any question, he can answer it.'

Gene came back to Micky and stared right into his face, 'A question? *Any* question?'

'Sure,' said John. 'Math, science, general knowledge, whatever.'

'No, no. He wants to work on our guidance systems. I want to know what he knows about our guidance systems. Night Hawk, for instance. What do you know about Night Hawk?'

Micky didn't even hesitate. 'Night Hawk can guide missiles in complete darkness, or fog, or the densest of smoke. It was first used in combat in Desert Storm, where it was used to knock out Iraqi armor through sandstorms and oil fires.'

'Tell me more,' said Gene, circling the table.

'You developed Night Hawk for the Hughes AGM-65 Maverick, which is a rocket missile powered by a Thiokol TX-481 solid-fuel motor. Night Hawk is an imaging infrared system – IIR – matched on the launch aircraft with forward-looking infrared – FLIR. It has a correlator which automatically slaves the missile to the target. It was

378

tested on 262 tank-size targets, and achieved a strike success rate of 96.2 percent.'

Gene looked at John, and then at Sara. Neither of them were smiling.

'This *isn't* a scam, is it?' he said. 'It's weird, but it isn't a scam.'

'You want me to tell you about your Talon system?' asked Micky. 'That's a mid-course beam rider with the terminal stage directed by CW interferometer semi-active homing. Or how about your EM passive homing system?'

'Please – I think that's enough,' Gene told him.

John held out his hand, palm upward. Gene stared down at it, and then said, 'What?'

'I believe I did what you hired me to do.'

'You want paying now? When that missile flies, *then* you'll get paid.'

'Unh-hunh. No pay, no fly.'

'I hired you to bring me William Cicero. That was our agreement. You want to sue me? You wouldn't stand a chance in court.'

'All the same. If I don't get paid, Micky won't plug in that guidance system for you. And let's be realistic here, Mr Broussard. You stand to lose a whole lot more than I do.'

Gene took a deep breath. He stalked up to one of his Franz Kline paintings, and ground his teeth at it, thinking. 'All right, I'll tell you what I'll do. I'll pay you $150,000 now, out of goodwill. The rest you get the second that missile hits its target. In fact, if it hits its target dead-on, I'll give you a $200,000 bonus.' He turned to Micky. 'Think you can do that, Micky? Hit that target dead-on?'

'Sure of it,' grinned Micky.

Gene stared at him for a long time. It was obvious by the expression on his face that he wanted to believe that Micky could get MiGR8 up and running; but it was equally obvious that he was finding it very, very difficult. But at last he said, 'All right, I'm willing to give you a try. We'll have to get you a security clearance in double-quick time, but I think I can swing it. I'll call Major-General Broadmore at USAF Tactical Air Command. I'll tell him we'll be ready to test MiGR8 by the end of next week.'

He paused for a moment. Then he came up to John and pointed a finger steadily at his nose. 'I'm only going along with this, John, because you came so highly recommended. But if your friend Micky here turns out to be a fraud; or if I find out that you've been trying to turn me over; then, believe me, you'll be sorry that you weren't sitting at that table with Kevin and Jesus, just to get it over.'

John said, 'Sure.' Then he turned to Sara and said, 'How about dinner tonight? You can pay. I think you owe me one.'

Gene arranged for them to stay at a private house close to Lake Poinsett. It was a huge, cream-painted mansion with a pillared portico and a fine red-tiled roof, deeply secluded in a grove of mature oaks. It could only be reached from the main highway by its own curving driveway, and electrically operated gates kept out accidental trespassers.

Two Broussard security men were posted to keep a 24-hour watch on the house, and a further two

380

were assigned to protecting Micky. They were much like Kevin and Jesus: ex-cops and former MPs. They were professional but they were also extremely bored, and so they over-dramatized every move they made, checking each corner as if they were making a drugs raid, dodging from doorway to doorway, and (much to Micky's irritation) forcing his head down and bundling him into the back of their car as if he had narrowly escaped an attempted assassination. And this wasn't just once: this was every time they went out.

John was given a large bedroom with a balcony overlooking the gardens, and the lake beyond. He opened the French windows and stepped outside for a while. The surface of the lake was ruffled by the Atlantic breeze, with pelicans bobbing on it like little paper boats. The gardens were overflowing with red and purple flowers. This was the way that John had always wanted to live. Wealthy, comfortable, and quiet.

He stepped back into his room. The walls were painted a restful shade of dove-gray, and there was a large oak four-poster bed, with a hand-embroidered quilt. He sat on the end of the bed, and then fell backward, so that he was staring at the ceiling.

He lay there for almost a half-hour, and began to doze. He had a vivid dream about Jamie. He could hear Jamie crying, but he couldn't open the door to see what he wanted. God, Jamie hadn't cried since the night he was shot! John had to get in to help him, but the door must have been deliberately locked and bolted, so that he couldn't. He knocked and knocked, but nobody answered, and Jamie went on crying as if he were the most miserable child on the planet.

It was then that somebody touched his cheek, and he jumped awake. He looked up to see Sara bending over him. Her eyes were wide and glassy, like somebody who has just witnessed a minor road accident. 'Are you all right?' she asked him. 'I did knock, but you didn't answer.'

He propped himself up on one elbow. He was soaked in sweat and his mouth felt like the inside of somebody's shoe. 'I'm fine. Tired I guess. Sorry. What time is it?'

'A quarter of six. I would've let you sleep but something's come up.'

'Believe me, whenever I want to sleep, something always does.'

'We've had a telephone call,' said Sara. 'It really concerns Micky, but I thought that I'd better speak to you first. I don't want to upset him if it's all a hoax.'

John stood up, and tugged his shirt away from his back. He walked out to the balcony, and held onto the rail, letting the early-evening breeze cool him off. Sara came up behind him. The pelicans had flown away now, and the lake was the color of sunset, and memories, and boysenberry jelly. Sara laid a hand on his shoulder, then lifted it away again, because he was so chilled and sweaty.

'What?' he asked her. She seemed so twitchy, so agitated.

'Does Micky have a girlfriend called Roxanne?'

'Yes,' said John. He turned around. 'Why? Nothing's happened to her, has it?'

'I'm sorry, John. We've had a call from some-body who wants to know where William Cicero has gone to. They say that they've kidnapped this girl Roxanne, and they won't release her till we tell them.'

'For Christ's sake. Did they say who they were?'

Sara shook her head. 'All they said was, they'll contact us tomorrow, at 7.30 a.m. If we don't tell them where William Cicero is, we'll never find out where Roxanne is, either.'

'Was it a man? Yes? What did he sound like?'

'I don't know. Gruff.'

'Where did he call you?'

'At the office, just after five. I came here right away.'

'How did he know that we were here?'

'He didn't say. Guesswork, I suppose. He called the main switchboard and asked to speak to Micky Frasier.'

'How do you know that it isn't a bluff? Maybe they haven't kidnapped Roxanne at all?'

'Well, that's why I came to you. I had no way of checking it out. But I must say that he *sounded* serious.'

John said, 'This is crazy. This is really crazy. Micky doesn't know where William Cicero has disappeared to; and neither do I.'

'You're still absolutely sure about that?'

'Of course I'm sure. And why are you still so worried about finding William Cicero, anyway? Micky can put MiGR8 together with no trouble at all. *Your* problems are over.'

And then he knew that he was right about Sara.

He pressed his hand over his mouth and stared at her without saying anything at all, while she looked back at him with increasing bewilderment.

'What's wrong?' she wanted to know. 'What are you looking at me like that for?'

Dr Lügner had warned him: *I'm sure there's an informer, somewhere in Broussard Guidance Systems. If I go back to Broussard, I'll be dead before I open my lunchbox.*

Maybe the mystery kidnapper had been guessing, but who had known *for sure* that he and Micky were coming back to Broussard this afternoon? Gene, and Sara, and that was all. The security staff hadn't been briefed until very much later.

Who had known that he was supposed to be meeting Kevin and Jesus at the Blue Pelican restaurant? Kevin, and Jesus, and Sara. And who had known what car he was driving, when those men in suits had identified him in the parking lot, and chased him all the way down the beach to the pier? Sara, and Sara's personal assistant, who had rented the car.

And who was still nagging him to know where Dr Lügner had disappeared to – with the threat of hurting Roxanne?

All right, the evidence wasn't completely conclusive. It could have been almost anybody. A secretary, a switchboard operator, one of Broussard's security division. It could have been one of those favorite perpetrators of sabotage and industrial disloyalty, a 'disgruntled employee'. But John had a feeling about Sara. She was panicking, and panic had its own distinctive smell, like ozone after a lightning strike, or the barrel of a recently fired Magnum, or a woman on heat. It suddenly made sense of Sara's discomfiture. She should have been delighted and relieved when John came up with a substitute who could fix up Broussard's guidance system. Instead, she was quivering with fright.

Launching the MiGR8 missile wasn't her first priority at all. Her first priority was finding Dr Lügner. A different agenda altogether.

He opened his traveling-bag and took out a clean shirt. Then he stripped to the waist. His body was lightly tanned, muscular, but slightly too bony for his height. He would have tempted any woman to feed him on steaks and chocolate cake for a month, to build him up.

'You want to know what's wrong?' he asked her. 'You – that's what's wrong.'

'I don't understand what you mean. We had a call . . . what does that have to do with me?'

'You had a call, for sure. But it wasn't anonymous. You knew exactly who it was.'

'What are you insinuating? Are you trying to suggest that *I*—'

'Yes, Sara, you. Who else could it be? And look at you now. You've got what you wanted – or at least you've got what you were *supposed* to have wanted – and you're hopping around like a bitch on cinders.'

'I don't know what the hell you're talking about!' Sara protested.

'William Cicero, that's what I'm talking about.

385

Or Dr Lügner. Or any one of all those names he uses. You want him, don't you? But you don't want him for Broussard Guidance Systems. You don't give a single-barreled shit for Broussard Guidance Systems. The only reason you started working for Gene Broussard was because his security people were looking for Dr Lügner – they were really *desperate* for Dr Lügner, otherwise Broussard Guidance Systems looked like going down the tubes. But you don't want Broussard finding him, do you? Or anybody else for that matter. You want him dead.'

'This is insanity,' said Sara, but she kept on pacing around the room. John was surprised how quickly she had revealed how terrified she was, how hysterical she was. She took out a cigarette and lit it with jumbling hands.

'Has Roxanne really been kidnapped?' John demanded.

'Yes,' she said, blowing out smoke.

'So who's taken her? Come on, Sara – who is it?'

'*This is insanity!* You're questioning me like *I* did it – like it's *my* fault! I just had to do what I was told!'

John was calmly unfastening the buttons on his clean shirt. 'Did you ever hear of something called OGRE, Ms Lake? And I'm not talking about Grimms' fairy tales here.'

Sara sat down on the edge of the bed. Her face was as gray as the walls. 'I can't take pushing in two directions, Mr Huntley.'

'Then you know about OGRE?'

'I've heard about it. Not very much, so there's

no point in giving me the third degree.'

'Dr Lügner believes that it's OGRE that's trying to kill him. They killed Kevin and Jesus, didn't they, and it was only by sheer luck that they didn't kill me, too. I think you set that up.'

Sara glanced at John and flinched as if he had struck her. 'After I first came to see you in San Francisco, I didn't want you to get involved in this at all. I tried to persuade Gene that he didn't really need you. But Gene was adamant. He wanted the best. There was nothing I could do.'

At last she'd admitted it. John leaned over her and said, in a deep, breathy voice, 'Like I said, I don't really know why those OGRE people want to kill Dr Lügner so bad. Maybe you do. But I can tell you one thing. I'm going to find out. And I'm going to track down whoever it is who's responsible, and for my own satisfaction I'm going to make sure that they're arraigned for killing Kevin and Jesus and a guy called Guido and a guy called Mario and a young guy called Mingus. And I'm going to make sure that they're tried. And I'm going to make sure that they're punished.'

Sara said, 'You'd be wiser – very much wiser – if you walked away.'

'Wisdom was never my strong suit. You remember what Benjamin Franklin said, "Some are weather-wise, and some are otherwise." I've always been otherwise.'

'John . . . they're absolutely determined to see William Cicero dead. Why do you think they went to all the trouble of arranging for me to work for Broussard? It wasn't easy, either. If Gene wasn't so

387

soft on rescuing strippers and hookers and other fallen women, I probably wouldn't have stood a chance.'

'*You* were a stripper?'

'No, and I wasn't a hooker, either. Not what *you'd* call a hooker, anyhow. Let's just say that I was lost and somebody found me, and gave me one last chance.'

'Somebody from OGRE? Why would they want to do that?'

'It wasn't "somebody" from OGRE . . . it was OGRE's director, Titan Blight.'

'Titan Blight? Well, *that* name rings a bell.'

'It should do. He's been tub-thumping about world government for decades. A couple of years back he was *Time* magazine's Man of the Year.'

'Yes,' said John. 'I read about him. He's financing some new computer system, isn't he?'

'That's right. Creative Software. He's already invested $280 million of his own money.'

'And Titan Blight is the one who wants William Cicero dead?'

Sara lowered her head and didn't answer, so John tipped her chin up with his finger and stared directly into her colorless eyes. 'He's the one who's holding Roxanne?'

'Yes,' she whispered.

'In that case, I think it's time we called the police, don't you?'

'No!' she told him. 'If Titan even *thinks* that you've called the police, she'll vanish, I promise you, and you won't ever see her again.'

'Don't tell me he's *that* influential.'

'Influential? He's the eleventh wealthiest man in Massachusetts, and he's practically God. If you have any idea where William Cicero is, you really ought to tell me. For Roxanne's sake, even if it's not for *my* sake.'

'How many times do I have to repeat myself? I simply don't know; and neither does Micky. Besides, even if I *did* know, what kind of moral dilemma would that put me in? I don't tell you, and Roxanne dies. I do tell you, and Dr Lügner dies. You really expect me to make a decision like that, and live with myself for the rest of my life?'

'I don't know,' said Sara. 'But if I were you, I'd try to find out where he is first, and think about the moral dilemma later.'

John stepped away from her. He really didn't know what to think of her now. She was still just as sexual, and she attracted him just as much. It was a shock to hear her admit that she had tried to have him killed, but in a perverse way that made her all the more interesting. He had once known a very beautiful woman who had been obsessed with a convicted multiple murderer, and strangely, he could almost understand the allure.

'What are you going to do now?' John asked her.

'I don't know. If William Cicero definitely isn't coming back to Broussard, then I'll probably be sent to look for him someplace else. Or maybe I won't. Titan isn't what you might call forgiving.'

'Does William Cicero *have* something on Titan Blight? I mean, does he know something about Titan Blight that Titan Blight wants to keep quiet?'

'If he does, then Titan's never discussed it. But

then he never discusses anything with me, except what he wants me to do for him.'

John said, 'Where do you think Roxanne is likely to be?'

'I *know* where she is. She's up at Twisted River. That's Titan's residence just outside of Boston. But it's no use going there. He has the tightest security you ever saw. Well, he has six Picassos, for beginners.'

'How come he's so rich?'

'Oh, he wasn't *born* rich. But after World War Two, he was sent out by the government to confiscate scientific and engineering patents from Germany and Japan. Most of the patents were handed over to Washington, like they were supposed to be. But dozens of *very* profitable patents kind of went astray. You've heard of Feisler Aspirin?'

'That's *his*? Jesus.'

'So is Nutrinol, and Slumberex. He brought back half of the Nazi pharmaceutical industry. Not to mention a whole clutch of patents for rocket fuel and rubber substitutes. By 1952 he was a multimillionaire. God alone knows what he's worth today.'

'Listen,' said John. 'I think you're right about finding William Cicero first. But there's no chance that I can do it before noon tomorrow. Do you think that you can convince Titan Blight to keep Roxanne safe for a few days longer?'

Sara said, 'I don't know. I could try, if you really believe that you can find him.'

'I found Dieter Waxman, remember?'

'What about your moral dilemma?'

'Just like you suggested, I'll think about that later.'

'Do you think you can trust me?'

'Of course I don't trust you. But I think that I can find William Cicero and I don't think that you or Titan Blight or any of your men in suits have a hope in hell. And so long as you need him so desperately, I don't have to worry about trusting you or not, do I?'

Sara stood up and tugged down the hem of her skirt. 'All right, then. I'll call Titan and see what he says.'

'Tell him one thing else. If he even *breathes* on Roxanne, I'll be coming after him, security or no security, and I'm going to break every one of those six Picassos over his head.'

Micky was asleep when John came into his room, sprawled across his bed as if he had fallen onto it from 50,000 feet. His mouth was wide open and he was still wearing his boots. John sat down beside him and loudly cleared his throat. The late-afternoon sunshine slanted across the wall, illuminating an antique dresser in dark bird's-eye maple, and the corner of a gilt-framed oil painting, *Lake Okechobee in High Summer*.

'Micky?' said John, and shook his shoulder. 'Micky?' he repeated, and shook him again.

Eventually Micky opened his eyes. 'Oh . . . it's you. I was dreaming.'

'Listen, I'm sorry to wake you, but I have to tell you something serious.'

'Something serious? That sounds serious.'

'It's Roxanne. It seems like those guys in suits have taken her away . . . kidnapped her.'

Micky immediately sat up. 'They did *what*? She isn't hurt, is she?'

'Not so far as I know. But they want to know where Dr Lügner's at; and they're not going to let her go until they do.'

Micky swung his legs off the side of the bed. 'That's it! They can shove their missiles where the sun don't shine! I'm not having any more to do with this! I'm the only person who can connect up MiGR8; and there's no way in the world that I'm going to do anything – not until Roxanne goes free!'

John said, 'Micky, calm down. This is nothing to do with Broussard.'

As briefly as he could, he told Micky about his conversation with Sara; and all about Titan Blight; and OGRE.

'If I can persuade Titan Blight to keep Roxanne safe until I've found Dr Lügner, then we have a much better chance.'

'What about the cops?'

'Too risky. From what Sara says, the only law that Titan Blight obeys is Titan Blight. The guy's a billionaire. He has six Picassos.'

'I don't care if he has six zits on his ass. I want Roxanne back.'

'You'll have her back, I promise.'

'How can you promise that, John? You'll have to find Dr Lügner first, and how the hell are you going to do that? He could be in fucking Tibet by now.'

'I'll find him, Micky, I swear to God. I'll get your Roxanne back.'

'So what if you find Dr Lügner? What are you going to do then? Hand him over so that this Titan Blight character can blow his head off?'

'Right now I don't exactly know *what* I'm going to do. But the number one priority is to find out what kind of game we're playing in. We won't have any leverage with Titan Blight until we know why he's so goddamned anxious to have Dr Lügner dead.'

'How can that give us any leverage? Dr Lügner knows what it is, but *he* doesn't seem to have any leverage. I mean, if Titan Blight is involved in some kind of terrible scandal, why hasn't Dr Lügner ever gone to the media with it? He wouldn't even tell *us* what it was all about, would he?'

'Well, my hunch is that Dr Lügner's never gone to the media about it for one reason and one reason only.'

'Because *he's* involved, too?'

'Exactly.'

Micky was so agitated that he kept sitting down and standing up again and thumping the dresser with his fist. 'If I could get hold of those bastards – I tell you, John, if I could just get hold of those bastards – I can do kung fu now, do you know that? I'd break every bone in their fucking bodies. Right down to their auditory ossicles.' He paused, and explained, 'The bones in their ears, the bastards.'

John said, 'There's nothing that you can do right now. You're going to have to leave this to me. Just carry on working on that missile and try to keep your hopes up.'

'What if Dr Lügner's *really* gone to Tibet?'

John shook his head. 'I don't think so. Come on, you're the one with the IQ. Think about it. He took all kinds of risks to teach you how to activate this missile, which means that he still has a very strong interest in how it's going to fire. My hunch is that he hasn't gone very far away, not yet.'

'I hope not. God, I hope not, for Roxanne's sake.'

John smiled, and gripped Micky's shoulder. 'Come on,' he encouraged him. 'I've got a hunch this is going to work out okay.'

'You've got more hunches than Quasimodo,' said Micky. He was trying to smile but he had tears in his eyes.

Roland was waiting for Sara in the bar of the Cocoa Beach Corinthian, looking out over the beach and sucking with drawn-in cheeks at a planter's punch with more greenery than Dominica.

He must have heard Sara's heels rapping on the floor but he didn't turn around. She perched herself on the edge of the green-painted basketwork chair opposite him and crossed her legs.

'Well?' he asked her.

'I could use a drink.'

Roland popped his fingers but the barman ignored him. He popped them again. In the end he had to get up, walk over to the bar and order the drink himself. He came back looking even more displeased. 'Schmuck,' he growled. 'They should turn this whole fucking hotel into a garage.'

Sara said, 'I've talked to John Huntley and Micky Frasier, together and separately. I'm 100 percent convinced that they don't know where William Cicero has gone to.'

'That's a disappointment. Well, it will be for young Roxanne. Pretty girl. Nice gazongas. Pity.'

'John Huntley doesn't want her hurt.'

'Who said anything about hurting her? She won't feel a thing.'

'Don't you understand? The point is, John Huntley has a real talent for locating missing persons who don't want to be located. He's prepared to bring us William Cicero, so long as we stay off his back, and so long as Roxanne stays alive. Listen – I know that Titan specifically ordered that you should find William Cicero before Roxanne is released; and that you should sanction him first. I know that he specifically ordered that nobody should have the chance even to talk to him before he was dealt with. But you haven't had much luck in finding him, have you? And if you can't find him, you can't deal with him, can you?'

Roland's mouth tightened but he managed to control himself. He picked up his planter's punch and viciously sucked it until the ice turned transparent. He had a fleeting fantasy of taking out the .44 Magnum that was holstered under his left armpit and blowing Sara's head off. Under different circumstances, he would have done. The thought of that classy, well-dressed, provocative body with no head on it quite appealed to him. Pipestem neck, blood pumping everywhere. But

Mr Blight liked her, more than she realized; and Roland didn't dare to touch her, any more than he dared to scratch his initials on the side of Mr Blight's Ferrari. Mr Blight never *drove* his Ferrari, but that wasn't the point.

'For fucksake I can find William Cicero,' he said. 'I was born with the nose.'

'Roland, you're good at what you do, and Titan knows that you're good at what you do. But John Huntley isn't just good. He's the very best.'

'Unh-hunh,' said Roland. 'Something's wrong here. First of all you wanted him sanctioned. Now you're all sweetness and light.'

'Nothing's wrong, Roland, it's a question of practicalities.'

Roland looked out at the beach. The sea was unnaturally bright. Lightning flickered, and there was tension in the air.

'How long does he want?' Roland asked, at last. Without sunglasses, his eyes looked piggy and small, and not at all threatening.

'Three days, max. Come on, Roland, it makes sense. Once he's located William Cicero, you can off the both of them, and take all the credit. Who's to know?'

'You, for one.'

'Don't be funny. You know my situation.'

'Well, I guess. And you know me. You double-cross me once, you never do it again.'

A waitress in an emerald-satin basque and fishnet pantyhose brought Sara a vodka-tonic with a slice of lime. The waitress wore teetering yellow high-heels and a ruffled yellow hat that was heaped with plastic bananas, plastic cherries, plastic grapes and plastic kumquats.

'Thank you,' said Sara.

'You're welcome,' said the waitress, and stood by their table, waiting.

'What?' said Roland, after almost a minute had passed by, and the waitress still hadn't left.

'*The waitress*,' hissed Sara. '*Give her a gratuity.*'

Roland looked the waitress up and down. 'Waitress?' he said, loudly. 'I thought you were dessert.'

Nonetheless, Roland called her at Broussard Guidance Systems an hour and a half later and said that Titan had agreed to extend his deadline for Roxanne's disappearance by three days, starting the following morning. Roland tried to sound disgruntled, but Sara could tell that he was relieved. He didn't want to incur Titan's wrath any more than she did, and if he could call Titan by Friday and tell him that William Cicero was dead, his life would be bonuses and shiny new Buicks.

Sara sat back in her white leather armchair and stared at her reflection in the window. Outside, the traffic crawled along A1A like beads on an abacus. Beyond the traffic was the beach, and then the sea, and she felt more than ever as if she were sitting on the very shoreline of human existence.

15

No passion so effectually robs the mind of all its powers of acting and reasoning as fear – Edmund Burke

The sky was gray when John flew into Minneapolis-St Paul airport the following afternoon, but there was enough watery sunshine to reflect from the IDS Building and the Norwest tower, and there were enough thermals rising from Long Meadow Lake to give the 737 an unpleasant jolting as it came in to land.

He walked out of the airport as quickly as he could, and hailed a taxi. The taxi driver steered with the flat of his right hand and quietly cursed everybody who got in his way.

'Why do I have the feeling that this job is getting on your nerves?' John asked him.

The taxi driver's eyes hovered suspiciously in the rearview mirror. 'It's sedentary, that's the problem. It's sedentary and it's stressful. It's bad for your health.'

'What's to stop you from taking some exercise?'

'I did. I went jogging last weekend but my body tried to kill me.'

The taxi driver took him along Hiawatha Avenue and then turned right toward the University of Minnesota. He parked beside a bland concrete laboratory block. Inside the neurobiology building, on the third story, John was taken by a lugubrious research assistant to a small corner office with a view of the gray, misty Mississippi. Dr Charles Bron was sitting at one of the neatest, most ordered desks that John had ever seen. His clock was *here*; his laptop was *here*; his notepad was exactly *here*; and *here* was a silver-framed photograph of a startlingly ugly baby. It could have taken the part of a Ferengi in *Deep Space Nine*, without even wearing prosthetic ears.

Dr Bron was 55 years old, with expensive rimless eyeglasses, an obsessively precise mustache, and a bald, tanned head that had the appearance of an antique copper kettle, well polished and slightly dented. He wore a white lab coat and blue pinstripe shirt, and a dark blue necktie with the crest of the American Neurological Institute.

'Mr Huntley? Won't you – ?' he said, and indicated the chair on the other side of his desk.

John sat down and looked around the office. There were shelves stacked with box files, and rows of identically bound books with titles like *Neural Inhibition* and *The Physiology of Commissural Fibers* – although, oddly, there was a copy of *Lolita* there, too.

John said, 'This is pretty much of a long shot, but

I've been hired by an electronics corporation in Florida to look for a certain neurochemist. He's, uh, gone missing, as it were.'

'Well, well. That sounds mysterious. What's his name, this certain neurochemist?'

'That's the difficult part. He's very eccentric – paranoid, even – and he goes under dozens of assumed names. William Cicero . . . Charles Babson . . . no? Dr Lügner? No? How about Walter Cera?'

'Sorry, none of those names mean anything to me. Is there any reason why they should?'

'All I know is that he worked with your father for a while, in the mid-1950s; and that he and your father carried out a series of experiments involving chemicals which were supposed to enhance your brain-power.'

Dr Bron sat back again, shaking his head. 'My father worked with *hundreds* of different people. They came from all over – France, Spain, Japan – even Russia. He was probably the world's leading expert on the chemistry of the human brain.'

'Did you meet any of these people?'

'Oh, for sure. Dad worked very long hours. But he used to bring some pretty interesting people back to the house. They'd stay weekends mostly, because Dad liked to talk and talk and talk, and a dinner party never lasted long enough.'

'You don't remember one guy in particular? Very thin, short-cropped hair, about 5 feet 6 inches tall.'

'I'm sorry. In those days, most research chemists used to look like that.'

John reached into his inside pocket and

produced a clear, striking drawing of Dr Lügner. It had been Micky's inspiration: he had speed-read two books on cosmetic surgery and maxillary reconstruction; and then he had drawn Dr Lügner from memory – but making him appear as if he were forty years younger. Dark-haired, lean, his upper lip unwrinkled and all the crow's feet around his eyes smoothed away.

'Byron Hemming,' said Dr Bron, without hesitation.

'You *know* him? Are you sure?'

'Of course I know him. He was the last neurochemist that Dad ever worked with. He stayed with us for nearly a month.'

'And you're absolutely positive that this is him?'

'No question. Where did you get that? I haven't seen that face since I was 14 years old.'

'What was he like, this Byron Hemming?'

'Dad thought the sun shone out of his ass, but I never liked him much. Boys of 14 have very sensitive antennae, you know? They can detect phoneys through solid walls.'

'You thought Byron Hemming was a phoney? In what way?'

'I don't know exactly. He was *shifty*, that was all. He never came to the house in daylight and he never left in daylight. My older brother Tom said that he was probably a vampire. I always felt that he was in some kind of a *hurry*, you know? He was out for what he could get and he didn't want any delays. He never stopped talking, either. He was the only guy I ever met who could out-talk my father. He would sit there with his soup getting cold, rattling on about the cerebellum until you felt like strangling him.'

John picked up the drawing and tucked it back into his coat pocket. 'You say that he was the last neurochemist who ever worked with your father? When was this, exactly?'

'Well, Dad died in February 1957, so what we're talking about is the late summer of '56.'

'Did your father give you any idea what kind of work they were doing together?'

'He probably mentioned it, but I don't recollect what it was.'

John said, 'I hope you don't mind my asking you this . . . but did you notice any *changes* in your father in the months before he died?'

'Oh, yes. Very much so. A dramatic change. My mother always used to say that he must have had some kind of premonition that he was going to die, because he seemed to have more of an appetite for life during the last quarter of '56 than at any other time I can remember. Before, he never used to play baseball with me, ever, but one day he took me outside in the yard with a glove and a ball, and we played out there for *hours*, right until it got dark. Not only that, he was *good*. His co-ordination was superb.

'He started to play the piano. Not just 'Chopsticks', you know, but proper classical piano. Mozart, Beethoven, Berlioz. We suddenly began to believe that he could do *anything*, and he could. Tom's Hudson Hornet broke down and he rolled up his sleeves and reassembled the gearbox. Didn't need a workshop manual, just did it.'

'Did Byron Hemming continue to come around?'

'Well . . . he did for a while, but then I had the impression that he and Dad had a real heavy-duty argument about something. I heard them one night in the library and they were really shouting at each other. I think I only saw Byron once after that. He came round to the house one evening to collect some research papers, and that was that.'

'Then what?' John asked him.

Dr Bron wheeled back his chair and turned it around, so that he was facing out of the window, looking down at the campus buildings and the rows of lime trees and the Mississippi beyond, flowing thick and tawny between its concrete banks.

'Two days before Christmas 1956 my father came down to breakfast and didn't know who he was. He didn't recognize any of us, either. He could talk, with a very limited vocabulary, but that was as far as it went. Complete memory wipeout. We took him to three different specialists and they all said the same: his memory and his reasoning had all vanished, just like a computer crashing – although that wasn't the way they put it in those days. His whole being, his whole personality, everything that made him what he was—' and Dr Bron popped his fingers.

John said nothing, but waited for him to continue.

'In the end, we had to send him to a home. It was a beautiful place, in Stillwater, on the St Croix River. He didn't know who he was, and he didn't know who *we* were, either. But there must have been some small part of him left – some small part that didn't want to spend the rest of his days sitting in a chair staring at the wall. He hadn't been there for more than three or four weeks before he cut his wrists with a broken glass.'

Dr Bron swiveled his chair back. There was a small, wistful smile on his face. 'Ebbed away,' he said, almost in a whisper. 'Just . . . ebbed away.'

'I'm sorry,' said John. 'That's a sad way to go. Listen, you don't happen to have any of your father's old research papers, do you? Anything that might give me a clue where Byron Hemming came from, and where he went to afterward?'

'They're all in the University Library. I can call up and have them accessed for you. I have an idea, though, that Byron came from Southern California. Dad and I were talking about fishing once, and Byron said something about the grunion spawning on the beaches, close to where he used to live. I didn't think about it until years and years later, when I saw a program on the grunion run on TV.'

'Well, thanks,' said John. 'That could turn out to be useful.' He stood up and held out his hand.

'I'm sorry if I upset you. These investigations have a nasty habit of turning up things that people would rather forget.'

'Hope you find your man,' said Dr Bron. 'Maybe, when you do, you can call me and tell me who he *really* was.'

Micky's security clearance didn't come through until late in the afternoon, so there was nothing he could do all morning but fret about Roxanne. He tried three times to contact John to ask him if he was any closer to finding Dr Lügner, but on each occasion John's phone was switched off.

He strummed for a while on an old Spanish guitar that he had found in a closet along with a collection of dilapidated tennis rackets. He tried to compose a song for Mingus, but he missed Mingus too much and he was too distressed about Roxanne.

At lunchtime he sat alone on the veranda with a plateful of grilled tuna and a glass of cold Chardonnay, but he had no appetite.

He went out into the garden with a copy of essays by Henri Louis Bergson, the early twentieth-century French philosopher. He was becoming increasingly interested in Bergson's ideas on the evolution of intellect; and his views on time and space. More than anything else, he was intrigued by the notion that, in time, there is no repetition, no recurrence, and that time is the continual creation of what is new.

The thought of this ceaseless creation made it a little easier for him to accept Mingus' death. You can't go back, you have to go on. But it didn't make him any less anxious about what might happen to Roxanne. He read three lines and tossed it aside.

When Sara arrived, Micky was still in the garden, creaking backward and forward in a large white-upholstered swing. She took off her shoes to walk through the bright green grass. She looked more confident today, in a short white linen suit and a bright pink blouse.

'Hi Micky.'

Micky sat up. 'How's Roxanne? Any news?'

'Nothing, not yet. But I'm sure she's still safe.'

'I'll evaporate those bastards, I mean it.'

Sara held up a shining Broussard security tag. 'Here. You're a Grade 5 now. I think it must have been the fastest security clearance in the history of US military intelligence. They sent somebody to talk to your schoolteacher. They sent people to talk to your landlord and your neighbors and your local drugstore. They even sent somebody to Tallahassee to talk to your grandma. I don't know what she told them, but the agent said that if *she* had Communist leanings then he was Fidel Castro.'

Micky reluctantly took the tag and dropped it onto the seat-cushion. Sara sat down beside him, swinging the seat two or three times, her bare heel kicking in the grass. 'What have you been reading?' she said, and picked up his book. '*Durée et Simultaneité*?'

'Bergson. Only in translation. He says that nothing ever happens the same way twice, so it's no use making plans.'

'Perhaps he was right. What are you going to read next? *Janet and John Get Philosophical*?'

'*The Relativity of Knowledge*, if I can find a copy.'

'Sounds gripping.'

'Well, it's all about noumena and phenomena. Like, a noumenon is what you call an object in itself, independent of its being perceived or felt or known about. A rock in the middle of a desert that nobody's ever seen. But so soon as you look at an object, or touch it, or feel it, the object changes as well as you. It becomes observable: it becomes a phenomenon.'

'Does the same thing happen with human beings? Before you knew about me, was I a noumenon? And have I changed, now you know me? Have I become a phenomenon?'

Micky looked at her for a long time. She *was* a phenomenon: a beautiful woman, with luminous skin and sun-lightened lashes and eyes that were cold and colorless like an empty seashore. She didn't give herself away; and maybe there was nothing behind those seashore eyes but selfishness and self-preservation. But here she was flirting with him and teasing him and making jokes about noumena and phenomena, and none of his girl-friends had ever been capable of doing that.

It suddenly occurred to him that he could have a woman like Sara. He had always been good-looking enough, in a young and predatory kind of way. Now he was intellectual enough, too.

Sara leaned close. 'Do you want to see your missile?' she asked him, as if it were the most erotic suggestion ever made. There were two tiny pink smudges of lipstick on her front teeth.

'I can see it now?'

'Of course. That's what I came here for. That's why we expedited your security clearance.'

He hesitated, and then he picked up his security tag. 'Just promise me one thing. I mean really promise me. You won't let those bastards lay a finger on Roxanne.'

Sara gave him an almost imperceptible nod, and

then took hold of his hand. 'Come on. It's time to get this show on the road, don't you think?'

At the gates, a black Cadillac Seville with black-tinted windows was waiting for them. A security man with a ginger mustache opened the door and they climbed in. Sara said, 'Gene's as twitchy as a pregnant father. I'll tell you something, Micky, if you can make this missile work, Gene'll make your bank balance look like the Federal Reserve.'

'I don't have a bank account,' Micky told her. 'Everybody I ever worked for always paid cash.'

She laid a hand on his knee. 'Some things are going to have to change, aren't they?'

They drove into Broussard Guidance Systems and around the back of the office building to the huge aluminum-sided workshops. They were stopped at a red-and-white-striped barrier by a bulky black uniformed guard, almost as big as the booth that he stood in. He checked their passes, giving Micky an especially beady looking-over, before he let them through.

They parked outside the very last workshop and climbed out. There was a small block of prefabricated offices on one side, with a sign that read GUIDANCE DIVISION – STRICTLY NO UNAUTHORIZED ENTRY. Sara rang at the doorbell and they were admitted by another security guard, who checked their passes again. Then she led Micky along a carpet-tiled corridor, through a pair of soft plastic dust-doors, and into the workshop itself. There were bright halogen lights shining everywhere, and a strong smell of highly refined oil, polyurethane, and fresh acrylic paints.

On both sides of the workshop there were benches crowded with calibrating instruments, trays of tools, banks of electronic diagnostic equipment and extraordinary pieces of highly polished pipework whose function couldn't even be guessed at. Even though Dr Lügner had given him so much information about MiGR8, Micky couldn't help feeling that he had wandered into one of those science-fiction movies where government agents are secretly dismantling a crashed UFO.

There were only five technicians working on the missile, serious-looking young men with cropped haircuts and pale blue zip-up suits in shiny nylon, and the missile itself was a disappointment. It was lying on a heavy-duty orange-painted jig, still mainly dismantled, with colored wires fraying in all directions, so that it looked more like a washing machine under repair than a cruise missile.

Sara took Micky around to the missile's mid-section, where a lean, suntanned technician was working on the turbojet engine.

'Nestor, I'd like you to meet Micky Frasier. This is the man who's going to make your missiles fly. Micky, this is Nestor Drysdale.'

Nestor wiped his hands on the cloth that was hanging out of his pocket, and shook hands. He looked more like a Blue Mountain moonshiner than a missile technician. His bright blue eyes were set slightly too closely together, and his nose could have opened a can of soup. When he spoke, it was with a tensile Virginia twang, well punctuated with 'mmhs' and 'mmh-mmhs' and 'yessirs'.

'Haven't I met you before someplace?' he asked.

409

'Didn't you used to work for Raytheon?'

Micky shook his head. 'Guido's.' He peered at the engine that Nestor had been working on. 'This is the tactical powerplant, isn't it? Teledyne CA J402 . . . 272 kilograms of thrust. Had any problems with it?'

'No way. I love it, *mh*. I love taking it apart, and putting it back together again, and hearing it whistle, yessir. And there's been plenty of time for that, up until now. None of the team thought this baby was ever going to leave the ground.'

'It will, I promise you,' said Micky, with exaggerated confidence. Over Nestor's shoulder, he gave Sara a lopsided smile. Sara turned away as if she hadn't even seen him. He was confused for a moment, but then he said, 'Who's in charge of guidance?'

A swarthy young man in Coke-bottle eyeglasses came forward. He had a fine black downy mustache on his upper lip which made him look about 12 years old. 'Manuel Ortez,' he said, holding out his hand. 'I'm real pleased you're here. Well, no I'm not, actually, because I should have been able to solve this problem myself, and I couldn't. So you'll forgive me if I'm a little short-tempered from time to time.'

Sara put her arms around Manuel's shoulders. 'Manuel is our boy wonder when it comes to guidance, aren't you, Manuel?'

'He invented Redeye,' put in Nestor.

'Redeye? You mean that imaging infrared seeker they used on Hecate missiles? Redeye can hit a target from 15 miles away with less than 0.5 metre error. Redeye is very impressive.'

'I know. But Redeye can't do what MiGR8 is supposed to be able to do. Redeye can see but it can't *think*. Redeye can identify but it can't recognize. Redeye can't make *judgements*.'

He took hold of Micky's elbow and led him over to a stainless-steel trolley. In an improvised frame was a shiny metallic device the size and shape of a turtle, lying helplessly on its back. Micky almost felt that if somebody turned it over, it could slowly crawl away. Instead of legs, however, it had two dozen protruding outlets all around its curved circumference, which looked as if they were plated in platinum.

'That's it, that's MiGR8,' Manuel announced. 'Doesn't look like much, does it? Smaller than Tercom, lighter than the Lear Siegler strapdown platform. But ever since we took over Hoshi, I've studied every book, every pamphlet, every diary, every CD-ROM. I've studied it and studied it, and *I've* got an honours degree in advanced electronics from MIT.

'I can understand what it is, and how it's supposed to work, but I can't understand how to *make* it work.'

Micky peered at the turtle more closely. Its shape was very familiar, like a turtle that he had seen in a recurring dream, but of course that was Dr Lügner's memories at work. Unlike Tercom, which looked like nothing much more than a collection of angular boxes, MiGR8 seemed to be organic, almost *alive*. It was dormant now, but Micky knew how to make it come to life, and to start thinking, and to start killing people, if it was called upon to kill.

He went back to the half-dismantled cruise missile and asked Nestor to show him where the MiGR8 system was supposed to be inserted. The guidance-system housing was scooped out so that the MiGR8 unit would fit into it snugly, and it was studded with platinum contacts.

Manuel leaned over the missile's opened-up nose. 'I thought that the contacts and the outlets would touch,' he said. 'Then I thought that maybe the signals would arc between them. But when that system's fitted in correctly, and all the screws are tightened, there's a gap between every guidance outlet and every contact; and no guidance signal can cross it. It's so small, this gap, you can't even see it without a microscope. But it's there, and unless we can find a way of bridging it, MiGR8 can't send out any messages to the missile's power-plant and the missile's control surfaces. It's like a genius who's had a stroke. He knows all the answers but he's physically incapable of telling you what they are.'

Micky nodded. He didn't say anything. John had advised him to act dumb – more like an idiot savant than a genius – and he could see the sense in doing that. This was a high-security project, teeming with security personnel, and if he started discussing Proust and analyzing modern American opera, as well as fixing the MiGR8 guidance system, sooner or later somebody was going to start asking how a failed rock musician and a mediocre dishwasher was suddenly cleverer than Einstein, Mozart, and Wernher von Braun all put together.

Manuel said, 'MiGR8 was fully programmed for its first test flight before we took Hoshi over. An air launch from Cape Canaveral Air Force base. Whoever that guy at Hoshi was, the one who developed MiGR8, he was inspired. Here, let me show you. I never saw cruise-missile flight data that was anything like it.'

Manuel laid a hand on his shoulder and guided him over to an IBM computer terminal. The screen was showing nothing but the Broussard logo; but Manuel rapidly punched an array of keys, and *MiGR8 Atlantic Test* appeared, followed by a graphic three-dimensional map of Florida, the Bahamas, and the West Indies.

'Okay . . . the missile is released here, just off Cape Canaveral. It flies downrange, south-eastward, until it reaches Isla Mona, in between the Dominican Republic and Puerto Rico, where it changes to radar and infrared imaging to locate a specific building. Inside this building is the target model. The missile identifies the target model, double-checks it, and then goes in for the kill.'

'Is it going to be carrying a warhead?'

'Oh, sure. Full conventional load with multiple fuses. You have to give the generals a big satisfying bang. That's arms salesmanship.'

Micky said, 'Do you mind if I play around with these computers for a while?'

'Be my guest. You're the one who's got to make this baby fly.'

Micky drew up a swivel chair and sat down in front of the screen. He punched up MIGR8 ATLANTIC again, and followed the launch data and the flight plan. Several US Navy vessels would be sailing across the Tomahawk's flightpath, attempting to jam its guidance system and to score 'hits' on it with radar-simulated anti-missile missiles. Dr Lügner must have been totally confident when he wrote these programs that MiGR8 would be light-years ahead of all existing guidance systems when it came to evasive aerobatics.

Manuel came back with two steaming mugs of coffee. 'You've checked out the flight plans? Now take a look at the target.'

He sat down beside him and directed the mouse to TARGET INDIVIDUAL on the screen. Instantly an eerie, androgynous face appeared, slowly rotating on the screen. It had sharp, distinctive features: an overlarge nose and widely staring eyes. Micky found himself leaning back, away from the screen. He didn't like the target's unblinking stare.

'The condemned man,' said Manuel. 'Created from a sculptor's imagination. A man who never was, molded out of clay. One man's eyes, another man's nose, a third man's mouth. But when they use this missile in anger, they'll be using a 3-D image of a real person, built up from photographs. All you have to do is scan it into the computer, and that person better start calling for a priest.'

'How about MiGR8 itself?' asked Micky. 'Did you access that yet?'

He asked, but he knew the answer already. MiGR8's brain wouldn't function unless it had been charged up with Synaptine. It was crammed with information, packed with facts. It knew every geographical feature on the planet, from the Grand Banks to the Gobi Desert. It knew how to fly at shoulder height over estuaries and wadis; and it could jink between snowcapped Alpine peaks and monumental redwood trees. It could make its way through the streets of any city or town, anywhere at all, from Austin to Zaporozh'ye. Just at the moment, however, it was technically unconscious – incapable of passing on its information to man or machine.

Manuel said, 'We've had five different computer analysts working on MiGR8, and this is where it gets embarrassing. We can't even *guess* how it functions, and we can't find out how the hell to access it. Look – there are indicators on the main computer that MiGR8 has been fully briefed and targeted, and that the whole system is raring to go. But we can't get MiGR8 itself to confirm it, and we have no idea how to fit it into the Tomahawk. I feel like a kid who's been given an erector set for Christmas, and can't put it all together.'

He dabbed at the switch and the ghostly target image vanished. Micky checked his watch. 'I'll get onto it tomorrow, first thing. Don't worry . . . from what I've seen here, we should have this missile up and running in 24 hours.'

'You sound pretty damned confident,' said Manuel; and not without a little bitterness.

Micky stood up. 'You know what Isaiah said, "In quietness and in confidence shall be your strength".'

415

★　　★　　★

As evening fell, they sat together on the heaped-up, powdery beach outside the Doral Hotel in Miami and watched the sky turn lilac. The wind was still warm, but Constance felt an occasional chill from the sea, and she wrapped her new pink cardigan around her shoulders. Lionel sat close to her, his shirtsleeves ruffling. He hadn't said much since they had arrived, but she knew how tired he was, and she knew that he enjoyed her company. She turned to him, and smiled, and he smiled back at her, and she could almost imagine that she had found somebody to love, somebody to stay with.

She adored art, and she adored her work; but old age was already breathing on the back of her neck; and the prospect of spending the last years of her life all alone, in Melbourne, Florida, 'the old woman who used to own the picture shop', was more than she could bear.

She didn't have to ask herself why she had left the gallery and gone off so spontaneously with John. Better a short, happy, exciting, terrible life, than years of tedium and sickness, suns that came up and suns that went down, and strained foods at lunchtimes, and visitors who couldn't stand the smell of impending death. She wouldn't have minded if she had died in Lionel's house in Winter Park; or Guido's restaurant; or Mingus' house. She had sat at her mother's bedside while she gradually disappeared, and clutched her hand, and right at the very end her mother had lifted her head and stared at her and whispered, 'What was it all *for*, Constance? What was it all *for*?'

Lionel said, 'Have you ever been to South America? Buenos Aires?'

Constance shook her head.

'You'd love Buenos Aires. It's the kind of city that brings you back to life. That's what you're looking for, isn't it? Life?'

'Yes,' she said. 'Life.' She watched a young blonde girl in a blue bikini running along the beach with a small dog dancing after her. 'I never believed that I would ever grow old. Then one morning I woke up and looked in the mirror and I *was*. And ever since then – well, I'm not afraid of dying, not a bit. What I'm really afraid of is *not living*.'

'Come with me, Constance. You and I could have really great times together.'

'To South America? Are you serious?'

'You came with me this far, didn't you? Where's the harm in going a little further?'

'I don't know anything about you, Lionel. Oh –' she laughed ' – I know that you're something of a genius, and some very dangerous men want to see you dead. But that's not very much, is it?'

Lionel shrugged. 'It's more than a whole lot of married couples ever find out about each other. But, listen, if you want to know all about me, I'll tell you, as we travel.'

Constance looked at him over her shoulder, so that he could see only her eyes. It was almost dark now, and lights glittered all the way along the oceanfront hotels. The gulls were screaming as if they could sense that something dreadful was about to happen.

Lionel said, 'Come with me, Constance. I never

met a woman like you before – a woman who just upped and did what she wanted.'

He hesitated, and took a breath, and then he said, 'It's been so damned lonely, all these years.'

Constance leaned over and kissed his cheek. He took off his spectacles and they kissed again, while the sea lapped and lapped as if it had seen all this before, and the gulls circled around their heads, higher now, and silent.

Titan Blight knocked on the door of Roxanne's room but walked in without waiting to be asked. Roxanne was leaning against the French windows, both arms raised, staring sightlessly at her reflection in the darkened glass. On the table her supper tray lay untouched – the shaved ice had melted beneath the shrimp, the roast monkfish was growing cold in its congealing pepper sauce, the piped cream was dripping from the pineapple tart.

Titan peered down at the tray, dipped his finger into the tart and licked it. 'You don't know what you're missing, sweetheart,' he told her. 'George is one of the best chefs in Boston. He'll throw a blue fit when he sees that you haven't eaten anything.'

He approached the French windows and lit a cigarette. He stared at Roxanne for a while, with smoke leaking out of his smile. Her face was half concealed by her hair, but he could see her pouting lips. She was wearing the same jeans and tight white T-shirt that she had been wearing when Roland had taken her away from St Cloud. Titan had offered her a change of clothes, but she had refused.

'I haven't heard from Mr Huntley yet,' he told her. 'I hope for your sake that he doesn't take too long. Why, you might have to start eating George's cooking.'

'Up yours,' said Roxanne.

'I wish,' Titan replied, blowing out smoke.

Roxanne turned and confronted him. 'You can't keep me here like this. It's against the law, and you know it!'

'It depends what you mean by the law. Some laws are greater than others – like the law of survival, and the law of progress, and the law of human destiny. In the general scheme of global importance, I'd say that the crime of keeping you here against your will rates just below driving a motor vehicle under the influence of Jack Daniel's and just above allowing one's poodle to poop on the sidewalk.'

He coughed and then he said, 'So long as I locate your Dr Lügner, you don't have anything to worry about. But there's been too much fuss down in Florida, sweetheart. Too much pandemonium, and pandemonium is always expensive and bad for public relations. So the simple answer is that instead of causing any more death and destruction, we keep you here till Mr Huntley brings him in.'

'Then what? You'll let me go?'

Titan reached out and slowly stroked her hair, his cigarette still burning between his fingers. 'I wish I didn't have to. You know that you're welcome to stay here as long as you like.'

'You have to be kidding,' she said, jerking her head away.

He didn't seem to be deterred. 'Tell me,' he said, 'do you wear any panties? Or maybe you're naked under those jeans. I'll bet you I can tell just by smelling them. Why don't you let me smell them?'

'Just leave me alone!' Roxanne snapped at him, and circled away, around the table. Titan followed her at a slow train-like shuffle.

'You shouldn't be looking a gift horse in the mouth, sweetheart. You could live here for ever, in total luxury. You could have anything you wanted, just by ringing a bell. You could have a sports car, and designer clothes, and jewelry. You could go on vacation whenever you wanted – Europe, Hawaii, you name it. And do you know what I'd ask in return? A little soaping in the shower, now and again, that's all I'd ask, and maybe a little friendly relief.'

'Get away from me, you're *sick*!' Roxanne screamed at him.

Titan stopped shuffling, and smiled, and nodded. 'You're absolutely right, of course. I'm sick. I'm a sick, sick person. I shouldn't be thinking about sniffing young girls' jeans at my age. I should be thinking about higher things, like the decline of religious observance in the Western World, and the social consequences of the Internet.'

He looked down at the supper tray thoughtfully. Then he picked it up, and hurled it against the wall, smashing the plates and splattering the silk-fabric wallpaper with sauce and ice-cream. Roxanne stepped back, shaking, her eyes wide in alarm.

Without another word, Titan walked out of the

room, leaving the door open behind him, and a swirl of cigarette smoke.

It was a gray, overcast morning in Boxboro when John arrived outside the Klein property in his rented Chrysler. Mrs Klein lived in a square, red-painted eighteenth-century house on top of a small hill. It looked like a house from a children's book, with a white picket fence and three strange knobbly trees beside it.

John rang the doorbell and the door was opened so promptly that Mrs Klein must have been watching him walk up the path.

'Mrs Klein? I'm John Huntley.'

'Well, you'd better come along in,' she said. She was a tall, wan woman in her mid to late seventies, with long white hair tied back in a ponytail. She was wearing a plain sleeveless dress in a large brown-checkered print, and her thin wrists were decorated with several heavy bracelets made of stones and beads. She was one of those women for whom the hippie era had come just a little too late, but who had wholeheartedly embraced it all the same, and who had been living it ever since. She smelled very strongly of vanilla musk.

Her house was small and cozy, with stenciled walls and furniture draped with brightly colored Indian blankets. There were white-painted shelves everywhere, with seashells on them, and china dogs, and framed family photographs, and an ocarina, and a native American sundance doll.

'Would you care for some ginger tea?' Mrs Klein asked him. 'I was about to make some anyway.'

421

'That's okay, thanks,' he said. 'Me and ginger don't agree.'

She patted a large sofa next to the fireplace. 'Take a seat, then. I was very intrigued that you called me. Up until now, people have scarcely ever mentioned Nathan's name, ever, not since he died.'

'Conspiracy of silence, huh?'

'Oh, no. I wouldn't call it that. But Nathan was the one of the best neurochemists that Brigham & Women's ever had, and I never thought that he was given the recognition that he deserved. After he died, it was just as if everybody had forgotten him. It was very sad.'

'Mrs Klein . . . I know this goes a long ways back . . . and I don't want to distress you or anything . . . but can you remember the last few weeks of Nathan's life? I mean, can you remember if he was acting abnormal in any way?'

'He was never better. That was why it surprised us so much when he suffered his stroke. He was working on some new kind of neurochemical project, and he was very excited about it. He was very energetic, too. He seemed to have re-discovered all of his old enthusiasm. He used to be quite a painter, when I first met him, but after he started at Brigham & Women's he gave it all up. Suddenly he went up to the attic and brought out his easel and his paints and started turning out portraits and landscapes and goodness knows what. And they were *very* good . . . much better than the pictures he used to paint when he was younger.'

'Anything else?'

'Oh, for sure. He made me a new kitchen

cabinet; and he built a Gothic kennel for the dog. He started up a barbershop quartet with some of our friends, and wrote all the songs for it. He started writing poetry, too. I never realized that he could write poetry. There was one that I learned by heart. "Each time you go/ You leave a space/ That's not a space/ But your own place/ Where flowers flourish, children play/ And sunshine sparkles every day." Well – that was one of the first ones he wrote. After that they got too difficult for me.'

John said, 'This new kind of neurochemical project you mentioned . . . was he working on that alone, or was he collaborating with anybody?'

'Oh, he was collaborating. I don't even think that it was Nathan's idea, originally, but he was helping to test it.'

'Can you remember who he was collaborating with?'

'Of course. It was Dr Zweifel. Nathan used to think the world of Dr Zweifel and Dr Zweifel used to think the world of him. Nathan said that he wasn't supposed to tell anybody . . . the work they were doing was top secret. But it was some kind of drug which would help the mentally retarded. Rather like L-dopa, I should imagine.'

'Do you happen to know if your late husband took any of this drug himself?'

'Well, I don't. I wouldn't have thought so. He was very careful about mind-altering drugs. One of his colleagues was sued once, for millions, for testing lysergic acid on a Down's syndrome child. Nathan always tested them on rats first. Mind you, he always used to say that they should have been tested on politicians.'

'But think about the way he was behaving in the months before he died – painting, and writing, and all of the stuff. That wasn't his normal self, was it? Do you think he could have been injecting himself with something? Like, some kind of mind-expanding concoction?'

Mrs Klein angled her head backward and sideways, and peered at John in deep suspicion. 'Do you know something that I don't?' she asked him.

'To be honest, maybe I do. Do you want to tell me how your late husband died?'

'Is this relevant? It was terrible.'

'Mrs Klein, losing somebody you love is always terrible. But it's really important that I find out how it happened.'

'Who did you say you were from?'

'Western Eye Industrial Investigations, San Francisco. We've been looking into some serious malpractice in the neurochemical industry.'

'You're not suggesting that Nathan did anything wrong?'

'Oh, no. Far from it. We think that Nathan could have been a victim of a serious act of incompetence. If we can prove it, you could stand to gain anything up to a million dollars' worth of compensation.'

Mrs Klein looked dewy-eyed. 'I don't care about money. I'd give up $10 million to have my Nathan back.'

'What about, uh – your second husband, Mr Klein?'

Mrs Klein sniffed defiantly, and sat up straight.

'That animal? I wouldn't give you a nickel for him. I threw him out six and a half years ago and I haven't seen him since. Do you know what he used to do?'

All John could say was, 'No. I don't know what he did.'

Mrs Klein leaned forward, took hold of John's hand, and hissed, '*He used to urinate in the wash-basins.*'

John tried to give her a reassuring smile. She wouldn't let go of his hand. In the end, he said 'Wow', and she released him, but carried on staring at him, and nodding her head, as if she had just made him a party to the foulest secret since the Salem witch trials.

'You want to know how Nathan died?' she asked him. 'He was driving me to dinner with the Buracks, in Littleton. We were only ten minutes from home when he took his hands off the steering-wheel and just let the car glide to the side of the road. I said, "Nathan, what's wrong? Aren't you feeling well?" and do you know, he just stared at me and said, "Who are you?" And do you know something, he'd forgotten who I was. He'd forgotten who *he* was, too. He didn't know where we were going, or why. He'd even forgotten how to drive a car.

'I managed to flag down a passing truck and the trucker called an ambulance for me. Nathan spent five weeks in hospital and I went to see him every day, but he never recovered his memory, and at the end of the fifth week he suffered a massive stroke. The worst part was that I was holding his hand when he died, but he didn't even remember who I was.'

Mrs Klein took out a tissue and dabbed at her eyes. 'It won't change anything, knowing why he died, or who was responsible for it. It won't bring my Nathan back. But, yes, if you manage to find out, I'd like to know who it was.'

'I think I may have a pretty good idea already,' said John. 'Did your late husband have any papers or diaries that I could look at?'

'Most of his papers are in the Mugar Memorial Library. But I still have his personal diaries. I suppose you'd like to see the very last one he wrote?'

'Anything covering the period when he was working with Dr Zweifel.'

Mrs Klein left him for a while. He waited impatiently, listening to the sociable chatting of the clock on top of the fireplace. This was too much of a coincidence: two research scientists with whom Dr Lügner had worked, *both* being afflicted by a sudden, total and inexplicable loss of memory. Maybe it was a natural side-effect of Synaptine . . . but Dr Lügner had taken Synaptine, too, so why hadn't *he* suffered from the same mental wipeout?

Maybe he had seen what had happened to Dr Bron and Dr Schoenman and altered the Synaptine formula to make it safe. Or maybe he hadn't. Maybe his genius had extended to devising a serum which would completely erase the memories of anybody who knew what Synaptine was, and how to make it. For some reason, he had never

426

registered the formula – but he had certainly made sure that he protected it.

Mrs Klein came back carrying a large ledger with a marbled cover and a yellow leather spine. 'Here it is . . . Nathan always kept up his diary. The man from the Mugar Memorial Library said that he wanted everything – notes, tape-recordings, and diaries, too. But the diaries were far too personal, far too precious. You'll see that he used to do little cartoons and sketches in them, and stick in news-paper cuttings and all kinds of things that interested him.'

'You wouldn't let me borrow it, I suppose?'

Sweetly but firmly, Mrs Klein said, 'No. But you can read it here, if you care to. Use the dining-room table if you want to make notes.'

John sat in Mrs Klein's gloomy dining-room for almost three hours. Dr Schoenman had kept such a detailed journal that it was amazing that he had ever found time to do any research. He had written down what he had eaten for breakfast, how he had dressed, what the weather was like, everything. If anything in the *Boston Globe* had caught his eye he had carefully cut it out and stuck it on the page, with his own comments written next to it. There were small sketches of the places he had visited during the day, as well as caricatures of the people he had met. There was even a recipe for Denver sandwiches, complete with illustrations.

Two-thirds of the way through the diary, how-ever, just when John thought that he was going to come up with nothing but menus and meteoro-logical reports and odd news items ('Boston Man

427

Memorizes 11,000 Telephone Numbers'), he came across a caricature that he instantly recognized as Dr Lügner. Underneath, Dr Schoenman had written, 'Lunched today with Dr Henry Zweifel from University of California at San Diego. He believes he has come up with a formula which will revolutionize human intelligence; and wishes me to assist him in a series of tests. He has already tried the formula on himself, and he demonstrated his extraordinary mental powers during lunch . . . I was skeptical when I started my soup, but by the cheese I was convinced. For instance, he was able to remember our entire conversation from the moment we had first met. He was also able to work out the 13th root of a 100-digit number in little more than a minute, which was not much longer than it took him to say it out loud.'

For the next two months, Dr Schoenman wrote very little more about Dr Zweifel, and nothing more about Synaptine. But it was obvious from his diary that his intelligence was increasing at a spectacular rate. One whole page was taken up with a philosophical discussion on human perception which was so baffling that it literally made John sneeze.

'Bless you,' said Mrs Klein, from the living-room.

Then, however, came a guarded entry which indicated that Dr Schoenman was starting to harbor suspicions about Dr Zweifel. 'I asked Dr Z several questions about how he had developed his formula. He was uncharacteristically evasive. In

428

fact he was so evasive that I decided to contact the neurochemistry department at UC San Diego for myself. I talked to Professor Fellows on the telephone, and he said that he had never heard of Dr Z nor was anybody in his department working along the same lines – although obviously he was very interested in the nature of Dr Z's project. When I confronted Dr Z he became angry and said that I had betrayed a trust. He had developed Synaptine with War Department funding during the war and therefore he was not at liberty to discuss it in any detail.'

However, Dr Schoenman was still not satisfied. He was taking the drug himself and obviously felt that he had a right to know more about it. He contacted a friend whose son worked for the National Security Agency in Washington. 'Clark went through some classified WW2 files and came up with the information that there had been considerable War Department interest in neurochemistry during WW2 for the purposes of interrogation and so-called "brainwashing". They were seeking to develop a chemical that could be introduced into the air or the water systems of Axis countries – a depressant which wouldn't kill or maim, but which would undermine the enemy's morale and their willingness to fight. There were other neurochemical projects, too, including a plan to induce total loss of memory on a nationwide scale. Can you imagine a whole nation suddenly forgetting who they are, and what they are supposed to be fighting for? Many of these projects seem very far-fetched, but I suppose we have to remember that we were fighting for our very lives in the 1940s, and losing tens of thousands of our finest young men, and even the most outlandish notions for bringing the conflict to a speedier close were given serious consideration.'

Dr Schoenman was told that 'all neurochemical projects were supposed to be handled by the Office of Global Research and Experimentation, known as OGRE. I tried to locate OGRE. They have a telephone number listed in Rockville, Maryland, but I have rung and rung and nobody ever answers. I talked to Ray Gatling, the science correspondent on the *Boston Globe*, and he said that he had heard of OGRE but its work was highly classified, even today. However he knew that its director had been Titan Blight, a very wealthy Massachusetts businessman who now lives in Dedham, on the Charles River. I attempted to reach Mr Blight, but I was told that he was on an extended vacation in Europe.'

Dr Schoenman's last few entries were much shorter and more perfunctory, although they clearly revealed his confusion. On the one hand, Dr Zweifel's formula appeared to open up a golden age of worldwide enlightenment. On the other hand, Dr Zweifel himself was becoming increasingly difficult and antagonistic, almost to the point of violence.

'Have suggested to Dr Z yet again that we publish a joint paper in *Neurochemistry*. His anger unbelievable. We had a scuffle in the laboratory and almost came to blows. I said that I would take no more Synaptine unless he agreed, but he must have known that I was bluffing. Synaptine has opened my eyes to a whole new world. Synaptine has made me, potentially, a god. How can I stop taking it, when it enables me to understand *everything* – even football, I might add, which I never understood before!'

The next entry was even more telling. It was one sentence, the only sentence on a page that was otherwise blank. 'Have discovered that "Zweifel" in German means "Doubt".' Followed by '???' Up to his old tricks, thought John. Dr Lügner the Liar might have been a genius, but he loved to tempt fate.

Then, the penultimate entry: 'I met Dr Z on the Boston waterfront today and told him that I was no longer prepared to continue our joint experiments. Also that I was considering talking to Ray Gatling and telling him all about Synaptine. At first Dr Z was furious but then he calmed down and begged me not to. He said that Synaptine had been developed at considerable human cost, rather like the GIs who were positioned close to the atomic bomb tests at Alamagordo. This might have been acceptable in wartime but it could now cause serious embarrassment to many senior figures in the Department of Defense. However I insisted that he come clean about it all and he promised that he would, provided that I gave him 24 hrs to talk to all involved. This evening I took my seventh and last dosage of Synaptine.'

And, the following morning, last of all: 'Had that strange dream about Manchuria again. It was raining and I saw the girl driving ducks. Again the number 731. I can never understand what this dream means and why it makes me feel so horribly guilty.'

John closed the diary. He knew that he was very close now to understanding why OGRE wanted Dr Lügner dead.

That night, in his marble-tiled bathroom, Micky gave himself his fifth shot of Synaptine. He looked at himself in the mirror and decided that he didn't look much like Micky any more – as if his expanding intelligence had somehow changed his face, too.

Who are you? he wondered. *And what do you want?*

He went to bed and tried to sleep but he couldn't. He kept thinking about Roxanne being touched – Roxanne being tied up – Roxanne being raped – Roxanne being suffocated. He went to the icebox for a Dr Pepper, but when he took his first swallow he realized, to his surprise, that he didn't like it any more. His palate was becoming as discriminating as his mind.

He tried to write another song but after ten minutes he tossed his pencil across the room. All he could think about was Roxanne, and that Roxanne was in danger because of him.

Toward dawn, still sleepless, he picked up Keller's *Theory of Reversion*, which postulated that as soon as they were dug out of the ground, and were no longer subject to intense pressure, diamonds gradually began to revert to their original state. In several thousand years, all of the finest jewelry in the world would be nothing more than heaps of worthless carbon. Even diamonds weren't for ever.

16

A thing which is not perceived cannot be known, and, not being known, cannot exist. The only intelligible cause of all phenomena is a mind. Neither pain nor pleasure exist apart from their being felt – George Berkeley

John flew back to Orlando on the red-eye. He sat next to a huge black Marine who fell asleep and rested his head on John's shoulder so heavily that his upper arm went dead. John arrived at the house just after 8.15. The morning was exceptionally hot and there were warnings of electric storms by mid-afternoon.

He found Micky in the living-room, watching *Power Rangers*.

'How's it going?' he asked. 'Any more news about Roxanne?'

Micky switched off the television. 'Nothing. They won't even let me talk to her. How about you? Did you track down Dr Lügner yet?'

'Not yet. But I'm making some interesting progress. I think I have a pretty good idea why those men in suits want him dead. You remember him

434

telling us that he was part of a huge program during World War Two to improve the human intellect? It seems like he told us the truth but not the whole truth. There may have been casualties.'

'Casualties? What do you mean?'

'People got hurt. And I mean *lots* of people got hurt. "Considerable human cost" – those were his exact words. I've read dozens of reports about the way the War Department used military personnel for testing nerve gases and biological weapons. You remember that movie *The Philadelphia Experiment*, where they tested some kind of invisibility ray on a whole shipful of seamen? That wasn't so far-fetched. About three years ago I was investigating a drugs company in Anaheim. Some dispute over foreign patents. Anyhow, it turned out that almost all of their basic research had come from human guinea-pigs during the war – young infantrymen who hadn't quite made the physical grade. And guess what they'd been researching? Cholera, for Christ's sake. They'd been injecting poor un-suspecting bastards with *cholera*.'

'So what do you think?' asked Micky.

'I think these guys who kidnapped Roxanne – these OGRE people – they must be implicated in Dr Lügner's experiments, too. OGRE was respon-sible during the war for finding out what new scientific research the enemy were into – especially biological warfare – and also for following it up with their own experiments, so that the US wouldn't lag behind. The question is, what happened when they started working on a brain-improving drug? My guess is that there were serious casualties, and Dr Lügner knows about it.'

'Any ideas what it was?'

'It could have been memory loss – that's what happened to Dr Bron and Dr Schoenman. Oh, yes, they both worked with Dr Lügner and they both tried Synaptine. It worked fine at first – they could paint, they could play the piano, all that stuff. But then both of them suffered from total instantaneous memory loss. One minute they were okay – the next, *whap*! – they didn't even know what day of the week it was. I'll tell you something, Micky, if you value your brain, I'd stop taking it.'

'I don't know. Dr Lügner takes it, doesn't he, and it hasn't hurt him? Maybe those other two guys took an earlier batch, before he could sort out all the wrinkles.'

'All the same, you never know . . . its effect may build up in your system. One more dose may be one dose too many.'

Micky checked his watch. 'I have to go to Broussard in a minute. The missile guidance system is all ready to be hooked up.'

'There's one more thing,' said John. 'You know that dream you keep having . . . that dream of being in Manchuria? The 731 dream? The one that always makes you feel so guilty?'

'Sure, what about it?'

'Dr Schoenman had it too. The very same dream. The same number, 731. And *he* felt guilty, too.'

'That's the Synaptine. Dr Lügner used his own brain impulses to activate it, and so it's still carrying some of Dr Lügner's memories.'

436

'Exactly. So what happened in Manchuria that made Dr Lügner feel so guilty that he passed his guilt onto two separate people, you and Dr Schoenman, and possibly Dr Bron, too?'

'I don't know. I don't understand the dream at all. In any case, man, how can it be connected with what Dr Lügner did during the war? He couldn't have been working in Manchuria, could he? It was occupied by the Japanese.'

Micky went to his room to dress while John went into the kitchen to perk himself some strong black coffee. Some tiny memory was nagging in the back of his brain. It was something about Manchuria . . . something about scientific experiments. He was sure that he had encountered some mention of Manchuria not so long ago.

Micky came out wearing a clean yellow shirt and blue jeans. 'Listen . . . I'll catch you later. Are you coming in to see Sara?'

'Wait, I'll come with you,' John told him. He could have used a shower but he didn't want to lose this tantalizing ghost of a thought. 'I'd like to see this missile of yours.'

'You won't be impressed.'

'I will be if it can fly 300 miles and hit somebody right in the mush.'

They were driven to Broussard Guidance by one of their taciturn security men, who performed the ritual of opening the car doors for them in such a way that he shielded them with his body. Micky went off to the workshops while John went up to his office. He had a single dried-up yucca plant, a curled-up NASA calendar, and a view of the

437

company parking lot, with dazzling reflections shining from a hundred windshields.

He sat down, stripped off his necktie, and switched on his computer. He logged onto his own files back at Western Eye in San Francisco, and was relieved to find that Danny hadn't yet changed the password to keep him out. He punched up the only two recent cases involving Japanese interests: Hashimoto Pharmaceuticals and Heart Felt, Inc.

He had dealt with the Hashimoto case himself: a long and frustrating investigation into a series of break-ins at a Bay Area drug research company, and the subsequent appearance of three of their most profitable formulae – different name, different packaging – in Japan.

He went through the Hashimoto file line by line, but the only mention that he could find of wartime research was the name of Ryosuke Murata, the former director-in-chief of the Japanese National Institute of Health. It was an open secret that, during World War Two, Murata used to be a member of the notorious human experimentation Unit 1644 in Nanjing.

John tried six or seven different leads, but in the end he decided that his Hashimoto hunch was taking him up a blind alley. He switched to Heart Felt instead.

Heart Felt, Inc., was a San Francisco-based blood bank which exported clotting agents for hemophiliacs. They were founded in 1980, and for three years they did good business all around the Pacific Rim – Indonesia, Malaysia, and Taiwan – and in Japan they were close challengers to Tokyo's biggest blood bank, Green Cross. But in 1983 there was an outbreak of AIDS amongst hemophilia sufferers, and Tokyo's health ministry imposed a two-year ban on the import of foreign blood products on 'safety grounds' – Heart Felt's included. This was in spite of the fact that Heart Felt always heat-treated their coagulants, to eliminate the HIV virus; while Green Cross allegedly didn't. There was no appeal. Heart Felt lost over $3.75 million of Japanese business.

In 1996, however, a Japanese lawyer called Tsutomu Shimuzu claimed to have discovered secret documents which clearly revealed that Green Cross had failed to heat-treat their clotting agents; and that the health ministry's ban on foreign blood had been imposed in order to give Green Cross time to develop heat technology. During the ban, nearly 2,000 people had been infected by tainted coagulants; and eventually the health ministry and five major drug companies were ordered to pay them compensation.

Western Eye had been hired by Heart Felt's lawyers to prove that there was a conspiracy between the founder of Green Cross, Ryoichi Naito, and the Tokyo ministry of health. It hadn't been necessary for John to fly to Tokyo himself: he had contacted Western Eye's Japanese agent, Ipi Sinkosha, and after six weeks of digging, Ipi had come up with his report.

John hadn't taken much interest in it at the time, but now he scrolled it slowly and read every word.

'The HIV victims suing for greater damages in the courts in Tokyo and Osaka say that the drug

439

companies and blood banks have shown a blatant disregard for human life. They say, however, that this is what anybody would expect from a medical establishment that over the past fifty years has welcomed the doctors of what were known during the war as "biological warfare units."

'The Japanese soldiers who built a fortified laboratory at Harbin in Manchuria told locals that it was a sawmill. Later they joked to each other that the *maruta*, the logs, were human beings. Inside this and other secret facilities in China, doctors recorded the effects of injecting Chinese prisoners with typhus and exposing them to plague-carrying fleas.

'When the *maruta* grew sick, the Japanese doctors sliced them open, often without anesthetic, and removed their vital organs to measure the speed at which they were deteriorating. One of the most notorious experiments was Operation Kashkoi (Japanese for "Operation Clever") which involved more than 1,100 people having the tops of their skulls sawn off while they were still alive, so that doctors could examine their living brains. In all, over 3,000 *maruta* are known to have died, probably more.

'As the war ended, the doctors became concerned for their own safety. The Soviets wanted to shoot them all. But Ryoichi Naito, a bacteriologist, went to meet Lt.-Col. Murray Saunders, the American charged with investigating biological war crimes, when he landed at Yokohama in 1945. Dr Naito begged for an amnesty in exchange for all of his research data.

'Lt.-Col. Saunders, fearing that an open trial would teach Stalin's scientists more about biological warfare, agreed. The Japanese experiments were hushed up, and after the war, the doctors built up spectacular careers. Several went on to head university medical faculties. At least four medical criminals joined the National Institute of Health, which advises on drug safety. Ryoichi Naito founded a blood bank with Masaji Kitano, a former frostbite researcher who used to freeze captives solid and break off their arms and legs; and Hideo Futagi, a human vivisectionist.

'I have talked to Professor Keiichi Tsuneishi, an expert on the medical atrocities that the Japanese committed during the war, and he says, "The way war criminals have been embraced by the medical community is indicative of a terrible moral sickness among Japanese doctors."'

It was the last sentence that affected John the most. It said simply, 'The existence of the Japanese medical unit was so thoroughly suppressed by the US Government that it will never figure alongside the names of Auschwitz and Buchenwald and Bergen-Belsen, although there are many younger Japanese lawyers who believe that it should do. The laboratory at Harbin was designated Unit 731.'

God, thought John. I should have known it, all along. Unit 731. No wonder Dr Lügner had felt so guilty. He must have worked in Manchuria with Dr Naito and Dr Kitano. He must have developed Synaptine from human guinea-pigs, opening up their skulls and seeing how their brains worked.

Operation Kashkoi . . . Operation Clever.

But how had he managed to get to Manchuria in the first place? An American, in a high-security facility, in a hostile, occupied country?

Had he been a traitor? And if he was a traitor, why did Titan Blight want him dead? All he had to do was report him, and have him arrested, and tried.

Unless the Office of Global Research and Experimentation had known about Operation Kashkoi right from the beginning, and had actually been involved in it.

Ridiculous? Unthinkable? He didn't know. All he knew was that he was beginning to cut very deep into the body of this mystery, and that its heart was much darker than he had ever supposed.

He was still working on his PC when Sara came in. She was wearing a blatantly scarlet suit with a clashing crimson blouse, and a large glittery marcasite brooch. She sat on the edge of his desk and watched him for a while.

'Micky told me you were here,' she said. 'You haven't found Cicero yet, then?'

'I'm getting there.'

She leaned forward and peered at the screen. He could see down her cleavage and smell body-warmed Ombre Rose. 'This is all about blood banks. He's not hiding in a blood bank, is he?'

'Just checking a little background, that's all.'

'I put a call in to Twisted River this morning. I thought you'd like to know that Roxanne's safe and well.'

'It amazes me that your Mr Blight thinks that he's going to get away with this.'

'Oh, he will. He always does. He has so many friends, you see. In the police, in the judiciary, up on Capitol Hill. Even if you managed to have him arrested, they wouldn't detain him for more than a day. While *you*, my darling man, would have to spend the rest of your life looking over your shoulder.'

She kissed him on the forehead, and then stood up. 'You ought to go down to the workshop. Micky's almost finished installing the guidance system.'

'Already?'

'He's making our technicians look like they're all thumbs.'

'When do they plan to test?'

'Two days' time.'

'That's pretty short notice.'

'Not really. Apart from the guidance system, we've been ready for months.'

John shut off his PC and stood up. 'Tell me something,' he said. 'What's a girl like you doing in a nasty conspiracy like this?'

She gave him a smile which actually made the hairs rise up on the back of his neck. 'Buy me dinner tonight and I'll tell you.'

Constance woke at 9.37 that morning and found that Lionel's bed was empty. She never usually slept so late, but she had been lying awake for most of the night listening to the tireless sound of the ocean and the sound of Lionel breathing and wondering if she were really doing the right thing, running off to South America with a strange man.

She was beginning to feel just the slightest tinge of homesickness, too. She would have done anything to be able to go back to the gallery for two or three hours, to make sure that her sister was keeping the books properly, and taking good care of the stock. But then she looked out of the Doral's salt-encrusted windows, down at the beach, and the rolling white surf, and she told herself not to be so cowardly. If she gave up on this adventure now, she would never have another. And think of the autobiography she could write!

There was a note waiting for her on the dressing-table. *See you by the pool whenever, love L.* She chose a plain light green linen dress, which she wore with white strappy sandals, a necklace of oversized white beads, and a white straw hat. Then she went down to the poolside to find Lionel.

It was another hot, breezy day; and the pool area was already crowded with sunloungers. Constance looked around but at first she couldn't see Lionel anywhere. At last she glimpsed him on the steps leading down to the beach. He was talking very earnestly to a young dark-haired girl in a zebra-striped bikini. She couldn't hear what he was saying, but by the chopping motions he was making with his hands it looked as if he were trying to persuade her of something. She nodded, and nodded again, and before she turned to leave him Lionel tapped the face of his wristwatch with his finger.

She ran off with a wave and Lionel climbed back up the steps and stretched himself out on one of the sunloungers.

Constance hesitated for a moment and then approached him. He was lying back with his eyes closed, his thin white chest glistening with sun-oil. She let her shadow fall across him, so that he opened his eyes and squinted up at her.

'Aha!' he said. 'The sleeping beauty! Here – there's a sunbed for you. How would you care for some breakfast?'

She sat down. 'You should be careful,' she said. 'You could get yourself burned.'

'Oh . . . I'm only going to sunbathe for fifteen minutes or so. Just to get rid of my anchorite's pallor.'

A waiter came over and Lionel ordered coffee and muffins and eggs Benedict. 'Today, we can relax. Tomorrow we can drive down to Key West. After that, a hop to Mexico . . . and then it's Buenos Aires, here we come.'

'Who were you talking to?' Constance asked him.

He frowned at her. 'I wasn't talking to anybody.'

'Yes, you were. Down on the beach.'

'Oh, that girl, you mean? She was asking me the time, that's all.' He paused, and then he took hold of her hand and smiled at her. 'You're not *jealous*, are you?'

John approached the jig where Micky was working, uncomfortably dressed in a Broussard Guidance Systems jumpsuit and a paper surgeon's hat. Micky – who was wearing not only a surgeon's hat but a surgeon's mask, too – was leaning over one of the missiles, carefully lowering the turtle-shaped MiGR8 unit into the scooped-out depression in the guidance system. Manuel Ortez and three other technicians were hovering over him, watching every movement intently.

'How's it going?' asked John, as Micky tightened the last screw that held MiGR8 into place.

'Walkover,' said Micky, stepping back from the missile and pulling down his mask. He turned to Manuel and the other technicians and said, 'Let's take five, guys, okay?'

John and Micky were left alone. Micky said, 'The guidance system was fully programmed and ready to run. The only thing these poor suckers didn't have was the right connection sequence, all the correct synaptic tolerances, and, of course, the magic potion.'

He produced a phial of Synaptine from his breast pocket. 'Here . . . put on a mask and watch this.'

John tugged a paper mask out of a box and tied it around his nose and mouth. Micky was already bent over the missile.

'The MiGR8 unit fits in here, right? Like a human brain into a skull-casing. All I have to do is unscrew this small inlet cap here, and pour the Synaptine into it.'

He emptied the phial, and screwed the cap back on again.

'Now, if we go back to the computer . . .'

On screen, John could see a multicolored image of the turtle-shaped 'brain' fitting snugly into its housing, all purples and greens with patches of orange. Gradually, he could see the Synaptine filtering through its capillaries – like the white tendrils of growing tree-roots. Eventually the Synaptine reached the microscopic interface between MiGR8's contacts and the missile's contacts, and filled it in.

'That's it,' said Micky. 'Contact. MiGR8 and the missile should now be able to talk to each other. Faster than any conventional computer – faster than any regular human brain.'

John said, 'That's amazing.'

'You think so? You wait till you see this mother fly.'

'Sara said you were test-launching in two days' time. Do you think you're going to be ready for that?'

'We could probably launch it this afternoon, if we were pushed.'

'Gene Broussard must think it's Christmas come early.'

'You'd better believe it. They're sending a full evaluation team from the USAF Tactical Air Command, including the Assistant Secretary for Programs and Acquisition.'

John said, 'I'm impressed. But listen – this Dr Lügner thing – I think I've made kind of a breakthrough.'

Micky listened with his head lowered while John told him all about Unit 731. When John had finished, however, he shook his head in bewilderment. 'I don't get it. We were at *war* with Japan, weren't we?'

'Sure. But most people don't realize that even

when there's a war on, business people and scientists still keep in touch with each other. It's my belief that Operation Kashkoi was partly or wholly initiated by OGRE. They knew something that the Japanese didn't – that there wasn't a hope in hell of them ever winning the war. OGRE were looking *beyond* the war . . . way into the future. But at the same time they exploited the very special opportunity of war to give them something which was essential for Dr Lügner's work – something which they could *never* have had in peacetime. Living human guinea-pigs, in any numbers they required.

'Dr Lügner did his research at Unit 731. He's never told anybody about it, for obvious reasons. But now that Titan Blight's so hot on his trail, he may decide that it's time to make a confession. Dr Lügner's pretty old now, after all, and if he fingered our friend Mr Blight for setting up Unit 731 in co-operation with the Japs, he could probably cop a plea. Better than a bullet in the back of the head.

'Just remember that Titan Blight is just about to launch this Creative Software business. The government is worried enough already about the power that it's going to give him. Who's going to regulate him? Who's going to know what he's doing? He's going to be able to move money from one country to another faster than you can blink. He's going to be able to trade expertise for information and who can control a barter like that? Or collect tax on it, for that matter. No law will be able to touch him – or anybody who subscribes to Creative Software. You're going to see the biggest black market the world has ever known. And it'll be Titan Blight's black market, believe me. Think about it. He's going to have more influence than Hitler and Stalin and Mao put together.'

'So this is why he wants to whack Dr Lügner?'

'It must be part of the reason, mustn't it? If Dr Lügner decides to make a clean breast of things, then Titan Blight isn't going to be running the most influential software company on the planet. He's going to be sitting in front of a grand jury, answering charges of collaboration with the enemy and conspiracy to commit genocide.'

'But whatever happens, none of this is going to help Roxanne.'

'Yes it is. I'm going to make sure that I get all the evidence I need that OGRE was involved in Operation Kashkoi. Once I've done that, Titan Blight won't dare to lay a finger on her.'

'But then he'll send his men in suits after *you*, too.'

'Those bozos? I'll worry about that when it happens.'

Micky looked around the workshop and wished that he didn't understand anything that was going on here. He wished he could still drink Dr Pepper. He wished he could laugh at *Home Improvement*. He wished he had Roxanne back.

Manuel came up and said, 'I don't want to interrupt anything, Micky, but we still have five hours of tests to run.'

John gave Micky a reassuring pat on the back and then Micky went back to work.

*   *   *

A little after one o'clock, Titan came back to Roxanne's room. She was sitting on the end of the bed watching television. Her lunch lay untouched on a tray.

Titan stood beside her for a while, smoking and watching Daffy Duck. At last he said, 'What would you like most in the world?'

'What do you think?' she said, without taking her eyes off the television. 'I want to get out of here, now, and go home.'

'Haven't you ever wondered what it might be like to be rich?' he asked her. 'You could have your own car. Which sort of car do you prefer? A Mercedes? A Ferrari? You could have all the beautiful clothes you'd ever wanted. You could travel. Have you ever seen the Iguacu Falls, or the sun rise over Angkor Wat?'

'I just want to go home,' she repeated.

He gave her a pat on the shoulder. 'Of course you do,' he said, benignly. 'But there's plenty of time to change your mind.'

As soon as it was morning in Tokyo, John put a call through to Ipi Sinkosha. Ipi was on his way into the city center from the suburb of Shibuya, and was stuck in a traffic jam. It was raining, and John could even hear the rubbery sound of his windshield wipers.

'John? What a surprise. I was talking to Danny only last week and he told me that you weren't working for Western Eye any longer.'

'That's right. But it doesn't mean I'm not working at all. Listen, do you remember the Heart Felt

450

blood bank investigation? That's the one. In your report you mentioned something called Unit 731 . . . that medical research laboratory in Manchuria. Yes. Yes, that's it. You also mentioned Operation Kashkoi, where they did tests on people's brains. Yes, that's it. What I'm trying to find out is, did any American doctor work on that program?'

'American? No, of course not. This was wartime. And Unit 731 was top secret.'

'Is there any possibility that an American doctor could have been smuggled into Unit 731 without anybody knowing about it?'

'I don't think so. After the war, US military intelligence interviewed all of the doctors who worked at Harbin. They released them, of course. That was part of the deal made with Lt.-Col. Saunders. But they questioned them very thoroughly. If an American doctor had been working there, I'm sure they would have found out. And is it *likely*, do you think?'

John hunched forward over his desk, the heel of his hand pressed against his forehead. Outside, the afternoon sunlight was sparkling on the sea. In Tokyo, Ipi had already slept through the night that was still to come, and woken up again. 'Is there any way you could check?' he asked. 'I'm really convinced that a US neurochemist was involved in Operation Kashkoi.'

Ipi said, 'I'm not sure. I could talk to Mr Shimuzu, the lawyer. He might have some more information.'

'How soon could you do it? This is real urgent, believe me.'

451

'I don't know. Today, I guess, once I get clear of this traffic jam. You're sure he wasn't German?'

'What?'

'This doctor you're talking about. You're sure he wasn't German? They had a German doctor at Unit 731. That's what it says in the US intelligence records. He worked on Operation Kashkoi, as well as some of the experiments they carried out on women. He disappeared during the war, though; and after five years they presumed that he was dead.'

'What was his name, this German doctor?'

'Oh, come on, John. How do you expect me to remember that?'

'You do have a record of it, though?'

'Sure. It's in the office. I guess I could call and have my secretary look for it.'

'Please, Ipi. It's important.'

John put down the phone. He sat still for a while, his hands steepled, thinking. Then he picked up the phone again and dialed the clinic in Santa Cruz.

'Mr Huntley? We're so glad you called. We've been trying to get hold of you since yesterday.'

'How's Jamie? Is everything all right?'

'He spoke, Mr Huntley. You mustn't get too excited. It may not lead to any great improvement, but he's actually managed to say something.'

'He *spoke*?' John felt as if the ground had opened up underneath him. 'What did he say?'

'He said "I want to go home".'

John put down the phone and sat quite upright, without even realizing that tears were streaming down his cheeks and dripping onto his shirt. He thought of calling Lorna, but he knew that he would sob, if he did, and that she in turn would act icy-cold. He thought of calling Maggie, but somehow he didn't want to share his excitement with Maggie. It was probably the first time that he recognized that their affair was genuinely over.

Instead, he went back down to the workshop, where Micky was sitting in front of a bank of computer screens, running a computer model of MiGR8's launch program. Time after time, MiGR8 guided the Tomahawk across the map in a red, unerring line. Time after time it found its target and hit it within a tolerance of less than six inches. As accurate as they were, even the newest Geosat positioning satellites couldn't guide a bomb to within less than 20 feet.

Micky looked up. 'John . . . what's happening? Hey, come on, man, what's wrong?'

John stood in the middle of the workshop, amongst all the weapons of war, and found that he could hardly speak. 'I, er – I – '

'What's happening, man?' said Micky. 'You look terrible.'

'I, er, heard just now that Jamie – well, he said something. He spoke. He said that he wanted to go home.'

Micky put his arms around him and held him close, saying nothing at all, while John silently and guiltily wept into his pale blue jumpsuit.

'It was my fault,' John said at last, wiping his eyes. 'He was only four years old and it was my fault.'

Manuel Ortez came up and said, 'I'm sorry,

Micky . . . we have to finish this orientation test.'

'No, shut it off,' Micky told him. 'We can finish it off tomorrow.'

John said, 'No . . . you go ahead. I'm okay. This is the first time in years I've ever felt that there might be some hope.'

He went back to his office. He dialed Lorna's number but as soon as he heard it ringing he hung up. Instead, he called Constance's number, in Melbourne. He hadn't heard anything from her; and he assumed that she had returned to her gallery. He had always found her easy to talk to. Eccentric and wacky, but caring, too. A mother figure for men who didn't have mothers any more.

'Carden Gallery, may I help you?'

'Constance? This is John Huntley.'

A slight pause. Then, 'Sorry, Mr Huntley, Constance isn't here. This is her sister Elspeth Walmer.'

'When is Constance going to be back?'

'Well, Mr Huntley, we're all asking ourselves that. She's taken an extended vacation.'

'On her own?'

'I'm not sure that I'm at liberty to answer that.'

'Ms Walmer, this is critical. I have to know if Constance was on her own.'

'You're not suggesting she's in any kind of danger, are you?'

'I don't know,' John told her. 'But if she's with somebody, and the somebody is the somebody I think the somebody is, then I need to talk to her, pronto.'

'I could pass on a message.'

'Please, Ms Walmer. I have to find out where Constance is, and who she's with, and I have to find out *now*.'

A longer pause. 'She'll *kill* me if I tell you.'

'Ms Walmer, you have to. I can't even start to tell you how urgent it is.'

An even longer pause. 'You won't tell her it was me?'

'Of course not. I'll tell her that I used a ouija board. I don't know, anything.'

'All right, then. She called me this afternoon from the Doral Hotel in Miami. She said that she had found a wonderful man and that she was going to spend some time with him in South America. Buenos Aires, to be precise. She said the man's name was Lionel, and that she thought she loved him.'

'Lionel? Is that all she told you about him?'

'Well, she said he was very clever. He was teaching her all about Renaissance art.'

'That's him,' said John. 'That's the very guy.'

'Is something *wrong*?'

'No, Ms Walmer. Everything's fine.'

He put down the phone. *Found him*, he exulted. *I've found him. All I need now is final proof that he worked for Unit 731.*

Almost as if it had read his mind, his fax warbled, and then a single message came over. It was from Ipi, and it had tomorrow's date. It read, simply; *'According to US military intelligence records, the only non-Japanese doctor who worked at Unit 731 at Harbin was German. He spent almost three years in Manchuria, and later moved to Tokyo, but no more was heard of him after the firebombing on the night of March 9/10, 1945. Since more than 80,000 people were killed that night and most of them were charred beyond identification, US war crimes investigators presumed him dead. During his time at Unit 731 he was primarily concerned with brain experiments, most of them carried out while their victims were still alive, still conscious, and still capable of feeling pain.*

His name was Dr Leo Versammlung. I can find no records of his previous career in Germany, although they may have been destroyed during the war.'

John punched up his German dictionary, and searched for *Versammlung*. It didn't even look like a real German name, more like a noun. And there it was, at last. *Versammlung, noun, feminine = Gathering.* Another joke, like 'Lügner' or 'Bakayaro'? But if it were a joke, it was a goddamned obscure joke. Why would he choose to give himself a false name that meant 'gathering'? Gathering what? Gathering who? Gathering your senses? Gathering your clans? Gathering ye rose-buds while ye may? Unlike all of the other names that Dr Lügner had used, this didn't seem to make any sense at all.

Unless, of course, 'Gathering' just happened to be his real name.

John decided to start with that premise. It wouldn't do any harm to check it out. Maybe it was absurd to think that Dr Lügner would have given himself a name that gave away his true identity so easily. But his behavior had often seemed paradoxical. On the one hand, he appeared to be determined to escape the men in suits, at whatever cost. On the other, he strewed so many obvious and provocative clues that anybody would have thought that he wanted them to catch up with him.

Maybe it was guilt, thought John. The same guilt that he felt for Jamie. The same guilt that everybody feels when they try to be God, and fail. After all, if Dr Lügner really *was* Dr Leo Versammlung, then he had a whole lot to be feeling guilty about.

From his talk about grunion, they had guessed that Dr Lügner had come from Southern California. If he had been old enough to undertake highly advanced research work in 1942, the youngest he could have been was 25, which would make him at least 80. A damned sprightly 80, though – with a body as fit as his mind.

John started with the student and faculty rosters at UC Santa Cruz, running right through from 1935 to 1942. Plenty of Gasparellis, Gates and Gatlands, but no Gathering. Then he tried California State at Fresno, and UC Santa Barbara. Two Gathers and one Gathercole. No Gathering.

He tried UCLA, and found one Gathering there, class of '40, but he was studying French. At last he scrolled his way through the records of UC San Diego, and there it was. Dr Lionel P. Gathering, class of '38, graduated with honors in biochemistry and stayed on at the university to lecture and to research. Winner of the 1940 Saltzman Award for contributions to scientific understanding. Twice winner of the Ford Foundation Award for biology.

John searched for the UC San Diego Yearbook for 1938. On page 27, upper right-hand corner, he found a photograph of Lionel Gathering at the age of 24. Dark-haired, plumper, with owlish old-fashioned eyeglasses. But there was no doubt about it. He was looking at a younger Dr Lügner.

'Got you, Doctor Liar,' said John, under his breath. All right – this wasn't conclusive proof that Dr Lügner/Gathering was Dr Versammlung, but he was making more progress than he could have hoped for. He tapped into the library of the *San Diego Tribune*, and initiated a search for the name of Dr Lionel Gathering. Then he picked up his phone and asked Gene Broussard's secretary to bring him a cup of coffee.

It didn't take long for the computer to locate Dr Gathering's name. The story in the *Tribune* was dated September 27 1942.

SD SCIENTIST'S WIFE
FOUND SHOT DEAD

Police were searching today for celebrated young SD biochemist Dr Lionel P. Gathering, 28, after neighbors found his wife shot dead in the bedroom of their home in Rancho Santa Fe.

Sheriff Wesley Briccus says that Dr Gathering has been missing since the night of September 24, and has to be considered a prime suspect in his late wife's murder.

Mrs Gathering, 26, was shot once in the head at point-blank range. Police experts called the killing 'an execution, rather than a murder.'

Dr Gathering has not reappeared at his

laboratory at UCSD since the incident, and his De Soto De Luxe remains in the driveway of the marital home on Paseo Delicias.

John found two more stories – SCIENTIST STILL MISSING and MURDER SUSPECT SCIENTIST 'PROBABLY DEAD' SAYS SHERIFF. The evidence for Dr Gathering's demise was a single sports shoe washed up on the beach at Cardiff-on-the-Sea bearing his name in mauve indelible marking-ink.

So Dr Lügner had murdered his wife in September 1942, and escaped from San Diego. All that John needed now were two last connecting links – positive evidence that Dr Gathering and Dr Versammlung were one and the same man; and positive evidence that would support his theory that OGRE had been involved in Operation Kashkoi.

He left his desk and went over to the window. The sky was filled with a fleet of thick white clouds, stately and slow. He thought *I want to go home*.

He picked up the phone and dialed the Doral Hotel in Miami. When he got through, he asked to speak to Ms Constance Carden. The ringing went on and on, but there was no reply. After more than two minutes, the switchboard operator said, 'I'm sorry, sir. Do you want to leave a message?'

His first instinct was to say no, in case Dr Lügner saw the message, too, and realized that John knew where he was. But as he turned around, he felt his pendant swing underneath his shirt – the blue enamel footprint that Constance had given him when he had first taken refuge in her gallery.

'Yes . . . I'll leave a message. Tell her that

Pythagoras called. Tell her to watch her footprints.'

'Excuse me?'

'That's all. She'll know what it means.' *And she'll know who it came from, too.*

That evening, Micky came back exhausted from the workshop and went straight to the icebox and found himself a can of Coors. He leaned back against the counter watching John chop up bell peppers.

'So you really had some luck today, hunh?'

'You bet. I could go pick up Dr Lügner first thing tomorrow.'

'So when are you going to tell Titan Blight? I mean, if you do that, Roxanne could be free tonight.'

'I know. But then Titan Blight will have Dr Lügner killed, you know that.'

'You think he *deserves* to live, after what he's done?'

'I'm not a one-man court of law, Micky. It's not my place to condemn him to death.'

'But it's not your place to condemn Roxanne to death, either. And Roxanne is totally innocent.'

John checked his watch. 'I think we can find a way around this. Sara's coming around for dinner tonight. I can ask her to pass on a message to Titan Blight. An ultimatum: either he releases Roxanne, like *immediately*, and he calls his hit-men off Dr Lügner, or else every TV station in the country will be running a lead story about OGRE's activities during the war.'

'What are you trying to do, commit suicide?

Come on, man. This Titan Blight is a dude who can send people looking for you with machine-guns.'

'He can, for sure, but I'm betting that he won't. He won't take the risk. For all he knows, I've already lodged all the information someplace safe.'

'Suppose Titan Blight calls your bluff? Suppose you're wrong, and he didn't have anything to do with Operation Kashkoi?'

'Then I guess I'll have to tell him where to find Dr Lügner, won't I? But I'm sure that he *was* involved. I can't think of any other reason why he should be so determined to eliminate Dr Lügner, can you?'

'But even if you're right, and Blight lets Roxanne go? Then what? You can't sit on a story like this for the rest of your life. And how do you know those assholes won't *still* come after you?'

'I'll worry about that when Roxanne's free, okay?'

Micky wiped the sweat from his forehead with the back of his hand. 'Okay,' he conceded.

John said, 'How's your missile shaping up?'

'It's ready. Forty-two hours from now, it should be flying.'

Micky had spent all afternoon checking MiGR8 – its launch guidance program, its in-flight detection sequences, its face-identification capabilities. All the Tomahawk needed now was fueling and arming, and then it would be taken to Cape Canaveral Air Force station during the course of the afternoon.

The countdown to the test launch had already begun, scheduled to take place at 1605 hours EST.

Bristle-headed military technicians had been loitering around the workshop for most of the afternoon, peering into the diagnostic screens and asking Micky endless questions about geomagnetic guidance.

Micky peered over John's shoulder. 'What are you cooking?'

'Jambalaya. You want to join us?'

'No . . . I'm bushed. I'll have some in my room.' He hesitated, and then he said, 'Listen, you know, about your son . . .' He held up his fingers, firmly crossed.

John smiled, and nodded, and went back to chopping onions.

After dinner at the Cuba Libre Restaurant downtown, Lionel took Constance back to the hotel, but when she climbed out of the back of the taxi, he stayed where he was.

'You won't miss me for an hour or two, will you? I promised to visit an old friend at Miami Shores. He's a professor of applied physics I used to know from MIT. Retired here. I could use a little complicated conversation. No offense meant.'

'You go right ahead,' Constance smiled at him. 'I can have a long hot soak in the tub.'

'You're very special,' he told her. The hotel lights reflected in his spectacles and turned both lenses blood-red.

She went up to their room and kicked off her sandals. The air conditioning was uncomfortably cold. A red light was blinking on the telephone to show that she had a message.

'A gentleman called you at a quarter after six,' said the operator. 'Mr Pythagoras. He said to watch your footprints. I hope that makes some sense.'

'Thank you,' said Constance, and put down the phone. She sat very still for a moment, thinking. She couldn't imagine how John had discovered where she was, but she knew that it had to be him. She also knew that he was warning her about somebody. Maybe the men in suits had picked up their trail, and he was trying to advise them to keep an eye open. But why had he chosen to be so cryptic? If Lionel had picked up the message, he wouldn't have understood it at all.

She felt even colder, and she actually shivered. Maybe John hadn't *wanted* Lionel to understand it.

She picked up the phone and dialed Broussard Guidance Systems. The switchboard was closed for the evening, but the call was picked up in the workshop by Manuel Ortez, who was watching the final reassembly of the Tomahawk's airframe.

'Do you happen to know how I can contact John Huntley? It's very urgent.'

'I don't have his number personally. But I should be able to have him call you. Who shall I say?'

'Just tell him the doctor's friend.'

'Is that all? The doctor's friend? No number?'

'He knows the number. Please try to make sure that he gets the message as soon as possible.'

Manuel left the workshop and went through to the main building. He found Sara standing in the lobby, talking to a tall man in a black squarish Emporio Armani suit. Sara herself was dressed in a slithery gray dress that seemed to cling to every curve of her body. The marble floor had just been polished and they looked as if they were standing on a frozen lake.

'Sara?' said Manuel, his voice echoing. 'You're going to see John tonight, aren't you?'

'I'm leaving right now, as a matter of fact.'

'Some woman called. Wanted us to give him a message.'

'Some woman?' interrupted the man in the black suit. 'What did she sound like? Young? Old?'

'Oldish, I'd guess. She sounded real worried.'

'And what did she say, this oldish, real worried woman?' the man persisted.

Manuel frowned at Sara; but Sara said, 'It's okay . . . Roland is one of our security people.'

'She said she was the doctor's friend. That's all.'

'The doctor's friend?' said Roland. He gave a particularly creepy smile. 'The doctor's *friend*?'

'That's right.'

Roland turned to Sara. His eyes were glittering like black beetles. 'I knew it. They're together. William Cicero and that old Constance Carden woman.'

'How do you know that?'

'Because Constance Carden still hasn't gone back home to Melbourne, and where else would she be? Can you get me the phone company record of all of John Huntley's calls? He's found Cicero, just like you said he would. But I'm going to make sure that I get Cicero first.'

'Hey,' said Manuel. 'I was supposed to give this message to John Huntley, not to you.'

'I'll tell you what it's all about,' said Roland. He leaned forward and grinned at Manuel and there was a shred of broccoli between his two front teeth. 'It's about truth; and justice; and the way that certain people want it.'

17

All rivers are at the edge of chaos. Their paths change by natural sinuosity, for which there is a mathematical formula. Stand on any river bank for long enough and you will drown – not because you fall in, but because the river will come to get you – Dr Steve Jones

Sara arrived with a chilled bottle of Cuvée Napa and a strange, almost hypnotized look on her face. She kissed John on the cheek and her perfume was very strong. Blonde by Versace. 'Something smells good,' she said, stepping into the hallway. 'I always like men who can cook.'

'My mother taught me,' John told her. He was wearing a plain blue Chambray shirt and chinos, and he knew he looked tired. 'She always said that if I could cook and make a woman laugh, I would always have all the female company I ever wanted.'

'But?'

'I can't make women laugh.'

She walked through to the kitchen. The lights were brighter there. She spun around on her heel and said, 'Well, you have plenty of other attributes.'

'Such as?'

'You know where Cicero is, don't you?'

John lifted the lid of the large green jambalaya pot, emptied a plateful of crawfish tails into the rice, and stirred it. 'I'm working on it,' he said, evasively.

'Can I taste some?' said Sara, standing close.

'Sure. I hope you like Cajun food. I was taught to cook it by a man called René Bofinger. He came from a swamp near Grosse Tête, Louisiana, but I met him when he was working for Lip Lickin' Foods in Cleveland, Ohio.'

Sara tasted a spoonful. 'I like it. It's good and spicy.' She watched John for a while, and then she said, 'Why didn't you tell us earlier?'

'What, where Cicero is? Because I didn't want to be an accessory to your killing him, that's why.'

'That doesn't really matter any more. We've found him ourselves. By tomorrow morning, he won't be troubling any of us, ever again.'

'Oh, I think he will. You see, if you kill him, I'm going to go directly to the media and tell them *why* you wanted to kill him.'

'You don't *know* why. Even I don't know why.'

John opened the Cuvée Napa and poured out two generous, effervescent glasses. He handed one to Sara and said, 'Here's to happier times, hmh?' Then, 'Why don't we go through to the living-room? We need to discuss what you're going to tell Titan Blight about this.'

She followed him through to the airy, primrose-painted living-room, with its huge linen-upholstered couches. She sat down and said, 'You

467

can't play around with a man like Titan. He'll see you dead first.'

'I'll take a chance on that. Why don't you give him a call right now, and give him an update. Tell him that we know where William Cicero has gotten himself to. Then tell him that he'd better not give anybody any orders to hurt him, and that he'd better let Roxanne go free. Tell him that he has two hours to think it over.'

Sara was looking pale. 'I can't tell him that.'

'Why not? He understands English, doesn't he?'

'He'll still kill Cicero, and then he'll kill you, and me, too.'

'Unh-hunh. He won't dare. I've left all the details of why he wants to kill Cicero in a place where he's never going to find it. If anything happens to Cicero or me, those details go to CNN. Then Titan Blight will go down with all flags flying.'

'What if he doesn't believe that you really know? This isn't some kind of crazy bluff, is it?'

'This is no bluff,' John told her. 'Just tell him Unit 731. He'll know what I'm talking about.'

He reached over and picked up the telephone. 'Go on. The sooner the better.'

'I can't. Even if he doesn't kill you, he'll come after me. He made me, John. He made me everything I am. If I fail him now . . . you don't even know what he'll do to me.'

'I'm sorry,' said John. 'You have to.'

Sara nervously licked her lips, staring at the telephone as if it might suddenly jump out of John's hand and bite her. 'Why don't you give me some time to think this through? Maybe there's a better way.'

'I've been thinking about it all day and I can't think of a better one.'

'Supposing we call William Cicero and warn him? That'll give him time to get away. Then supposing you and I just disappear, too.'

'And then what? Take on false identities and live in a cabin in the Yukon for the rest of our lives?'

'John, I'm begging you. This isn't a good idea.'

'Shooting Kevin and Jesus wasn't a good idea. Trying to shoot me wasn't a good idea. Call him.'

'For God's sake, John. You know how I feel about that. I was caught between a rock and a hard place.'

'Then call.'

At last, Sara reached out and took the telephone. She punched out a number that she had obviously punched out many times before. She waited while it rang, picking at a thread on the couch-cover. Eventually, she said, 'Victor? It's me. I have to talk to Titan. No, I have to. Tell him it's about Cicero and it's urgent.'

'Don't forget,' John prompted her. 'Unit 731.'

After a long, tense wait, Sara said, 'Titan? How are you? No, I didn't just call to ask you that. We have a problem down here. Yes, a serious problem.'

John couldn't believe how flustered and evasive she was as she told Titan Blight what had happened.

'Unit 731,' he coaxed her.

'I can't.'

'Tell him,' said John, leaning close to the receiver. 'Or I'll tell him.'

Sara licked her lips, and then she said, with a catch in her throat, 'John Huntley says to mention Unit 731, whatever that is.'

There was a moment's silence, followed by an audible roar of rage, followed by a stream of semi-coherent blasphemies. In the end Sara had to hold the phone away from her ear.

John took hold of the receiver. 'Mr Blight? John Huntley here. Yes. I just want to give you a little ultimatum.'

There was more roaring and cursing and in the end John handed the phone back to Sara. 'Two hours, remind him,' said John.

Titan slammed down the phone, and Sara was left white-faced and shaking. 'God knows what he's going to do now.'

'Don't worry about it. He can bluster as much as he likes. He doesn't have any options.'

'John – you're underestimating him so badly. You don't understand how *powerful* he is. He has hundreds of influential people in his pocket. Police, government agents, congressmen, senators. He plays golf with the director of the CIA.'

'Unit 731,' John repeated, and confidentially tapped the side of his nose. 'Now, how about some of that jambalaya?'

'I couldn't eat anything. Not now.'

John filled her glass. 'Have another drink. Relax. This could be the most memorable evening of your entire life.'

After the drink, Sara began to calm down. John

took a plate of jambalaya in for Micky, but Micky was already fast asleep, breathing thickly into his pillow. He lit two candles on the dining-room table, put on some soft, warm background music, and he and Sara ate their meal together and tried to talk about anything except Titan Blight.

He thought about Jamie, and he was still thinking about Jamie when Sara laid her hand on top of his. 'Something wrong?'

He shook his head. 'No . . . sorry, I was miles away.' He looked at his watch and there was one hour eleven minutes left to go.

'We still have time to run away together,' said Sara. 'But I guess you wouldn't want to. I seem to cause you nothing but trouble.'

'No,' he said. 'People cause their own trouble. It's no use blaming anybody else.'

The stereo began playing a smooth, lyricless version of Randy Newman's 'Falling in Love'. Sara said, 'How about a dance?'

'I'm the world's champion toe-treader.'

All the same, she stood up and pulled him up after her. He took hold of her, and they began to shuffle around the dining-room table, with the candles flickering on the walls all around them.

'Let's pretend we've just met,' she told him. 'Let's pretend I didn't come to San Francisco and ruin your relationship with Mrs Scarbeary, and that I didn't try to have you killed, and that neither of us have ever heard of Titan Blight.'

He didn't say anything. He was very conscious of how warm and close she was, and of the way that her dress slid over her hips, and her breasts touched

471

his arm. Her mouth was very slightly open, as if she had just recovered her breath from making love, and the candlelight shone on the curve of her lower lip.

'Let's pretend that we don't know anything about each other at all,' she said.

'That's not difficult. I don't know anything about you anyway.'

'You know how much I like you, don't you? I liked you the moment you came walking up the steps of your house.'

'You had a pretty idiosyncratic way of showing it.'

She smiled, and kissed him very lightly on the lips. Then she watched his face to see how he was going to react. He knew that he shouldn't. He knew what game she was playing. But she was beautiful, and they had drunk half a bottle of wine each, and for all he knew Titan Blight was already sending men to blow him away. He kissed her in return, just as lightly as she had kissed him, and then more forcefully. She clung closer, as if she were trying to mold herself around him, and slid her tongue into his mouth. The feeling of her bare skin underneath that slithery dress was electrifying. He could feel that she wasn't wearing panties, and that aroused him even more.

They danced slower and slower, until they were standing still, locked in a kiss.

The music stopped and they stopped kissing, although they remained close together.

'Are you always so assertive with strangers?' he asked her.

'Life's too dangerous to wait for what you want.'

He kissed her again, even though he hadn't yet forgiven her for what she had done. This time their tongues wetly wrestled together before John penetrated Sara's mouth. She bit his tongue until they could both taste blood; and when he tried to take it out she wouldn't let him go. He felt himself rising against her thigh. The harder she bit, the harder he rose. He wasn't thinking about Titan Blight now. He was thinking about nothing but the challenge of this warm, soft, sensual woman. He thought that she was going to bite off his tongue and make him mute. He thought that she was going to suffocate him with her perfume. He thought that she was going to rape him, and then arrange to have him killed. She was right. Life was too dangerous to wait.

He lifted her dress up to her waist and caressed her bare bottom with both hands. Slowly she released her teeth from his tongue, but he kept on kissing her, and now their kiss became even deeper and even more greedy, as if they wanted to swallow each other. John could see Sara reflected in the night-black glass of the dining-room windows, and his own fingers straying down between her round, gym-toned cheeks. It was like watching a silent erotic movie, filmed through the darkest of lenses.

He led her through to the living-room. He unzipped her dress while she kissed and kissed him with increasing intensity. The dress slipped to the floor, and Sara stepped out of it. She was wearing nothing but a white lacy bra, through which her areolas flushed pink. John kissed her mouth, and then her neck, and then cupped his mouth over her bra and breathed warm breath over her left nipple. She kissed the top of his head, and then she reached behind her and unfastened her bra. Her large breasts swung, and her nipples crinkled and knurled.

She lay back on the couch. There was the strangest look in her eyes – as if she were highly excited, but dead, too – as if all of her sexual pleasure had come from people who were using her, rather than people who cared. John stripped off his shirt, unbuckled his belt, and pushed down his jeans. His cock stood very hard, swollen-headed and upcurving, and it cast a shadow on the couch cushions like a single antler.

Sara whispered, 'Fuck me. Go on. What are you afraid of?'

He looked down at her, and he could scarcely breathe. There was a moment of high tension between them, when he almost turned away. But then she bent her right leg until she could take hold of her ankle with both hands, and she twisted it up until her foot was right behind her neck. She did the same with her left foot, so that she was doubled up, with her knees under her armpits, her breasts squashed against her thighs. Between her legs she was opened up wide, very pale pink, the color of pink lilies, and filled with bright clear dew.

In a way, her contortionism was frightening, but it was highly erotic, too. It must have taken intense self-discipline for Sara to keep her body so supple, yet the pose she had adopted was totally submissive – her legs tied up in a human knot, her breasts bulging, her vagina completely exposed. John knelt over her, his cock in his fist, and guided its purplish head between her lips.

She continued to look up at him with that excited, dead look. 'Go on,' she murmured, almost inaudibly. 'You know you want to do it. So do it.'

John leaned over her. His back was as taut as a bow. He looked into her eyes and he saw her for what she was, and he thought to himself: *I can't do this*. But his mind said one thing and his body said another. He sank his cock into her, and she was so wide open that he buried himself inside her, as deep as he could possibly go.

Her eyelids drooped and wavered and she let out a little gasping noise like a strangled bird. He took himself halfway out and then plunged himself in again, and again.

There was perspiration on her upper lip. She was trembling with the pleasure of it. 'Don't stop, John,' she whispered. 'Don't stop, or I'll kill you.'

It was then that the phone rang, and they knew that it was Titan Blight.

At the same time, Roland was driving south on Route 1 through a series of squally showers. He had just passed Port St Lucie with another two and a half hours to go before he reached Miami. He had decided to carry out this assignment alone. William Cicero had made a fool of him too many times, and he considered this killing to be personal.

He was driving a tan Ford Aries, because he wanted to be as unmemorable as possible. His black coat was swinging from a hanger in the back.

A plaid tennis-racket case lay on the seat beside him, containing an Ingram Mach 10 and three clips of ammunition.

Rain lashed the side of the car, and the road glistened red with reflected rear lights. The radio was playing 'A Boy Named Sue', and every time Johnny Cash reached the chorus, Roland joined in and slapped his hands on the steering-wheel.

He enjoyed killing. He enjoyed the surprise on his victims' faces. He enjoyed the way they danced and spun when he shot them. Most of all, though, he enjoyed the feeling of a job completed. He couldn't abide loose ends. It had particularly infuriated him that William Cicero had managed to escape from that colored boy's house. Now he had the chance to make things neat. Tie things up. He sang along happily with Johnny Cash.

One hundred thirty miles to the south, Constance was lying in bed still waiting for Lionel to come back. She had bathed, washed her hair, and manicured her nails. She had ordered herself a mimosa on room service, and all she could do now was watch television and drink it in solitary splendor. She had been alone ever since her divorce, and she had persuaded herself that she enjoyed being alone. But even though she and Lionel had only been together for two days, she found that she resented him going out. She could see herself in the dressing-room mirror and she decided that she simply didn't want to be alone any more.

She was wondering whether to order another mimosa when the door abruptly opened and Lionel came in, looking flushed. His hair was sticking up at the back and his necktie was crooked. Without a word, he went across to the bathroom, and she heard him splashing water onto his face. He came out drying himself with a handtowel.

'How long will it take you to pack?' he wanted to know.

'What do you mean?'

'I mean that we have to leave. I saw one of their cars waiting outside. They've found us.'

'But it's nearly eleven o'clock. We can't just *leave*.'

Lionel tugged open the closet doors and tossed their bags onto the bed. 'It's an occupational hazard, I'm afraid. We should be okay, once we get to Buenos Aires.'

'Are you *sure* it's them?'

Lionel pulled the drawers out of the closet and tipped them upside-down over his traveling-bag: socks, shirts, neckties, shorts. 'Of course it's them. If it's not one variety of them it's another. There's always a them, when you're somebody like me.'

'Lionel, I can't. Not now.'

'Of course you can. It's a case of getting out of here *prontissimo*, or else it's a case of sudden death.'

'Lionel, I'm not sure that I want to carry on running.'

He dropped one of the empty drawers onto the floor and stared at her. 'What do you mean? You knew what my life was like. Come on, Constance, we'll be safe once we get to South America.'

'I'm not sure that I really want to go to South America.'

'Of course you do. You'll love it. Carnivals, beaches, sambas.'

'Lionel . . . before we go any further together I want to know why these men want to kill you so badly. The truth. I think I have a right to know.'

'Just now, I don't have the time to tell you the truth. We have to get out of here, Constance. Ten minutes tops. The last bus for Key West leaves at 11.45.'

'I have to *know*, Lionel.'

'In that case, I'll tell you while we're traveling. I promise, okay. But pack.'

Constance reluctantly climbed out of bed. She glanced at the telephone, hoping that John would call her before they had to leave. She looked back at the bed, and wished that they could stay here and have a good night's sleep. She was beginning to feel very tired.

'Come on,' Lionel urged her. 'Let's get on with it!'

She took one of her neatly folded skirts out of the drawer and laid it in the bottom of her bag.

Titan said, 'I apologize for losing my temper, Mr Huntley. I've had a difficult day, that's all. And I'm afraid that you're not the first person who's tried to put pressure on me.'

'I'm not trying to put pressure on you, Mr Blight. I simply want Roxanne released and Dr Gathering to be left alone.'

'I'm afraid that there's nothing simple about this situation, Mr Huntley. But I have a suggestion. Why don't you come up to Twisted River and we can talk it over.'

'What good will that do?'

'Well, for one, I can help you to make a much more informed judgement about what you're asking me to do. I can tell you the full story about Unit 731.'

'I'll only agree to come if you let Roxanne go free.'

'Mr Huntley, the lovely Roxanne is the least of your problems. Once you and I have had a chat, she can go free whenever she wants to.'

John thought for a moment, and then he said, 'Okay, then. I'll come. But don't forget that everything I know about Unit 731 is on file. If anything happens to either of us—'

'Mr Huntley, please,' Titan interrupted him. 'Who do you think I am? Attila the Hun? Come up in the morning. I can arrange for a private flight for you from Melbourne airport. Ms Lake will take care of all the details.'

With that, Titan put down the phone. John looked at Sara. She was making a concentrated face in the mirror as she reapplied her lipstick.

'What are you going to do now?' he asked her.

'Whatever Titan wants me to do. Everybody does what Titan wants them to do.'

He took hold of her shoulders and turned her around so that she was facing him. 'Tell me something,' he said. 'Is there a *you* in there?' he asked, staring directly into her eyes.

She said nothing. He couldn't read her expression at all. 'I'm sorry,' he said, at last. 'I had no right to ask you that.'

She turned back to the mirror, leaving him feeling as if he had tried to kill *her*, too.

*   *   *

Roland reached the Doral Hotel at 1.37 a.m. It was still raining and he was over a half-hour later than he had expected. He parked on the opposite side of Collins Avenue, and pushed his way into the hotel through a laughing, chattering crowd of silver-haired men and women in evening dress. He went directly to the reception desk and produced the only picture of Dr Gathering that he had: a photograph taken at a picnic at UC San Diego in 1941, and aged by computer graphics to make him look 80.

'Did this gentleman check in here the day before yesterday?' he asked the receptionist. 'He could have been going under the name of Dr Lionel Gathering.'

The receptionist glanced at the photograph and said, 'I'm sorry, sir. We don't give out any information about guests. Hotel policy.'

Roland laid a $100 bill on the counter and placed his hand flat on top of it. 'Did this gentleman check in here? All I need is a yes or a no.'

'Yes, sir. He did. But if you're looking for him, you just missed him. He checked out about two hours ago.'

'Shit,' said Roland, and punched his fist into the palm of his hand, giving the receptionist the opportunity to whip the $100 off the counter and into his pocket. 'Did he say where he was going?'

'Sorry, sir. No forwarding address.'

'Shit,' Roland repeated. But then he said, 'How did he leave? Did he have a rental car or what?'

'No, sir. He asked me to call him a taxi.'

Well, that helped a little, thought Roland. If he

480

didn't already have a rental car he had probably gone either to the airport or the bus station. If he had gone to the airport he could have flown anywhere, but it would take only a couple of hours of canvassing the various airline desks to find out where, and Dr Gathering would know that. Even if he had gone to rent a car, Roland would be able to track him down. No – it was Roland's instinct that he had opted for the bus, and that he was continuing to travel south. On almost any of the Florida Keys he would be able to find himself somebody who would sail him to Mexico, no questions asked – and once he had done that, he would be almost impossible to locate.

Roland called Twisted River on his mobile phone, and left a message. Then he drove south on Route 1, his tires sizzling on the rain-slicked blacktop, his windshield wipers monotonously bumping from side to side. His blood was up; and he was in a killing mood now.

Micky slept and dreamed of Manchuria. His hand lay curled on the pillow and his fingers twitched when the duck-girl appeared, driving her little flock. He heard somebody saying, '*Unit 731*,' and then somebody else laughing. He felt as if all this had happened a very long time ago.

Close to dawn, when the sunlight was flooding through the curtains, he had another dream, too. A strange, fleeting dream; but very much fresher than the dreams about the duck-girl. He dreamed about faces, one on top of the other, like paper-thin tracings; or a palimpsest, one face drawn over the rubbed-out image of another face. For some reason, he felt that this was critically important. One face, concealing another.

He woke up, and for one split second he felt sixty years older: physically drained, physically depleted, as if he would never be able to get out of bed. He went into the bathroom for a glass of water, and as he drank, he looked at himself in the mirror. *One face, concealing another.* He couldn't work it out.

John arrived at Melbourne Regional Airport at 6.55 the following morning, carrying an overnight bag. The rain had cleared and the morning was hot and windy. The silver-painted Lear Jet was whistling and ready to go. John's bag was taken from him by an expressionless male flight attendant with mirror sunglasses and a sooty six o'clock shadow. He had barely buckled up before the door was closed and the airplane pivoted on its stand, ready to go.

They took off toward the west, over Lake Washington and the swamps, and then turned northward over Titusville and Daytona Beach. The sun was shining so brightly on the sea that John had to draw down the blind.

By the time they approached Norwood Memorial Airport to the south of Boston, however, it was well past ten o'clock and the skies were overcast. A few drops of rain spattered the windows as they taxied toward the terminal, and off to the west the clouds were the color of wet slate. John stepped down from the plane onto the windy tarmac, and Titan Blight's shiny black limousine was waiting for him. He climbed in, his pants squeaking on the leather upholstery, and the car swept him away as soon as he had closed the door.

'Hope you had a pleasant flight, sir,' said the chauffeur.

'Sure. Yes. Thank you.'

'Last flight we had up from Florida, two geese flew into the engines.'

'No kidding. Anybody hurt?'

'Two dead, that's all. Three survived.'

'Pretty good going.'

The chauffeur's hand spun flat on the limousine's wheel like a peeping Tom wiping a window. He had a silver skull ring. 'Comes to us all, sir. That's what they say. Comes to us all.'

They arrived at Twisted River and swept up toward the house. The clouds had passed over now and the morning was beginning to brighten up. Half a dozen gardeners were crouched in the flowerbeds putting in bedding plants, and a bright green John Deere tractor was driving up and down the long slope that led to the river, towing a wide grassmower behind it. As John stepped out of the limousine he could smell the aroma of freshly cut grass, and it reminded him of his childhood.

Titan Blight kept him waiting for twenty minutes. He paced around the huge living-room, trying to curb his impatience, and trying to evaluate from Titan's paintings and possessions what kind of man he might be. On top of the grand piano stood a bronze statuette of a woman being ravished by a grotesque horned demon, and maybe that said it all.

Titan eventually appeared wearing a loose black kimono and black slippers. His hair was wet and combed back as if he had been in the shower. John had seen news photographs of Titan, but nothing had prepared him for his height and his bulk and the slablike crudity of his features. Nothing had prepared him for the *atmosphere* which surrounded him – not just wealth, and power, but suppressed violence, too.

'So you're Mr John Huntley,' said Titan, sitting down in the largest chair in the room, and lighting himself a cigarette. 'You've been giving my people quite a lot of difficulty, Mr Huntley. Appreciate your coming up here. Maybe we can settle one or two things.'

'First of all I need to see Roxanne.'

'Roxanne's in prime condition, take my word for it.'

'I don't care what condition she's in, you're still holding her here against her will.'

Titan blew out a long stream of smoke. 'You've put me in a very difficult position, Mr Huntley. I hope you realize that.'

'There's nothing difficult about it. Either you release Roxanne or the full story of Unit 731 goes to the press.'

'Half the story, Mr Huntley. Only half the story. There were more people than me involved in OGRE's activities during the war. Most of them are dead now; but there are still one or two very important reputations that you and your friends are putting in jeopardy.'

'Why should I care?'

'Because you're an American, Mr Huntley; and I presume you're a patriot, too.'

'And what's so un-American or unpatriotic about telling the media what Dr Gathering was doing in Manchuria?'

'Some secrets are better left secret, that's all. The Office of Global Research and Experimentation was originally set up to monitor foreign scientific advances and to develop for our own benefit those projects which looked as if they might have some military value. The atom bomb was a classic example, but there were scores of others. However, *I* didn't look at OGRE's work in quite the same way that the politicians did. It was obvious from the outset that Japan couldn't conceivably win a war against the United States. So I continued to co-operate with Japanese scientists throughout the war; and they continued to co-operate with me. I could see far beyond a few years of petty conflict over trade and territory to a time when science could bring us a genuinely global society, and a genuinely lasting peace.'

'Not to mention an enormous profit.'

'You shouldn't be so cynical, Mr Huntley. It was a dream, and you can't say that it was a bad one. It's still my dream today, which is the reason why I'm funding Creative Software.'

'But the work that Dr Gathering was doing – he was torturing people, and killing them.'

'Mr Huntley, they were going to be tortured and killed in any event. As it is, they suffered and died usefully. They were sacrificed in the hope of a far better future for the rest of the world.' He stood up, and walked slowly around and around the chair in which John was sitting, encircling him with smoke. 'Dr Gathering was in close contact before the war with Dr Ryoichi Naito. Dr Naito had been charged by the Japanese military with producing a drug which would enhance human intelligence. Their idea was that a small team of geniuses could be produced to work on new and highly advanced weaponry – which would be their only chance of winning a war against a country as powerful as the United States.

'But Dr Naito reached an impasse in his work. He shared all his data with Dr Gathering, who managed to make the critical breakthrough. There was just one problem. Just as the Austrian neuro-physiologist Otto Loewi had discovered in 1921, the drug could only be prepared using chemicals taken directly from a stimulated human brain. In other words, the drug could only be prepared by killing people.

'Of course, Dr Gathering abandoned his project. But then I heard from our intelligence agents about the Japanese scientific units in Manchuria. I re-alized that if Dr Gathering could be sent to Unit 731, he would be able to use living brains for his experiments and complete his work. Hopefully, of course, he would be able to devise a way of preparing his drug synthetically.

'It sounds impossibly callous, doesn't it? But this was over fifty years ago and the whole world was at war. Life seemed cheaper then. Not only that, here was an opportunity which would probably never arise again in Dr Gathering's lifetime. As many living subjects to work on as he needed, with complete freedom to do whatever he wanted to them. Mutilate them. Electrocute them. Saw the tops of their skulls off, anything.'

'You're really telling me that Dr Gathering agreed to go to Manchuria and do that voluntarily?'

Titan laughed and coughed, both at the same time. 'Of course not. Dr Gathering was always such a sensitive soul.'

'So how did you manage it?'

'Everybody is susceptible to one pressure or another, Mr Huntley. Why are you here? Because of the adorable Roxanne. And because of your ego, too. You're going to be paid for this job, aren't you? Why should you care what happens to Roxanne or what happens to me? Why don't you just go back to San Francisco and pick up your life where you left off? You're vain, that's why. You want to save Roxanne like a knight in shining armor; and you don't want to see me get away without being punished. I've met people like you before. Principled people. Little guys with bullish attitudes and no brains.'

Titan paused for a moment to crush out his cigarette and to light another. 'On September 24, 1942, a team of Japanese commandos landed on Solana Beach in Southern California, from a submarine stationed offshore. They headed inland and kidnapped Dr Gathering from his house in Rancho Santa Fe. I suggested that raid myself. After all, there was no other way that Dr Gathering could be persuaded to go.

'He was taken to Kyoto, first of all, and then to

487

Unit 731 at Harbin. He was told that if he refused to carry on his research into a "genius" drug his wife would be summarily shot by Japanese agents. What he didn't know was that his wife had already been shot on the night that he was abducted.

'Later in the war, he was moved from Manchuria to Tokyo. After Tokyo was firebombed, our people lost track of him, and we thought he was probably dead. It was only when we started to get wind of some mysterious polymathic genius working in the Far East that we began to suspect that Dr Gathering might have survived. Four or five times we almost located him. And twice, before he slipped away, he left a dead body behind him. Well – three times now, if we count the girl he murdered at Winter Park.'

'You mean Suna, that maid of his? Dr Gathering killed her?'

'Of course. You can't get hold of human brain chemicals any other way.'

'So he never managed to produce his drug synthetically?'

'It doesn't look that way, does it? But all the evidence we have so far is that the drug wears off if you don't take it regularly. And the only way to guarantee a regular supply is to extract its ingredients from living brain tissue. Dr Gathering has been working for years on producing his drug synthetically. We have evidence of that. We think that he may be close to succeeding – and if he does, of course, that would be another serious irritation.'

'Of course,' said John. Now he understood. 'If Dr Gathering can market his "genius" drug commercially, then Creative Software will be obsolete overnight.'

Titan gave him a queasy smile. 'Nobody would *need* a computer any longer, would they, except as a simple tool for writing letters and producing diagrams. Everybody would have full access to the fastest, most creative computer that's ever been invented – their own brain.

'At the moment, people's scientific and political thinking can be controlled by whatever software they have available to them. But if they can abandon commercial software and start to use their own minds . . . well, you can imagine. It'll be worldwide anarchy.'

'Or worldwide freedom?'

'That depends on how you view people's ability to determine their own lives, Mr Huntley.'

'But so far, Dr Gathering can only derive his drug from living brains?'

'That's right. You can be a genius but you have to leave a trail of corpses behind you.'

John suddenly thought of Constance. 'Listen,' he said, 'maybe I can make a phone call.'

'To warn Ms Carden?' smiled Titan. 'She and Dr Gathering have already left the Doral. We don't exactly know where they are now, but one of my people is going after them.'

'You'll make sure that he doesn't hurt her?'

'Mr Huntley, let me tell you this. Dr Gathering isn't the same as you or me. He's a psychopath. What he had to do during the war . . . well, you can imagine what it must have done to his mind. Then he came back to the US to find out that his wife had been dead all along, ever since he was kidnapped. He's not only a psychopath, he's a vengeful psychopath, and he's a genius, too. We don't know how many people he's killed since he came back to the US after the war, but it probably runs into hundreds. One every couple of weeks, to keep him in supplies of this drug of his.

'So far, he's been way too clever for any law enforcement officers to connect up his killings, and what I'm telling you is only speculation. But he has to be stopped, Mr Huntley – even on the evidence of the killings that we *can* prove.'

John said, 'I can't believe this. Everything that Dr Gathering's done . . . You've admitted yourself that *you* were responsible.'

'Of course I was responsible. But what's the point in making matters worse?'

'Why can't you put the FBI onto him? Why do you have to kill him yourself?'

'My God, Mr Huntley. I thought you were some kind of hotshot. If he's arrested and goes for trial, then all of this business will have to come out in the open. Some very distinguished heads will roll, including mine.'

'Well, at least you're honest.'

Titan sat down again. 'You don't have to be sarcastic, Mr Huntley. I know what I did. Of course I wouldn't be at all happy if this Unit 731 business got into the media. But let's stop fretting about the past and think about the future. This whole world will be a far better place once people have access to Creative Software. It will also be a far better place when Dr Gathering is no longer in it.'

'So what do you propose to do now?'

'I'm not going to beat around the bushes. I propose to offer you a very substantial bribe. The deal is, you take the money and you go away and you never mention Unit 731 to anybody, ever again.'

'And Dr Gathering?'

'You let me deal with Dr Gathering the way that Dr Gathering needs to be dealt with.'

'And Roxanne?'

'Ask Roxanne for yourself. But, yes, she's free to go if she wants to.'

John's mouth suddenly felt dry. He knew that it was wrong; he knew that he shouldn't be saying it; but he found himself asking, 'How much?'

'Would two make you happy?'

'*Two?* You call that substantial?'

Titan irritably flicked ash onto the carpet. 'All right. Two and a half.'

'Forget it.'

Titan said, 'Three. And that's my final offer.'

John stood up. 'What the hell do you take me for? You think I'm going to sell myself out for $3,000?'

Titan stared at him as if he were retarded. Then he reached into the pocket of his robe and produced a checkbook and a fountain-pen. He balanced the checkbook on the edge of his wine-table and began to write, and John watched in silence as the zeroes seemed to go on and on and on.

Titan held the check out. His hand trembled slightly. John realized that he was in the presence of a man to whom death felt very close, and who needed to fulfil himself before he died.

'Let me ask you one question,' he said. 'Are you telling me the truth about Dr Gathering?'

Titan said, 'What do you think?'

'Well, I think that you probably are.'

'So take the money, Mr Huntley, and go in peace.'

'There's just one more thing,' John told him. 'I want you to let Sara go, too.'

Titan's fingers visibly tightened on the check. 'You're asking for something that you don't have any right to ask for, you know that.'

'Yes,' said John, and waited for an answer.

At almost the same moment, the Tomahawk missile was arriving by truck at Cape Canaveral Air Force station. It was driven into the brightly lit hangar where a gleaming white-painted A-6E Intruder was waiting to receive it. The countdown for the test launch had reached T minus 4 hours 13 minutes and 53 seconds.

18

Discovery consists of seeing what everybody has seen and thinking what nobody has thought –
Albert von Szent-Györgyi

Lionel had been edgy ever since they had reached Key West. He had found them a room at the Blue Marlin Motel, a cheap and anonymous concrete building off Flagler Street with a single dried-out yucca and a swimming pool that was globular with suntan oil. The owner looked like Popeye's pappy, and had a tattoo on his hairy forearm that reminded Constance of *The Scream* by Edvard Munch.

Outside their room, the sky was so blue that it was almost purple, and the sun beat down like a hammer. But Lionel stayed inside, tense and silent and fretful.

'What's the matter?' Constance asked him. He kept pacing to the window of their room and peering out through the venetian blinds. 'You don't really think they've managed to follow us, do you?'

'Well, you never know,' said Lionel. 'They're not as stupid as they look. They're persistent. And they don't care what it takes.'

'They couldn't have known which way we were heading, could they?'

'I don't know. I don't know. I'm just – stressed out, that's all.'

'Why don't you have a rest and watch some TV and I'll go find us something to eat?'

'They'll see you.'

Constance laid her hands on his shoulders and said, quite firmly, 'Calm down, Lionel. You're being paranoid, that's all. I can understand why, the way they've been chasing you for so long. But we're safe now. Relax, and I'll bring us back some Chinese take-out.'

Lionel stood rigid for a moment, thin and rigid, but she gently pushed him and he sat down on the edge of the bed. 'Okay, you're right,' he said, taking off his glasses. 'I'm letting this whole thing get to me. I'm sorry.'

'You like crispy shredded beef?'

'Whatever, unless it's chop suey.'

Constance left the room and walked along the shaded concrete balcony to the steps. A man with a big red belly was lying on a sunbed reading *Vogue* and she thought how incongruous that was. He lowered his magazine, lowered his sunglasses, and watched her with bulging blue eyes. She went down the steps quickly, feeling as nervous and paranoid as Lionel.

A newspaper vending machine was baking in the street outside the motel, almost too hot to touch. Constance glanced at the headlines as she passed by; and then stopped; and walked back. Inside the machine was today's *Miami Herald*. The lead story

494

was GIRL, 22, FOUND DEAD ON SHORE. Underneath the headline was a photograph of the girl to whom Lionel had been talking on the beach.

Constance took out a paper and stood in the street reading it. There was no doubt in her mind at all. The girl's hair was the same, her face was the same, and she was wearing the same distinctive zebra-stripe bikini. She had been found dead on the beach not more than a quarter of a mile north of the Doral Hotel. As yet, Miami police had issued no statements about the possible cause of death – not even a guess. The girl had been lying on a towel as if she had been sunbathing and fallen asleep – except that she couldn't have been sunbathing, because she was discovered just after eleven o'clock in the evening.

Eleven o'clock. That was the time when Lionel had rushed into their room and insisted on packing. Maybe he hadn't seen a car outside the hotel after all. Maybe there had been a different reason why he had been in such a panic to get away.

She finished reading the article and then she walked a little further along the street and threw the newspaper into a trashcan. There was a red-painted Italian restaurant opposite, La Veranda, and a craft gallery, and a telephone booth. She couldn't see a Chinese restaurant anywhere at all. But she looked around her, just to make sure that she wasn't being followed or watched, and then she went across to the telephone booth. She punched out her sister's number and waited.

★   ★   ★

At T minus 3 hours 55 minutes, a car arrived to take Micky to Cape Canaveral Air Force station. It was driven by a young USAF corporal called Hudsecker. He had a haircut like the landing deck of an aircraft carrier, and he spoke with a strong West Virginia accent.

'When they said go get the egghead in charge of the Tomahawk launch, I was expecting some old geezer in a white lab coat. I sure wasn't expecting nobody like you.'

'That's because there isn't anybody like me.'

There was a pause as they turned onto the main road. Then the corporal said, 'You don't seem too happy about it, if that's not being too personal.'

'Well, what would you do, if one day you were just a corporal, the way you are now, and then suddenly you were the brainiest guy in the known universe?'

'How should I know? It's not exactly likely to happen, is it?'

'Yes, but supposing it did. Supposing you could suddenly write like Shakespeare and paint like Rembrandt and work out the most difficult math problems in your head?'

'Well, I don't know. I guess I'd go to Atlantic City and try a spot of card-counting.'

'You wouldn't do anything . . . I don't know, *responsible*? Like try to find a cure for cancer; or work out a way to save the rain forests? Or help the Air Force to develop the most accurate missile ever?'

The corporal shook his head. 'Nobody never did nothing for me. Especially the Air Force. Why

496

should I do anything for anybody else? Anyhow, I don't think I'd want to be the brainiest guy in the known universe. I like beer and baseball and girls with big boobs, and you don't need no brains to enjoy none of those. I prefer to leave the thinking to people who like thinking. I'm happy the way I am.'

They drove through the perimeter gate and around the back of the main administration building toward the control tower. Heat shimmered from the concrete apron, and Micky could hardly hear himself think as two F-16s taxied past them, heading for the runway. It was good not to think, just for a moment. He had been doing nothing but thinking ever since he had taken the first of Dr Lügner's injections, and his brain was so crowded with statistics and theories and advanced ideas that he felt as if it were coming close to meltdown.

Just to be stupid again, for a day or two. Just to wash dishes and make a mess of playing the guitar. Just to be happy the way he was, the same as Corporal Hudsecker. Just to have Mingus back.

When Corporal Hudsecker led Micky into the control tower, they found it already crowded with Air Force officers and guidance technicians, as well as more than a dozen personnel from Broussard, including Nestor Drysdale and Manuel Ortez. Through the dusky-tinted windows, Micky could see the white twin-engined Intruder out on the runway, as ground crew made final adjustments to its Pratt & Whitney J52 turbojets. Sara Lake came over, smiling.

'Micky . . . how's everything?'

'Could be better.'

'Well, *this* will make you feel better. We've located Dr Gathering, and Roxanne should be on her way back to Florida later today.'

'Can I talk to her?'

'So soon as we know that Dr Gathering as been – ah – *dealt with*.'

'She's okay, though?'

Sara smiled. 'Mr Blight says he's very sorry for everything that's happened. He hopes you'll understand.'

'He's more of an optimist than I thought he was.'

'Come on, Micky. Don't take it so hard. We had to find Dr Gathering, no matter what it took.'

'So where is he?'

'Key West. Roland's driving down there now.'

'And Constance, she's there too?'

'I can't tell you any more right now. Ah, look. Here's Major General Broadmore. He's leading the Tactical Command procurement team. General – I'd like you to meet Micky Frasier, our guidance systems genius.'

Major General Broadmore was lean and tensile, with a large nose, a clipped white mustache, and an expression in his eyes like a gunslinger trying to decide exactly when to draw. He had medal ribbons from Vietnam to the Gulf. He held out his hand and gave Micky the standard-issue USAF metacarpal-crusher.

'Seems like our guidance systems geniuses are getting younger and younger,' he barked. 'Or is it me growing older and older?'

Micky gave him a slightly goofy shrug.

'Anyway,' said General Broadmore, 'why don't you give me a comprehensive rundown on how this MiGR8 system operates?'

Micky took him up to the computer terminals that would monitor the Tomahawk as it flew toward its target. He showed him how it could sweep the immediate target area with radar and infrared to locate and identify an individual human being. 'It doesn't do anything that a human being couldn't do with any of the standard equipment available today, but it does it a thousand times faster.'

'Well, I'm sure looking forward to seeing it work,' the general told him, clapping him on the shoulder. He checked his watch. 'All our observation ships and AWACs will be on station in about sixty minutes' time, and they'll be following that baby all the way from launch to ground zero.'

The clock on the computer screen said T minus 3 hours, 6 minutes, 22 seconds and counting.

She came back with the Chinese food to find Lionel sitting on a wicker chair on the balcony outside their room. He took off his glasses as she approached, and there was an odd, unamused look on his face.

'Something wrong?' she asked him. 'I brought lemon chicken, too. It's their specialty.'

He followed her into the room, and stood close beside her as she set the brown paper sack down on the table. As she was taking out the chopsticks and the napkins, he said, 'Who did you call?'

'What are you talking about? I didn't call anybody.'

'Don't lie to me, Constance. I know all about liars. I've been lying for fifty years, remember.'

'I promise you I didn't call anybody. I don't want those men to catch us any more than you do.'

'I followed you, Constance. I changed my mind and thought we might go out for lunch instead. I saw you go to the phone booth and make a call.'

'I wanted to talk to my sister, that's all. I couldn't get through.'

'Oh, no? So how come I saw you talking for so long?'

'Lionel – I'm sorry. But I can't go on living like this. I can't go on running.'

'You're going to have to go on running. In fact, you're going to have to start running again now. Titan Blight's people may not be geniuses but they aren't stupid. They must have a bug on your sister's line. And that means they could be here in 3 hours and 26 minutes, which is precisely how long it takes to drive from Miami to Key West. Or of course a damned sight faster if they come by air.'

Constance sat down. 'I'm sorry, Lionel. I don't want to go any further. I know I wanted an adventure, but this isn't a proper adventure. This isn't *going* anyplace at all: it's running away.' All the same, she didn't think it wise to mention the headline that she had seen in the *Herald*.

Lionel turned away; and then turned back again. 'You can't give up on me now, Constance. You don't know how lonely it is, leading this kind of life.'

500

Constance didn't say anything. She had nothing to say. She had learned that even danger can become monotonous, after a while. She had also learned that very few things turn out the way you expect them to; especially adventures.

Lionel reached out with finger and thumb and tilted her chin upward, so that she was looking directly into his eyes.

'You'll get used to it, believe me,' he told her. 'Now let's get packing before they arrive.'

'Lionel—'

'You're coming with me, Constance. I've made up my mind.'

Roland sped across the causeway between Long Key and Conch Key with the sea glittering on either side like smashed champagne glasses. His tires sizzled on the concrete; the warm wind buffeted through his open window and made his shirtsleeve flap. He was feeling pleased and excited, not least because his hunch had turned out to be correct. Only a few minutes ago, Sara had called him and said that Roland's electronics team had intercepted a call to Constance's art gallery in Melbourne from a phone booth in Key West.

A check of motels and hotels in the immediate area around the phone booth had come up with three elderly couples who had checked in early this morning, but only one couple had fitted Lionel and Constance's description to the letter. They were staying at the Blue Marlin Hotel, Room 216. Roland could almost imagine he was there, kicking down the door, and opening up with his Ingram

Mach 10. One thousand, one hundred rounds per minute – enough to chop two old people into corned-beef hash.

He slapped his hands on the steering-wheel and sang. When he overtook a bus on a long straight stretch of the causeway, he lifted his hand and waved at the young girls who were sitting in it. They all waved back, and some of them blew him kisses.

It was a long, difficult and tedious afternoon. Micky sat in front of the monitor screen for most of the time, running over the guidance program again and again and again. Something was worrying him but he didn't know what it was. All the flight and target data appeared to be correct. All the circuits for jamming, confusing, and spoofing enemy radar were fully functional. The facial-feature recognition system was responding perfectly.

Yet as T minus 13 minutes and 17 seconds approached – the time when the Intruder would take off toward the west and then circle back over the Atlantic Ocean in preparation for launching its missile – Micky was becoming increasingly anxious.

It was intuition, more than technology. He kept having the same feeling that he had experienced before – the feeling of a face on top of a face, like two people staring into opposite sides of the same window, and each seeing their own reflection superimposed on the face of the person they were staring at.

A memory? An intuition? Or maybe it was nothing more than tiredness.

Major General Broadmore came up to him and said, with pride, 'Looks like we're ready to launch.'

Gene Broussard came up, too. His white suit was crumpled and his banana-yellow silk tie was tugged loose, but he was so excited that he kept on letting out little staccato laughs.

Outside the control tower, the Intruder boosted its engines and rolled away from its stand. 'This is it,' said Gene. 'This is where we take weapons into the twenty-first century.'

Even Sara came up and stood beside them as the Intruder maneuvered its way onto the airstrip, pivoted around on its undercart, and then built up still more thrust. In the distance, a flock of pelicans took to the air in alarm.

'T minus 13 minutes and 17 seconds, and it's a go,' intoned the Air Force flight director. The Intruder sped along the runway, and lifted almost immediately into the afternoon sky, its tailpipes flaming hot orange.

Micky sat staring at the screen in front of him. He still couldn't rid himself of the feeling that something wasn't right. He thought about the very first moment that he had seen Dr Gathering (or Dr Lügner, or whatever his name was). He thought about the way in which Dr Gathering had lived so many lives, and created so many different characters for himself. He was always so devious. He couldn't even pass on a simple message without creating an imaginary golf resort, with himself in it.

He was so complex, so strange, so tortured with ghosts. And it was because of this complexity that Micky was worried, and couldn't stop worrying.

At Twisted River, the telephone rang, and Titan
picked it up. From where he was sitting he could
see John and Roxanne sitting among the palms in
the conservatory, talking. They went on talking but
Titan could tell that they were half listening to what
he was saying.

'It's Roland here, sir. I've located them. In about
twenty minutes your troubles will all be over.'

'Excellent. But do try to be less theatrical this
time, will you? You don't have to turn the whole
place into Swiss cheese. Just take them out
someplace quiet and put one between their eyes.
I've already called in too many favors with the
Florida State Police.'

'Whatever you say, sir,' said Roland, with undisguised disappointment.

Titan put down the phone. Then he eased
himself out of his chair and walked through to the
conservatory. John looked up at him but Roxanne
kept her eyes on the floor. She was wearing a simple
white dress and there were plum-colored circles
under her eyes.

Titan lit a cigarette, coughed, and said, 'Twenty
minutes and we can all breathe easy.'

The Intruder circled over the Banana River, its
cockpit winking in the sunlight. Then it turned
toward the ocean, headed due eastward. The time
was T minus 1 minute and 14 seconds, and it was
scheduled to release its Tomahawk exactly 8.3
nautical miles offshore. It would already be
traveling at well over 400 m.p.h. when it was

dropped, while a ground-launched missile would have needed a tandem booster engine to get it up to flying speed.

'*Bird Base the Atlantic bird is fully armed and ready.*'

The control tower fell quiet, except for the repetitive instructions from the guidance officers and the soft, quick rattling of fingers on computer keyboards. An occasional nervous cough from Gene Broussard.

T minus 1 minute. Sara glanced across at Micky and gave him a cool, strange smile.

T minus 30 seconds. Major General Broadmore cracked his knuckles together in anticipation. Twenty-five . . . 20 . . . 15 . . . 10 . . . 5.

'*Atlantic bird . . . released, fully clear, engine ignited.*'

There was a pause, then, '*Bird Base. We have migration.*'

There were whoops of delight from the Broussard team. Gene punched the air and said, 'Yes! Yes!' again and again. Everybody crowded around the monitors to watch how the missile would make its way to the target, dodging through some of the most sophisticated anti-missile systems ever devised.

Micky kept his eyes closely on the two screens in front of him. On the left screen he could follow the missile, still heading due eastward, as it was supposed to, before it veered south-eastward toward the West Indies. It was flying at Mach 0.72, close to its maximum operational speed, at an altitude of less than 500 feet.

On the right screen he could follow the streams of guidance information that were pouring out of MiGR8's artificial mind – every shift in windspeed, every slight alteration of the light. MiGR8 was flying the Tomahawk as if it were a seabird, as if it had a spirit of its own.

Gene stood behind Micky and said, 'Look at it go. I never saw guidance so responsive. I mean this baby is *smooth*.'

Four minutes and 37 seconds into the test, the nuclear cruiser *Long Beach*, stationed 43 miles offshore, locked onto the Atlantic Tomahawk and used its Aegis weapons system to simulate a close-range anti-missile attack. Without hesitation, the Tomahawk swerved upward in a graceful curve, and performed an extraordinary barrel-roll that would have left any pursuing missiles scattered behind it in electronic confusion.

Its shadow raced across the sea, momentarily joining the darker shadows of the sharks.

'They can't stop it,' said Gene. 'Look at it, look at it, holy shit, they can't stop it.'

Major General Broadmore looked across at him and said, 'You don't know how glad I am that this is *our* system, Mr Broussard.'

But it was then that Micky frowned and peered closely at the figures on his display screen.

'Anything wrong?' Gene asked him.

'Look at the left-hand screen. The Atlantic bird is one degree off course, northward. But then look at the right-hand screen. All the figures say that it's still following its pre-programmed trajectory without any deviation.'

'One degree? That's negligible. It could be cross-winds, anything.'

'MiGR8 is intended to fly like a bird. It's supposed to take account of even the slightest crosswind.'

'So what's the problem?'

'The problem is that these missiles are programmed to fly 100 percent on course, regardless of weather conditions.'

Gene said, 'It's not a serious glitch, though, is it? I mean, one degree? It's probably nothing to do with MiGR8. It's probably a minor fault in the control systems.'

Micky slowly shook his head. This was beginning to worry him more and more. The Atlantic bird went two degrees off course, then three. Then suddenly it described a wide, swooping semicircle, and started heading northward. The right-hand screen still continued to insist that it was flying straight and true.

'What the hell is going on?' Major General Broadmore demanded. 'Is this missile on course or not?'

'Yes,' said Micky, furiously punching buttons. 'But not on the course that *we* set for it.'

Reams of figures scrolled down the screen, but now they had been joined by algebraic symbols, too. Σ's and O's and x's and y's.

'Do you understand any of this?' asked Gene. He could see the Atlantic bird speeding even further northward now, flying straight and true towards Isla Mona. If it stayed on the same heading, it would cross the coast over the Isle of Palms, near

Charleston, and head on over South and North Carolina. And it was armed with enough explosive to demolish a ten-story building.

Micky activated the guidance scanner so that the reams of figures and symbols would be printed out. 'I think I know what's happened here. Dr Lügner's hidden a rogue guidance program inside the main guidance program.'

Major General Broadmore studied the screens for a moment. 'You can't bring the bird back on track?'

'I'm trying,' said Micky. 'But this isn't an ordinary guidance system. It has the capacity to think for itself.'

'Meaning what?' demanded Major General Broadmore.

'Meaning that if you program it with a wide range of choices, it can decide for itself which is the best choice to make.'

'What the hell are you talking about? Computers can't *think*.'

'This isn't exactly your garden-variety computer, General. It has a chemical element which gives it the ability to make up its own mind what it wants to do.'

'You mean it can disobey orders?'

'Well, that's one way of putting it.'

'So do we have any way of knowing what or who it's decided to hit?'

Micky's fingers flew over the keys. 'Not unless it decides to tell us. The original flight data was a mask – a way of hiding what this missile was *really* supposed to do. Look here – you see this instruction? It's what you call a tripswitch. A specified time after the Tomahawk was launched, the original data was discarded, and it went off hunting for somebody else.'

'Abort,' ordered Major General Broadmore. 'No question about it. Hang the expense, and abort, before it reaches the coast.'

Micky punched out BUZZARD. REPEAT BUZZARD which was the abort code. They waited, and waited, but nothing happened. The white line continued to creep north-westward across their monitor screens. Atlantic bird was now less than thirty-five seconds away from crossing the South Carolina coastline.

Micky tried BUZZARD for a second time. Still nothing happened, and the missile continued to fly.

'Shit, Micky,' said Gene. 'Isn't there *any* way you can stop it?'

Major General Broadmore turned around and shouted, 'Bring me a phone, will you?' Then, to Gene, 'I'm going to call Myrtle Beach and Seymour Johnson and have them send up some F-16s.'

'Major,' said Micky. 'You're wasting your time. Whatever that missile is doing now, it was planned, pre-programmed, at Dr Lügner's leisure; and whatever countermeasures you're thinking of taking against it now, he's thought about them already, months ago, even *years* ago, and he's made quite sure that he's going to outsmart you.'

'So what in God's name do we do now?'

Micky tore off a long sheet of printed-out data and frowned at it. The missile's new heading was encrypted, in a code that he had never seen before.

Yet there was something about it which he recognized. Not so much the repetition of specific letters, or any kind of discernible pattern, but a certain indefinable *logic*.

'So what the fuck has our Dr Lügner done?' asked Gene, sitting back in his chair. 'I mean, where the hell is that missile *going*?'

Micky said, 'It won't respond to any of our overrides. It hasn't broken off communication, but it won't respond.'

'Well, try to *make* it respond, damn it!'

'It's still headed north-westward on the same course, General,' said a disembodied voice in the background. 'It hasn't flinched an inch so far.'

'Shit,' Gene repeated. 'We can't abort it. We can't shoot it down. And we don't know where the hell it's going to come down. You want to see Broussard Guidance Systems go down the toilet? I just pray to the Lord my God it doesn't kill any innocent people.'

Micky said, 'In 2 minutes and 11 seconds it'll be passing over Wilmington, North Carolina, population 44,000.' He turned to Gene and added, 'That's if it *does* pass over.'

Lionel and Constance walked down to the quay, where dozens of small boats were bobbing. They passed two boat-sheds that were closed before they came to a green-painted wooden shack full of fishing tackle. A small man in a striped T-shirt was drinking beer out of the can and listening to country and western music. He was so suntanned that he looked more like a monkey than a man.

'Help you?' he wanted to know.

'Possibly. My wife and I were thinking of taking a boat trip to Mexico.'

'I could help you with that. Cost you $400.'

'That sounds okay to me. How soon could we leave?'

The man checked his watch. 'Have to fuel up first, and take on water. Why don't you come back in a couple of hours?'

'You can't make it any sooner?'

'No, two hours is all right,' said Constance. 'Why don't we go have something to eat? After all, we wasted all that Chinese food.'

Lionel thought for a moment, and then reluctantly nodded. 'Two hours then. No more.' And as they walked away from the quay, he took hold of Constance's arm and added, 'You won't be making any more phone calls, though, will you? And you won't try running away?'

Constance shook her head. But all the time she was wondering whether she was still agile enough to climb out of a restroom window.

19

If it comes to that, how can any man be called guilty? – Franz Kafka

Micky had been working on the missile's face-recognition unit for nearly an hour, and his blueberry Bubblicious no longer had any blueberry flavor to it at all. Atlantic bird was still flying steadily north-westward, and had almost reached Providence, Rhode Island.

Major General Broadmore had altered the entire anti-missile defense system all along the eastern seaboard. Four F-16s had been scrambled from Myrtle Beach AFB and were shadowing the missile as it flew north, but Major General Broadmore had given the pilots strict instructions not to attack it while it continued to fly steadily – especially since most of its journey took it over heavily populated towns and cities.

Micky punched in CONFIRM PRIMARY TARGET LOCATION.

PRIMARY TARGET LOCATION ISLA MONA 18 DEGREES 4 MINUTES N 67 DEGREES 58 MINUTES W. SEEK AND STRIKE SIMULATED TARGET #001.

CONFIRM SECONDARY TARGET LOCATION.

A moment's pause. A flicker. Then, NO SECONDARY TARGET PROGRAMMED.

YOU ARE NOT HEADED FOR PRIMARY TARGET. WHERE ARE YOU HEADED?

UNABLE TO RESPOND AT THIS TIME.

'What does that mean?' Major General Broadmore demanded. 'Don't tell me it doesn't know where it's going.'

'It's possible that it doesn't,' said Micky. 'Not yet, anyways. It may not receive its final target data until it's almost at ground zero.'

'And you still don't have any idea what that final target might be?'

Micky shook his head. 'All I can guess is that it's somebody that Dr Lügner wants to get even with. He's not short of enemies, after all.'

'What about all this data?' said Major General broadmore, picking up the printouts. 'Doesn't this give you any kind of a clue?'

'I don't know. It's very deeply encrypted. It's nothing like any code I've read about.'

'We can decipher it, can't we? Schuhmacher – get onto Colonel Hawsley in Intelligence – at the double.'

Micky ran his pencil down the lines of numbers and figures. 'I can't be totally sure, but I was reading *Logic and Axiomatic Theories* a couple of days ago, and it looks to me like this code could be based on set and subset theory.'

'That's math,' said Gene.

'That's right. Like, Set A could be all the States in the Union; and Set B could be all the first words

513

of all the chapters in the Bible; and Set C could be all the rivers in the United States that run west to east. Then subset a could be all the States in the Union that have buildings over 44 stories; and subset b could be all the first words of all the chapters in the Bible that have asses mentioned in them; and subset c could be all the west–east rivers that begin with an M.

'I mean, these are just examples. To break the code you'd have to work out what the sets and the subsets actually are.'

'Which would take how long?'

'Days, at the very least. Weeks, even.'

'Weeks? You're kidding me. We don't even have *minutes*. We'll just have to shoot it down, if we can.'

'I don't know . . . we may not have to break the code at all. MiGR8 is intelligent enough to question its own programs. The idea of that is to allow it to adapt to rapidly changing situations during combat. Like, if its primary target's already been hit, MiGR8 will assess that fact and won't try to hit it again.'

'And that's going to help us to stop it?'

'I won't pretend that it's going to be easy. But I guess we could make it doubt the whole validity of what it's been told to do. We can make it question its data so much that it loses confidence in its whole mission, and decides to call it off.'

'Oh, yes, and how do we do that?'

'We have to show MiGR8 that a program coded in mathematical sets and subsets isn't necessarily 100 percent logical.'

'Now, why didn't *I* think of that?' said Major

514

General Broadmore, with heavy sarcasm.

Micky turned back to the keyboard and typed BUZZARD. REPEAT BUZZARD. TARGET AND GUIDANCE INPUT ANOMALY.

MiGR8 promptly replied: BUZZARD DENIED. NO CONCEIVABLE ROOM FOR ERROR.

QUERY PROGRAM CODE LOGIC.

PROGRAM 100 PERCENT LOGICAL NO CONCEIVABLE ROOM FOR ERROR.

'Just what I was hoping,' said Micky. 'There are some well-known illogicalities in set and subset theory. Russell's Antinomy, the foundation of Boolean algebra. But obviously Dr Lügner didn't want to use up too much valuable memory by telling the guidance system what they are.'

He typed in CHECK CODE LOGIC EXAMPLE. Then he entered

$$B = [x \sum A \mid x \not\sum x]$$

'So what's *that* all about?' asked Major General Broadmore.

'It's a paradox,' said Micky. 'It says that Set A contains all sets including itself.'

'How can a set be a member of itself?' asked Gene.

'Well, it's kind of unusual. But suppose Set A is a set of abstract ideas. That's an abstract idea in itself so $A \sum A$. Now suppose that Set B contains all sets that are *not* members of themselves. Set B should be a member of Set A, right, because Set A contains all sets. But by definition Set B contains only sets that are not members of themselves, so Set

515

B can't be a member of Set A.' He paused, and then he said, 'That's the simple way of explaining it.'

Major General Broadmore pulled a face. 'I *think* I get it.'

'No response so far,' said Gene, looking at the screen.

Micky waited for a while, biting his thumbnail. He kept thinking about Roxanne, and praying to himself that nobody had touched her. He couldn't bear it if anybody had touched her.

Eventually he punched in BUZZARD. REPEAT BUZZARD.

'Come on you son-of-a-bitch,' breathed Major General Broadmore. Gene sat back in his chair and simply looked defeated and sad.

Micky sent the instruction again. BUZZARD. REPEAT BUZZARD.

MiGR8 replied BUZZARD DENIED. But then – after a few seconds' pause – REQUIRE GUIDANCE AND TARGETING DATA DIAGNOSTIC.

Micky said, 'That's it! *Yes*! We've made it question what it's doing.'

'So why won't the damn thing abort?' asked Major General Broadmore.

'My guess is that Dr Lügner programmed it *not* to abort. But the main thing is that it won't try to complete its mission until it's sure that its targeting data is correct.'

He typed in RUN TARGETING DATA.

There was a long and noisy outpouring from the printer, an endless torrent of numbers.

'This tells us squat,' said Major General Broadmore.

'Wait,' said Micky. 'If MiGR8 has been targeted to hit a specific person, we should get a face.'

They waited. The minutes ticked past, and more and more figures gushed out of the printer. But then the figures came to an end, and a picture started to assemble, line by line. It gradually built up into the image of an elderly man, with a face like slabs of rock. His mouth was grim and his eyes seemed to challenge anybody in the whole world to regard him as anything except a minor god.

'Do we *know* this guy?' asked Gene, tearing the paper off the printer.

'Never seen him before,' said Micky. He held the picture up and said, 'Anybody recognize this dude?'

Sara came up to the console. There was an unreadable expression on her face, but by the way she was standing Micky could tell that she knew who it was.

'Titan,' she said, in the quietest of voices. 'It's Titan.'

Micky stared at her. 'Titan Blight? The missile's programmed to hit *Titan Blight?*'

'That's him all right. No question about it. And the missile's headed toward Boston, isn't it, where Titan lives?'

'But Roxanne's there!'

'I can't help it, Micky. That's where it's going.'

'Jesus! Roxanne's there, and John's there, too!'

'Listen,' said Sara. 'Don't panic. I'll call Titan right now.'

'Don't panic? How long before Atlantic bird reaches Boston?'

'At its present speed,' said Gene, 'a little under four minutes.'

Micky hurriedly punched up a detailed map of the Dedham area and superimposed the Tomahawk's projected flightpath. The Tomahawk was still flying at its maximum operational speed of Mach 0.72, which meant that it was going to reach Twisted River in 3 minutes and 44 seconds.

Major General Broadmore came up and Gene briefed him. He said, 'We've already scrambled six more F-16s from Pease AFB . . . if they can't bring that thing down, then nobody can. But we're going to have to hit it before it reaches the suburbs.'

'You hear that, Micky?' asked Gene. But Micky was too busy typing. BUZZARD. REPEAT BUZZARD. CONFIRM YOUR GUIDANCE CODE FLAWED.

Major General Broadmore said, 'You have 2 minutes 11 seconds left, before that Tomahawk reaches Boston.'

'Have you got through to Titan Blight?' Gene asked Sara.

'I'm still trying. Nobody's picking up.'

'Let me try,' said Manuel. 'I have a knack with phones.'

'Micky – I'm going to authorize an intercept,' said Major General Broadmore. 'But you keep on concentrating on turning that missile around.'

Micky nodded. On the display screen in front of him a small shoal of F-16s approached the missile from the north-east, triangular white blips. They converged on the Tomahawk at nearly 600 m.p.h., firing seven AIM-9L Sidewinder missiles at it. The Tomahawk spun and skipped and avoided them all.

There were 2 minutes and 15 seconds to go.

'Ten seconds. Five.'

In the conservatory at Twisted River, John and Roxanne were sitting close together in basketwork chairs, with a tray of drinks and nuts and miniature pizzas untouched beside them.

'Do you *trust* this guy?' asked Roxanne. She was looking very tired.

'Do bears go into the woods and dress up as women? Of course I don't trust him. But the real question is whether he trusts me.'

'What do you mean? He's paid you $3 million, hasn't he?'

'He's given me a check for $3 million. But I keep asking myself, if I were him, would I give me $3 million? And even if I would – would I trust me never to say anything to anyone? I don't think so.'

'So what are you saying?'

'I'm saying that we should seriously think about getting out of here as soon as we can.'

'He said he'd let us go, didn't he, once they caught up with Dr Lügner.'

John stood up and walked across to the conservatory window. Outside, on the sloping lawns, the lawnmower plied its way up and down, leaving immaculate stripes behind it. John wondered why such a corrupt and ugly man should insist on keeping such a beautiful garden.

'I don't think he's going to let us go. I think he's keeping me alive just in case his own people can't find Dr Lügner.'

'But he can't keep us here for ever, can he?'

'He can if he offs us.'

Roxanne said, 'He wouldn't do that – would he?'

'I've seen people killed for a gravy recipe.'

'But if we disappear . . . doesn't all of your information about Dr Gathering go to CNN?'

'That's the idea. But Titan Blight has friends in very high places, and we won't be around to make sure that it isn't spiked.'

Victor came in. He was wearing a black silk suit and a ruffled white shirt. He glanced at their tray and said, 'You haven't touched your daiquiris, Mr Huntley.'

'I only accept drinks from friends,' said John.

Victor hesitated for a moment, and then he said, 'The alarm beams are off, while they're mowing the grass.'

'Oh, yes?' said John. 'And what does that mean?'

'That means that if a deer were to run across the garden and into the woods, he would have a pretty fair chance of reaching the perimeter fence before Mr Blight's game-wardens spotted him.'

'Oh, really? And why should you care?'

Victor shrugged. 'Because I like to see animals running free. Especially since I will never be free myself.'

John came up to him and stood very close – so close that he could see the diagonal crimson scar on Victor's neck. 'Tell me,' he said, 'are we at risk?'

Victor gave him a noncommittal shrug. 'Everybody who has dealings with Titan Blight is at risk. To start with, it always looks so simple. But before you know it, you get drawn in. You might have thought that you were dependent before you met him. On drink, on drugs. But when you try to get out, that's when you discover what dependency really means.'

John looked at Victor for a long time. Then he said, 'Do you want to come with us?'

'Me? No. I couldn't. I need Titan more than I need my freedom. There's one thing you could promise me, though. Don't let Sara come back.'

John said nothing. Victor waited for a few moments longer and then he left the room. John walked over to the drinks tray, picked up one of the daiquiris, and drank it. Then he held out his hand toward Roxanne and said, 'Let's get the hell out of here, while we can.'

Micky punched in BUZZARD. REPEAT BUZZARD.

BUZZARD DENIED the MiGR8 system retorted.

Micky typed MISSION DATA INACCURATE. BUZZARD.

Major General Broadmore stood behind them and counted the last few seconds.

'Five . . . four . . . three . . . two . . .'

RERUN MISSION DATA CHECK.

'It's too late,' said Major General Broadmore.

Gene leaned back in his chair and tossed his pencil across the room. 'That's it. Ground zero. Kerblam.'

Sara's face was strangely haggard. Micky felt a surge of bile in his mouth. He took off his earphones and unsteadily stood up. He knew that Roxanne had to be dead – blown into bloody smithereens – and John, too. It was even worse knowing that it had been his arrogance and his newly found intellect that had killed them both. He pressed his forehead against his keyboard and closed his eyes. Oh, Roxanne. Oh, Roxanne.

John went over to the conservatory door and tried the handle. Without any effort at all, it opened. He gave Roxanne a quick jerk of his head and whispered, 'Here! I think he's left it open for us!'

'What?' said Roxanne. She came over, and as she did so, John opened the door wide. They breathed in wind and roses and newly mown grass.

'Do you really think he was serious?' asked Roxanne. 'This isn't some kind of a trick, you don't imagine? Like they shoot us and pretend that we were trespassing.'

'I think that's a risk I'm prepared to take. Let's get out of here.'

He was just about to step out of the door when a harsh, whispery voice said, 'Going someplace special?'

They both turned around, and there stood Titan Blight, wearing a huge white silk bathrobe which did nothing to conceal his breasts and his belly and his saddlebags. He was smoking a black cigarette. Beside him stood Sebastian, wearing dark wraparound glasses. When he took them off, he had the watery-eyed look of somebody who has recently vomited.

Titan looked at the open door. 'Thinking of strolling?' he asked.

John said, in a slightly strangulated voice, 'It's a good evening for it.'

'You're right. It *is* a good evening for it. So why

don't Sebastian and I come along too? I can give you the guided tour.'

'Well, I'm not so sure. I think we might have changed our minds.'

'No, no. I insist. Come along, now. Why don't I give an arm to both?'

Sebastian came up to them with an expression of undisguised malevolence. He wore a crumpled linen suit and a navy blue T-shirt. 'Shall we go?' he suggested, raising his arm; and as he did so, John saw that he was wearing a shoulder-holster with a Colt automatic swinging in it.

They stepped outside, and Titan hooked his arms through theirs, one on each side. Every now and then he lifted his cigarette to his lips, so that Roxanne had to lift her arm, too. Sebastian followed them closely, and a little to the left. John kept glancing back at him. He didn't like having armed men behind him.

'I have some very good news for you,' said Titan, as they walked down the long sloping lawn that led to the river. 'Roland called me and assured me that Dr Lügner was all but in the bag. So I don't think that I have to detain you good people very much longer.'

John said, 'Fine. Terrific. Maybe your driver can take us to the airport. Or maybe you can call us a cab.'

'You're not going to rush off, are you?' said Titan. 'I was going to offer you dinner.'

'We'd rather rush off,' said Roxanne.

Titan turned to her and drew her in close. He gave her a long kiss on the cheek, and John was sure

523

that he was licking her. Roxanne squeezed her eyes tight shut and said nothing.

The lawnmower was approaching them across the grass. Titan said, 'It's too noisy out here. Let me show you the rose garden. That's real quiet and secluded.'

He almost pulled them through a stone archway decorated with gargoyles and statues of hooded nuns. Inside, there was a geometric rose garden of more than half an acre, with covered walks and pergolas and carved stone fountains.

In the very center of the garden stood a stone well, with a bucket and a chain. Titan released their arms and said, 'From the bottom of that well, you can see the stars, even at noon. From the top, you can see your destiny.'

Roxanne cautiously peered over the edge. John held back.

'You know something?' said Titan, with huge self-satisfaction. 'You could fire a gun in this rose garden, and nobody would hear you. You could drop two bodies down this well, and nobody would ever find them.'

'You'd really dare?' John challenged him.

Titan lit another cigarette and blew out a long stream of smoke. 'It isn't a question of *daring*, Mr Huntley. It's a question of being able to do it.'

John stepped a little way back. He was acting calm but his mind was racing like MiGR8's guidance computer. 'I thought that $3 million was a little too good to be true. I mean, I never have luck like that.'

'It's only money, Mr Huntley – and I can tell you

from bitter experience, money never brought *me* happiness.'

At that moment Sebastian opened his coat, unbuttoned his shoulder-holster and took out the nickel-plated automatic. He stepped up to the well and pointed the gun unwaveringly at Roxanne's left temple. Roxanne said, '*Ah!*' and tried to shy away, but Sebastian snapped, '*Don't*. Don't make me nervous.' John had never seen anybody less nervous in his life.

'You're not seriously going to do this?' said John.

Titan looked at his watch. 'I have to be getting back. I'm expecting a call from Washington at any minute.'

'You can't do this!' John shouted at him. 'What have we ever done to you to deserve anything like this?'

'If I worried about niceties like that, I would have been behind bars years ago.' And with that, Titan turned his back and walked away. Sebastian waited until he had passed through the stone arch and then thumbed back the automatic's hammer. Roxanne was staring at John in disbelief.

There was a moment when John really believed that they were both going to die. To his own surprise, he was annoyed rather than afraid. Why does it have to be here, and now, and in such a brutal and squalid way?

He took a step toward Sebastian and Sebastian lifted his automatic toward him and John knew that he was going to fire.

But as he took another step he heard a thundering noise in the distance – a thundering noise which rapidly grew louder and louder. Without warning, the Atlantic bird flew over the rose garden at a height of less than a hundred feet, the roar of its engine blotting out everything.

Sebastian instinctively ducked. As he ducked, John kicked out at his automatic, sending it flying out of his hand. Then he punched him on the bridge of the nose, very hard, twice, and kicked him in the stomach.

Sebastian staggered backward with a Hitler mustache of bright red blood. John seized his lapels and punched him again and again. Sebastian lurched back against the well, his arms flailing for balance. Roxanne said, '*No!*' but Sebastian tilted over the low stone wall, and before either of them could do anything to save him, he had vanished. He gave one echoey shout and then all they heard was a splash.

John looked up. The thundering noise had diminished now, but he caught sight of a sleek, dark shape circling the house and then heading off south-westward. He quickly searched for the automatic but it had disappeared into the rose bushes somewhere. He took hold of Roxanne's hand. 'Now – let's get out of here before Titan sets the dogs on us.'

They jogged out of the rose garden. Roxanne said, 'What was *that*? It looked like a rocket!'

'Cruise missile. And I think I can guess where it came from. Come on, let's get down to the lake.'

They started to run down the newly mown slope toward the water. They hadn't gone more than fifty feet, however, before they heard a roar of rage. John glanced over his shoulder and saw Titan standing on the corner of the patio, both fists raised in fury.

'He's seen us . . . Jesus, he's coming after us!'

It would have been logical for Titan to call up more of his security guards, but his anger was so overwhelming that he was lumbering after them himself, his silk robe flapping like a tent in a hurricane.

'Come on,' said John. 'We can outrun him easy.'

They carried on running down the slope. But Titan didn't come directly after them. Instead, he cut across at an angle and flagged down the gardener who was mowing the lawn. John could see him shouting and pointing at them. Then he climbed up behind the gardener, and the gardener wheeled his tractor around and started roaring down toward them.

'Hurry!' John urged Roxanne. Together, panting, they raced toward the lake, but already they could hear the tractor coming closer. Looking back, John saw Titan standing triumphantly behind the gardener like a Roman centurion on a chariot, with huge fountains of mown grass pluming up behind him.

'Christ, he's going to run us down!' John shouted.

They ran harder still. Roxanne stumbled, and John had to stop to help her up. 'My ankle!' she said.

'Forget your ankle, this guy's trying to turn us into chopped liver!'

As they neared the edge of the lake, John saw a small stand of pines over to his left. He gave

Roxanne one of his piercing taxi-whistles, and beckoned her to follow him. Hop-skip-jumping on her twisted ankle, she did so. The tractor was less than thirty feet behind them, and over the harsh snarling of its overheated engine, John could hear Titan whooping in triumph.

They had nearly reached the first few pines. John looked back, and then looked back again. It was a gamble, and he couldn't be sure that he had judged his distances correctly. But the tractor was so close now that they didn't have much of an alternative. Snatching hold of Roxanne's hand, he dodged sideways between two of the smaller trees and the tractor came bouncing after them.

His judgement had been right – by less than six inches. The tractor sped between the trees but the left-hand wheel of the mower-trailer struck the trunk of one of the trees so that the whole rig swung around in a wild, jolting semicircle. Titan was dislodged by the collision and fell straight backward into the mower.

He screamed like an injured bull as his robe was dragged into the scissoring blades, and then his arms. Blood and fragments of white silk were spewed out of the mower along with the grass. Then his head and his trunk were dragged in, and pieces of flesh flew everywhere – fingers and toes, lungs and stomachs, livers and legs. The gardener jammed on the tractor's brakes so hard that it toppled sideways, its engine still roaring. He stood helplessly beside the mower, in which Titan's grisly remains were so entangled that he would have to dismantle it completely to get him out.

Only Titan's great Romanesque head remained intact, staring out of the mower-blades with a bloody-lipped look of rage and frustration. He was angry, even in death.

John looked at the gardener but all the gardener could do was stare back at him in shock. He took Roxanne's arm and together they walked around the lake and up toward the woods.

'So it didn't go for Titan Blight,' said Major General Broadmore. 'Where's it headed now?'

'I don't know,' Micky told him, furiously punching at the keyboard. 'But it's definitely headed back south.'

'Try another buzzard.'

'I have. But it won't respond.'

'What does that mean? It's just going to go on flying until it runs out of fuel?'

'Well, it might. But before it does that, I think it's going to have a try at hitting somebody else. My guess is that Dr Lügner programmed it with a whole list of targets. If it doesn't hit the first one, it's going to go onto the second. And so on, and so on. As I say, Dr Lügner had a whole lot of enemies. If he couldn't get even with one, he'd try to get even with another.'

'So where do you think it's headed now?'

'Washington, DC, by the look of its present co-ordinates.'

Major General Broadmore wiped the perspiration from his forehead with the heel of his hand. 'You have to bring this mission to a close, Mr Frasier. You absolutely have to stop this missile whatever the cost. If this damn thing lands on Washington – I mean, for Christ's sake, it could be targeted on the White House! It could have the President's face in its memory banks! It's pretty clear that this Dr Gathering is looking for revenge, and who knows what a vengeful man is capable of – particularly when he's a goddamned genius?'

'I'll try my best, sir,' said Micky. 'But whatever instructions I give it, MiGR8 always seems to have an answer for everything. And now look at it – it's using a different kind of code altogether – all letters.'

'No chance of cracking it, I suppose?'

'In the time that it's going to take for it to fly to Washington? My guess is that it's some form of Vigenère code. But very difficult to break, if you don't know the key text.'

'Shit,' said Major General Broadmore.

A young lieutenant came up and gave Major General Broadmore a snappy salute. 'I've just heard back from the Florida State Police, sir. They sent two officers around to the Blue Marlin Motel and it looks like Dr Gathering and his lady friend have gone. Looks like they left in a hurry, too. They left a couple of bags. Three witnesses say they saw them on their way to the quay. They've alerted the coastguard to stop and search any small boats.'

'Thanks, Grant,' said Major General Broadmore. Then, to Micky, 'It looks like we've found him. Pity it's too damn late. All we can do now is pray.'

'*Pray?*' said Micky. And he suddenly thought of Dr Lügner on the very first evening he had met him, saying, '*I feel like I've lost my faith. But I still pray sometimes . . . I still pray for peace of mind. "The Lord is my shepherd, I shall not want . . ."*'

His fingers hurried over the keyboard. His mind was in overdrive. He had never been able to think so quickly or so logically, ever before. It was like magic. Using Psalm 23 as his key text, he gradually began to decipher single words, and then whole sentences. Within minutes, he had unraveled enough of MiGR8's new instructions to be able to find out where it was targeted. He thought he could divert it, too.

But there was one chilling caveat: IN ABSENCE OF TARGETING DATA STRIKE BIRD BASE.

Micky stood up. Sara brought him a bottle of cold Evian water and he took two or three gulps. 'Do you see that?' he asked Gene.

'I see it, but what does it mean?'

'It means that unless we tell MiGR8 to hit *some-body*, it's going to assume that it's been tampered with, and it's going to fly back here and hit *us*.'

Major General Broadmore said, 'It's less than fifteen minutes away from Washington, DC. Is that where it's programmed to strike?'

Micky nodded.

'And are you going to tell me *who* it's programmed to hit?'

'Who doesn't matter. What matters is that we can divert it to hit somebody else instead.'

'Can't you just send it out over the sea?'

'It won't go, General. It's been programmed to kill an individual and that's what it's going to do.'

Major General Broadmore took a deep, flaring

breath through his nostrils. 'Then what about the fellow who programmed it? This Dr Gathering of yours.'

'He's not alone, General. Even if he's on a boat to Mexico, he has Constance Carden with him, and the boat crew, too.'

'I'm sorry, Mr Frasier. If what you say about this missile is correct, then we're going to have to take some casualties. But the fewer we can take, the better . . . and if one those casualties happens to include Dr Gathering . . . well, I have to say that there's some justice in that.'

'But you can't ask me to kill Constance. I know she's old, but she was just discovering herself. She was just finding out what life is all about.'

'Who is it programmed to hit in Washington?' Major General Broadmore asked him.

Micky hesitated, then punched it up on the screen.

'Jesus,' said Broadmore. 'I don't think we have any choice, Mr Frasier. A direct cruise missile hit on the White House isn't going to do any of us any good.'

Micky sat down again. He knew that Broadmore was right. 'There are two or three good likenesses of Dr Lügner back at the house,' he said. 'I drew them for John when he went to Minneapolis. Can you send somebody to get them, as quick as you can? And get me the map co-ordinates for Key West.'

After a quiet and nervy meal of grilled bluefish and salad at La Veranda, the Italian restaurant, Lionel and Constance went back to the Blue Marlin to collect their bags. It was evening now, and the sky was streaked with lurid oranges and bombastic purples. A soft warm wind was blowing from the south-west.

Lionel opened the motel door and let them in. Constance went into the bathroom to collect her toothbrush and her make-up, while Lionel checked the drawers to make sure that they hadn't left anything behind. He didn't want to leave any evidence that he had stayed here.

When he had done that, he reached into his blue paisley-patterned washbag and took out a large hypodermic syringe and attached a six-inch needle to it.

'I hope I don't get seasick,' said Constance, from the bathroom.

'Don't worry, you won't. I guarantee it.'

Lionel went to the bathroom and stood in the doorway, with the hypodermic concealed behind his back.

'I've never been to Mexico before,' she said. 'Do you think I'll enjoy it?'

'Mexico? It's great. So free and easy after the States. If you don't do something today, you can always leave it till tomorrow, and not do it then.'

Constance laughed. Lionel came up behind her and laid his left hand on her shoulder. He could see himself in the mirror, and he was surprised to discover that he was smiling.

'You wait, Constance,' he said. 'The big adventure starts here.'

He lifted the hypodermic and held it up behind

her, where she couldn't see it. He was still smiling. He was right on the verge of throwing his arm around her neck when there was a sharp, polite knock at the door.

Constance turned. 'Who do you think it is?' she whispered, fearfully.

Lionel was completely thrown. He managed to drop the hypodermic into the inside pocket of his coat, but he couldn't say anything that made any sense.

There was another knock. A voice said, 'Need some clean towels, sir?'

'Er – no, we're fine, thanks,' Lionel called out.

But then the door swung open, and there was Roland, leaning against the door-jamb, admiring his latest manicure. Black suit, sunglasses.

'I think this time we can call it quits. What do you say, Dr Gathering?' His cool was supreme. He kept on running an orange-stick inside his nails.

Lionel lowered his bag to the floor. He looked suddenly exhausted. 'I think you're right, whoever you are. I think that we've all done enough running.'

'Me too,' said Constance.

Roland stepped inside the room. 'Looks like I just caught you, doesn't it? Titan's going to be pleased.'

'You're not going to hurt us, are you?' Constance asked him. 'Please – we won't give you any trouble.'

'Hey, I'm not interested in you,' Roland told her. 'I've been told to leave you alone. So you just stay there, like a good little old lady, okay, and me and Dr Gathering here, we're going to take a walk.'

'No!' Constance protested.

'Sorry,' Roland grinned at her. 'In the midst of a sun-drenched vacation we are in death, right?'

'You can't do this!' said Constance.

'Oh, yes I can,' Roland told her, with a toothy grin. 'And if I were you, I wouldn't bother to call the cops, or you might just find yourself in more trouble than you're in already. You know what I mean? The police find the guilty guilty unless they're proved innocent, which is when they beat the crap right out of them for kicks.'

Lionel turned to Constance and said, 'You stay here. I'll be okay. I think it's time I stopped running, don't you, and faced the music? I'm an old man, now, after all. I don't want to go on running until I die.'

'Never heard nobody speak a wiser word,' said Roland.

Lionel walked toward the door. Roland looked at Constance and gave her a wink. It was then that Lionel whipped the hypodermic out of his coat and stabbed Roland right in the Adam's apple. Roland sprang back in surprise, then tried to shout out, but his larynx was pierced by the six-inch steel needle, and all he could manage was a high-pitched gurgle. Lionel pushed him so that he fell back onto the bed, and then he snatched up his bag and said, 'Come on, Constance! Let's go!'

But Constance stayed back, her hands clutched together in fright. 'No, Lionel, I'm not coming! Not now, not ever!'

Lionel hesitated for a split second, and then hurried out of the motel room and along the

535

balcony. He ran down the steps and past the office.

'Hey!' called out Popeye's pappy. 'You're not thinking of leaving us without paying fer the room, are you? Hey, you! The cops were here, looking for you!'

Lionel kept on running, out into the street, and down toward the beach. It was almost dark now, and he could circle around to the quay without anybody seeing him.

Panting, he jumped down from the concrete parapet into the warm white sand. He couldn't run any further, but he managed to keep up a steady dogtrot.

He hadn't gone more than a hundred feet, however, before he thought he heard thunder. A deep, growling, indigestive rumble. He stopped, and listened. He realized then that it wasn't thunder at all, but the sound of an approaching aircraft. An aircraft that was flying very fast and almost insanely low.

He was about to carry on trotting when the Atlantic bird appeared, flying at treetop level, its exhaust flaming, and circled slowly around the beach, like a shark. Lionel dropped his case and watched it in absolute horror: he was enough of a genius to guess what must have happened.

The Tomahawk thundered around the beach one more time. He knew that MiGR8's cameras and infrared equipment were identifying his facial features, and matching them to the CFR images in its memory. It could recognize him as easily as one human being can recognize another, and from a hundred times further away. He knelt down in the

536

sand and clasped his hands together, because there was nothing else he could do.

The Tomahawk turned, twisted, and came thundering toward him. It filled up his entire world. Then it struck him in the face at a closing speed of more than 350 m.p.h.

A devastating explosion sent columns of sand up into the sky, and broke windows for half a mile. It echoed and echoed across the sea, as if somebody were walking through a house, slamming all the doors. Then there was nothing on the beach but the burning wreckage of the missile's fuselage, and Lionel Gathering's few remaining possessions, two books and a pair of pajamas, flapping in the breeze.

Micky and Roxanne returned to Canoe Creek Road to find that Orbison was waiting for them, madly wagging his tail.

Rhett said, 'As soon as the clinic told me he was better, I went and picked him up. I guess I'd kind of gotten used to the guy.'

They went into the living-room and it was airless and musty. Micky took Roxanne into his arms and gave her a long, deep kiss; while Orbison limped around the house, snuffling under all the furniture.

'How about a drink?' said Micky, going through to the kitchen. 'I still have that bottle of wine that Guido gave me.' He took out of his shirt pocket the last remaining ampoule of Synaptine.

Roxanne leaned on the counter and picked it up. 'You're not going to take this, are you?'

'I don't know. I thought I might as well finish the course. Maybe I can work out how to produce a

537

synthetic version of it, and make some more.'

'If Dr Lügner couldn't, do you think you can?'

'It's worth the try.'

'I wish you wouldn't. I preferred you the way you were.'

'Oh, yes. And how was that?'

'I don't mean to be rude or anything. But kind of dumb.'

'*Dumb?* I was never dumb, even when I was dumb!'

'I just mean I'd like you more if you weren't a genius any more.'

He looked at her. He didn't know what to say. He thought of all the mathematical formulae that he had been able to solve, and all the music that he had created in his head. He thought of his drawing skills and his prodigious memory. He knew that he wouldn't be able to bear to lose it. It would be worse than being struck blind.

'We'll see,' was all he could manage to say.

John flew back on the early-morning flight to San Francisco. He felt exhausted when he got home and turned the key in the door, but quietly contented. He put a pot of coffee on to perk, then he slung his bag and his coat into the bedroom and went around opening all the windows.

When the coffee was ready, he took it out onto the deck and sat with his feet up, watching the sun gleaming on the TransAmerica pyramid.

As he sat there, a car drew up in the street below him. After a while, the door opened and a woman in a short red dress climbed out. She walked up the steeply sloping street and climbed the steps to his deck.

'Hello, John,' she said, with the sunlight shining in her hair.

'Well, well. Don't tell me you were just passing through.'

She sat down close to him. 'I wanted to say that I was sorry.'

'Oh, yes?'

'I didn't want you to go through the rest of your life thinking bad things about me.'

He shrugged. 'It's all over now, isn't it?'

She took out a cigarette and lit it. He watched her blowing smoke and said nothing.

After a while she said, 'What are you going to do now?'

'You mean right this minute? I'm going to finish my coffee and unpack; and then I'm going to go through my mail.'

'I mean what are you going to do with your life? Are you going to keep Titan's money?'

'I think I deserve it, don't you? I'm going to use part of it to set up a new surveillance business, just like I did before Jamie got hurt.'

'Only part of it?'

'Most of it I'm donating to the children's clinic at Santa Cruz. A Jamie Huntley memorial ward. Something to make this whole damned mess worthwhile.'

'How is Jamie?'

'Better . . . making a little more progress every day. I'm going to make a visit tomorrow.'

There was a pause. Then, Sara said, 'Do you

think we could see each other sometime?'

'I don't know. You tried to kill me once. How do I know you won't try it again?' She looked at him and she could see by the look on his face that he was only half joking.

'I'm a different person now,' she told him. 'The last three years of my life – well, I've erased it. I've forgotten it already.'

John suddenly frowned. *I've erased it. I've forgotten it already.* Her words brought back a thought that had been niggling him ever since he had left Florida. He should have warned Micky again not to take the last ampoule of Synaptine, because the chances were high that it wasn't Synaptine at all. Both Dr Bron and Dr Schoenman had taken a full course, and look what had happened to them. Massive attacks of amnesia, and death.

He hadn't thought that Micky would actually take the last dose, now that everything was over, but he remembered him saying, *'Synaptine isn't addictive . . . but genius is.'*

He got up, opened his briefcase, and rifled through it for Micky's home telephone number.

'What's wrong?' asked Sara. 'What did I say?'

'You fitted in the last piece of jigsaw, that's all. I just hope to God that I'm not too late.'

Micky was in the kitchen when the phone rang. He had bound his left arm with his guitar strap and he was probing for a vein with his hypodermic. Roxanne was in the living-room, fooling around with Orbison. Although she wasn't paying any

540

attention, Dan Rather was on the news, announcing that the launch of the 'wonder computer system' Creative Software had been postponed indefinitely pending federal investigations into Titan Blight's finances.

'Roxanne, will you get that?' Micky shouted, over the noise of television and barking.

'You get it!'

'I'm busy, for Christ's sake!'

'Well, me and Orbison are busy, too!'

Micky found a vein and slid the needle into it. Even if his genius was going to fade away, he was going to write as many songs as he could before it left him. He was going to be the greatest rock singer that ever was. And maybe the greatest country-and-western singer, too.

He was just about to inject the liquid into his arm when Roxanne appeared in the doorway. Her face was white.

'*Stop*,' she said.

'What?'

'Stop. John's on the phone.' She walked up to him with her hand held out. 'He says that Dr Lügner probably fixed the last dose. If you take that dose, you won't be a genius. You won't have a mind at all.'

'What is this? You're kidding me, aren't you? You just don't want me to take it.'

'You can talk to John yourself. He said there could be something in it like the South American Indians use on their poison arrows.'

'Curare?' He looked down at the hypodermic in growing horror. If injected into the bloodstream, curare would paralyze large areas of the brain, particularly the temporal cortex affecting memory. The result would be total and irreversible amnesia, if not instant death.

Roxanne gently took the hypodermic out of his hand and laid it on the draining-board. She put her arms around him and kissed him.

'Go talk to John. He'll tell you all about it.'

'Sure. Thanks. Hey . . . I love you for that. I love you for ever.'

'I love you too, stupid.'

There was a knock at the door. Micky went to answer it and in came Rhett, in a violent purple shirt and a voluminous pair of shorts. He was carrying a plate covered with a cloth.

'Well hi, Rhett,' said Micky. 'How's things going?'

'Just fine. Heard this morning that my kid got straight As in school. *My* kid, can you imagine it? You just wait and see how far that boy goes.'

'Hey, congratulations,' said Micky.

Rhett lifted the cloth from the plate to reveal two large pork chops, well-browned. 'My wife cooked too much for dinner so I brung these over.'

'That's really neighborly of you,' said Roxanne. 'Here – take them through to the kitchen.'

Rhett followed her. But as she opened the cupboard to take out two plates, he walked out through the back door into the yard. He gave a sharp whistle and called, 'Here, boy! Look what your Uncle Rhett's got for you!'

Orbison came bounding up with his tail wagging

and Rhett flung him one of the chops, which he caught in his mouth.

'Never thought I'd ever get to like that mutt so much,' Rhett beamed. 'Just goes to show . . . if you save somebody's life, you get tangled up with them for ever.'

Micky thought of Dr Gathering. He put his arm around Roxanne's waist and together they watched Orbison tearing the meat right down to the bone.

A SELECTED LIST OF FINE WRITING AVAILABLE FROM CORGI BOOKS

14242 5	THE LEGACY	Evelyn Anthony	£5.99
14168 2	JIGSAW	Campbell Armstrong	£4.99
14169 0	HEAT	Campbell Armstrong	£5.99
14496 7	SILENCER	Campbell Armstrong	£5.99
14353 7	BREAKHEART HILL	Thomas H. Cook	£5.99
14518 1	THE CHATHAM SCHOOL AFFAIR		
		Thomas H. Cook	£5.99
14578 5	THE MIRACLE STRAIN	Michael Cordy	£5.99
14377 4	THE HORSE WHISPERER	Nicholas Evans	£5.99
13823 1	THE DECEIVER	Frederick Forsyth	£5.99
13990 4	THE FIST OF GOD	Frederick Forsyth	£5.99
13991 2	ICON	Frederick Forsyth	£5.99
14293 X	RED, RED ROBIN	Stephen Gallagher	£5.99
14472 X	CONFESSOR	John Gardner	£5.99
14224 7	OUT OF THE SUN	Robert Goddard	£5.99
54593 7	INTO THE BLUE	Robert Goddard	£5.99
14225 5	BEYOND RECALL	Robert Goddard	£5.99
13678 6	THE EVENING NEWS	Arthur Hailey	£5.99
14376 6	DETECTIVE	Arthur Hailey	£5.99
14622 6	A MIND TO KILL	Andrea Hart	£5.99
14584 X	THE COLD CALLING	Will Kingdom	£5.99
14302 2	LITTLE BROTHER	David Mason	£5.99
14136 4	THE WALPOLE ORANGE	Frank Muir	£4.99
14478 9	AUTOMATED ALICE	Jeff Noon	£6.99
14392 8	CASINO	Nicholas Pileggi	£5.99
13094 X	WISEGUY	Nicholas Pileggi	£5.99
14541 6	AMERICAN GOTHIC: FAMILY	William T. Quick	£4.99
54535 X	KILLING GROUND	Gerald Seymour	£5.99
14143 7	A SIMPLE PLAN	Scott Smith	£4.99
10565 1	TRINITY	Leon Uris	£6.99
14561 0	THE SLEEPER	Gillian White	£5.99

Transworld titles are available by post from:

Book Service By Post, PO Box 29, Douglas, Isle of Man, IM99 1BQ

Credit cards accepted. Please telephone 01624 675137
fax 01624 670923, Internet http://www.bookpost.co.uk
or e-mail: bookshop@enterprise.net for details

Free postage and packing in the UK. Overseas customers: allow £1 per book (paperbacks) and £3 per book (hardbacks).